PUGILIST FROM SHANDONG

師祖李昆山

PUGILIST FROM SHANDONG

~ The Life and Times of Lee Kwan Shan ~

THOMAS J HAASE

Thomas J Haase

1702 W. Cass St. Tampa, FL 33606

Printed in the United States of America

First Edition 2019

ISBN: 978-1-7332759-0-3

For ordering information contact:

Thomas J Haase.com/orders

Website: Thomas J Haase.com

Cover art: Map: Between 1855 and 1870loc.gov/item/gm71005076

Lee Kwan Shan image: Thomas J Haase

Chapter Art: Guillo Perez III (guilloperez3.com)

With the past pushing us onward and out of the dark,

Each step we take is into the unknown.

Step by step, life's journey leads us on,

And from moment to moment we move ever closer to the light.

Thomas J Haase

Contents

Preface

As I began my training, the mystique of the Chinese martial arts and the depth of its associated philosophy intrigued me and stirred me to think about all the generations of teachers and students that had gone before. I thought about all of the students and teachers who had spent years training and learning a way of life, a way of thinking and being. Occasionally these teachers would pass on their art to future generations so they too could benefit, grow, and impart it to others.

As my own training eventually became exposed to Lee Kwan Shan and his style of Kung Fu, I became more intrigued by the similarities of his life to mine, and the idea that I was now becoming immersed in a way of life experienced by my Kung Fu grandfather (Sigung).

Being raised on a small farm, I could in a small way connect with his life at home and as he traveled: the openness, quiet, solitude, and connection to nature were an integral part of his life and mine. Many aspects of his life, I can only dream about or hold in a sense of perpetual wonderment and awe, but the moments of the solitary man wandering in a vast wilderness somehow rings true within in my heart and I am one with it.

Eventually, as my training began to transition from student to student/teacher, I realized a greater and greater sense of benefit and learning from all that I had heard and knew about Lee Kwan Shan's life. Consequently, I understood the importance of documenting and passing on the information to future generations.

Little by little, I gathered information and in 1993 came to another realization — the best way to pass on the information would be in a book.

So here we are, stepping back in time to an era long since gone, but to a way of life that still lives on. A time when survival depended upon the use of any and all means, including the body, during physical confrontations.

The world has changed dramatically in the last 150 years, and for the majority of readers, this way of life will seem extremely foreign if not impossible. Yet, a few remain who personally knew of those who lived during this tumultuous era and we are fortunate that they are willing to pass on their knowledge for the benefit of us all.

Acknowledgements

A special thank you to the following people, for with all their help and talent this story has been allowed to be told.

Grandmaster Chan Poi: for the many years of training and countless hours of discussion about life in China.

My wife Cynthia Haase: for your countless hours of patience and understanding along with the willingness to read, edit, and see this through to completion.

Elizabeth Swann: for all your hours of patient reading, polite critiques, and editing to help correct and rearrange my thoughts.

Susan Edwards: for your editorial expertise and professionalism. I knew your talents were right for this book.

Ray Eales: for bringing your writing experience and arranging this controlled chaos into a sensible storyline.

Pattie Breckinridge: for all your initial editing and propelling this book forward.

Shelley Durrell: my good friend who offered invaluable criticism, which helped create a book far above my expectations.

Guillo Perez III: my talented student and amazing artist. The pictures, Wow, just Wow!

Richard Cummings, Guill Rios, Mike Kirn, Tommy Maurer, Christine Myers, Amy Marbut, Leander Williams, Kevin Woodworth, Jim Bailey, and Tony Sweatt: for all their years of dedication and support.

Prologue

It is not easy to introduce this story to today's Western audience without first telling something of the conditions in which the story unfolds. The story that will be told here is based on the life of Lee Kwan Shan (a.k.a. Lee Yu Tong), father of the Wah Lum Kung Fu tradition in the West, and his life journey.

We begin in China where Lee Kwan Shan was born more than 150 years ago. China was a very different place then, so the process of gathering information for this story was a long one. Countless hours were spent researching the terrain, geography, economic fluctuations, weather impacts on the land in regard to crop production, political uprisings and their outcomes, military campaigns, and international disagreements that occurred regularly during this time period and how these factors affected a person's life.

Consequently, the reader will find items that have been added or expanded upon to assist you in more fully understanding the overall scope and struggles of Lee Kwan Shan's life journey around China as it was then. I hope this information will give the modern reader a feeling for the world in which Lee Kwan Shan was born, lived, learned, and died.

Chapter 1

~ The Middle Kingdom ~

China is a place of immense beauty, culture, and treasure; yet for eons it was a land barely known to most of the world.

It is secretive, primitive, illusive and strangely advanced, with mountains holding firmly to the ground while reaching beyond the clouds that seem to make time stand still. Vast cultivated fields of green crops cover the landscape growing slowly to maturity to be harvested as food for the multitudes. Beyond the fields, dense lush forests seem to extend forever sustaining innumerable species of life in total obscurity.

In distant regions of the country, the land is barren and lifeless, tamed only by the bravest of souls. In stark contrast, China's cities of millions resemble controlled chaos where everything is continuously in motion.

From the high mountains of the west and southwest to the inhospitable deserts and windy plateaus of the north, China's garment is hemmed to the south and the east by the sea. Along this gently curving coastline, villages and towns are scattered, earning their living from the sea and the land. The warm waters of the South China Sea near Vietnam give way to the colder waters of the Yellow Sea across from Korea. It is along these northern shores in a small town called Pingdu in the Shandong province that our story begins.

In ancient times, explorers informed the rest of the world about this country isolated by natural boundaries. The deep, dark waters on one side of China were protected from sea invasions by the dragons lying deep within. An endless mountain range on the other side supporting the heavens was guarded by legendary tigers, which protected all of China from any invasion across the endless and unforgiving frozen terrain.

Many great inventions came from this obscure land long before the rest of the world was ready. Gunpowder, suspension bridges, acupuncture — all from a place few knew existed. One of the most intriguing developments from this land of extremes was a system of close combat known as martial arts.

Throughout the centuries, many martial artists became great warriors who lived, trained and died in almost total anonymity. Some of them chose obscurity in order to avoid the burdens of societal pressure; others were unknown by accident or by the ploys of corrupt officials.

These warriors achieved greatness in their art, yet few people even knew their names. Today we know of their existence only through the stories passed down from the ancestors who briefly encountered them and in turn passed on their experiences to future generations.

Still, many of them left their mark on society and are remembered. From them, we gain a glimpse of a society that undoubtedly produced many others whose stories will never be told.

PUGILIST FROM SHANDONG

To the modern world, the abilities and training regimen of such warriors would seem incomprehensible. They devoted their lives to their training, attaining physical feats of speed, strength, endurance and longevity that come from daily practice. These were the people from whom legends were fashioned and many are still alive in classic Chinese literature, even though most outside China view them as mere fairy tales.

One societal structure stood throughout China for the past 1500 years as a place to teach, meditate, and learn both the spiritual ways and the martial ways of the warriors of China. These were the temples and they served as sanctuary from both political and social turmoil. These places of solitude were often sought out as a haven of last resort when for whatever reason a man or woman had to abandon their home and family and go into hiding.

The Shaolin and Wudang temples are the best known in the West. They served as spiritual, temporal and training centers for the martial arts in China. There were other temples, less well known than these; one such lesser known temple was called the Wah Lum Temple, which carried on its own traditions, legends, and stories of extraordinary fighters.

The following pages are a journey through China, through time, through life. This story is a path.

Chapter 2

~ An Era Begins ~

Springtime in Pingdu is a time when the cold winter begins to loosen its grip on the land and make amends for the months of barrenness. One fading winter, the white blanket of snow covering the hills slowly melted and eased its way down to the valley below, signaling to all that life could begin again.

Green shoots of grass began peeking through the last remnants of snow trying desperately to hold out as long as possible before it disappeared into the soil from the warmth of the midday sun. A multitude of birds busily searched the ground to salvage twigs and fallen leaves for their nests. Squirrels scurried about after much time in idle repose.

With the harshness of winter coming to a close, the annual Spring Festival inaugurated the coming season. This year's festival seemed to arrive with an air of added freshness. The New Year arrived the morning after a lunar eclipse, an auspicious omen indeed. With the moon slowly creeping into the darkness, all of the memories from the previous year's poor harvest seemed to vanish and be forgotten. The moon's return after the eclipse showed the promise of a bountiful year.

As the cold gray mists of dawn gradually dissipated, the sharp cries of a newborn child abruptly interrupted the early morning stillness on the outskirts of town. The child was taking its first gasp of air, beginning the long journey of life.

This was not an easy time to be raising another child in China, to his parents, he represented hope for continuing their family lineage but also the burden of another mouth to feed, another body to clothe and care for through the long nights. Still, with the arrival of a boy, they looked forward to the possibilities of what this new wonder might bring to the clan. Eventually they decided to name the boy Yu Tong, which translates to Jade Mountain, an auspicious title in response to his birth in 1866, the Year of the Tiger.

As a young child, Yu Tong was very inquisitive and energetic, showing signs of mental and physical toughness at an early age. His days were filled with amazement and wonder as he scurried about through the large open courtyard and each of the adjoining rooms, which were all appointed in different color schemes. These laps around the delicate furniture kept his family alert as they tried to keep him from breaking everything in sight. Yu Tong would race from one colored room to another, and then change his route to experience a different sequence of colors.

When he ran through the open compound, he threw stones on the red-tiled roofs and watched them roll back toward the ground. With their sounds still echoing through the courtyard, he quickly ran back inside where the smooth floors made sliding easy and fun.

PUGILIST FROM SHANDONG

Eventually his small body would tire from his efforts and he would find a cool shaded spot beneath one of the large willow trees along the wall. And there amid the long delicate branches slowly swaying in the cool breeze meandering through the open courtyard, he would lie down and sleep.

Later, when his older sister, Zhang Jie, and the elders retreated to the back courtyard for their afternoon Kung Fu practice, Yu Tong would awake to watch intently. He became so keenly interested in the movements that he imitated the hand and foot gestures practiced by his elders.

Even as a young child, Yu Tong did not have an easy life; on the contrary, there were many hardships. The year was 1866 and this was China. Hardship was commonplace for most of the population. If you were not royalty, you were working hard to survive.

"Yu Tong! Bring your older sister Zhang Jie and come in quickly so we can bow to our ancestors," his father began lighting the incense to place in the ancient urn.

"Why are we burning that incense?" Yu Tong asked as soon as he stepped inside the doorway and observed his family standing at the small table with the pictures of their ancestors neatly positioned along the back.

"Because our family heritage is very important, so we pay respect to them every day by burning incense," his father replied while carefully holding the three fragrant sticks.

"How come?" the boy asked.

"Well, Yu Tong, now that they are gone, they still need some sort of food and drink and the only way they can get them is from us. So we keep food and water on the table for them.

"It was through their efforts that we are here today, since they struggled and survived to bring us into the world.

"Also, they learned a special style of Kung Fu and carefully maintained it to pass down to our parents so they could teach it to us." He placed one hand on his son's shoulder.

"So burning the incense every day helps to make sure we always keep their memory alive, continue the family line, and thank them for all they did.

"Ready? Turn towards the table and put your feet together so we can bow," he said as he turned and humbly raised and lowered the incense sticks nine times and then carefully placed them in the urn.

"How long will we be doing that?" Yu Tong asked once they were finished.

"We will do this every day for our entire lives," his mother replied as she placed both her hands on his shoulders.

"And then one day it will be your turn to do the same for us."

"Now go outside and play," she said as she turned him toward the door and gently nudged him forward.

Yu Tong's family always had food to eat and though their clothes occasionally showed signs of wear, they never became like the rags worn by street beggars. Home furnishings were not the exquisite caliber of the emperor but were comfortable and well maintained.

Yu Tong's family had owned and operated its own security or courier service for the past four generations, providing protection to caravans and merchants sending goods to and bringing back purchases from various cities. Originally, his ancestor had worked for another courier service and after accumulating sufficient experience, decided to open a business.

PUGILIST FROM SHANDONG

During the last two centuries there was much lawlessness and highway bandits were common, so shipping goods from city to city had become an ongoing hazard due to the increasing number of robberies brought about by the onslaught of famine and drought. Caravans were seemingly easy targets, so Yu Tong's clan gained a comfortable existence by protecting shipments and merchants from having their goods stolen and their lives taken by highwaymen. This degree of financial independence also allowed the elders sufficient time to devote to the vital role of educating the clan's youngest members.

Chinese parents who could not afford to send their children to the village school sent their children instead to work in the fields. The education of these children often consisted of little more than vocational training, which rarely included learning China's written language. For those whose parents were poor and illiterate, mastery of the Chinese written language was usually unobtainable.

"Yu Tong, have you finished practicing your writing?" his aunt asked the moment she saw the young boy standing outside throwing rocks on the roof.

"Yes, Auntie, I did."

"I want you to bring it to me so I can check it and make sure." She pointed at the door.

"But I just said I finished," Yu Tong said as he stomped toward the door.

"Okay, but I want to see it!" his aunt sternly replied.

"Here it is," he said when he returned.

"Do you know why we spend so much effort writing these characters?" she asked while reviewing the hurried scribbling on the paper.

"I don't know."

"Well these characters are really old and each one is a picture of something in life," she began as they walked to the shade of the large tree.

"See, each one of these has a sense of its own individual life, yet each has a need to be connected to the others.

"They are not just a bunch of squiggly lines thrown together in hopes of creating a meaning.

"When writing the characters, it is as if the linking of the characters yearns to form a poetic and emotional meaning and reflect it on the delicate paper." She showed Yu Tong a properly formed character.

"I have heard in some countries the characters are very lonely by themselves and can only be useful when put together with others.

"Each character is a story by itself. Just like our art, philosophy, and medicine, our writing is connected to the earth. The characters resemble the roots and limbs of a large tree and go out in many directions with countless associations, while still being connected to the core." She drew an image in the fine soil at their feet.

"For a young child like you, learning such an intricate, expansive language will take years of daily practice. It is necessary for you to write each character repeatedly while reciting the sound of each word with perfect tone and inflection.

"Eventually you will begin to learn the meaning of each word, but only after you have perfected the writing and speaking sufficiently to satisfy your teacher." She handed the paper back to Yu Tong.

PUGILIST FROM SHANDONG

"Yes, Auntie, I will go and try harder," he said as he walked back inside.

For Yu Tong the rigors and discipline required for learning the language were soon diverted to another purpose. When Yu Tong was old enough, he began learning the family martial arts style of Tam Tui or Seeking Leg Kung Fu that had been passed down from generation to generation. Training in Kung Fu was difficult; it required long hours of practice in basic movements that helped stretch and strengthen every part of the body.

Tam Tui is one of the more demanding types of Kung Fu. The rigorous leg training of Tam Tui is unequaled by many other styles. So for Yu Tong this meant hours of continuous practice to achieve proficiency in each movement. The Tam Tui style of Kung Fu demands that the practitioner spend countless hours developing, strengthening and stretching all the muscles in the legs in order to execute movements that regularly change points of attack from the very top of the head to the bottoms of the feet. It takes years of diligence to reach proficiency.

"Yu Tong, three years ago Zhang Jie began learning our style when she was your age.

"Now that she is older and taller, she will be learning other material.

"But today you are going to learn the basic patterns in our Tam Tui system," his father slowly walked toward the training area.

"In our family style we have twenty-four basic patterns or forms" he continued as he began stretching his legs.

"Each pattern is designed to strengthen the body while teaching a specific series of movements.

"These patterns are the basis of our family style, so I want you to practice them diligently." He pointed his finger at his son.

11

"The first pattern goes like this." He demonstrated the sequence.

"Now you try."

As Yu Tong imitated the series, his body struggled to properly execute the series.

"No! Yu Tong, that is not correct," his father scolded. "You are not moving like you are serious; you look like you are only playing!"

"Yes, Father, I will try harder."

"Your hand is over your head for a reason, not just to keep the sun off your face.

"When you punch, you must make your fist like a rock or it will never be of any use.

"Right now at your young age, your body is still relaxed and that is good. But you must learn how to tighten your muscles when you attack and defend." He showed his son how to squeeze the arm muscles to punch correctly.

"Like this, Father?" Yu Tong asked while trying to make his fingers form the correct posture.

"No not like that. Make sure the thumb is on the outside and squeeze harder. When your hand is by your side it should be relaxed and continue being relaxed until you punch.

"If you tighten your hands too early, it will make you slow and use all your energy for nothing."

"When is too early?" his sister asked.

"Only tighten them just before you make contact," his father said as he demonstrated when the tension should begin to build up during a punch.

PUGILIST FROM SHANDONG

"And as soon as you are done, relax them again so that you can save your energy and move quicker to the next technique."

"Like this?" Yu Tong asked while throwing several punches.

"No, that is too early you must wait until the very end.

"Watch how long your sister waits before she tightens her fist."

"Oh, okay I see what you mean Father," Yu Tong replied.

"Also, when you attack you must move as fast as you can; this will teach you how to act in a fight." He demonstrated a series of quick movements.

"And if you want to move faster, you must stay relaxed longer. Like I just said, only tighten up just before you make contact.

"Yu Tong, follow your sister, she has the proper spirit. See how her body is relaxed as she moves and then it suddenly tenses when she punches?" He leaned over Yu Tong's shoulder to watch Zhang Jie.

"Wow, this is going to take some practice," Yu Tong said, wiping his forehead.

"Now do your routine like she did."

As his father turned to walk to the shade tree, Yu Tong glanced at his sister and caught her sticking her tongue out at him. Instantly his temper began to rage and drive him to perform the routine better than his sibling.

"Yes, that is much better, Yu Tong!" his father said as he performed each movement in unison with his children while sitting under the tree.

"Now you are using the muscles correctly and your techniques are much stronger.

"Do not forget to always watch where you are trying to punch and kick, otherwise you will only be punching the air.

"And make sure you punch through your target as if you are hitting the back side and not just up to it. Otherwise the technique will not have any impact and it will just be a wasted movement."

"Like this, Father?" she asked as she finished the basic routine.

"That is better," he said.

"Now do the routine again, but this time even stronger and with more spirit and focus."

For the next hour, the two young siblings continued practicing diligently while their father watched and occasionally adjusted their techniques or postures.

"Next I want you to perform the series slowly so you can see each detail."

"Like, where am I hitting, how is my body positioned when I hit, and are my feet rooted to the ground when I hit?

"Moving slowly will help you learn how to coordinate your muscles better and teach you precision about your target."

"What size should the target be?" Yu Tong asked.

"Try and make it as small as your thumbnail.

"Now your spirit will help you understand what you must feel when you are fighting.

"Move your body like you are actually fighting but do not let your mind allow you to become angry and make you lose control of the moment.

"Your mind will either help you win the fight or it will make you lose.

PUGILIST FROM SHANDONG

"If you are fighting and you let your anger control the situation, the fight is already lost." He looked directly at both of his pupils to make sure they understood this important point.

"When your mind follows your direction, all things are possible. But when you follow your mind, all is lost. Do you understand?"

"Father, I do not totally understand what that means." Yu Tong replied as he scratched his head while looking at the sky.

"Okay, let me explain it another way," his father said and gestured for his children to follow him to the shade of the large tree. Sit down here and drink some water and we will talk about what I just mentioned.

"Now, your mind is a very powerful tool." He began as he looked into their eyes.

"But it needs direction and that comes from your discipline to control it.

"Your mind does not care if you focus or not; it is happy with whatever decision you make.

"If you choose to let your mind wander and not focus, it is happy. Also, if you choose to train your mind to focus, it is just as happy. The decision is all yours.

"When you are fighting, success will come from a disciplined and focused mind, not from a mind that has no control." He pointed at his temple.

"As you practice, you must imagine you are in a real fight, so that your mind will connect to the feeling of fighting. But always be careful not to let anger become your guide.

"When you are angry, you do not think clearly and in a fight that will cause you to make bad choices."

"Father, you said we should root our feet to the ground. What does that mean?" Yu Tong asked.

"When you are moving from one position to another, your feet must feel as though they are buried in the ground so that you can transfer the power from the ground, up through your legs and out into your hands and feet." He stood up to demonstrate.

"If you allow your feet to slip and slide when you move then you will only be able to develop half of your true punching and kicking power."

"Why is that?" Yu Tong asked.

"Because when they are not solid to the ground, half of your power is leaking out the bottom of your feet.

"It is like when you want to push the cart that we load supplies in. If your feet are not solid, then you slip and fall and the cart does not move." He gently pushed against the tree trunk to demonstrate.

"Now, how do you develop this principle? Well, this all begins in your mind.

"You must visualize the idea of your feet being buried and as you practice, the feeling of sinking into the ground will begin to arise in your body.

"You must also train your mind to pay attention to what your feet are doing and focus on making them stay planted on the ground."

"All the time, Father?" his sister asked.

"No, only when you are hitting, kicking, or blocking. Otherwise you will not be able to move very fast or smoothly.

"With more and more practice, the feeling will become so strong that your mind believes you are buried in the ground up to your ankles and eventually, it will feel like you are buried up to your waist."

16

PUGILIST FROM SHANDONG

"Also, you must learn to use your waist to generate torque from the power rising up from your feet when they are rooted." He twisted his waist as he punched to demonstrate the proper technique.

"These principles will take years of practice, but it will happen if you practice diligently.

"Once you have developed these principles, your punches and kicks will be deadly because you will be using the ground to drive the power up into your waist and then out into your fists and feet." He showed them what their punches would look like after they achieved perfection of the idea.

"Even the great masters from the Water Margin all had to train and develop these skills to become heroes.

"Now, go practice some more and try to use what I have just said."

Instantly, the refreshed students jumped up and began practicing the routines with added vigor and excitement, and moving through each series with a stronger understanding and purpose.

"Yu Tong!" his father yelled as the boy finished the series of movements.

"Yes, Father?"

"You need to try harder! Remember you are not that tall and some of your future opponents will be much taller than I am. You cannot let them beat you on size alone.

"Use your size to your advantage. Since you are smaller and more agile, you can move in and out of their range much faster. Do not let them scare you because they are bigger. If you are smart, you will figure out how to use their size against them.

"Remember, Yu Tong that fear is the biggest obstacle." He pointed at his heart.

17

"If you are afraid of them because they are bigger, then they will always win. But if you make them afraid, no matter how big they are, you will win.

"You are strong and smart and can win any fight if you can maintain control of the situation correctly, always remember that." His father patted Yu Tong on the back and walked over to the shade tree with his children.

"Father, do you remember when those people were fighting against the government?" Yu Tong asked as they sat down.

"Yes I remember how Ching Yeung and others from the Nian rebellion were fighting against the rulers," his father replied.

"My friend Ching Yeung was born in 1790 and when he was young there was a rebellion by a group who called themselves the White Lotus Society and he remembers how the officials tried to solve the situation. Ever since that time he says he has never trusted the officials and has been continually rebelling."

"What were they mad about that made them want to fight?" Zhang Jie asked.

"Well, for many years they did not like how the rulers were running the country, so they began to rebel. Then in 1851the Yellow River banks burst and flooded many miles of farmland, killing many, many people. Afterwards, the rulers were really slow about fixing the problem and did not do very much to help everyone.

"The efforts the rulers made towards cleaning up the disaster were really slow and then the river broke through the banks again! It killed thousands of people and destroyed all the farmland down in Jiangsu Province."

"So what did they do?"his daughter asked.

"I heard they tried to get the foreign devils to lend them the money to fix the problem, but that did not work out.

"So since they didn't get the disaster fixed, the rebels started to fight back by saying the foreign devils were contributing to the struggles of our people and that the government was incapable of effectively running the country." He leaned in close as if the words he was saying were a secret.

"My good friend Ching Yeung from the Wah Lum Temple was right in the middle of all the trouble and revolt.

"He traveled all over the province with the resistance. Often he would travel disguised as an escort for our business." He looked around to see if anyone else was close enough to hear.

"You helped the rebels fight the government?" Yu Tong exclaimed.

"Not directly, I just allowed the fighters that Ching Yeung and I totally trusted to act as escorts for our caravans."

"Wow! So some of those guys I have seen helping were also fighters in the resistance?" Yu Tong's sister asked.

"Yes they were."

"Wow!" she exclaimed, looking around to make sure they were alone.

"What happened to all those guys?" Yu Tong inquired.

"Actually, quite a few of them are living at the temple with Ching Yeung."

"Wooow!" Yu Tong said in a soft voice as he leaned forward towards his father.

"Once all the fighting was over, they had to go somewhere to avoid being arrested. So they came here and entered the temple."

"How come they came to this temple?" his daughter asked.

"Remember how I told you that about one hundred years ago they burned the Shaolin Temple?" he said.

"After that happened, all the fighters and people wanting to live and train in a temple needed someplace to go. So the Wah Lum Temple became the new training area and refuge for those trying to avoid the authorities." Her father explained.

"Father, you said Ching Yeung was your good friend. How long have you known him?" she asked.

"His family has lived in this area for quite some time and my father knew him as well. Also, his family has done business with us for many years."

"Oh, so that is why you trusted him so much to allow him to work as an escort while he was a rebel?" she asked.

"That is correct, if I had not known him for a very long time, I would not have trusted him enough to get involved in his cause."

"Father at the temple, what kind of Kung Fu do they practice?" Yu Tong asked.

"Some people living there have trained in many different styles, but the only one I know of for sure is the Praying Mantis that my friend Ching Yeung practices."

"What style of Praying Mantis does he practice?" the young boy asked.

"The Jut Sow or Wrestling Hands style."

"Wrestling Hands?" Yu Tong asked.

"Yes, from what Ching Yeung explained to me, it is focused on the wrestling motions a praying mantis uses when subduing his prey." His father replied.

PUGILIST FROM SHANDONG

"Okay, enough resting under the tree. I want you two to go practice your two-person hand form." Their father stood up and began walking back out to the open grass area.

"Yu Tong!" he yelled the moment the boy began the opening movements.

"You are not trying very hard!"

"This is serious. If you ever expect to be able to use these techniques, then you need to act as though you are fighting a real enemy." He demonstrated the proper way to execute the movements.

"See how I place my foot when I move in and grab her arm?

"Also, look how I grabbed her elbow so that she cannot hit me with it.

"When you grab, you always grab too high or too low and that leaves the elbow exposed so she can still use it.

"Now try again and do it the way I just said."

"Yes, Father." The boy replied as he lowered his head and walked back to the beginning position.

"You need to practice your movements until they are natural, because only then will they be effective.

"If you are doing the movements and you still need to think about it, then it will not be of any use when you are fighting."

He said to his daughter, "When he does not try very hard, then I want you to try harder, because it will make him focus to avoid getting hit."

She glared at her brother, and he could tell she was going to try as hard as she could to hit him.

"Ready, try again," her father commanded.

The moment the pair finished their opening salute, his sister instantly charged forward, making every effort to hit her brother."

Thud!

"Ouch!" Yu Tong yelled the moment he hit the tree.

"What happened?" his father asked while trying to act surprised.

"She made me hit the tree," Yu Tong replied.

"Were you paying attention to where you were going?" his father asked.

"Well, I was worried about her hitting me!"

"Don't blame her; you need to always know where you are when you are fighting. That could have been a cliff or another opponent."

As Yu Tong stood rubbing the back of his head, his father smiled at his daughter and winked to signal his approval of her efforts.

Then as he began walking to the side to observe, Zhang Jie looked at her brother and gave him a slight smile while glaring with her eyes as if to say, *just wait until this next attack.*

Yu Tong began to get nervous because he knew what happened when she had that expression on her face.

"Father, is she going to attack like that again?"

"Yes!" his father yelled, looking at his daughter.

"Yes but—"Yu Tong began.

"No talking! Get ready."

Again once the opening salute was finished, his sister charged forward with even more intensity than before.

PUGILIST FROM SHANDONG

Thwack!

"Ouch!" Yu Tong yelled as his head hit a low branch.

"What did I tell you?" his father asked while trying not to smile.

"I was trying to watch but she continued to attack harder and—"

"Don't give me any more excuses, just pay attention." His father exclaimed.

"Yes, Father," Yu Tong grumbled as he slowly walked back to the center of the training area.

Suddenly a sharp breeze rushed between the trees, causing the leaves to shudder and swing wildly and filling the air with a fine cloud of dust.

The distraction pulled Yu Tong's focus away from his sister's attacks and concentrated his thoughts on what his father just said.

Slowly a quiet sense of calmness filled his entire being, and he felt himself becoming totally focused.

"Okay, let's try it again," Yu Tong said, calmly readying himself without the slightest fear of the barrage his sister was about to unleash.

"Ready?" she asked as she watched her younger brother prepare for the next series of techniques.

"Yes," he answered calmly.

The moment she finished her bow, she instantly launched into her attack. Kick, kick, kick followed by a sequence of punches and then a single block; bombarding her brother.

For a moment, it appeared as if this encounter was going to be a repeat of the previous attempts, but Yu Tong suddenly jumped up and spun in a semi-circle, landing behind his sister. The moment his feet touched the ground, he swung his left fist back and hit his sister in the back of her head.

"Ouch!" she yelled as her hand instantly reached for the point of impact.

"What did you do that for?" she screamed while rubbing the bruised area.

"You were not focusing," Yu Tong flatly replied as he stood motionless and looked at his sister.

"That was much better!" their father said as he watched his children trade cold emotions.

"Now before you two kill each other, I think we should end our training for today." He motioned for his pupils to respectfully bow to each other and let go of all the feelings they experienced during the previous exchanges.

"Thank you for this practice." They each said in unison while bowing to respect their father's wishes.

As they began walking towards the compound the wind that had blown the ground into a dust storm earlier suddenly stopped, leaving the entire area completely quiet and without a single leaf moving.

"Yu Tong, I want you to contemplate what happened during today's practice and what you need to do to improve your awareness," his father said as he motioned for his children to head toward their respective rooms.

"Yes, Father, I will think about everything that happened today and try to figure out how to change it for the better," Yu Tong said as he bowed to his father and then turned toward his room.

The next day, as they walked to the practice area, his father asked, "So how did your thinking about yesterday's practice turn out?"

PUGILIST FROM SHANDONG

"I was sitting in my room trying to visualize what happened and how I could have acted differently, but every time I got close to coming up with an answer, my mind kept jumping to the Praying Mantis style that you said Ching Yeung practices," Yu Tong replied with exasperation.

"Hmm, it sounds like you are developing a special connection to this unique style," his father replied.

"I guess so. This style just sounds so interesting," Yu Tong said.

The moment they arrived at their training area, Yu Tong's father placed his well-worn sword against the tree and turned to his pupils.

"Today before we begin I would like to talk to you about the correct way to jump and how to jump higher," He said as they all began stretching their legs.

"When you are jumping, if your mind is not focused correctly you will not be able to jump very high."

"How should it be focused?" Zhang Jie asked.

"You need to first believe that you can jump."

"Otherwise your body will barely leave the ground."

"Let your mind believe you can jump as high as the treetops. Then it will free itself from thinking about being too high off the ground.

"Then as you begin to jump in your forms, you will be relaxed and will not get scared about being in the air." He pointed at the birds effortlessly floating in the sky.

"How high can we jump?" Zhang Jie asked.

"Again, that will be determined by how you think," He responded.

"As far as the body motions, the technique should follow this pattern. First in order to go higher, you must use the knees. Drive them as high as possible because this will help to give your body a direction while beginning the lifting process.

"Then once this is activated you can use the muscles to help you jump.

"Always remember, if you do not lift your knees very high you will never be able to jump very high." He demonstrated how to drive the knees upward.

"This means the only kicks that will be effective are the low ones." He executed a low kick at Yu Tong's foot.

"Look, look, over there," he said, pointing at the large hawk taking off from the grass nearby.

"See how his movements and even his thinking are consumed with getting up into the air?

"The same must be true of our actions.

"Now I want both of you to practice your kicks and focus on trying to get higher in the air when you jump."

As they approached the middle of the training area, several startled mourning doves suddenly took off and reminded the children of what their father had just explained.

"I have an idea," his sister said. "Let's go over there by those low branches and see if we can jump up and kick them."

"Yes that's a great idea," Yu Tong replied.

For the next several hours the siblings took turns trying to kick the leaves and with each attempt the other sibling would explain how close the kick was to the leaf.

"Okay, I think that will be enough for this morning's practice," their father said as he stood up and began walking back towards the compound gate.

PUGILIST FROM SHANDONG

Each day after the basics and forms were finished, Yu Tong was required to practice special exercises that further developed specific areas of his body. Some days it would be the hands, to help strengthen the fists for the many types of punching techniques. These exercises required Yu Tong to spend hours hitting a variety of surfaces — from small moving targets that would teach him to follow his opponent and attack or defend at oblique angles, to static targets which honed his ability to focus on a single point and attack through his opponent so that any movement executed would become a lethal attack. Other days the practice would focus on jumping and kicking.

His greatest challenge was learning how to focus his mind to overcome the continual pain from the previous day's training. It took remarkable discipline. Every day there was a new experience of pain in some part of his body. Every day he would learn another technique to help overcome the sensation.

The conditioning required countless repetitions of hitting objects to toughen the body. The continuous tightening of muscles took its toll on his body, so his mother made him stretch repeatedly throughout the day to relieve the pain, but also to open his joints and lengthen the muscles.

His sister was also required to learn the family art and having her as a training partner taught the young boy a great deal about fighting strategy so the two spent much time together. Even though she was more experienced, Yu Tong could still get the upper hand at times, but only when he resorted to brute strength. Often, his sister would use her ability as a smaller, weaker opponent to outwit Yu Tong with angles and cunning. This taught him to not assume a person's size was a disadvantage.

"Father, how come Zhang Jie knows some different stuff from me?" Yu Tong asked as he watched her practice a special routine.

"Well, someday your sister will leave our house and go live with her husband and his family. Her children will be descendants of her husband's family and they will worship his ancestors.

"Also, all the training she does now she will take with her and then add it to what her husband knows, so it will no longer be in our family.

"Because of that, we teach our sons differently so they can eventually maintain the art and pass it down to our descendants and continue our family heritage.

"Do you understand?" he asked as he looked into Yu Tong's eyes.

"I think so," he replied while scratching his head and trying to grasp all that he just heard.

During the many hours of training, the aspect that bored Yu Tong the most involved the fingertip techniques his father taught him.

I don't know why I am required to do so many of these every day ,he thought while trying to maintain enough focus to complete the exercise.

Unbeknown to him was the fact that these were secret techniques known only to his family. They eventually would become one of his most notable trademarks as a famous martial artist.

"When you practice your hitting with the fingertips, you must focus your mind and train your eyes to only see one small spot," he could hear his father say from the back of his mind.

"Do not let your mind wander, force it to stay focused; otherwise your techniques will not be correct or precise."

PUGILIST FROM SHANDONG

"When I hit, my mind starts to drift off before I can get to the target," Yu Tong remembered telling his father as his frustration grew.

"Try harder!" he heard his father yell as he hit him on top of the head. Now try again, this training is very ancient and extremely important."

"As you hit the spot, make your mind visualize the power moving up from the ground and out to the fingertips.

"The more you visualize the power, the more you will feel it travel to the target." his father said as he showed him how to hit a smaller and smaller spot.

"Yes Father, I can tell when I focus more it does not hurt as much on my fingertips," Yu Tong remembered saying as he hit the tree harder without flinching from the pain.

Gradually, after years of training, his body and mind were developing to the point where the training no longer affected him. He had become so conditioned that his mind and body acted as one. He could move in and out of each position with total ease.

Additionally, Yu Tong pursued intensive training on his own, seeking to master his family's art. Consequently, the training began to occupy more and more of his day, since all of his waking moments were filled with the desire to become a master.

"Yu Tong, are you finished with your morning training?" his father asked the moment he opened his office door, stepped outside and caught the boy hurriedly heading towards the compound archway.

"Yes, Father, I have," he replied.

His father stood by the door with his hands on his hips and a scowl on his face. "Then you need to come in here and help load the wagon for our next delivery instead of going out there to always play and waste time."

"Okay," Yu Tong answered as he lowered his head and kicked a small rock on the ground.

"When you are finished, you and your sister can go outside with your friends for a short time."

Whenever they were allowed outside, they spent time playing with neighborhood friends, chasing and wrestling each other to the ground in the street near the family business. Sometimes the boys ganged up on the girls, forcing them to follow them and imitate every movement the boys showed them. At other times, the girls would retaliate, coercing the boys into skipping rope or playing some other game that only the girls wanted to play.

Occasionally, Yu Tong would sneak out of the house early in the morning, avoiding his daily chores in order to play with his young friends or go fishing in the nearby stream. The boys spent many days playing in the vacant fields behind the old brick factory, chasing each other through the dirty abandoned shelter that long ago had been a thriving business. The factory walls had become caked over time with thick soot from the furnaces that once blazed.

On other days, the boys would gather with their homemade bamboo fishing poles that they had carefully stripped free of all small branches. Old string served as fishing line. Old nails bent into a curve held energetic night crawlers as bait to draw the attention of the big fish casually swimming in the murky water of a favorite stream.

Whenever he skipped his chores, Yu Tong would devise a strategy to blame his sister for the lapse in duties and allow her to take the punishment. Inevitably, the truth was uncovered and the young boy would be required to take care of his sister's duties along with his own for an entire week.

"Father, can you tell me why people have to wear their hair in a queue?" Yu Tong asked when he returned from playing with his friends.

"It is because the Emperor Taizu, who was from Manchuria, wanted all Han men to submit to his rule after he defeated the government," his father said.

"Why do you ask, Yu Tong?"

"I see everyone has to cut their hair the same. I heard that if people do not obey the law they will be killed for treason."

"Yes that's true. It's because they do not want any trouble from anyone," his father replied.

"With all the bribery and corruption of the judges, everyone knows that the punishment and torture are very severe for even the smallest crime, especially if you are a criminal. Then it will be death.

"It's been the same routine for centuries. With each new emperor came numerous rules forced onto everyone to make them submit to the new ruler."

"And each time, people were executed to make an example of them.

"There's been so much fighting and killing over so many centuries that everyone has become slightly immune to it," he continued as they sat under the tree in the courtyard.

"Now they just accept it." He shook his head.

Chapter 3

~ A Tie Once Bound ~

Life in Pingdu was as rhythmic as the seasons, so as Yu Tong grew to manhood, the early morning workouts, then courier work, and the afternoons of practice continued without break.

He was a naturally fearless fighter; a childhood of training with his wiser and cunning older sister only served to enhance these abilities. She had learned his strengths and weaknesses, his favorite techniques, and ways to exploit his short temper. As they reached the threshold of adulthood, she had also learned not to give in to his intimidation. Occasionally, Yu Tong would retaliate by practicing one of the family forms against his sister that his father had taught only to him.

Ancient tradition dictated that the teaching of forms be based upon gender. Some forms, because of their nature and movements, were specifically taught only to women, while others were only for men. Still, through all the defeats at the hands of his sister, he developed into an expert fighter.

Often, when his father was teaching them, Yu Tong would have to fight both of them at the same time to hone his skills at fighting multiple opponents. Afterwards, they would each find their own favorite spot and spend an hour practicing their favorite forms from the family's style.

One day, with the short noonday break over, as the sun began to make its slow descent towards the horizon while the shadows gradually crept out from under the small recesses, Yu Tong's sister angrily searched for her absent helper. He had been across town most of the morning training with his friends without realizing how long he had been gone.

They liked to rise early, long before the sun came up, to meet near a small grove of trees to exchange techniques, discuss fighting strategies and spar with each other. Sometimes they would practice fighting one-on-one. Other days, they would practice fighting against two opponents at once to experience the difficulties of multiple opponents.

This particular afternoon, as the young man slowly made his way back to the family compound, he stopped along the way to look in the windows of the shops and gaze at their wares. Some things he stared at longingly, trying to figure out how to get the money to buy them. Others seemed like strange and useless pieces of junk. When he turned the corner near his home, he heard his father calling for him.

"Yu Tong, Yu Tong! Where are you?"

"Here I am," he said from off in the distance.

PUGILIST FROM SHANDONG

"Yu Tong, please come quickly," Zhang Jie said, glaring at him for being gone too long.

Yu Tong wondered what could be so important. As he opened the large front doors of the family house and stepped over the tall threshold, he saw his sister.

"Where've you been? Father is looking for you," she yelled, shaking her finger at him as she drew closer. "I've been out there in the barn working all morning. I not only did my work but yours as well."

"I've been busy," he said calmly without offering any explanation.

"You wait. I'll get even with you for that! Father is inside, and he's been waiting," she said as he walked away.

Not affected by her words, he headed down the walkway through the large open courtyard, lined with small, neatly trimmed shrubs that were just beginning to show signs of impending bloom.

Behind the soft curb of delicate green was an expertly designed fishpond covered with large broad-leafed lily plants. Ancient koi of different colors and sizes lurked beneath the surface. They followed Yu Tong as he walked past them.

Over the years, the young boy had befriended the fish with early morning feedings of fresh scraps from the kitchen. The slow-moving water gently rolled over layers of stone carefully arranged to create the soft sound of tranquility that helped calm aggressive energy that might find its way into the peace and harmony of the open courtyard.

He entered the main room at the center of the house, stepping through the ornate circular opening with its delicately carved rosewood lattice commonly called a "moon door" because of its resemblance to the moon rising over the horizon.

35

"Yes, Father?" he asked as he removed his shoes.

"Where have you been so long?" his father asked sternly. "I have been looking for you for such a long time! Come over here and sit down with us. We would like to have a talk with you."

The elder motioned for his son to sit on the stool between him and his mother. Tentatively, Yu Tong made his way over to the small antique rosewood stool with its ornately designed peach blossom pattern of Mother of Pearl molded into the seat and dragons carved into the legs. This small unobtrusive stool situated on the left and slightly behind the large high-backed chair, signified a position of reverence and deferment to the occupant of the large chair. The large chair, carved with a dragon and phoenix coiling up the legs and around the rim of the high back, helped to bring good fortune to the owner or the person occupying the seat.

"Your mother and I have been discussing your future," he began as soon as Yu Tong sat down, his face immediately changing from its harsh expression to one that was warm and caring.

"We've been thinking about how you can help expand the family business when you are a few years older. You must be able to protect yourself when you are escorting the valuables.

"You are twenty years old and some of the bandits are very experienced.

"If you were able to learn the Jut Sow Praying Mantis Style, you would be an invaluable asset to us. So we have decided to send you to train with Abbot Ching Yeung at the Wah Lum Temple."

Yu Tong suddenly felt a rush of total exhilaration.

PUGILIST FROM SHANDONG

"Calm down and listen. I know how much you have wanted to study this style." His father said.

"We have a very unique style of the Tam Tui system that has been in our family for generations. This Praying Mantis style should make a great addition.

"I will write you a letter that you are to give to the abbot the moment you arrive." He stood up to walk over to his writing table.

"He's been a very good friend for many years and I will respectfully ask him to allow you to live at his temple."

"Yes, father, I'll do as you wish." Yu Tong replied, as he watched his father write the formal letter while trying to contain his emotions. His feet wanted to run outside so he could tell his friends about the lifelong dream soon to come true, but he knew he had to sit patiently and wait until his father dismissed him.

"I'll finish this later after I find an auspicious day for 1886 that you can arrive at the temple, but for now you need to go and complete your training and chores," his father said as he put the brush back in its holder and glanced up at his son.

"Yes, Father," Yu Tong said and bowed respectfully.

This is great! He thought as he moved closer to pay his respects to his parents. He then sprang up from the small stool and was almost out the door before the delicate antique tipped over and crashed to the floor, just missing his father's foot.

"I don't believe it," he said when he was outside. "After all this time of asking about the temple, they have finally given in to my greatest wish." Quickly he finished with the few remaining chores and then rushed out of the compound to tell his friends the news.

Yu Tong knew about Ching Yeung, who was the master in charge of the small and solitary temple, through the stories his father and the parents of his friends shared in the evening after work.

His father would tell stories of years long ago when Ching Yeung had been a member of the infamous Yi Hua Team, (Righteous and Harmonious Fist) a group of loyal and dedicated patriots who sought to change the oppression imposed upon the common people by the vicious, corrupt Ming government.

For years, the government had been struggling with a number of crucial issues throughout the country. Additionally, it had been neglecting the onslaught of foreign devils wanting to engage in trade relations with China. Finally, after many failed attempts, the foreigners seized a number of crucial ports, forcing the Middle Kingdom to not only relinquish ownership of the cities but also to make reparations to the invading country and allow the advent of trade.

This cost the Chinese dearly, for with the trade arrived more opium and more foreign devils. Now the local people were beginning to revolt. They wanted their country back, the foreigners out and the opium gone. Additionally, they wanted the corrupt officials out of office.

Meanwhile, there was a population explosion, which nearly tripled the population of China. The explosion stemmed in part from increased grain yields, along with a vast migration to the many areas now able to yield a profit from the land. This helped to stimulate an interest in farming, but with so many more mouths to feed, the severe droughts, famine, floods and disease strained the country's resources and the government began to break down.

Soon, even the gentry's managers had to take on the task of famine relief. Furthermore, the disorderly transition from the Ming Dynasty to the Qing Dynasty, followed by the White

PUGILIST FROM SHANDONG

Lotus Society rebellion in the late 1790s, had exacerbated the suffering.

This erosion of conditions continued for years, resulting in the birth of more and more rebellious groups. Unfortunately, their efforts were largely ineffective and many of the groups' leaders died in the struggle or sought refuge in remote temples to avoid prosecution.

~~~~~

The next few months passed very quickly as Yu Tong began preparing for the trip. Meanwhile, his father was so busy preparing new shipments of cargo to Qingdao and Weifeng that he was completely oblivious that his son was barely able to contain his excitement.

When it was time for young Yu Tong to leave, his mother helped him pack his few belongings, trying her best to conceal her feelings about the departure of her only son. For many years, she had instilled her values deeply in this young child, and her husband, even though he was the leader and final decision maker in the household, always allowed his wife to do so.

Fused together in a young man bursting with the energy of a young explorer on the verge of departure. Were the ideals from an ancient society ruled by Confucianism mixed with the more modern ideals from Buddhism. His youth had been consumed with mastering the intricacies of a complex style of Chinese martial arts with roots deep in the past. Now he was a courageous young fighter with the mental and physical training that would help him endure long, lonely nights and dreary days throughout his life.

Yu Tong had become a seasoned practitioner at only twenty years of age. He was now brimming with energy and strength, his mind sharp and quick, his understanding of a wide variety of fighting techniques quite astonishing. His eyes were keen

39

and focused from the countless hours of moving through a series of prearranged movements connected together to simulate a fighting sequence. The muscles, tendons and ligaments throughout his body were strong, lean and completely flexible, so his manner of movement was very smooth and stealthy, like a large cat stalking its prey. The reflexes in his hands and feet were instantaneously responsive to any change. He also had the confidence necessary to survive in the feudal world of ancient China.

He knew he was talented. His body told him so each time he moved. Yet he was not a braggart; he never reminded others of his abilities. Still, his pride sometimes sparked a short fuse. On more than one occasion, his temper forced him to prove his talent. This was the ignorance of youth mixed with the confidence from years of training. Most of the time he won these challenges, but occasionally he had to accept defeat. This only made him train harder so he could neutralize the techniques used to defeat him.

Yu Tong usually rose early to complete as much training as possible before the sun got too high in the sky. On the day of his departure into an unknown part of his life, Yu Tong slept in. When the growing illumination of the sun in the room finally made it impossible to sleep, he began the task of packing his belongings. After the small bundle of clothes and personal belongings were neatly wrapped and tightly secured, Yu Tong heaved it over his shoulder and slowly walked outside. His mother was close to his side, silently communicating her love and support but also grappling with the feeling that their reunion might be far off in the future.

The air on this early spring morning was brisk, yet it carried a faint sense of change. Soon the warmth of the summer sun would be approaching and everyone in the town would be busy in the fields, caring for the young plants.

Suddenly, Zhang Jie came running from her bedroom in the back of the compound where she had spent most of the night

PUGILIST FROM SHANDONG

knitting a wool cap. As she passed through the large round archway leading to the front courtyard, she looked to see if her brother was still inside the compound. Not seeing him, she continued to the alley and looked in both directions before heading for the corner, where the town's main street led to the family's business. As soon as she turned the corner, she saw him with their mother.

"Little brother," she yelled with outstretched hands. "I want you to take this with you. I stayed up all night so that I could finish it for you."

"Thank you," he said as he removed his belongings from his back and began to make room inside for the gift.

Once he finished closing the bundle, he turned to his sister and exchanged goodbyes. Then he turned to his mother, looked into her eyes, and saw the beginning of an outpouring of emotions and quickly said goodbye before she began to cry.

He glanced at his sister, who for so many years had been his friend, classmate, teacher, and sparring partner. Now she too was beginning to show signs of emotion as she watched her little brother begin a journey of unknown length. He knew she would have loved to be the one going on this journey, but even though she was older and more experienced, he was much more talented. Yu Tong possessed a special gift for comprehending the fighting strategies of their family's Kung Fu style. He also was the only male child, which meant it was his duty to learn that style and safeguard it for life.

After saying his goodbyes, Yu Tong headed for the building where he knew his father would be working, the worn, aged structure that had for the last several generations been the source of the family's income and social status. Just before he arrived at the door, his father emerged with a small package under his arm and an elegantly wrapped letter along with a simply folded envelope between his callused fingers.

41

"Here, son, I want you take this with you." He handed the package to his son. "And here is the letter for the abbot along with a small map showing you where the temple is located. There also is some money in there for your trip."

"Thank you, Father," Yu Tong said, putting the package and letter in his backpack and the map in his pocket. "As soon as I arrive, I will be sure to give the letter to the abbot."

"When you get to the temple, make sure you are very respectful and spend as much time as possible mastering this Praying Mantis Style," his father instructed him.

"My friend the abbot has much he can teach you." The older man reached out to straighten the pack on his son's back.

"I will, Father. I know how important this is to you, to the preservation of our family style, and to the family business," Yu Tong said, looking into his father's eyes. He could tell that his father wanted to say more, to express how he felt for his son, but that was not how he was raised or in line with the teachings of his ancestors.

The two slowly bowed in unison, turned and headed in opposite directions. After just a few steps, Yu Tong heard the door to his father's office squeak as he opened it and made his way back inside. Quietly, he sighed deeply, adjusted his pack and began to make his way toward the edge of town.

Chapter 4

~The Road Less Traveled ~

Traveling northward, Yu Tong soon crossed the Hsien Ho River that slowly meandered its way around Pingdu from the south and eventually found its home in the foothills just north of the city. As he crossed the slow-moving stream imitating a dragon casually and quietly making its way through the tall grass, he turned and glanced back at his home one last time, reflecting on his childhood.

For a moment, it saddened him to think about leaving the security of his family and a life predetermined by his ancestral heritage, but his life was leading him elsewhere. This was a new beginning. He could sense that his destiny was not within the safe confines of the family compound, so as he turned and stared off towards the distant hills, he accepted that he was now on his own.

For days he walked with the knowledge that soon he would be fulfilling his dream. Eventually, he could see the faint outline of high peaks stretching into the deep blue sky and the thick emerald blanket of trees that covered the hillsides. These were not the revered five sacred mountains of China, but they still posed an impressive site.

He spent his days walking along small paths separating fields and hills, stopping to eat and sleep under one of the large shade trees. He would watch people stroll by as he sat on the side of the road in Kung Shachuang or Shanghui to rest from the hot sun.

Each day the terrain became more and more rugged. Soon hills and then taller peaks replaced the flat stretches of ground covered by fields of grain. Occasionally the earth allowed for a small parcel of land to level off enough for yet one more field of grain and then just as suddenly, the earth rose upward again.

Day by day, the separation from his family continued to grow as did his excitement about reaching the temple. The thought of living and training with a great master and friend of his father absorbed him, gradually diverting his attention from the outside world.

He knew, according to his father's map, that he was nearing the area where the temple was located. As the anticipation of arriving grew, he picked up his pace. At last, he left the main road and began the long walk up a narrow winding path through thick underbrush and low-hanging tree limbs.

As he climbed the mountain towards the temple, he was surprised at its size. This small, solitary structure did not project the strength of the Shaolin Temple, the oldest of the martial arts fortresses, which had been built more than 1,400

PUGILIST FROM SHANDONG

years earlier and survived numerous dynasties with their fluctuating attitude towards its value.

As each new group of rebels took control of the government, they viewed the temple either as an ally to be treasured and capitalized upon, or a dangerous enemy that needed to be strictly watched and if need be, exterminated.

Now, here he stood just a few feet from the Wah Lum Temple and face to face with history from China's distant past. From a distance, all he could see were tall trees creating a canopy over well-worn rooftops. Near the front entrance, large bamboo groves hid the stone walls. He thought the winding path, well-worn from daily trips to the village by the monks, would never end. But he was drawn forward by the knowledge that this was where he needed to live and train if he wanted to learn Jut Sow (Wrestling Hands) Praying Mantis Kung Fu.

Throughout his entire life, Yu Tong's family had told him stories of this remote temple hidden deep within the forests of Shandong Province. Only those in close contact with the monks living there knew about the temple and its unparalleled training in Praying Mantis techniques. Yu Tong's father knew the abbot through their associations prior to the abbot entering the temple.

Even though many people would have liked to reside in the temple, for most it was not a possibility, since residence was granted to you only if you were known and respected in the community. Furthermore, the family requesting permission needed to be financially stable so they could compensate the temple for the cost of food, clothing and necessary repairs to the buildings. Yu Tong was fortunate that his father met all of these criteria.

Walking slowly with the confidence of a trained martial artist, Yu Tong thought about the many hours of training he had received from his father and other family members. He also thought about what his father had told him about the abbot,

Ching Yeung, who fought the Ming government for years to help overthrow corrupt officials.

The time passed so quickly while he was reliving those memories that he soon found himself just a few yards from the temple. It was not the building that first caught his attention but the sound of the two acolytes standing at the large wooden gates. They were yelling at him. "Hey, where do you think you're going?"

"What?" he asked.

"I said, where do you think you're going?" Chang De, the older monk replied.

"I came here to see Abbot Ching Yeung," he answered.

"What is your name?" Chang De asked.

"I'm Lee Yu Tong from Pingdu City."

When the young visitor reached the gates and started to head inside, the younger monk stepped in front of him to cut him off.

After the long climb in the hot afternoon sun, Yu Tong was in no mood for a confrontation. So he stopped abruptly within a few inches of the monk and looked directly into his eyes.

"I have been sent by my father with this letter to ask permission to live here!" he said. "Would you please inform the abbot that I have journeyed far and would like to enter these doors and begin my training?"

"You stay right here and I will inform the abbot of your arrival," the older monk replied, turning to instruct the younger monk to make sure their visitor stayed put. As soon as the older monk left, Yu Tong glared fiercely at the young monk, exhaling deeply in a low groaning voice from deep in his stomach.

The young monk, already intimated by this confident young man, began to chant to try to calm himself while sweating profusely.

Once inside the temple gates, Chang De the senior monk, headed across the small open courtyard and past the main training hall, then around the large fishpond filled with water lilies, lotus flowers, and koi fish older than anyone could remember. Beyond the courtyard were the individual buildings arranged in an eight-cornered Bagua symbol with the abbot's personal quarters in the center.

Each building consisted of a simple stone structure with a tightly woven straw roof tied with rope and vines. The windows were small irregular openings spaced evenly around each side, covered with rustic wood lattice shutters. The monks slept inside on wooden frames covered with a layer of straw. In the middle of each building was a small wood stove used for warming the sharp night air.

Next to the sleeping quarters was the eating hall. This room was the identical size and shape as all the others in the temple, with a wall separating the kitchen from the tables arranged in a circle.

As he made his way around one of the sleeping quarters, the senior monk heard the sound of water gently falling over rocks into the small pond in front of Abbot Ching Yeung's personal quarters. As far as anyone knew, this pond was built when the temple was first constructed 100 years ago and the original fish inside were still alive. Large lily pads covered most of the pond's surface. Ferns and moss blanketed the rocks on the waterfall. Around the pond, small flowers bloomed between the rocks. Stone statues were strategically placed, facing outwards, to scare away the evil energy.

Beyond the statues, neatly manicured Chinese evergreen bushes lined the walkways surrounding the abbot's personal quarters. Each bush was trimmed identically to the next, no more than knee high and just as wide, with all the dying or dead branches removed to keep the Feng Shui energy strong. Centrally located in each section between walkways were large groves of bamboo that stretched high into the open air, gently bowing and partially covering the small stone paths.

Just as Chang De was about to knock on the ornately carved wood door, the abbot called out from inside, "Please enter."

The monk pulled his hand back in surprise, wondering how the abbot knew he was at the door. As he opened it, he started to inform Ching Yeung who he was, but the abbot interrupted him.

"I know it's you. I could hear your footsteps from over by the sleeping quarters." Ching Yeung said."How can I help you?"

"Abbot, we have a visitor at the front gate who claims to have a letter from his father asking permission to live and train with us."

"What's his name?" Ching Yeung asked.

"He says his name is Lee Yu Tong from Pingdu City."

"Well why didn't you ask him to come in and pay his respects? If he says he has been sent by his father and has a letter asking permission for residence here, then you should have brought him in to see me."

"I didn't because he acted very rude and disrespectful," Chang De replied.

PUGILIST FROM SHANDONG

"So I left him out by the gate with my assistant until I confirmed with you whether he was telling the truth."

"Yes, he is who he says." The abbot put his calligraphy brush back in its folder. "I have known his father for quite some time. He helped us on many occasions to resist the corrupt Ching officials.

"Sometimes he carried supplies or messages for us from the south. Other times he allowed our troops to act as guards on his caravan, so we could survey the status of our enemy's positions throughout the province.

"His family has an excellent reputation in the province. They've been in the security guard business for years, and young Yu Tong is their fifth generation. Go now. Fetch our guest and apologize for your actions."

"Yes, Master," the monk replied and left hurriedly.

As he entered the main courtyard, he could see by the expression on the junior monk's face that he had returned just in time.

"Wait, wait," he yelled as he saw Yu Tong readying himself to attack the frightened-looking guard in his path.

"So you've returned," Yu Tong stated coldly as he turned his attention to the senior monk.

"Now tell me, am I allowed to go inside or have you come back to get some of the beating I was about to give your assistant?"

"I'm sorry for our rude actions, sir," Chang De replied, slowly pulling his assistant out of harm's way.

"It's just that we get so many visitors who try to gain entrance into our humble dwelling. I have spoken with the abbot and he wants you to go directly to his quarters and pay your respects. Please follow me. I will show you the way."

He turned to the junior monk and instructed him to fetch some tea and pastry and take it to the abbot's house.

When they reached the abbot's private quarters, the senior monk knocked on the small wooden door.

Instantly, he heard a response from inside.

"Come in," the strong, disciplined voice said.

As the monk and the guest entered the room, the lone figure standing at the opposite side stepped out from behind a small candle sitting on a table.

As he did, Yu Tong was momentarily taken aback as the fighter he had heard so much about finally came into view. At this moment, he knew his dream had come true.

The aged warrior spoke. "So you're the son of my good friend from Pingdu City?"

"Yes, Master, I am," Yu Tong answered.

"So tell me, how is my old friend?" the abbot asked, slowly stroking his long, white beard.

"He's doing well."

"My student tells me you have a letter from your father?" the abbot said in a questioning tone, then extended his hand in anticipation of the formal tradition.

PUGILIST FROM SHANDONG

"Yes I have." Yu Tong removed the pack from his back, opened it, and carefully pulled the elegant envelope from inside.

He handed it to his host.

Slowly and methodically, the abbot first untied the bright ribbon holding the envelope closed and then carefully removed the contents. As he read the letter, he placed the envelope on the table, walked over and sat down in his chair. When he finished, he looked up before addressing his guest.

"So your father wants you to train with me because he feels I can teach you many things. I know of your family style, a very effective fighting style. So why does your father want you to learn this Praying Mantis style?"

"Well, I guess he thinks this is a very advanced system of Kung Fu," Yu Tong said.

"He knows how much our Tam Tui style would benefit from combining it with the Praying Mantis style. He has always spoken very highly of you and your abilities, so I'm sure that was also a consideration."

The abbot stood up and walked toward his guest while saying nothing. In the silence, Yu Tong nervously awaited a response, knowing his lifelong dream stood in the balance.

Ching Yeung was now in his mid 90s and the warrior rebel turned recluse had begun years earlier to pass on his mastery of the Praying Mantis style to a few respectful students of the next generation before the techniques were lost forever. Now, standing here in front of him was someone wanting to live and train with him and he needed to decide if he was willing to take on another student at his age.

"Well, I guess if your father has so much faith in my humble style of fighting and abilities at my age, it would be very disrespectful to send you home with nothing," the abbot said as he turned and returned to his seat.

"Take our newest pupil and show him to his humble quarters."

Quietly the two men turned and left the small house, leaving Ching Yeung to resume his calligraphy painting.

Once they arrived at the simple dwelling where all the monks lived, they went inside and Chang De showed Yu Tong where he would be sleeping.

The new student put his personal belongings away before the senior monk took him to the front courtyard where both men joined the rest of the inhabitants in their afternoon workout.

Chapter 5

~Seclusion ~

B ong... Bong... Bong...rang the large bell as it pierced the thick early morning air.

Each morning before the first light, all the residents gathered in the eating hall for their small vegetarian meal before beginning their chores of cleaning, washing and repairing various structures.

Afterward, their daily routine required everyone to gather in the courtyard for training, which always began with a standing meditation and breathing exercises. This helped to stimulate their bodies and prepare them for the rigors of training by improving their concentration.

Next, they began with the basic exercises to help develop the stances, balance, flexibility and endurance required to correctly practice each hand form and use of each weapon. These prearranged sets of movements (called *forms*) were an essential part of the training. They were the foundation for applying the techniques for self-defense and for developing the spontaneous flow of one movement to another in any situation.

Following the basic exercises were the two-person sets for hand and weapon combat, which helped hone the skills of spontaneity and relaxation necessary for fighting.

"Everyone, I would like to introduce our newest member to you." Ching Yeung said as he walked near the students and placed his hand on Yu Tong's shoulder.

"This is Yu Tong from Pingdu. I have known his father for many years and now that he's a student here, we'll teach him our Praying Mantis style.

"Ready, feet together. Bow." he said, leading everyone through a formal salute to show their mutual respect for the temple's newest member.

"Xiawu, I'd like you to take Yu Tong to the side and show him our basics. Everyone else, I want to see your most recent weapon routine." Ching Yeung walked towards the shade tree.

"Okay, Yu Tong," said Xiawu, "this is how we begin each series. We refer to it as Yu Bei Shi or Ready position." Xiawu demonstrated the hand motions.

Yu Tong was shown all the basic stances, punches and kicks. Many of them were very similar to what he already knew, but others were completely new. With each movement, he was taught the formal name used to describe the technique and then the simple exercises that would be a foundation for the more intricate Praying Mantis forms to be learned later.

PUGILIST FROM SHANDONG

"Okay, now this one is called 'Praying Mantis Catches the Cicada," Xiawu said as he carefully adjusted Yu Tong's hands and fingers into the proper position.

"See, you are grasping your opponent just like a mantis grabs its prey." He said.

"Oh, okay I see how this works," Yu Tong replied. "Wow that's so effective! And I see how you can move faster from here into your next technique."

"When you strike, you can use the fingertip to attack vital areas." Xiawu explained.

"Great! Now I can incorporate the finger conditioning and years of training my father required when I was younger." Yu Tong was excited.

Gradually, as the months passed, the young guest became an accepted addition to the small secluded temple. Eventually, a few of the more senior monks displayed signs of interest toward their classmate's proficiency in learning the new style. One of them, Xiawu, began to spend most of his training time paired with Yu Tong.

As they taught Yu Tong the Praying Mantis style, he demonstrated his family's style of Kung Fu. Thus, as they taught him, he taught them.

This new theory of movement and application at times perplexed Yu Tong with all of its strange hand gestures, unusual foot movements, and unconventional applications. It was challenging after years of training in one style to learn another style. No longer were the techniques of his family style the most effective in all situations. The new fighting techniques he was learning forced him to re-evaluate his family's Kung Fu arsenal.

"This afternoon I want to teach you some of the fighting theory and philosophy that are unique to the Praying Mantis style," Abbot Ching Yeung said one day to the group of young men training in the open courtyard.

"This style is based on a more solid stance and the use of the hands to act as a mantis as it wrestles its prey into submission.

"In its natural surroundings, a mantis cannot move about very quickly. Its four feet stay rooted to the ground or limb, so its hands can wrestle with the opponent." He executed some of the typical low stances.

"I know other Praying Mantis styles use the footwork of the monkey to a high degree to give them more mobility. And when you encounter someone who knows another style of Praying Mantis, you will see that his movements reflect this idea."

"But we like to imitate how the praying mantis actually defends itself and controls the opponent without the fast stepping of the monkey." He demonstrated some of the hand gestures as he maintained a low fighting stance.

"Also, there are twelve basic characteristics that you must use when fighting with this style." He gestured to his students to follow him.

The sweat-drenched students followed him to a nearby tree to sit in the shade.

"Xiawu, please stand up," The abbot said, and the young man jumped up to help him demonstrate the characteristics.

The remainder of the group formed a semicircle and sat on the ground with their legs crossed.

PUGILIST FROM SHANDONG

"The first, second and third characteristics in Praying Mantis are called Gou, Lou, and Cai, meaning Hook, Grapple, and Pluck, and they are employed like this."

As Xiawu began to punch with his right arm, Ching Yeung grabbed it and yanked it forward, causing Xiawu's head to whiplash and his body to lose its footing.

"When a praying mantis strikes, it is excellent at this technique. It wants to neutralize the opponent's force as quickly as possible, then draw the opponent off balance so it can gain control of the situation," he said.

The moment Ching Yeung released his grip; Xiawu rubbed his neck and glared at everyone on the ground as they chuckled at what they had just witnessed.

"Now, everyone choose a partner so we can practice this series of movements," said Ching Yeung.

"For those who are attacking, make sure you are trying to hit the chest. Your opponent will not learn how to apply the movement properly if you are not serious with your attack.

"Xiawu, since Yu Tong is just learning this technique only attack with enough force to make light contact.

"As he gets better at using the movement, you can punch with more force."

Throughout the afternoon, the group practiced the series, taking turns acting as attacker and defender. As the sun sank below the distant horizon, everyone was thoroughly bruised and tired and eager to end the practice.

Over the next several days, Ching Yeung made his way through the entire list of twelve techniques. He demonstrated how each was used in application and where it could be found in the forms they were learning. Numerous hours of practice each day ensured the concepts were beginning to become natural reactions.

"Today I want to discuss what are called the eight key points of Praying Mantis," Ching Yeung said as the group finished their morning warm-up exercises.

"The first key point is this: The art of Praying Mantis is that of a process and continuous movement, with each technique giving birth to the next.

"You must think of fighting in a series of movements rather than trying to finish the fight with a single move," he said while demonstrating several basic techniques.

"When you encounter an opponent, the situation tends to flow back and forth between the two of you until one side gains the upper hand.

"Attack and defend simultaneously since all actions are neither exclusively offensive nor defensive," he told his students.

"Any action always contains the potential of its opposite. Reversing is the way of the universe.

"As you practice, you need to research every movement that you know and find out how to use each of them as both an attack technique and a defensive technique.

"When you reach out to grab your opponent, you are not just trying to gain control of his attacking arm. You are also attacking his other arm just prior to grabbing the attacking arm." He demonstrated every move he was describing.

"The third point is: Stay relaxed and change the stepping pattern.

"Be aware that in any confrontation, your body naturally develops more energy from the adrenal glands. This tends to make you anxious if you're not careful. You must stay relaxed to maintain control of the situation, to see everything your opponent is going to do. Only when you anticipate correctly will you make the right move.

"Also, be aware of your footwork," he added while executing a series of stances with varying rhythms.

"In every form that you know there are many unique types of stepping.

"Sometimes you may use a series of small quick steps, which are designed to confuse the opponent while closing the distance between you.

"Other times you may use a combination of long straight or twisted steps that allow you to close quickly and deceptively on your opponent.

"Learn to utilize many variations spontaneously while fighting, because an experienced opponent can predict your next move just by watching your footwork. That's why you have to change your footwork — to keep them guessing.

"Now, practice all the different types of stepping you know and then use those steps with different hand movements.

"Try not to always use the hand and foot movements exactly like you learned in the forms, change them up."

When the sun began to sink below the trees, everyone knew it was time to begin the evening chores, and Ching Yeung dismissed his students.

Over the next several weeks, everyone focused on these new lessons. Gradually, they became aware of new techniques within the techniques they already knew, along with a whole new series of applications for all the old movements.

"Master, may I ask you where this style of Praying Mantis came from?" Yu Tong asked one day when everyone was warming up their muscles for the morning workout.

"Years ago when I was working for your father as an escort, I trained with Lee San Jin and he was kind enough to teach me his style." Ching Yeung explained.

"Lee San Jin from my village?" Yu Tong was surprised.

"Yes. I know he's a relative of yours."

"Yes, he's a cousin of my father's," Yu Tong replied.

"I hear he's retired and living back in your village again." Ching Yeung said.

"I'll need to ask my father." Yu Tong replied as he began stretching his legs.

"Today I would like to tell everyone a story about a famous Shaolin monk who lived about 900 years ago," Ching Yeung said as he walked over and sat under the large tree standing sentry over the fishpond.

"Che Kong, who lived during the Northern Song Dynasty which was from 960 – 1127 AD, was an exceptional master of the White Crane style."

"He could direct his qi to any part of his body and occasionally he would demonstrate this ability by using it to close the pores in his skin so tightly that a mosquito couldn't withdraw its stinger."

"Master, when you say his qi, what exactly do you mean?" Yu Tong asked.

"Qi is that life force that runs through your body. There's the physical or nourishing portion of *qi* that makes up the air, water, and food that we take in. The other aspect of *chi* is more insubstantial. It is the vital fluids and the energy itself that flows through our bodies.

"It sustains all the organs and gives the body life.

"If you asked him where his energy originated, he would say his power came from fluidity of movement through a relaxed body and open mind.

"Hardness occurs when the body is tense and the mind is closed in fear," Ching Yeung explained.

"Ultimately, when a person's qi flows freely, there will be power, since all power comes from qi and when one's qi is controlled, one's power will be clearly expressed throughout their techniques.

"If you don't have qi, where does your power come from?" he asked, looking at each student to see their expressions.

"The power of the average person comes from coarse, violent movement created by a lack of control of their inner energy. The average person lacks direction and intent along with the mental ability to control and focus their mind. The average person's power floats on the surface only and does not sink to their very core.

"The power of a true master arises from the depths without his awareness, all at once, and it sinks downward as heavily as a mountain. The power of an average person floats on the surface and is without substance, but that of a master sinks and is real, since it comes from his center and encompasses his entire being.

"If you practice for a long enough time, you will see the light and experience the essence of true power. In a battle when you use your hand the qi is focused in three places: the shoulder, the elbow, and the heel of the palm. Upon raising your hand, all of the power in your body rushes to the place where the qi is collected. The qi follows your mind as fast as the speed of light. If you practice properly you will experience this.

"Over the years, you will encounter many different styles. I wanted to explain to you one aspect of the Crane style so you will be better prepared to fight anyone who uses it.

"The Crane style is useful for dealing with difficult situations. The crane's strength lies in its legs, and the essence of its spirit is silence. A student of this style will concentrate solely on the strength in their arms and gather their energy

"Empty spirit and empty will, forgetting oneself, standing alone like an ornamental column, or an 8,000-foot hanging wall are ways to describe the feelings you develop as you master this style, but this mastery does not occur quickly."

~~~~~

Time passed slowly in this set of small, secluded buildings, but with each new day came lessons about more techniques, forms and fighting strategies. Yu Tong also learned an assortment of body conditioning exercises.

His favorite exercise was designed to strengthen the fingers. It made him think about how his father had made him practice a series of drills that included fingertip techniques known only to the family members. When he was younger, that aspect of his training was of little interest to him. All he wanted to learn was how to punch, kick, and roll on the ground.

"Everyone come out into the open area so I can explain some basic weapons theory." Ching Yeung said as walked past the large tree where the students were resting from the recent meal.

"Now, here's the basic theory for the differences between the stick and straight-sword or Jian." He began once all the students were seated in a semi-circle.

PUGILIST FROM SHANDONG

"The stick is the grandfather of all weapons and should be compared to an umbrella," he continued.

"To properly execute the stick techniques, it should be frequently angled away from the body. It's extended away from you because it has reach.

"Your body should be like the central shaft of an umbrella, while the stick represents the sheltering cover of the parasol.

"Just as the parasol of the umbrella will shelter you from the sun or the rain, so should the staff shelter you from the blows of your enemy.

"Sometimes a parasol is opened, sometimes it's closed; sometimes the stick is close to the body, and other times it's thrust outward.

"But, just like an umbrella, the action of opening and closing is caused by the hand's leverage. The shaft and the ribs of the parasol are distinctly separate parts. They're always working at opposing angles to one another." He demonstrated the concepts as he spoke.

"The stick must not be held rigidly in your fists, but must be manipulated with the palms and fingers. When you bring the stick on a downward strike, you are emphasizing the pressing movement of the forward palm.

"Now the straight-sword is the mother of all weapons and can be most properly compared with the dragon." He placed the stick on the ground and picked up the well-worn sword.

"In contrast with the stick, its characteristics are virtually opposite.

"The stick is always a separate implement, whereas the sword must have total unity with you, the practitioner.

"With this weapon, there's no distinction between the two: man or weapon. You're both as one. Together, you must twist, turn, coil, leap and fly like a celestial dragon in the clouds.

"When you take up your sword, do not treat it like your stick. You and your sword must become a single entity. Your limbs are a part of that unit.

"All concentration must come brightly to bear on the very tip of the sword. Let the blade shine, for here is the dragon seeking its way." He slowly demonstrated several basic movements.

"In contrast to the stick, the straight-sword is seldom extended all the way, and it definitely lacks the stick's reach. Consequently, the movements are predominantly whirling ones, with the blade held close to the body.

"Inspired by their use in combat, the parries are executed at close range, with the body and legs turning frequently to lead the edge of the sword in angled, slicing cuts. When you thrust the sword outward, it returns by cutting its way along a different angle rather than simply being pulled back. The sword sets should have a liveliness that is reminiscent of the dragon's serpentine motion.

"Few movements with the straight-sword are two-handed, and your free hand is never allowed to simply move around.

"It, too, has precise movements to perform." He demonstrated the prescribed hand gesture of the index and middle fingers straight and the ring and little finger curled under the bent thumb.

"This hand posture is not simply an imitation of the sword for the sake of symmetry; it was originally thought to be a talismanic protector. The early swordsmen believed that each time the blade passed near or above the head, the mystical power of the sword could injure the soul." He demonstrated several postures utilizing this hand position.

"The sword has always been an integral part of life. Even the emperor and officials had beautiful swords inlaid with jewels. Noblemen fought with swords rather than coarser weapons like maces and axes.

"Even the great poet Lee Po was an expert in swordsmanship. Swords are believed by some to possess individual per-sonalities, supernatural powers, and even their own destinies. Originally, a peach-wood sword was considered so mystical that certain Taoist sects used it for special exorcism ceremonies." He glanced from one student to the next.

"A stick set has very different characteristics from the sword sets. The stick teaches how to coordinate both sides of the body. You must move it and align its length to particular angles, turning it alternately from left to right, thrusting it outward to a predetermined distance.

"The sword teaches you grace, poise, posture, and positioning. Its execution cannot be as physically powerful as the staff because it is lighter and more fragile by nature. Instead, its emphasis is on pinpoint concentration and precise cuts and parries.

"A straight-sword isn't used to directly block a weapon — it will break. Consequently, this characteristic has influenced the movements of the forms so the practitioner twists, turns, jumps, and crouches low in an imitation of a dodging swordsman aiming for the smallest opening.

"Both of these weapons are taught in a variety of weights. Initially, the weapons are lightwood. Then as you progress in ability, you will be given heavier weapons in a system of graduated weight training, the heaviest ones weighing twenty-five pounds or more.

"After you achieve a high standard with this weight, you will be given a very light weapon of approximately one or two pounds. In this way, you can perform the set with drama, expression, strength, and blinding speed — just like when you are in a fight." He pointed at each student with the sword to drive home the point.

"As with all weapons, this process is designed to be extended over a period of years. In this way, you and your body will gradually attain a very high level of proficiency. As you gain proficiency, you will become more and more one with the sword.

"The use of weapons training is not only for the sole purpose of teaching you how to kill your opponent. At times, this is of vital importance, but in addition to this, you are taught how to project your qi out into the very tip of the weapon. In this way, you can expand your range of sensitivity to an area as broad as the weapon that you are using," he explained while demonstrating several postures.

"Also, the use of these weapons teaches you how to extend your awareness out away from the body. Through continual practice, you will gradually develop a very acute sense of concentration, balance, and sensitivity, along with learning how to develop the mental imagery to become the specific animal that corresponds with each individual weapon." He slowly bent down to pick up the remaining weapon.

"Okay. Now let's go inside and reflect on these ideas for the night."

The following afternoon, Yu Tong was summoned to the abbot's quarters.

"I would like to talk about your training," Ching Yeung said when he arrived.

PUGILIST FROM SHANDONG

"I've been observing your training and keeping a close watch on your mental development."

"Thank you, Master," Yu Tong answered.

"I know that you plan to return to your family village and help your father, but if you are going to be guarding the shipments, you will need additional training to assist you while on the road." He poured the hot water into his teacup.

"What kind of training could we add to the Praying Mantis, Master?" Yu Tong asked.

"Your father and I discussed your future years ago, and we agreed that you would need special skills to successfully defend the cargo being transported from city to city.

"And when you were young your father had you practice for hours to develop your fingertips but he never told you why.

"I think it is time for you to know why that training was important and what it will be used for.

"I'm going to teach you the Shaolin art of Dim Mak or Death Touch." Ching Yeung leaned forward on his chair and looked at his guest.

"I've heard stories about that art from my family, but I've never seen it." Yu Tong replied.

"The Shaolin training manual said that the student should practice touching the walls and trees with their fingertips and gradually the pressure increases until after several years they will be able to hit the tree and leave a mark," Ching Yeung said, imitating the motions in the air.

"As you continue your practice, when you hit a piece of wood you should be able to make a hole in it. And if you hit someone, there will be immediate pain or death."

"So that's why my father always made me practice those finger exercises!"

"But you must be very careful," Ching Yeung said. "This art is very dangerous, so very few people will ever learn it and they must always be aware of how the training is affecting their mind.

"And that's why I've waited so long before I decided to teach it to you.

"I needed to see how your mind was developing and how much you could focus." Ching Yeung reached out to touch Yu Tong on the forehead.

From that day onward, Yu Tong spent time daily learning the secretive art of Dim Mak from his teacher.

Now after all the years of training and practicing techniques, forms and free sparring, expertise was beginning to show for Yu Tong. He knew all the ways of attacking and at the perfect moment most times seemed to disappear and reappear behind the incoming technique. Additionally, through the secret training from his family he was also capable of hitting with pinpoint accuracy.

Vast numbers of people trained in Kung Fu their entire lives but only a select few ever had the opportunity to glimpse at the Dim Mak art. Fewer still would endure the demanding lifelong training and master the art.

Many times masters would try to teach this art to a select few. Often, they would stop the teaching due to an incompatibility between the student and the art. Over a period of years the student would be carefully observed for signs of danger. This was usually indicated by shifts in mental focus, uncontrollable emotional outbursts or even gradual shifts in personal viewpoints. To the neophyte all this appeared trivial, but to the trained eye these were all telltale signs of impending danger.

PUGILIST FROM SHANDONG

Occasionally, someone would be sent into town to pick up supplies. Usually the abbot would send two people so they could protect each other from local bandits along the way.

"Xiawu. When you're finished with your morning chores, I need you to go into town for some supplies."

"Master, may I take our newest student with me for the trip?"

"Yes. Also, Yu Tong has never been introduced to our friends who kindly help us with our supplies. When you arrive, make sure to introduce him to everyone, so next time they will remember where he is from." The abbot handed the bags to Xiawu to carry the supplies in.

"Yes, Master. I'll be sure to stop by every store where we get our supplies."

After their initial trip into town to introduce Yu Tong to all of the friends of the temple, the pair routinely found ways to persuade the abbot to let them make the trip to replenish the temple's supplies.

Their trips into town often took longer than anyone else because they wanted to meander through town to check out all the stores and visit the magistrate's office to see if any wandering fighter had challenged a local fighter to a match. Eventually, they would pick up the supplies needed at the temple and head back.

They always stopped along the way at their favorite old oak tree, which beckoned them to practice their movements in the cool shade of its large limbs. Before they knew it, dusk would fall and the two would make a frantic dash back to the temple before the gates were closed, lest they be reprimanded by the abbot for being irresponsible.

Whenever he had the opportunity, Yu Tong would seek out a place of solitude and sit quietly under the large magnolia tree just outside the temple. The tranquil spot had also become his favorite training area over the years with its broad leaves spreading outward to grasp the rays of sunlight while its long twisting, outstretched branches patiently covered the surrounding area, providing relief from the heat.

The area was filled with an assortment of trees — magnolia, boxwood, bamboo, elm, cypress, spruce, palms, oaks, and occasionally a solitary birch. Each struggled to survive in its own part of the universe, tirelessly reaching outward to find a small amount of moisture and sunlight for sustenance.

The trees showed a number of impressive qualities that man in his hurried pace would be wise to adopt. They did not strive to destroy each other. They did not cheat, steal or fight. Theirs was a life of survival through balance, patience, and self-sufficiency.

Each tree was a soul unto itself, solitary, majestic, beautiful, diligent, unique, and humble. Its branches stretched outward, calling to the world to come and enjoy its splendor. The soft cypress branches hung like feathers floating in the air while the long, slender bamboo leaves fluttered like delicate silk. Nearby, the oaks stood strong and steadfast.

One day as he sat contemplating the series of movements from the most recent form he had learned, a small squirrel began to inch its way down the branch towards the acorns lying at the base of the tree, directly beside the young warrior's leg. The squirrel would take a few steps, stop to survey his surroundings, shake its furry tail, pause, and then shake it again. The creature was nervous about the possibility of predators, but impatient to find food.

The closer it got to the food, the more nervous it became since the acorns were lying right next to Yu Tong's leg. When the visitor was within a few feet of him, Yu Tong looked away but kept very close track of his progress.

Gradually, the small creature grew closer and closer to Yu Tong, its fear diminishing as hunger drew it to the acorns. One by one the squirrel picked up the nuts and delicately held them in its front paws while eating small pieces from one side. When that side was picked clean, the front paws slowly turned it over so the other side could be eaten.

Within moments the meal was over and the creature began looking around for its next feast. Suddenly another companion high up in a neighboring tree began chattering at its friend on the ground as if to say, "Come on back up here where it's safe."

Immediately, the squirrel turned toward Yu Tong, shook its tail a couple times, turned, and in a flash raced across the ground and up the tree. The whole experience only lasted a few moments, but it seemed like hours to the perceptive warrior.

Yu Tong returned his focus to his training. He stood up, walked into the open area between the trees, and began reviewing all the movements from the Praying Mantis hand forms he had learned.

He practiced one particular routine unique to the Praying Mantis style for hours. With each move, he focused on the various ways to apply it. He knew the forms were taught in a specific manner and were not to be changed; that way future generations could learn the style as he did, in its purest form. They could be taught to understand the basis for the style and comprehend the meaning of its fundamental movements and applications. He also knew that true appreciation of each movement would come only with time and practice. To truly understand each movement's complexity required many hours of personal practice. His father had instilled this discipline early in his life but he was only now beginning to understand its beauty.

He realized that to master martial arts, he must treat every technique as a question to which he must find an answer. This was something he had to do on his own. To rely on others would mean never being more than a shadow of someone else's ideas and understanding.

Yu Tong's solitary training sessions continued for hours while the sweat poured down his face and soaked his clothes. With each move, his body increasingly imitated the actions, gestures, and mannerisms of a praying mantis fighting for survival. His thoughts began to transcend human conception, evolving into the knowingness of an animal in its natural surroundings using its instincts.

He then began to get a glimpse of what Wong Long experienced when he first began to develop the deadly Praying Mantis style. Its movements were very different from anything Yu Tong had ever experienced. The rhythm of the movements, the concepts for defending, redirecting, controlling, and attacking — all in the same technique — were unlike any in his family style.

His new understanding of how to use angles in conjunction with footwork to control an opponent fascinated Yu Tong. The more he trained, the more his excitement grew. Soon he began to incorporate the strong-hand techniques for attack and defense along with their grappling ability into his family's art. This eventually gave him the advantages of both the leg superiority from his family's Tam Tui style and the superb hand control from this unique style of Praying Mantis.

The sun had set before he realized the day was over. Lost in his dedication to master the martial arts, he hadn't noticed the long shadows of night quickly smothering the last remaining rays of sunlight. An owl's call far off in the distance alerted him to the time of day. Slowly he gathered his things and began the long walk back to the temple.

Chapter 6

~ Exit into the Unknown~

Throughout his ten years at the temple, Yu Tong made many trips into town with his older Kung Fu brother Xiawu. They typically bought food and supplies, and occasionally watched a challenge match between two rival masters.

As they continued to refine their skills during their daily practice, they began to discuss challenging some of the wandering martial artists who visited the town.

One day, a stranger arrived and posted his challenge on the doors of all the main avenues to the city, boasting that he would quickly defeat anyone who accepted his challenge. The following day Xiawu and Yu Tong happened to be in town to pick up materials and find out more about this stranger, having heard about the challenge from a visitor to the temple. As soon as Xiawu read the notice, he signed an acceptance to the bottom.

"Xiawu, are you serious?" Yu Tong asked.

"Yes, I think I'm ready," he replied, while placing his hand on his friend's shoulder.

"Who will you take to help out?"

"I would like to go by myself so no one else knows about it."

The next morning, he left the temple before the sun began to creep above the horizon in order to arrive at the designated location early and begin preparing for the challenge.

As soon as the stranger arrived, the two men stepped into a small open area and exchanged formal salutes. For a moment, neither of them moved as each tried to determine what the other was going to do.

In the background, a steady stream of owners and customers gathered around the pair. Suddenly, Xiawu charged forward with a series of kicks and punches in an attempt to catch the stranger off guard.

Unfortunately, this opponent was no novice and was not fooled or startled. He waited patiently until his aggressor was within range and then casually stepped aside and countered with a sweep to Xiawu's legs.

Xiawu's body spun in midair and he landed face first in the dirt next to the stranger's feet and momentarily lay motionless.

The stranger stepped back and readied himself in case Xiawu wanted to continue.

PUGILIST FROM SHANDONG

Startled by his opponent's ability and embarrassed by the outcome of their first exchange, Xiawu jumped up and once again charged forward with another series of techniques.

The stranger once again waited until Xiawu drew close and sidestepped the attack while countering each move.

Unfortunately for Xiawu, the stranger's experience delivered him back to the ground in the same position as before, but with more serious bruises to his side and leg from the kicks of his opponent.

As Xiawu's anger and embarrassment raged, he jumped to his feet to ready himself for the next exchange. He wiped the mud from his eyes and glared at the stranger while trying to hide the pain in his side.

Again the pair stood motionless, gathering energy while formulating a strategy for the next exchange. As they stood face to face, Xiawu's inexperience and fatigue must have been evident to the older spectators because they turned and headed back to their business, already knowing what the outcome would be, leaving only the young to learn the fate of this overconfident young monk.

Without warning, Xiawu's opponent rushed forward with a series of multiple level kicks. The moment the first kick was withdrawn, the second came speeding in, followed by the third and fourth. Startled by this sudden barrage of kicks, Xiawu froze momentarily and by the time he regained his focus, the challenger was landing the first of several kicks to his chest. The first one drove Xiawu backwards and before he could regain his balance, the next kicks sent him tumbling to the ground and landing with his face in the dirt.

Slowly Xiawu stumbled to his feet, and any remnants of confidence he had when he arrived were past memories. His eyes no longer held the steel stare of a young fighter's confidence; now they showed the signs of prey resigned to defeat and eventual death.

"Go home, little boy, you're not ready for my techniques," the stranger said as he turned away to go sit in the shade of a large tree.

"Today I'll spare you, since you are not at my level, but don't try again," he added without looking up while brushing the dust from his jacket.

For several minutes Xiawu stood motionless in the hot sun and tried to decide his next move. The crowd gradually disappeared, and when he lifted his head to look around, he realized he was alone. First, he turned toward his opponent in one last vain attempt.

The stranger just shook his head sternly.

Xiawu slowly backed away; accepting his defeat, then turned and slowly limped back to the temple.

Over the next year, Xiawu slowly regained his health and practiced with even more determination, driven by the goal of evening the score with the seasoned fighter who had defeated him. Every day he practiced the techniques he had tried in the fight to figure out how they could have been neutralized so easily. As he did, he focused on the response the stranger had for each movement, hoping to find the opening he was leaving for his opponent.

Eventually, he heard about another notice that was posted and once again quietly made his way into town to accept the challenge. The following day he arrived especially early for the fight so he could loosen up and prepare his strategy.

When the appointed time arrived, so did his rival. Upon seeing who his challenger was, the stranger stopped and shook his head.

PUGILIST FROM SHANDONG

"Are you here for another beating, or just to watch?" the stranger asked as he set his jacket on the ground and rolled up his sleeves.

"You got lucky the last time. I'm here to even the score," Xiawu yelled as he stormed into the middle of the street.

"Well, let's see who this fine morning brings the luck to," the stranger replied.

Again the two fighters stood motionless for what seemed like an eternity. Suddenly, both challengers charged forward with their differing styles of movements. The instant they came within each other's reach, the blocks, counters, grabs, punches, and kicks seemed to be never ending.

As the stranger threw a series of techniques designed to fell the best of his opponents, Xiawu instantly had a response to neutralize every movement.

Then Xiawu took the offensive and unleashed his attack. The insights he had gained after his previous defeat greatly improved his techniques and precision.

His skills took the stranger by surprise and caused him to retreat. "Whoa, I see you've been practicing," the stranger said.

"Yes I have."

Again Xiawu pressed the attack and began driving the stranger backward. Suddenly without warning as he was retreating and countering each of Xiawu's techniques, he stopped all backward movement and began pressing forward while still defending all the incoming attacks.

The surprise change of strategy caught Xiawu off guard. He had been feeling confident in his revisions, but now he began to lose focus and his precision began to slip. As he continued to retreat while countering, the stranger suddenly swung his fist overhead in a large circular motion and caught Xiawu squarely on the top of his head. The shock wave from the blow traveled all the way down his spine and caused his knees to buckle.

The stranger seized the opportunity and kicked Xiawu in the chest, sending him rolling backwards and again landing with his face in the dirt.

For a moment Xiawu lay motionless and then slowly regained his fighting position.

"You'll pay for that," he said as he wiped the sweat-soaked soil from his face.

"Really?" the stranger replied in a sarcastic tone as he smiled.

As Xiawu charged forward, the stranger remained motionless waiting until the moment Xiawu was within range. Then he suddenly began spinning like a whirlwind until he was behind his young adversary.

The stranger kicked Xiawu in the back with a loud thud, again sending him face first towards the dirt.

Xiawu coughed as he struggled to stand up.

"Do you mean like that?" the stranger chided as he watched his weary opponent try to prepare himself for another lesson.

The stranger stomped the ground with a boom and charged toward his unprepared adversary. He pummeled Xiawu with an unending barrage of kicks, punches, blocks, grabs, and finally a body throw that took every ounce of Xiawu's spirit and sent it flying back to the temple.

PUGILIST FROM SHANDONG

For several minutes Xiawu lay on the ground trying to find a place on his body that was not injured and trying to gather enough energy to attempt to stand and face his opponent.

"Go home and don't come back! I will show no more patience for a beginner like you," the stranger said as he stood and waited for Xiawu's next move.

Without saying a word, Xiawu gradually rose to his feet and turned to make the long painful trip back to the temple.

The stranger walked to a large tree and sat beneath it. "Now who will be next? I guess there are no worthy opponents in this town," he yelled as he looked around to see if anyone else had the courage to challenge him.

Xiawu neared the temple gates, hoping to avoid everyone inside and go straight to his bed.

"Xiawu! What happened?" Yu Tong asked the moment he saw his friend struggling toward the temple gates.

As Yu Tong drew closer he could see the seriousness of Xiawu's injuries.

"Was this from your fight in town earlier?" Yu Tong asked as he helped Xiawu to his room.

"Yes, but don't tell the abbot, please!" Xiawu replied as he slowly lay on the well-worn bed.

As soon as Yu Tong had his friend comfortable in the bed, he walked outside and without saying a word, he stormed out the front gate and headed for town.

Who does this guy think he is? He raged to himself while racing toward town.

Does he not have any respect for his Kung Fu brothers?

81

Throughout the trip his mind kept boiling about the beating he observed on his friend and what kind of martial artist could do such an act.

When he arrived at the edge of town, he found an acquaintance, asked where the stranger was, and learned he was sitting under the big tree around the corner. Furiously, he picked up his pace and headed for the small, secluded area set up for the earlier challenge.

"Today is going to be your last!" Yu Tong yelled, pointing his finger at the stranger when he saw the fighter casually sitting in the shade.

"And who are you to come here and yell at me in such a manner?" The stranger stood up to face his aggressor.

"I'm Yu Tong from the Wah Lum Temple and that was my friend you beat up so badly this morning." Yu Tong screamed while continuing his forward charge.

"Oh, that young inexperienced kid is your friend?"

"Yes, and I'm here to teach you a lesson!" Yu Tong removed his jacket.

"Oh really?" the stranger asked as he slowly walked towards the middle of the street.

"Your friend said the same thing this morning when he arrived and look how that turned out."

"Well, I'm not Xiawu and it's I who will be giving the lessons now." Yu Tong glared at the stranger.

Without saying a word, the stranger stood motionless and finally offered Yu Tong a formal Kung Fu salute to say he accepted the challenge.

PUGILIST FROM SHANDONG

Yu Tong courteously offered a salute in return.

For several moments the two fighters stood silently gathering their energies. Suddenly as if choreographed, the two squared off in their favorite fighting positions.

The stranger circled the young, hot-tempered challenger.

Yu Tong recognized the traditional Crane style the stranger was using. He slowly turned in a very small circle to keep face to face with his adversary.

The stranger suddenly attacked.

As the stranger grew closer, Yu Tong stood his ground and found openings in the barrage to launch his family's Tam Tui style techniques, eventually sending his opponent to the ground with a well-placed kick.

The moment the stranger hit the ground, he jumped back to his feet, as if demonstrating that the kick did not hurt him. Yu Tong knew from his years of training that the kick had a definite impact on the stranger's chest.

"Are you okay?" Yu Tong asked sarcastically.

"That barely touched me," the stranger replied, but Yu Tong could see he was trying to hide the pain.

As the two fighters stood facing each other, the locals began lining the sides of the street. Moments passed without either fighter moving, and then suddenly the stranger pressed the attack with a series of kicks meant to catch Yu Tong by surprise.

As the kicks approached Yutan's chest, he blocked the first three but misjudged the block for the last one. He flew backward and landed on his shoulders just before rolling over.

"Oh, I hope I didn't kick you too hard." The stranger smirked while Yu Tong got up and brushed the dirt off his face.

"That was nowhere near as hard as I am going to kick you," Yu Tong snapped as he readied himself for the next exchange. He exhaled forcefully to reset his breathing and charged forward with a series of powerful Tam Tui kicks and sweeps.

The stranger was able to defend them and as Yu Tong tried to sweep his leg, the stranger jumped up out of the path and kicked Yu Tong in the back, sending him rolling to the side from the impact.

"Oh, that must've hurt! Are you okay?" the stranger asked.

Without a word Yu Tong stood back up and tried to ready himself as his anger neared its boiling point.

When fighting never let your anger be your guide and kick through your target. He heard his father's wise words in his mind.

He began to relax and release the anger while contemplating his next attack.

He remembered the abbot's fighting instructions. *When using the Praying Mantis techniques change up your footwork, do not continue using the same stepping style, because it will be easy to interpret.*

He began to attack his opponent but with a very erratic style of stepping. As he did, he observed the confusion on the stranger's face and attacked even more vigorously. Eventually he created a gap in his opponent's defenses and returned the favor of sending him face first into the dirt from a well-placed kick.

PUGILIST FROM SHANDONG

"I held back some power that time because I didn't want to hurt you too badly," Yu Tong said as he watched the stranger ready himself after getting back up.

The stranger stood silently for a while, a look of shock and confusion on his face. Suddenly, he lunged forward.

Yu Tong recognized the technique the stranger was employing in his attack. It was from a series his teacher had experienced while fighting the government and had later taught his students at the temple. Yu Tong realized that in using this technique the stranger meant to kill him. He stepped back momentarily, stopping the fight.

He stared at his frustrated opponent, exhaled deeply and resigned himself to what he had to do. He knew this fight would not end until someone was dead, and based on his teacher's stories, once he killed this stranger, there would be an investigation and he might go to jail.

Never let anger guide your techniques, he heard his father whisper in his mind.

While he stood contemplating his next move, the stranger suddenly lunged forward to catch him by surprise. As he drew near with his attack, Yu Tong easily countered his opponent's palm strike, and instantly sent a Tam Tui-style Heart Piercing Kick deep into the man's chest, stopping his forward momentum and sending him backward in midair.

The stranger landed on his head, rolled on the ground and clutched his chest. As he did, Yu Tong stood quietly by his feet. Within minutes, the man was dead.

With expressions of disbelief, the crowd closed in on the lifeless body. As they did, Yu Tong silently picked up his things and turned toward the path to the temple. He knew he must leave the temple and become a lonely wanderer.

The moment he left the small dirt street and headed into the open expanse of the Shandong countryside, his rage slowly subsided and as it did, he began to experience a strange sensation slowly welling up in the pit of his stomach. As he walked, he tried to focus on something other than the previous moments, like the following day's training and all the techniques he wanted to hone to a razor's edge. But no matter how hard he tried, the strange feeling grew stronger and stronger.

Soon he was overwhelmed by the feeling, to the point that he could no longer sustain any other thoughts. Without warning, his eyes swelled with tears and he began to sob uncontrollably. It was then that he realized the feeling was guilt from having taken someone's life. Yu Tong had heard many stories from friends, relatives, and his teacher about what it felt like to kill someone, but he hadn't grasped the depth to which it had affected them. Now he was sinking into an unfamiliar darkness with no seeming end.

Slowly he continued his journey back to the temple. The darkness of the night deepened, his arms and legs grew heavier, and walking became laborious. With each step, the image of the lifeless body of the stranger flashed before him – the eyes still open but showing no emotion, the hands still clutching tightly to the worn clothes covering the chest where the foot had extinguished life.

Yu Tong kept wondering what he could have done differently to keep from killing this stranger. Yu Tong was so lost in his thoughts that his arrival at the temple seemed sudden. Once inside the front gate he headed straight for the abbot's private quarters to inform his teacher of the events, sure that the authorities would come to question everyone. Unfortunately, the light from the Abbot's single candle was already out, so he turned and walked to his room.

All night he laid awake thinking about the fight and how the abbot would react in the morning. His temper had once again gotten him into trouble and now he wondered what the outcome would cost him.

As the sun began to break through the dark night and welcome a new day, Yu Tong slowly walked to the abbot's quarters.

He politely and cautiously tapped on the door.

"Who's there?"

"It's Yu Tong, Master"

"Shouldn't you be eating and preparing for your training?"

"I must talk to you, Master."

"Okay, enter."

When he entered the humble quarters, he focused his eyes on the abbot, who was writing next to his candle. From his position at the door, the candle cast a large silhouette of the abbot on the wall, creating an impression of a much larger person. Respectfully he bowed and then waited for the abbot to finish his writing.

"Now, what's so important at this hour?" Ching Yeung asked as he finished and turned towards his student.

"Yesterday Xiawu returned from a fight in town."

"Yes I already know about it."

"Well when he returned and told me what happened, I lost my temper and ran into town to confront the guy who beat him."

"Yes, I know about that too," he replied.

"During the fight I had to kill him, because I could tell by the way he was fighting that he was trying to kill me." Yu Tong bowed his head to look at the floor.

"Was it your intent originally to go there and kill him?"

"No, Master. I just wanted to teach him a lesson."

"You know there'll be an inquiry?"

"Yes, Master."

"When they find out you live here at the temple, they will come here looking for you and want you to go into town for an interview."

"Yes, Mastery Tong sighed.

"I also know if I stay until they arrive, and go with them for an interview, I will be arrested until it is settled."

"Yes that is true." Ching Yeung said and leaned back in his chair. If you want to avoid going to jail, then your only option will be to leave the temple."

"Yes."

The room was filled with a thick silence as the two pondered what should happen next. The silence seemed to last for hours, though it was only a few minutes. Yu Tong stood silently with his head bowed, patiently waiting for his teacher's response.

The abbot, still sitting by the candle, stroked his long thinning beard. Eventually, he rose from his small chair and walked over to his despondent student.

"I think it would be best if you gather your belongings and leave this morning." He put his hand on his student's shoulder.

PUGILIST FROM SHANDONG

"When they arrive, I'll tell them you left and no longer reside here. They'll fuss and yell at me for not keeping you here, but that's all they can do.

"Afterwards, they'll storm out and begin searching for you. So from this day forward, you'll need to keep moving and never stay too long in one place.

"I know how sad this moment feels to you. When I was young, I had to roam also to avoid arrest by the government." The abbot looked into Yutan's eyes.

As Yu Tong listened to the voice of his aging teacher, he felt a deep sadness and realized this would be the last time he would ever see his teacher. Slowly he bowed, then stood at attention to give his teacher one last formal salute before turning to leave the small residence.

"Be sure and finish your duties before packing today," the abbot said without looking back as he returned to writing on a delicate scroll.

Later that morning, Yu Tong finished neatly packing his belongings inside the small maroon and turquoise satchel his mother had made for him years earlier. He threw the pack over his shoulder and walked out to the front gate where everyone was waiting.

He removed his pack and said goodbye one by one, first to the newer students, then to the seniors. After he finished, he put the backpack over his shoulder and turned to see Abbot Ching Yeung walking toward the group. He removed the pack, stood at attention and respectfully saluted his teacher, who returned the formal salute for an extended period to signify his mutual respect for his student.

Slowly he returned the pack to his back, bowed to his teacher for what might be the last time in his life, turned and slowly left the small solitary temple to start his long journey down the mountain and into the busy world below.

As he journeyed down the small winding path, he remembered the events of the day when he first arrived ten years earlier, the feelings of anxiety and sheer exuberance over beginning a new chapter in his life. The time had passed so quickly, and his life had changed immeasurably from experiencing the discipline of intense training and learning a new style of Kung Fu to meeting new friends and studying with a master who had caringly and meticulously taught him about survival.

Yu Tong knew he would not be safe in this area for quite some time. The local authorities would come looking for him once the villagers told them what had happened and who was to blame. If they found him he would surely be taken to jail to await an official inquiry. Afterwards, he would undoubtedly be sentenced to prison or death based upon what the court felt was an appropriate punishment.

He knew that what he had done was justified, everyone watching also knew, but when everything was laid out on the table and all the various stories were taken into consideration, he intuitively knew what would happen. He had seen it many times before. All parties would be brought in for formal questioning, they each would be required to testify as to what occurred and then a verdict would be rendered.

Unfortunately, if those directly involved weren't from a reputable family or didn't have direct ties to the community, they would be executed. So with a slight sigh of exasperation he chose to travel far to the western side of Shandong Province, where no one would know anything about the situation.

Author's Note:

PUGILIST FROM SHANDONG

*~The Importance of Temples in China during the Time of
Yu Tong ~*

*During the 1800's and early 1900's the main factors that
composed the fabric of Chinese life were the family and its
lineage, village/city hierarchies, and the numerous political
allegiances. However, there was another aspect that endured
centuries of political and social upheavals: the temples.*

*In addition to promoting religious beliefs and meditative
practices, many of them also served as places of refuge.*

*Ongoing political and social turmoil forced many people to
seek out a place to escape the forces that sought them, and
these temples were usually their last resort.*

*The Shaolin and Wudang temples are the best known to
Westerners and served as spiritual, temporal and training
centers for the martial arts in China. There were other less
well-known temples, one of which was called the Wah Lum
Temple, which carried on its own traditions, legends, and
stories of extraordinary fighters.*

*Throughout the numerous political changes in China, the
temples were very often at the center. Those individuals who
were attempting to overthrow the old ruling power often
sought the assistance of the monks. In exchange for their help,
the monks and the temple to which they were attached would
receive the new ruler's favor. This favor typically meant
money, power or simply being left alone.*

*On the other hand, if the rulers considered the monks to have
been allied with the losing factions, then they would do what
they could to suppress the prestige of the temple. This kind of
disfavor typically meant keeping a watchful eye on everyone
and everything inside the temple walls. In this case the monks
were held in suspicion but these rulers knew from centuries of
experience that they could control their enemies more
effectively if they kept them alive, gave them a small amount of*

freedom, but still maintained control of their daily lives in a subtle manner.

The temples were and still are to some extent a place of cultural and personal advancement. Many of the ideas first perceived by the monks, sitting quietly in their meditations, were gradually spread to the local community who then proceeded to take the information everywhere.

The power of the temple teachings in physical, mental and spiritual areas was formidable. After being taught by the monks in these temples, people who had been subservient to the higher classes began to gain independence and personal autonomy.

In these temples were simple and humble monks, living a meager life while demonstrating that life had much more in store for those who were willing to set aside a few useless worldly attachments and strive for a life beyond the crude and barbaric physical existence.

Many rulers found that this entire concept ran against the grain of their personal agendas and so they rigorously opposed the existence of the temples. Rulers changed often in China and typically as soon as a new regime took control, the old rulers' views were swept away as the new regime asserted its dominance. Thus the temples fell in and out of favor but never so much as to completely end their influence on society.

Chapter 7

~ The Deadly Black Tigers ~

Several years after being asked to leave the temple, Yu Tong was still reminiscing about the extraordinary time he had spent inside those simple walls. The knowledge and training from that experience had shifted his perception and understanding of the world around him. He now looked at people and their daily struggles through less judgmental eyes instead of from the sheltered perspective of his family.

There had been opportunities to appreciate broader realities in his home town of Pingdu where neighbors sometimes failed in their struggle to keep from being lost in the masses of poverty-stricken wanderers. But his family's routine protected him from seeing those realities. They worked every day to sustain the family business, and used the rest of their day to learn, perfect, and carry on the techniques of the family's system of self-defense.

Now, moving from city to city, he observed the emotional, physical, and social devastation instilled by the Japanese after they defeated China in 1895 in the most recent war. This time it involved the loss of the peninsula of Korea from Chinese rule. For centuries this small extension of land surrounded by the Yellow Sea and the Sea of Japan had been under the complete control of Chinese rulers. Now the Japanese, after defeating their rival Middle Kingdom neighbors, were forcing the Korean people to relinquish their ancient customs and allegiances.

Additionally, China had been forced to concede vast amounts of land, goods and money in reparation for damage inflicted upon the invading French, Russian, German, Japanese, English and American forces during their repeated invasions. As he traveled throughout Shandong Province he observed the signs of this foreign invasion; the landscape was worn, tired, and abused from the continual bombardment of exploding bombs and marching troops. The small villages that at one time had been meticulously cared for were now mere shells of a former life with no signs of hope. People sat or stood motionless and broken as if frozen in time with no idea or energy to rebuild their lives and restore their heritage.

At the temple, Yu Tong had spent nearly every day in complete tranquility. Chirping birds announced the new day and there were few other sounds than the chanting of temple occupants deep in meditation. Training occupied the remainder of his day. This new reality of the world as it was outside those walls was a very harsh contrast to the life he had been forced to abandon.

Yu Tong traveled continuously throughout the province in search of adventure to supply breaks from his solitary lifestyle. Occasionally he heard rumors about the status of the ongoing investigation by the magistrate of Pingdu County, as his office continued to search for the young fighter who had killed a reputable member of an upstanding family. The officials wanted to find the culprit so that he could be prosecuted for the crime, and the family wanted him caught so their family honor could be vindicated. However, they had been given a vague description of the fighter which produced unrecognizable sketches, and with Yu Tong's continual roaming, no one was able to connect him to the crime.

Solitary life was hard, but he was young and curious. He visited many cities, towns, villages, and personal dwellings throughout Shandong province and the fringes of the neighboring provinces during the years following his departure from the temple. In each place he discovered a new series of adventures. Qingdao was one of his favorite places to visit and he enjoyed exchanging ideas and techniques with fellow Praying Mantis martial artists.

For centuries Qingdao had survived as a fishing village, and then in the late 1800s, the government seized control of its strategic location and ice-free port to establish a sailing fleet that turned the city into a major seaport. Unfortunately, by the end of the century, Germany would invade this beautiful city and force China to relinquish the area for a period of ninety-nine years.

This old city was a refreshing contrast to Pingdu, but it also was filled with the realities of the new world. Foreigners, whom Yu Tong regarded as foreign devils, continually invaded this ancient city since the first act of complacency by the Chinese government. The Chinese government, when they accepted defeat from outsiders who wanted to continue smuggling opium into the country, lost effective control of their own destiny. The sheer size of this city was initially frightening to Yu Tong, as was the influx of foreigners and their strange languages, mannerisms, and style of dress. He sensed a feeling of personal invasion. The foreigners scurried about the city as if it were their own. Natives were treated as outcasts.

Barbarians from a faraway land called Germany were the first to begin inhabiting this small seaport. They brought their strange architecture to Qingdao, which used strange angles and unbalanced lines with no sense of harmony with the surrounding landscape or ancient buildings that had stood for centuries. Additionally, they brought their business of brewing beer, a beverage with a strange taste to natives of the Middle Kingdom and were peddling it on every street corner.

Early each morning, Yu Tong sat quietly in a Lotus position, trying to erase the noise of the outside world long enough to find his true inner self. There he experienced a sense of oneness that filled his entire being like a dense fog slowly sinking to the ground while blanketing everything beneath it. Practice allowed him to focus on a single thought until he felt total connection to the universe.

His understanding of the world slowly changed and his compassion and patience expanded. When he had completed his meditation, he would gradually open his eyes, casually stand up and begin his day. His life was remarkably different from when he was living inside the security of the walls of the secluded temple. Here, everyday, he had to find food to sustain him and shelter for the night. Most people around him seemed to be in a hurry, their response to the stress of daily survival perhaps. Fortunately, the abbot had taught Yu Tong that life was long, so there was no need to hurry.

Each city had a special story to tell, yet each left him searching for more. But on one morning he woke and felt the call of home in his mind. After many months of living a solitary and hidden life, he decided it was time for him to return home. Yu Tong would return home, to track down old childhood friends, to see his father, mother, and sister and settle down to a steady job serving as an escort for his father's caravans. He wanted to move on with his life.

On the day he set off for the long trip home, he reviewed the lessons he had learned. As he began along the road from Jinan towards Pingdu, he looked at the strangers around him differently than he would have years earlier. Now, he understood that home is where you make it. He started remembering his childhood, particularly the joyful moments he had spent with his sister playing in the courtyard, visiting friends down the street, training for hours. They had learned many things during those grueling hours about life, self-defense, themselves, and each other. Now as he traveled the narrow dirt path leading from one town to another, his daydreams drifted through his mind like a slow-moving mist engulfing the countryside.

In the evening, as the intense heat retreated, shadows lengthened and the moon appeared, he would find an unused cave in a hillside to rest his mind and body. These caves were a very familiar sight throughout the provinces. For centuries, masses of field workers counted on these cavern dwellings as their only possession and their only way to provide a home for their families. Some families eventually saved enough money to construct structures at the entrance to keep out drifters and wild animals looking for an easy meal, or birds and bats seeking shelter. Those who could not afford this had to deal with the outside world as it came on a day-to-day basis, never knowing in what condition they would find their cave each evening when they returned from the long day of labor in the fields.

When he could see the outline of the city of his birth in the distance, his memories became more vivid. With each step, the feelings of long ago flooded his body, creating a sense of nervous anticipation. Unknowingly, he quickened his pace until he reached the road leading into town. When he could see the street leading to his home, he stopped, surveyed familiar sights, then slowly closed his eyes and breathed deeply to smell the familiar scents.

The feeling of being home sank deep into his soul, awakening his younger self. He even began to faintly detect the aroma of his mother's cooking, an aroma easy to detect since she used a blend of herbs and spices very different from other households in his neighborhood.

As he was enjoying the feelings of his youth, he saw his sister step out of the main archway on her way into town. He knew she routinely looked in both directions to see who was out in the street. He watched as she caught sight of him standing at the end of the street just beyond the shadows of the mid-day sun.

"Yu Tong!" she yelled in disbelief, running toward him as her scream echoed throughout the compound. When his mother reached the front door, she gasped as she saw her son.

"Mother," Yu Tong called out, his arms outstretched, as his mother drew near.

"My dear son has returned home," his mother said with tears in her eyes, wrapping her arms around him for the first time in years. For the next few minutes, time stood still as the three huddled together in the center of the path. Eventually, without saying a word, they returned to the compound.

As they neared the main entrance, Yu Tong looked at the ornate archway. His experiences of the last few years had taught him to appreciate everything around him. As a child, he had considered the entrance just another passageway into the outside world. He never really stopped to inspect the craftsmanship of each piece of brick placed exactly upon the next, the detail of the expertly carved characters vertically lining the opening, or the message they spoke to the world: "Tsai yun nan hsien (Colored clouds are rising in the south; the family is being blessed by good heavenly signs.) As he read the words, he remembered how his mother made him wipe off fingerprints from the ornately carved stone placard that he and his sister had left there during one of their many adventures.

For the first time, he also noticed the elaborate hand-carved woodwork connecting the two lintels of the gateway, superimposed from side to side with numerous geometrical and realistic designs painted in different colors to enhance their features before being varnished.

PUGILIST FROM SHANDONG

His eyes moved upward to the tiled roof with its arched corners pointing to the heavens to keep the evil spirits from landing. He never realized as a child the tiles curved up and down to give the appearance of a rolling sea, with the ends closed off with a decorative cap to seal out small animals. Slowly his gaze turned to the roofline, where a series of dragons and other small ceramic statues were strategically placed along the outermost corners to help ward off unwanted spirits. He remembered as a young boy, he loved to throw rocks at the distant figures, which had no meaning for him at the time.

As he alternated between memories and his new appreciation of the surroundings, his mother and sister stood quietly, waiting for Yu Tong to resume their retreat into the compound. Within minutes, his father came running into the courtyard, alerted by a family member to Yu Tong's arrival.

"Father!" he shouted as soon as he saw his father, instantly jumping up to head towards the patriarch of the family.

"Yu Tong," his father said in his strong steady voice, which didn't show any sign of the emotion he was feeling at this moment.

As family members returned home for the day, they joined in the celebration and continuously asked questions about his travels.

"How many cities did you see?" his uncle asked.

"Oh! There have been quite a few; some big, some small," Yu Tong answered.

"Which one did you like the most?" his mother asked as she handed him another bowl of fresh vegetables and rice.

"I would say my favorite was Qingdao," he replied while nodding his head to say thank you for the food.

"What was so special about Qingdao?" his sister inquired.

"I really enjoyed the people I met and the time spent exchanging information and techniques with them about Praying Mantis."

Slowly the evening festivities celebrating his arrival came to a close. One by one the relatives all returned to their homes, leaving Yu Tong and his sister sitting in the moonlight talking about all of his adventures.

For the next few months, Yu Tong was required to spend all day practicing his family style and the new style of Kung Fu his father had sent him to learn. His sister was always conveniently available to help whenever he needed a partner. She was mesmerized by the new movements her younger brother now performed. Subsequently, she no longer had the advantage when they practiced their fighting.

One afternoon as they practiced the new style of fighting and Yu Tong was explaining the applications, his sister could sense a certain melancholy in his manner.

"Little brother, what's wrong?" she asked as she stepped back and looked into his eyes. "I can sense that even though we're just practicing these new movements, you're upset about something."

They walked to a nearby tree and sat in the shade to rest.

"Well," he began as he wiped the sweat from his forehead, "while I was living at the temple, I got into a fight with a fighter from a nearby village and ended up killing him in order to save myself." He gazed off into the clouds slowly beginning to peek over the distant hilltops.

"What? Does anyone else in the family know about this?"

"I suspect the abbot has sent word to father about the fight, but I'm not sure about anyone else."

His sister sat quietly and watched her younger brother as he struggled to contain his emotions.

100

PUGILIST FROM SHANDONG

"I never realized how much it changes a person after they've ended someone's life," he continued after several moments of silence. "Everything I was taught about that moment and all the years of training in preparation for the time when it might happen, were never quite enough."

For the remainder of the afternoon the two just sat and barely spoke at all. The birds continued their chirping, the sun slowly moved across the sky and began to sink, everyone on the street continued their daily routines, but here in the shade of a large oak tree, two young souls sat speechless as their minds drifted off in reflection about the revelation.

Throughout the following weeks, Yu Tong's body language exhibited signs of how the taking of the fighter's life had affected him. No longer was he as carefree and casual about the exactness of the techniques. Now everything seemed to fall into a place; everything had a place and a reason for its preservation throughout the generations. It was through the continual perseverance, practice, and research on the part of the practitioner that made every technique worthwhile and useful in the ongoing struggle to survive.

After several more weeks of personal practice and reflection, Yu Tong began working for his father as an escort guarding shipments of precious goods from one city to another. This meant he now had to use everything he had been taught by his father and Abbot Ching Yeung. It was going to be a major test of how well he had absorbed their lessons.

The people he would encounter while guarding the cargo would prove to be a part of society all to themselves. Their focus and objectives were to steal anything and everything they could acquire, with no concern or emotion toward the victims.

As the months passed, Yu Tong began facing various challenges in his new assignment. Occasionally, a solitary bandit hiding along the road would make a futile attempt to rob the caravan he was guarding. Unfortunately for him, his fighting skills, did not measure up to his desire to relieve others of their goods, so Yu Tong easily sent him limping on his way empty handed.

Gradually, the caravan gained a reputation regarding the success of the products always arriving at their destination, which also helped the family business flourish.

Eventually, with the increased reputation the bandits had to resort to more drastic measures. One day, three of the known thieves joined together to finally rid the area of this young guard who was becoming a hero in the county by continually thwarting their attempts to steal the caravan goods.

The caravan had left Pingdu several days prior to deliver a cargo to Weifeng. The trip began quietly and uneventfully. The only people seen along the way were farmers working in their fields. As Yu Tong and his assistants traveled the well-worn road, everyone on the cart was enjoying the warmth of the midday sun, thinking only of the nights ahead that would be spent in a familiar town with friends not seen in months, causing their fear of danger on the road to lapse.

It was a bright summer day with but a few clouds in the sky. The gentle breeze strained to diminish the heat from the sun high overhead, while the cloud of dust trailing the caravan seemed to hang in the air as if waiting for someone to carry it away to another place and time.

Yu Tong's mind wandered. He began to wonder about how old this well-worn path actually was and how many secrets it must contain — secrets of mystery, war, birth, death, love and hate. He became fixated on the question of what had happened along this stretch of roadway 200 years ago. Had there been a robbery gone awry, a great battle between warlords and a group of visionaries attempting to overthrow the corrupt government, or possibly a meeting between two great Kung Fu masters trying to maintain their reputations as great warriors? Like a loyal friend to all who traveled it, this pathway did not divulge its secrets.

PUGILIST FROM SHANDONG

The mid-summer day continued to pass slowly as the small, horse-drawn wagon inched its way through the countryside along the rough, winding path. A soft breeze gently drifted through the trees, giving the travelers a moment of reprieve, while lifting the large leaves as though to look quietly underneath, then moving like a wave out across the fields of green. But the breeze only offered momentary relief from the sun, which was directly overhead. The birds and small animals had found refuge hours earlier in their usual hiding spots, waiting for the cool evening to resume their foraging for food.

Passing a small group of houses huddled together as if trying to fend off the inward pressure from surrounding fields, the road suddenly made its way around a large rock formation that seemed to appear out of nowhere. The rock appeared to be upside down and travelers could not see this unique force of nature from afar because large magnolia trees and bushes of bright crimson blocked the view. The contrast of tall trees, low-lying bushes and bright flowers provided a refreshing change from the miles of green, open fields.

Suddenly, without a sound, three masked bandits jumped down from the top of the large rock formation, landing within a few feet of the caravan. Yu Tong sprang from the seat on the small cart and landed between the bandits and his cargo as the driver tightened the reins to stop the horses. As Yu Tong faced the robbers, he kept his left side partially turned to hide the twin broadswords behind his right leg, while standing motionless and waiting for the first sign of attack.

The three bandits stood directly in the path of the horse, with drawn weapons and an air of confidence. Moments passed slowly; no one from either side moved.

"Hey you little man, we are the Black Tigers.

"I am Monghai from Outer Mongolia, these are my friends Yuhua from Shanxi and Linshu from Hebei and we want all your valuables." The stranger pointed at Yu Tong.

Monghai, the largest and most brazen, stood six feet tall and was distinctly of Northern Chinese and Mongolian descent. His tattered clothes strained to contain the broad chest and thick muscles beneath them. His skin was dark and covered with thick black hair. A dense beard covered his face from ear to ear and his shirt was open from top to bottom. He clearly aimed to intimidate the caravan with his large stature.

His clothes showed signs of age but still retained the intricate patterns that had been brightly visible when the outfit was new. Green dragons, now faded from time, still coiled their way around the jacket from top to bottom. A large and still-fierce tiger clawed its way down each sleeve, even though numerous holes and tears had made havoc of the predator's body. His pants were also faded and torn. His feet bore tattered shoes with remnants of an elaborate design of clouds circling around the moon.

His two accomplices, standing just behind him on either side, were a mix from different regions of China. The first — a tall man with a slender build, very thin hair, and nervous twitch — was from Shanxi Province and was called Yuhua. He had escaped prosecution from the local authorities for stealing in his hometown, by fleeing to Northern Shandong Province. The other man; a short, stout figure with a mean disposition and the mentality to match, was from Hebei Province and liked being called Linshu. He too had avoided prosecution by escaping to a distant land where no one knew his name or his crimes. Eventually, all three ended up working together to increase their odds of stealing valuable goods from the many caravans crossing the province.

These two bandits wore a hodgepodge of fabrics, garments and ornaments which they had acquired from previous robberies along this very road. Both wore finely tailored silk jackets that Yu Tong guessed probably once belonged to an important businessman. They were cut off at the shoulders, and they now barely covered the large frames of the two bandits. Each wore a different style of pants they had stolen, cut off at the knees to allow the thick, tanned, scarred legs easy mobility.

PUGILIST FROM SHANDONG

In contrast to this trio of brash and unkempt bandits, Yu Tong, who stood a mere four feet-nine inches tall, had his queue tightly wrapped around his neck and tucked neatly inside his shirt. His shirt was clean and intact with no holes or tears; the fabric was still bright with only a simple pattern of peach blossoms decorating the sleeves. His pants fit comfortably and proudly displayed the dragons clawing their way down each leg.

"I am Monghai and we are fearless." the leader of the bandits yelled from behind his dirty unkempt beard.

"My friends Yuhua, Linshu, and I have traveled this entire area and robbed many caravans." He glared at Yu Tong and shook his fist.

Yu Tong stood motionless without saying a word, waiting for their next move. A slight breeze moved through the trees as if trying to quell the tension of the moment by rustling the leaves. The horse pulling the cart stirred nervously. Without looking back, Yu Tong reached up and patted the horse's nose, quieting the animal.

Moments passed slowly before the bandits appeared to realize their intimidation strategy wasn't working, so their leader tried a different approach.

"The caravans we attacked in the past always had more than one guard, so I guess today is going to be really easy. Just give us all your cargo and we will let you go home alive." His hand twitched on the spear by his side.

The caravan driver and his son were frozen to their seats, staring at Yu Tong to see how their escort would respond.

Yu Tong remained still and silent.

"How can he just stand there and let these bandits take our cargo?" the driver whispered to his small, frightened companion.

The silence from Yu Tong seemed to last an eternity and was making the bandits visibly nervous. Soon, the leader of the bandits became impatient; his hand was continually changing position on the grip of his well-worn spear. The other two also revealed signs of nervousness, repeatedly exchanging glances. Yu Tong knew they were not accustomed to this kind of response from their victims. Usually everyone on the caravan dropped to the ground and let bandits take what they wanted.

"Are you that young kid everyone has been talking about who has been chasing all our friends away before they could steal your cargo?" Monghai screamed as he inched his way closer.

Success in a fight comes from a disciplined and controlled mind, Yu Tong heard his father say as he remained silent while still hiding his twin swords.

Finally, the trio attacked. The leader lunged forward with his razor-sharp spear in an attempt to drive it deep into Yu Tong's chest. But just as the spear neared his body, Yu Tong stepped to the side and kicked the man directly in the ribs. A loud crack echoed through the air as the ribs gave way to the force of his foot. The bandit was propelled backwards, crashing to the ground between his two friends before rolling into the thorny shrubs along the roadside.

As the other two bandits lashed out with their own weapons, Yu Tong dropped to the ground and swept the feet out from under Yuhua; sending him face first toward the dusty path and stirring up a cloud of dust that temporarily made him disappear. Yu Tong then jumped up and kicked Linshu in the chin. Linshu had stumbled backward and landed next to his leader.

PUGILIST FROM SHANDONG

When the dust cloud settled, Yu Tong could see that the two were in so much pain that they had released their weapons and grabbed their sore face and legs.

By the time Yu Tong finished with the last bandit, their leader had recovered from the kick, finished pulling the thorns out of his back, and was beginning to close in for another attack. The pain from his broken ribs forced him to change strategy and look for an easy opening to attack Yu Tong.

Again Yu Tong stood his ground, completely motionless while hiding every indication of his next attack. The moment Monghai's spear drew near, Yu Tong spun to his right, pulled two broadswords from his back and chopped down on top of the flexible wooden shaft as it sped past his body; just missing his hip.

Monghai changed direction and whipped the spear around in an attempt to cut Yu Tong's leg. As he did, Yu Tong elevated his leg high into a single-leg stance to avoid the sharp metal tip, while using a single sword to chop outward and block the spear. Then he swung his other sword downward, catching the middle of the wood shaft in a move that cut a deep gouge halfway through the flexible weapon.

Monghai spun around and tried to strike his opponent in the head with the handle of his spear. Yu Tong jumped forward to avoid the hit and rolled behind his attacker. As he stood up Monghai twisted and again tried to thrust the spear tip into his chest. Yu Tong twisted into a low sitting position while blocking the spear with the swords.

Thud! Echoed through the air as the swords cancelled the spear's direction.

Yu Tong swung one sword around slashing the bandit's face and cutting a deep gouge from ear to chin.

While Monghai was reacting to the sword striking his face, Yu Tong came over the top of his head with the next technique; a movement he had practiced thousands of times. He stepped to the right with a circular block from the left sword and chopped low with his right sword to attack the bandit's exposed lower limbs. *Thwack!* The sword sliced the back of the joint on one knee, cutting through the torn pants, then the muscles and tendons, severing them completely.

His opponent dropped his spear, fell to one knee, and clutched the other with both hands to stop the bleeding. As he did, Yu Tong swung his left sword as hard as he could; hitting his opponent between the neck and shoulder. Blood from the wound spewed in every direction as Monghai fell to the ground, rolling and clutching his leg. The rolling made the wounds become encased in soft dirt which quickly turned to dark red mud.

The remaining two bandits had recovered from their hard fall to the ground, but the sight of their seriously injured leader left them in shock. Soon the shock turned into rage and with no more than a glance, they decided to avenge their leader's demise.

"Ai-yaa!!" Yuhua yelled, as he ran toward Yu Tong holding an axe high above his head with one hand while the other one was clenched in a fist that was waving wildly.

Yu Tong calmly stood his ground. The moment his opponent was close, he dropped down on his left leg as his right leg slid in front of the attacker. Instinctively the bandit looked down in response just in time to see the young warrior shift forward and swing the razor-sharp blade across his exposed thighs, cutting each leg to the bone. Yuhua fell to the ground, stared in disbelief at the damage and then suddenly screamed from the pain exploding throughout the severed muscles.

Yu Tong spun around, ending up behind his defenseless adversary and caught him in the back of the neck with his right sword, dealing him the same deadly blow as his friend. The axe dropped from the bandit's hand as he collapsed to the ground and settled into the soft dirt. Now there were two bodies lying on the ground with only a few short moments left in their current life, and a single opponent left to contend with.

Before Linshu could recover from the sight of his friend being critically wounded, Yu Tong rushed forward to attack him. First he swung his left sword over his head in a circle as though he were going to hit his opponent on top of the head. This was a diversion to draw his victim's weapon upward so that he could attack his legs.

This bandit was inexperienced and so he was easily tricked. As he raised his blade in an attempt to stop the blow, Yu Tong casually stepped to the side and swung his left sword down upon his opponent's left leg, cutting deep into the thick tissue. Before the bandit could grab the injured leg, Yu Tong drove a heart-piercing kick into his exposed chest.

Crack! Was the sound coming from the bandit's chest as his feet left the ground from the impact.

The kick propelled him backward through the air and he landed on the edge of the path. His weapon still lay in front of Yu Tong. Gradually the remaining bandit struggled to his feet and attempted to make another charge. As he took his first step, the injured leg collapsed and once he again lay in the dirt while moaning from the pain.

"Do not get up again!" Yu Tong said as he watched the crippled opponent vainly attempt to stand and attack.

Linshu apparently didn't hear Yu Tong's command through his pain, and eventually stood up to face his enemy.

"I am not done yet!" he snapped and shook his fist at the fighter standing in front of him.

Yu Tong stood silently and shook his head, then suddenly jumped forward and kicked the battered bandit directly in the center of his chest. *Crack!* The ribs echoed as the bones in the bandit's chest gave way to Yu Tong's foot crashing through the chest into the cavity housing the heart. Linshu was lifted off the ground and sent flying backward. He was dead before hitting the ground.

Yu Tong remained motionless for what seemed an eternity, as he witnessed the outcome of the bandits' poor judgment. Then he slowly stepped back, looked around the area to make sure there were no other bandits and when he was convinced they were alone, he began to relax and wiped the blood from his swords and the sweat from his forehead.

When he finished, he took one last look at the three dead bodies lying lifeless in the blood-soaked soil, shook his head, and felt saddened by what he had been forced to do.

Turning toward the cart, he noticed the driver and his son hadn't moved a muscle since the fighting had begun. Both still had the same frightened expression on their faces.

He said to the boy, "Hey, kid, go out there and drag those bodies off into the weeds so that we can continue on our journey."

"Yes, sir," the teen said and jumped down from the seat.

Exhaling deeply, Yu Tong grabbed the side of the cart, pulled hard and swung himself up into the spot where the boy had been sitting. Without looking at the father, Yu Tong just pointed at the path in front of them as if to say, "Let's go."

Gently the man tapped the horses with his whip. The cart and his heavy cargo made their way to the location of the fight. The boy had finished dragging the corpses into the bushes. As they passed by, he jumped up into the remaining seat next to his father.

PUGILIST FROM SHANDONG

When they made it to the other side of the large rock formation, all visual signs of the recent events were out of sight. The three were relieved to be heading back into the open fields once more. Slowly, the tension and fear drifted off into the far away hills. For the rest of the day, nobody spoke about the incident. A few hours later, they arrived at their destination and unloaded their cargo.

"So, did you have any trouble along the way today?" the owner asked. All three looked at each other with knowing eyes, but nobody answered.

When they finished unloading, Yu Tong headed to the local teahouse to relax and separate himself from the day's ordeal.

By the next day, the entire city knew about the fight. People continually approached Yu Tong, asking him for the full story and offering to buy him food and tea. Several days later, the trio was ready to head home with another load of valuables. As they left town, the owner yelled for them to be careful of other bandits who might be roaming their path. He might have meant them well but his tone made it clear to Yu Tong that he cared more about the safety of his goods than the welfare of the father, son and young warrior.

Months passed without further problems, so the trips from one city to another were slow and uneventful. The only highlight was the anticipation of arriving at each destination to hear the tales being told about the fight. As the story evolved, the bandits' numbers and statures grew as did their martial prowess to a point that even the gods would have been hard pressed to defeat them in battle. Each time he was confronted by someone with a more fantastic story, Yu Tong abruptly corrected their fantastic version with the truth. Unfortunately, most people preferred to believe the more fanciful story.

Chapter 8

~ China Wars ~

As far back as 2600BC, when Huang Di defeated the Yan Emperor and throughout every century since, China has been at war within its own boundaries. Countless warlords were continually trying to usurp power from the current ruler to further their own personal agenda. Those who failed were killed and those who succeeded only survived a short time longer, until the next coup.

During the 1800s, China was once again immersed in a long and costly warring phase. This time it was with the lowly foreign devils. For so long, China had been able to keep them out, and only trade on their own terms, but this would soon come to an end with the influx of the deadly opium. The first Opium War began in 1839 when China tried to stop the

English from importing the deadly drug into China's southern ports.

For years China never had a desire for any goods from the English, but England continued to buy up vast amounts of Chinese goods. Consequently, these lowly foreigners had been smuggling in small quantities of the addictive drug, and slowly but steadily the demand continued to increase.

Eventually, the English East India Trading Company developed a monopoly on the market and steadily increased the amount imported. Their initial port of entry was Canton and gradually it began to find its way into a number of the major cities. Finally in 1839, China grew tired of the drugs being imported and attempted to stop all incoming merchant ships and confiscate their illegal drugs. Unfortunately, the small Chinese junks were no match for the British cannons.

In battle after battle, China tried in vain to thwart the influx but continually lost to the superiority of the British gunships. Eventually, after eighteen losses, the Chinese government formally accepted defeat, and on August 29, 1842 signed the Treaty of Nanking, which included the cession of Hong Kong.

Unfortunately for China, this treaty never explicitly spelled out a solution for the opium problem. Consequently, this would not be the end of their war with opium or the British. A few short years later in 1857 they were once again at war. This time the English wanted even more treaty ports and sought to legalize the opium trade. China was forced into yet another treaty and even higher reparations to the foreign devils.

In 1875 war's ugly head surfaced once again when the foreigners wanted more. Japan, France and Britain wanted to expand into China's vast territory. They slowly began to dismantle the tributary states that China owned, through a series of short but decisive wars that brought them under their own rule. Finally, in 1879,Japan acquired the Ryuku Islands, France claimed Vietnam in 1885, and in 1886 the British took

PUGILIST FROM SHANDONG

Burma for themselves. In 1894, Japan pressed again and won Korea's independence and separation from China.

Finally, after more than twenty battles with the foreigners from 1875 to 1890, the Chinese view of superiority and their isolation from the rest of the world was making life progressively harder and harder for the common workers. They not only had to endure the continual taxation by the government to pay for their losses in the many wars but the internal jockeying for position by the numerous groups that wanted to gain control of the Imperial Palace setup conditions in which little attention was paid to the common person.

To further complicate the situation at the time a series of devastating famines, droughts and other natural disasters made conditions much worse.

The people were tired, poor and frustrated and were looking for a way out of poverty, a way out of the internal bickering among the political groups, and a way out of the continual and costly wars with foreigners. Unfortunately, there would not be an answer for many years to come. Until then, the country would suffer many more atrocities and lose millions more lives.

As a solitary wanderer, Yu Tong had witnessed first-hand the condition of the country and its people. Everywhere he traveled he saw the effects of the wars, the drought, the famines, and the internal feuding. Fortunately, he had learned how to live simply, through the use of herbs, meditation, and his years of martial training. He could survive on much less than the ordinary man, his daily requirements were much lower, and his direction in life was different. He didn't have a need for success and position. He just wanted to survive.

People everywhere were starving. As he walked into each town or city, he saw countless homeless people sitting on the side of the road with an expression of total loss, defeat, and desperation on their faces. Some had not eaten in weeks and just sat, begging from whoever would turn and listen, while on the verge of starvation. Others had already resigned themselves to the completion of this life, and were just waiting for their final release so they could come back and start over.

It is over this bleak backdrop that our story continues to unfold.

Chapter 9

~ A Duel to the Death ~

The many months following the fight with the Black Tigers had proven to Yu Tong that if he wanted to survive he would need to find a different occupation. He knew that eventually there would be an opponent who would end his life as he had to do to others before. His father had reminded him so many times when he was younger and would always say: "Yu Tong, you need to be careful with your training. If you continue to brag and boast about how good you think you are, someday someone will come along and put you in your place.

"You are the torchbearer for our family and you need to carry on the family name. So watch what you do and who you challenge."

When he woke the next morning, Yu Tong realized he would not be safe in this area for long. His reputation as an escort was escalating, and the bandits all wanted him dead. He also knew once the villagers told the local authorities he was to blame for the killing of someone of reputation years earlier they would soon come looking for him. So with a large sigh of exasperation he chose to travel far enough away so that no one would know anything about the situation.

He knew now was the right time for him to retire from the escort business. The next day when they returned from a trip to Weifeng to deliver some merchandise, he walked into his father's office, sat down to give him a report about the trip and gave him the bad news.

"Well, I know everyone here will miss you on the road, but it is also for the best if you want to survive. I know there are bandits out there who would like to try and prove that they are better than you in order to boost their reputation." His father leaned back in his chair and sighed.

"What are you planning to do if you quit this job?" his father asked as he leaned forward to put his hand on his son's shoulder.

"Well, I was thinking about traveling around for a while and seeing some of the other parts of China." Yu Tong said as he sat up straight to try and show his courage about what he was saying he would do.

"How will you survive?" his father asked with a tone of concern in his voice.

"I figured I would take some of my weapons with me and when I need money I would perform a demonstration in the streets for the local people," Yu Tong replied.

"Do you think it will be enough to survive on?" his father asked.

"I don't really need much to survive on. While I was at the temple we learned to get by with very little and still be happy."

PUGILIST FROM SHANDONG

"When will you be leaving?" he asked as Yu Tong stood up to leave.

"In a couple days," he replied. "I don't want to linger around here and be a burden to you and Mother."

Without knowing where he was going to go at first, Yu Tong knew it had to be far, far away from everything, including his home and family. So he just began walking south. Heading first towards Anhui Province, he thought that this might be safer than going through Jiangsu Province, since he may have to pass by or through Shanghai and since it is a busy, more modern city with connections to the north, someone may have heard about the incident in Shandong and reported him to the authorities.

~~~~~

Author's Note

Walking from Northern China south toward Vietnam is by no means an easy task. First, the distance of approximately 1,800 miles is reason enough not to attempt the feat. Furthermore, this is not a smooth, even terrain that you can easily stroll through without effort. It involves navigating over or around numerous mountain ranges, vast open plains of field after field of a variety of crops, rivers too wide to wade through that you must swim or search for a bridge to crossover, and mile after mile of complete and isolated wilderness with a variety of wild animals continually looking for a meal.

~~~~~

As he began the long journey to a place he had never seen, he decided to stay off the main roads for a while until he was out of the province, decreasing his chances for possible recognition.

119

Walking along the small, worn path he noticed the season was changing. The fields of corn that had been planted months earlier were now tall and majestic and showing their splendor. They gloriously announced to him the arrival of their new bounty and filled his senses with their sweet aroma. These fields of corn were ripe with corncobs full of kernels golden yellow topped with silk of dark brown announcing their maturity.

Caretakers would soon arrive and continue the cycle by cutting the stalks one by one, bundling them neatly on a small hand-drawn cart. Soon the cart would be overflowing and then be taken to the village where the other family members would carefully remove the cobs and the outer layers of husk to reveal the bounty deep inside.

Walking quietly and alone along the small footpath separating the fields that were trying to overtake the barren ground, he could smell the scent of ripe wheat wafting through the air and lightly hanging in the midday sun as if suspended by some unseen string.

No one seemed to notice his presence. He might have been a local out checking his fields during a slow time in the season, or someone from a neighboring village on their way to visit an ailing relative. Unsuspecting to all, here was a solitary soul in route to a distant land many miles from his home. Soon, he would turn down another path that would lead to a small village around the bend and out of sight forever.

Later as he made his way along the quiet road from Huainan to Anqing, he looked down and solemnly noticed the event occurring beneath his feet. Each step along the dirt path had left a temporary mark of his existence and journey. The soft fine almond colored dust covering the road like a warm winter blanket effortlessly gave way as he rhythmically continued on his journey.

PUGILIST FROM SHANDONG

Within moments he could no longer detect the imprints left behind from only a few feet away. All traces of his existence through this area and any imprint on the land would soon be at the whims of the wind gently blowing across the green fields.

The wide fields of rice were separated by an occasional fish pond filled with carp of every color and covered with broad-leafed lotus plants that helped shade the occupants from the heat and protect them from predators like the egrets standing at the water's edge with their skinny legs and long slightly curved beaks, patiently waiting for the occasional victim swimming too close to the surface.

Traveling from city to city, Yu Tong found the road was sometimes very lonely and uneventful; for days he would walk and not see anyone. No one working in the fields or carrying harvested crops piled precariously high on a tired and shaky old cart. On those days it seemed the air was still and thick without enough of a breeze to even ruffle the delicate bamboo leaves gently hanging off the long thin spires reaching toward the sky.

The few solitary clouds far off in the distance seemed to have stopped and were resting near the cool air coming up over the mountaintops and diminishing the sun's onslaught of heat attacking them from overhead.

Other times it seemed as though he never got a moment's peace. People were working their crops in the fields and would momentarily stop to see who was walking by, while others carried the bounty freshly harvested in small wooden carts stacked dangerously high over the rough and narrow roadway. As they moved slowly along the path, each small bump caused the load to shift from side to side and come close to toppling into the small overgrown ditch along the roadside.

Scattered occasionally between the carts traveling to and fro were other solitary drifters like him, each with their own story, their own destination and reason for leaving wherever they came from.

The continual traveling in the provinces had taught Yu Tong immensely. While spending time in various villages he had seen how fierce the competition between Kung Fu masters had always been. When he was young, he heard many stories from his older relatives about the challenges to gain or maintain control of a local Kung Fu school that often ended only when one fighter was dead. Occasionally a fighter would concede the fight and leave town, allowing the victor to take over the teaching in the village. Now he was seeing it with his own eyes, feeling the thickness of the energy during the match with his body and hearing the losing fighter's last gasp for air just before his life ended.

He was hearing from strangers and seeing for himself how numerous villages would search for the best master in the area and hire him to come and teach and protect their families. After their new teacher was settled into his new position, the village elders would secretly go out and recruit bandits to come and challenge the new master in order to assure everyone that they had a qualified teacher who was still able to maintain his reputation as a fierce fighter.

~~~~~

Sitting along the roadside while trying to make some money so that he could eat from selling herbs that he learned about at the temple, Yu Tong had observed many daily routines along with an occasional unique occurrence. Throughout the day he always noticed the same group of family members heading off to their crops in the fields, each carrying a different implement to use in the care of the tender young sprouts emerging from the fertile soil.

Later he would see a group of men pulling their small wooden carts overloaded with manure to the fields and carefully spread over the delicate plants.

Occasionally, he would see an elegantly carved and hand-painted covered cart hurry past with one of the town's officials tucked inside and hidden behind a veil of fine silk woven into a beautiful scene of dragons chasing a pearl while dashing in and out of the turbulent sea. The same coach would come rushing back about an hour or so later, still appearing as though they only had a few hours to save the world.

As he continued to watch the same scenario day after day, he noticed a gradual increase in activity next to the main entrance of the compound of one of the city's more prominent families. Throughout the day more and more people seemed to be hurrying in and out of the archway, carrying an array of equipment.

Meanwhile, a group of about ten boys were busily digging up the hard-packed roadway that had slowly worn down to become a high ridge in the middle of the road with two wheel tracks on either side just wide enough for the narrow wooden wheels of the small horse-drawn carts. Furiously they dug with their old, worn and rusted shovels and hoes to try and loosen the resistant soil. Others worked to break up the large chunks of dirt into a fine layer of loose soft earth.

Throughout the entire process, it appeared as though there was some sort of urgency about their project in the street and everything happening inside the compound as well. Eventually the boys finished their project. As soon as they picked up their tools and headed off through the large archway, one of the elders yelled for them to put down their shovels and begin moving the lumber from in back of the guest quarters to out in front where they had just leveled the dirt. As they hurriedly carried the old, worn and cracked boards to the front, some of the elders began constructing a large square platform.

Hour after hour they worked until finally the stage was finished and all the equipment was taken back inside.

The sun was slowly sinking behind the horizon and the shadows were beginning to take over the land as Yu Tong began packing up his things.

THOMAS HAASE

One of the boys who had helped to level the ground was walking by, so Yu Tong stopped him and asked, "Hey, boy, what is going on down there by your house? It seems like everyone was in an awful hurry to get that platform finished."

"Oh, that's because some fierce fighter is coming to town tomorrow to challenge our teacher Master Lou," the boy said as he stopped to watch Yu Tong finish packing. Are you going to come and watch?"

"No probably not. I can see all I need to from down here," Yu Tong replied as he lifted the bag onto his shoulder and reached down to pick up his weapons.

"You should come down and watch; they say this guy used to kill tigers up north for money." The boy replied as he stared at the array of weapons the stranger was carrying.

"We'll see," Yu Tong said as he turned and began walking away.

The next morning after Yu Tong finished his training in the nearby woods he headed towards his usual spot on the street to sell the bruise medicine he had mixed months earlier. As he finished setting up his wares, the sun slowly began inching its way above the horizon. Looking off in the distance he saw how one by one the rooftops, then the trees, then the hillside, then the faraway mountains and finally the clouds began to appear while continually supporting each other in an unending attempt to reach the sky and become one with the heavens. Each one seemed to be holding up the next taller in an unending chain and finally the clouds were able to reach into the darkness of the faraway heavens, feel and experience the vastness of space and time and then in some small subtle way send back the knowledge gained to those far below.

The scene was one he had seen countless times in his life and each succeeding image seemed to strike his very core and give him a sense of connection to all; both above and below. Slowly he was beginning to understand more and more about what his parents and Grandmaster had told him over and over when he was young.

"Life is a long journey to be experienced moment by moment and all things in the universe are connected, from the smallest insect crawling along the ground to the largest planet speeding through the vast corners of the galaxy. Each is an entire universe unto itself."

He was beginning to realize the complexity of life with the simplicity hidden deep within and only visible to those who would take the time to stop and observe everything in its natural surroundings.

After what seemed like forever, Yu Tong's attention returned to the present and the task at hand; survival. As he turned toward the large compound at the end of the street, the young boy who had befriended him came rushing around the corner of the main entrance and straight toward him.

"Hey, mister! Hey, mister!" the boy yelled as he drew closer.

"And good morning to you too!" Yu Tong replied with a slight tone of intolerance towards the young boy's lack of respect for his elders.

"The guy is here, the guy is here. He showed up early this morning and told my father he was ready whenever Master Lou got the courage to challenge him," the boy said.

"So I guess they'll be fighting on the platform later today, huh?"

"Yes, my father says they will probably start in a couple hours before it gets too hot."

"Who do you think will win?" Yu Tong asked.

"I don't really know for sure," the boy replied with a puzzled look on his face.

"Well, tell me, which direction did the stranger come into town from?" Yu Tong asked as he slowly settled into his shaded spot and leaned back against the wall.

"I think from over that western mountain," the boy pointed to the snowcapped peak far off in the distance.

"That's not good for him," Yu Tong said as he dropped his head down and slowly shook it from side to side.

"Why?"

"Because it would have been good luck to come in from the east; he would be coming from the direction of the rising sun and carrying the strength of the sun on his back. Also, he would appear really tall and strong as the sun tried to shine around his body. Plus, anyone who saw him would have difficulty recognizing him because they would have to look directly into the sun as it gradually rose above the horizon," Yu Tong said as the boy sat down and listened intently.

"Also, if the stranger had arrived from the east when he approached the platform his shadow would have been cast completely across the stage, and the platform would have been charged with his energy; giving him an advantage when they began to fight."

The young boy slid closer and became totally engrossed with the words he was hearing.

Yu Tong shrugged and continued. "Unfortunately, it seems this stranger is not too well versed in the old traditional ways of good fortune."

"Wow!" the boy replied as he looked down the street in the direction of his house.

For a moment neither of them said a word while pondering the outcome of the fight. Eventually, the boy could not contain himself any longer and suddenly jumped up, turned, and ran back home without saying a word.

PUGILIST FROM SHANDONG

Several hours passed without a single member of the family coming out of the compound. Then as if summoned into the street by the emperor, everyone came through the main archway all at once and surrounded the large platform.

Moments later Master Lou slowly walked out into the open street, looked in both directions and then back into the compound, turned and stepped onto the stage. He began going through a series of traditional stretches and exercises followed by short sections of a number of the forms that he was taught. After several minutes he paused to look around the area and as he glanced down the road leading out of town he, saw the outline of a large muscular man heading his way.

As the foreigner finally approached the platform, he rudely pushed people aside without saying a word. When he reached the stage, he threw off his coat and shirt and stood motionless, staring at his opponent.

Meanwhile, Master Lou continued his routine as if nothing had happened. When he finished, he turned to look directly into the eyes of the brazen stranger. Time seemed to stop momentarily and everyone waited to see who would attack first and more importantly, who was going to win.

A cool breeze from the north drifted through the area. The leaves on the trees suddenly began to ruffle and whisper faint sounds of the coming change of season. Everyone's shirt sleeves fluttered wildly creating a sudden burst of noise and trying in vain to diminish the tension building on the platform.

As the breeze continued through the crowd, a solitary cloud crept across the barren sky and slowly began blocking the sun from raining its rays down on the crowd. Moments later a long shadow crept up over the heads of the impatient spectators, along the ground, up the side of the platform and onto the stage. Inch by inch it continued across the stage until the entire half by the unkempt challenger was covered in gray.

Hmm, it doesn't look good for the challenger, Yu Tong thought as he quietly sat and watched the entire ordeal from down the street.

A large dark cloud that crosses your path when you are in the middle of a challenge is a sure sign that your chances of winning are slim and your days are soon to come to an abrupt end. He sat back against the wall and tried to catch the last few moments of shade before the sun crept higher across the horizon and chased all signs of relief under the edges of the buildings.

Master Lou stood motionless. Suddenly, as if by some unseen cue, both fighters simultaneously ran toward each other. As soon as they were within range, each threw a flurry of techniques both offensive and defensive while continually circling each other. As one would throw a technique from their style that usually disabled their opponent, the other would throw an equally effective move to counteract the incoming blow. Back and forth the two fought, each using more and more deadly techniques. For a short period no one could determine who was going to be the victor.

Then from out of nowhere Master Lou began using a series of techniques that Yu Tong had never seen before. With each new technique, Yu Tong saw the stranger slowly begin to lose his advantage as Master Lou began to take control of the fight. Desperate to win the stranger tried to hit him with more and more attacks that Yu Tong recognized as killing techniques. Unfortunately, all his attempts were in vain and within minutes his rage became obviously uncontrolled.

He charged towards Master Lou while throwing deadly techniques Yu Tong knew would kill the largest tiger.

As he drew near, Master Lou casually stepped backwards to give the impression of retreating, a disguise Yu Tong had used many times, while setting up his opponent for a specific technique. Step by step Master Lou backed up towards the edge of the platform then at the moment when it seemed he

128

was going to fall off the edge, he dropped down to one knee and struck upward into his opponent's abdomen towards the heart with his fingertips. The moment his fingers hit the man's heart, the large fighter who for years had killed tigers in Northern China for money with no fear of death, stood frozen.

Within seconds his face began to change color while the facial expression gave every indication about what was beginning to happen. Suddenly, the stranger dropped forward, followed by a loud *Thud!* As he fell dead on the floor and lay motionless with Master Lou standing over him looking down at his most recent victim.

The crowd anxiously stood waiting to make sure the event was finished, and then one by one, they began to meander back inside the compound. Soon only the dead stranger and Master Lou were left on the platform.

As suddenly as the solitary cloud had drifted into the area it moved on. Its shadow crept down off the platform, out along the small dirt path leading out to the open fields, and up towards the top of the nearby hills.

The following day a couple of the men from the compound arrived to dispose of the body and dismantle the stage. By the time the sun began to sink behind the distant mountains, the entire area had been cleaned up and all traces of the previous day's events were but a memory.

Months later, Yu Tong would finally pack his belongings and move on, just like he had in every other city. Occasionally, he would stop for a day or two in various cities and towns and while there he would try to make some money by demonstrating his Praying Mantis techniques or weapons prowess. In one city he might demonstrate his ability to throw a small iron bird from inside his sleeve at a target, usually twenty feet or more. This was one of the many martial talents he practiced regularly and his skill at hitting a target was superb. He would always hit his target, sometimes exactly where he said, other times it was just to the outside of the mark, but he always hit the target.

In other places, he would exhibit his ability to defend himself with his favorite double broadswords by allowing the passersby to throw rocks at him. His training served him well and no one was ever able to touch him with a rock. Over the years of continual practice, his ability to defend himself with these two faithful companions had become exceptional and this proved on many occasions to be a life-saving asset.

While trying to make his way to Hefei before nightfall he came upon in a small, secluded village tucked deeply within the fields and decided to stop for the day. He would wait until tomorrow before continuing on toward Hefei. This was one of the many small villages that for so long never had a proper name; it was just called the small village over the hill in the middle of the field.

The next day he rose early and began his trip long before the sun rose above the majestic mountains far off in the east. This day began like so many others: rise long before the sun and train in the Kung Fu he had learned over the past thirty years then set out on another piece of his journey. In a few hours the day would come to a close in the same manner: Just before dusk, he would seek out a quiet, out of the way corner where he could be alone, rest and then finally fall asleep. The following day it would all begin again.

Occasionally, he would stop for a day or two in various cities and towns, and while there he would try to make money by selling medicinal herbs or giving demonstrations.

Stopping in Bengbu (Pearl City) gave Yu Tong the opportunity to try some of the city's unique cuisine and view the fresh water pearls grown there that he heard so much about during his travels. This city had been established about 7,000 years earlier and remained a continual civilization ever since. Throughout the eons, numerous cultures had evolved and eventually succumbed to outside warring factions. Yet the city remained and continued to flourish, eventually receiving its revered nickname as a producer of quality pearls.

Walking down the well-worn street heading deep into the heart of the city, Yu Tong was amazed at how many signs were hanging from the storefronts promoting the freshwater pearls. Each sign claimed to own the best and largest pearls in town. Yet, when Yu Tong looked inside the store he saw the exact same pearls as the last stores.

"Hey! If these are better than everyone else's, how come they look exactly the same?" he asked the owner as he pointed at the display.

"Do you want to buy or not?" the owner snapped.

"Not today," Yu Tong replied as he turned and headed toward the door.

All morning he walked further and further into the city, noticing the promotion of the best, cheapest, and biggest pearls became bolder and more and more grandiose as the price crept higher.

Eventually he arrived at the King Yu Temple and sat in the shade of a large old tree.

King Yu lived 2100 BC, and was revered for his expertise at flood control and upright moral character.

I think I will demonstrate some of my Kung Fu; I should get a few coins and when I tell them about my herbs I should get a few more, he thought while watching all the people come and go from the temple.

A young boy and his mother walked by as he prepared for the demonstration.

The boy suddenly stopped to stare at the array of ancient weapons. "Wow!" he said.

His mother pulled on his arm.

"Mom, can I go over and look at those?" he asked while pulling on his mother's arm and staring at his discovery.

"Okay, just for a minute," she replied as she looked to see what had grabbed his attention.

The boy ran across the street and stopped within inches of the weapons Yu Tong had recently laid out.

"Wooowww!" he exclaimed in a long exaggerated tone as his eyes tried to take in everything in front of him.

He didn't notice when his mother walked up and put her hand on his shoulder to keep him contained.

"I guess he likes Kung Fu weapons," Yu Tong said.

"Yes, this is Er Weilu and he has always been amazed by them and begs to learn," she replied, patting her son on the head.

"That is good." Yu Tong smiled. "We need to continue our long heritage to honor the art and our ancestors. The young ones who are interested are where we should focus."

"I agree," she said.

"If you stay around, I am going to demonstrate some of my Kung Fu." Yu Tong looked the boy in the eyes.

"Really?" Er Weilu exclaimed.

PUGILIST FROM SHANDONG

"Yes." Yu Tong stood up and began to perform a series of warm-up basics to help loosen all his joints and stimulate the energy flow through his muscles.

"We will stay for just a short time, so he can watch," his mother said.

As a group of curious passersby began to gather around Yu Tong, some were store owners standing in the doorway of their business looking for customers; some were locals heading to the market with their wares; others were just leisurely sitting on the walkway doing nothing.

"Hey, Master, look!" the young boy yelled as he pointed at the crowd watching his warm-up exercise.

"Thank you all for stopping by to see my Kung Fu," Yu Tong said while walking around the small performance area and saluting everyone.

"My style is the ancient Tam Tui and it has been passed down in my family for generations.

"I am also an expert in the Praying Mantis Kung Fu from the Wah Lum Temple in Shandong Province.

"First I will show you several of the exercises I use to prepare for training.

One by one Yu Tong demonstrated the basic routines while explaining their purpose.

"This one is called Iron Bridge. It helps loosen the spine and strengthen the back, shoulders and legs." He arched backward and placed his palms on the ground to imitate a bridge.

"This next movement is called Kiss the Toe. It opens up all the muscles in the legs, hips and back" He arched forward and placed his chin on his toe.

"Wow!" Young Er Weilu shouted.

"Now that I am finished warming up, I will show you an ancient spear routine passed down from the renowned Fan Lihua." He said, picking up the well-worn weapon.

As suddenly as the first rays from the sun would cast a shadow on the ground, Yu Tong's spear sprang to life. The red tassel seemed to be dancing everywhere like a small fairy flitting through the air, then just as suddenly; dead stillness. Followed by a series of pokes, jabs, and cuts all executed with deadly accuracy.

"Great, great!" the audience yelled when Yu Tong finished.

"Now I will show you the strength and power of my family style." He stomped on the ground to signal the beginning of the hand routine.

Boom! Echoed through the air; momentarily startling everyone. As the dust settled from the stomp, Yu Tong jumped into the air while executing five kicks. The moment he touched the ground his body spun through a series of circular sweeps moving across the ground like a large broom clearing away the leaves. Each movement merged seamlessly with the next and appeared to be as effortless as brushing away a mosquito trying to land on the arm.

Throughout the entire performance, the young boy stood with his eyes fixed on every move. His mother tried repeatedly to pull him away, but the youngster was adamant about staying.

"Fine, but when we get home there will be no play time for you!" she said.

"That's okay. I'll help you with everything to make up for letting me stay." he said, maintaining his focus on Yu Tong's performance.

PUGILIST FROM SHANDONG

After several more routines, the audience began to lose interest in seeing only a weapon and hand routines and kept asking for more than just a few fancy jumps and kicks.

"What else can you do?" he heard someone ask from the back of the crowd.

"We have seen this type of performance before," another blurted out with an impatient tone.

"Okay, okay, I'll now show you something new that I know you'll like," he said as he set his long sword on the ground. "I'll need someone to hold up a plate in the air."

"I'll hold it for you!" the young boy said and ran to the center of the performing area.

"Good! Take this plate and walk down the street until I tell you to stop," Yu Tong said, pointing in the direction of an opening in the street.

Excitedly the boy grabbed the plate and began running towards the distant street corner.

"Okay, that'll do," Yu Tong yelled when he thought it was a good distance.

"I'll now show you how Zhang Qing** would attack his opponents," he said as he readied himself in a strong stance.

Zhang Qing, or Featherless Arrow, was a character in the Chinese classic book *Water Margin*, renowned for his rock-throwing ability.

Yu Tong gazed intently at the crowd and then suddenly began a series of steps with large arm swings and body twists. With each step, he gathered more and more power and focus for the next series of attacks. Suddenly he turned away from the boy holding the plate, jumped high up in the air, twisted in midflight and shot his arm forward toward the plate. Before he landed, the crowd heard a loud *crack* and saw the plate break in half and fall to the ground.

Er Weilu stood with his eyes wide open and a large smile on his face over what he had just seen.

For a second everyone just stood in amazement and then, "Great, great!" they yelled as they clapped enthusiastically.

"Thank you, thank you," Yu Tong said humbly as he saluted everyone watching while walking to where the boy was standing. He picked up the intricately carved stone bird.

"You did a good job holding the plate," he said to the boy while patting him on the shoulder.

Er Weilu's face beamed with excitement and his steps seemed to barely touch the ground as he raced back to his mother to tell her about what he had done.

"Now I'll show you my double broadsword techniques," Yu Tong told the crowd.

Picking up the two razor-sharp swords, he moved them around his body in perfect unison. Each defensive move was instantly followed by a precise attack, creating a defense impossible to penetrate. Every jump forward or backward was executed with the swords swirling around his body as though they were a tornado. When the swords defended the right and left sides of his body, a kick would suddenly come from nowhere and a loud *crack* would startle the crowd as the kick found its imaginary chest target.

"Great! Great!" The crowd yelled again as he was finishing the routine.

PUGILIST FROM SHANDONG

"I need several volunteers to help me this time," Yu Tong said while picking up a handful of rocks.

"I'll help, I'll help," he heard several people yell as they raised their arms.

"Come over here so I can give you these," he said.

Excitedly the volunteers rushed over to where he was standing, collected the stones he was handing out, and patiently waited for his instructions.

"I want you to stand in front of everyone else and when I tell you, I want you to throw those stones at me one by one," Yu Tong said with a strong confident tone as he looked each volunteer in the eyes.

The volunteers nodded, walked over and stood side by side in front of the crowd, waiting for his command.

Yu Tong picked up his double broadswords and began swirling them around his body.

"Okay, you can begin throwing the stones," he said without the slightest fluctuation in his technique.

One by one each volunteer began throwing stones at him. *Crack, crack* could be heard each time as he blocked a stone with the sword. Occasionally, someone would try to break through his defenses by throwing the stone at a part of his body that appeared to be undefended. Those attempts ended as all the rest, with the familiar *crack* as the stone was blocked away. Soon all the volunteers were finished with their rocks and Yu Tong stood unharmed, having blocked every single stone.

The crowd cheered as he stopped his sword movements and pointed at the stones lying on the ground around him and then at his body to show that no stone had hit him.

137

"Thank you, thank you, I am glad you liked my performance," Yu Tong humbly saluted each spectator.

"I am also very experienced with herbal medicine, so if you have any questions or want to see my special herbs, please ask." He said before the crowd lost interest.

"What do you use for shoulder cramps and arm pain?" an elderly man asked as he walked closer holding his wife's hand.

"Well, tell me about your shoulder cramps," Yu Tong inquired.

"I have had this problem with my shoulder for some time now and it never seems to get better," he rubbed his shoulder.

"Do you remember how it started?" Yu Tong asked.

"I think it was several months ago when I was lifting some boxes of merchandise in my store and the next day I could barely use this arm," he responded. His wife nodded her head in agreement.

"I have developed a special herbal patch that you can use every day and it should be better in a couple days." Yu Tong pulled a small package of tightly wrapped herbal patches from his pack.

"Put one piece on the shoulder right here." He pointed to the location on the shoulder where he thought the main problem originated.

"Oh, thank you very much," the man handed Yu Tong the coins for the herbs.

"I am glad I could help." Yu Tong bowed to the couple and smiled.

PUGILIST FROM SHANDONG

As the couple turned and made their way back towards their store, Yu Tong began to gather all his belongings and secure them inside his pack. As he did, everyone graciously walked past his weapons and dropped several coins into his small cup and then abruptly returned to their daily routines

Only Er Weilu remained. He stood nearby in complete awe over the performance. "Where did you learn all that stuff? "he asked.

"Oh, I have been training since I was your age." Yu Tong replied as he finished packing and sat on the ground next to the weapons.

"Where can I learn that?"

"Isn't there anyone in this city who can teach you?" Yu Tong asked.

"I don't know," the boy shrugged.

"If you ask your parents, I am sure they can find someone who is qualified to teach you."

The boy smiled.

"But you must be willing to train every day and very hard." Yu Tong said, giving the boy a stern look. "This is not something you can do with a casual attitude; you must be willing to train seriously if you want to succeed.

"Kung Fu is hard work, but it will teach you many things and your body will be able to perform amazing techniques. But only if you are dedicated and never give up."

"Okay, I will train really hard because I want to be like you." Er Weilu stood up and tried to demonstrate one of the postures he saw during the performance.

"Good, good, that is the attitude I had when I started." Yu Tong patiently watched the boy demonstrate his techniques.

"I wanted to be as good as my teacher," he continued.

"Er Weilu come here!" his mother called from down the street. "We must go home now!"

"Go now, and always remember what I told you about your training and you will go far."

As he gathered all his belongings, he looked down the street to see young Er Weilu trying his best to imitate the movements he had seen while frantically trying to keep up with his mother as she hurried toward their home.

Ahh, the uninhibited and never-ending enthusiasm of youth, he thought, remembering how he had felt at that age.

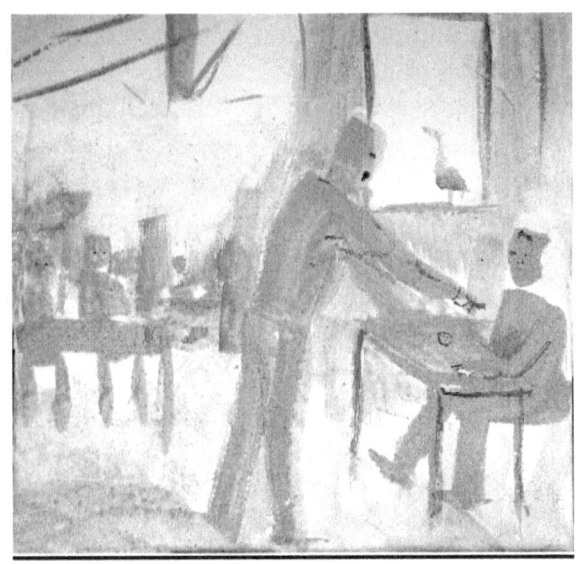

Chapter 10

~ Tearoom Conundrum ~

Hefei – *Junction of the Fertility River The name Hefei was first given to a county set up under the Han dynasty in the second century BC. Because of its location on a mountain saddle between northern and southern states, Hefei was frequently fought over in the fourth to eleventh centuries AD, and changed rulers several times.*

Yu Tong continued at a steady pace toward Hefei for several weeks along the dirt roads, witnessing the effects of previous wars and desperation on the faces of so many impoverished people. At last, in the distance the faint outline of the ancient city. He quickened his pace, hoping to make his way to Hefei before nightfall.

Several hours later he realized he would not arrive in time to spend the night in the city. So he found a small secluded area among the trees to settle down for the night. A gently moving stream trickling past his camp whispered just enough from the water tumbling over the rocks to break up the quiet and offer a sense of a distant companion. The sun had already disappeared below the horizon before he arrived, so by the time he was settled in for the night, the darkness had enveloped the entire sky.

I think tomorrow will be a good day for another performance, he thought while looking at the night sky splashed with the universe of distant stars.

Soon, the soft whispers of sleep gently began to tug at his tired body and his grip on the day loosened until he finally fell off to sleep.

The early morning light arrived in what felt like a single moment. He had no more than closed his eyes and now the joyous songbirds in the trees were suddenly announcing the onset of another day. As Yu Tong gathered his belongings and secured them in his pack, he decided to walk to the edge of the city before stopping to satisfy the hunger pangs growing in the bottom of his stomach.

Making his way back to the dirt path, he was greeted by several locals on their way to the fields to begin tending their crops.

"Good morning," said a woman carrying a bundle of tools.

"Good morning," he replied.

After walking for several hours he observed a small restaurant signaling the outskirts of the city. The hunger pangs had grown considerably since he woke up, so this location would need to suffice.

"Morning, what can I get for you today?" he asked as he neared the table.

PUGILIST FROM SHANDONG

Yu Tong asked for hot tea and a small bowl of soup.

The owner, who had introduced himself as Mr. Lin disappeared into the kitchen and quickly returned with the items for his customer.

"Will you be wanting anything else?" he asked as he set the tray containing the small teapot, one glass and a large bowl of soup with the spoon on the table in front of Yu Tong.

"No that should be all for now, thank you." Yu Tong answered as he inspected the items.

Quietly Mr. Lin returned to the kitchen, leaving the few customers to their business; two gentlemen were having an intense conversation completely oblivious to the world, while Yu Tong slowly sipped his hot tea in between spoonful's of soup.

Three young men wandered into his restaurant and began yelling, "Hey, old man Lin, where are you? We have been waiting here forever and you haven't come out to take our order?" said one who appeared to be the leader.

Mr. Lin appeared from behind the old door and said in a stern voice, "I know you just came into my store, because I heard you when you were talking outside."

"Hey, are you trying to give us trouble?" the smaller of the three said as he stepped out from behind the leader.

"No, but don't come in here yelling at me about being slow," Mr. Lin said as he motioned for the three to have a seat.

They found their way to the table close to the door. Mr. Lin quickly set the utensils at each seat, followed by teacups and saucers, and then dispensed jasmine tea into each cup.

As the three settled into their seats, they talked loudly among themselves.

For the next thirty minutes all was calm as each table was immersed in the task of the morning meal. Soon, the three finished their food and looked around at the other customers in the restaurant.

The smallest of the group noticed Yu Tong sitting off in the corner and quietly observing everyone else in the room.

"Hey! Do you see that little guy over there in the corner? "The smallest bandit asked his friends. They laugh and talk about how small Yu Tong is. Soon the conversation turns to the idea of how easy it would be for them to walk over and take all his money.

"I'll bet it will be so easy" the leader said, staring at Yu Tong and devising a plan.

The leader was the biggest of the group and stood about six feet tall with very broad shoulders and dark skin, indicating northern Chinese ancestry. His hair was long and unkempt and his clothing was typical of the attire from the far Northern provinces.

"If I go over there and yell at him and demand his money, I'll bet he will give it to me because I am so much bigger than he is" he said.

"Yeah, yeah, that's it!" the two subordinates gleefully replied.

He got to his feet and said to his friends, "You two wait here; I'll be right back with our loot."

His two companions were both small in comparison and they were definitely followers. Neither of them was over five feet three inches tall, one was no more than skin and bones while the other was extremely overweight.

144

PUGILIST FROM SHANDONG

The leader glared down at Yu Tong with an evil grin.

Yu Tong occupied himself with looking out the window across the room at the tall egrets standing along the edge of the water patiently waiting for an unsuspecting fish to come within range.

After a few moments of not being recognized, the leader yelled at Yu Tong to get his attention. "Hey you, little boy!"

Yu Tong continued to watch outside as the first egret drove its beak down into the murky water and came out with a small minnow, ignoring the unkempt Mongolian for being so rude and arrogant.

"Hey you, little boy I'm talking to you, so quit looking out the window," he yelled again with more attitude and sarcasm.

Again Yu Tong ignored him and finally after a few moments he turned very slowly towards the stranger and without saying a word, glared back at him.

Yu Tong was only about four feet nine inches tall and very lean from all his years of training. Each muscle in his body had been honed to a very fine edge. The speed, timing, agility and strength had all been developed to their utmost ability. Unfortunately, as he sat at the small quiet table trying to escape from the chaos out in the streets and enjoy a peaceful meal before beginning another long journey for the day, he realized that he would soon be forced to teach another ignorant thug a lesson in manners.

Eventually the leader reached out and put his hands on the table, leaned over and said to Yu Tong, "I want you to give me all your money and if you do I won't have to hurt you." He pointed his finger in Yu Tong's face.

"I think you should go back to your table and leave me alone." Yu Tong answered and then went back to looking out the

145

window. He picked up his teacup to finish the hot liquid inside.

The leader stood frozen.

If he comes back, I'll use my iron bird.

During his years at the temple he had learned many of the special arts from the Shaolin Temple that had been passed to outsiders through the generations. He liked the jumping arts to develop strength to jump from the ground to a rooftop and the power it gave him for his kicks. He also liked the throwing arts and could hit a very small point from a far distance with his specially made iron birds; both of which he practiced to an exceptional degree of proficiency, but his favorite was the art of Dim Mak or Death Touch art.

This one he practiced religiously every day; no matter what else he needed to work on he always found time to continue this special art. He had begun by striking an urn filled with water to develop the hand and finger strength and condition the fingertips. Next he had progressed to a container filled with fine pellets or sand. Later, he struck larger rocks and finally moved on to hitting just one large rock or the bark on trees and now after all these years his fingers had become like steel rods that could penetrate even the toughest tree bark.

After a period of thick, stifling silence, the large man leaning on the table straightened up, turned around and headed back to his friends.

"What happened, what happened?" the two men asked as soon as their friend came back and sat down.

"I told him to give me his money and all he did was tell me to go away. He didn't even look the least bit scared when he said it either." The big man picked up his teacup and drank the remaining liquid.

PUGILIST FROM SHANDONG

"You mean you didn't get anything from him?" his fat friend asked as he poured more tea in everybody's cup.

"No, I didn't."

"Well are you going to let him get away with that?"

"I don't know," he stared at Yu Tong.

It was now time for the shops along the street to open up for business, so the other two gentlemen in the restaurant paid their bill and hurried out the door without saying goodbye. All they seemed to have time for was a quick wave of the hand overhead as they stepped over the threshold and headed off in different directions.

Now the only people left in the restaurant were the three thugs and Yu Tong.

Mr. Lin hadn't come out of the kitchen for quite some time.

Eventually, the leader jumped up out of his chair and began screaming at Yu Tong. "You better get ready because I'm coming over there and teach you a lesson. Nobody talks to me that way and gets away with it, especially someone as little as you!"

Project through your target, Yu Tong heard his father whisper in his mind.

Calmly, without saying a word Yu Tong drew his arm back and flicked it forward. A small iron figure shot forward from inside his sleeve; hitting the rude stranger directly in the forehead.

The large Mongolian stopped in his tracks, staring blankly at the wall in front of him before falling straight backward like a tree and with a loud thud, crashing to the floor. His large thick head hit the floor first. A small trickle of fresh blood appeared next to his ear.

His friends watched in disbelief. They sat there frozen for what seemed like an eternity. Suddenly his fat friend seemed to realize what happened and rushed to help his unconscious leader lying on the floor.

His skinny friend joined him, and together they feverishly tried to revive their leader, but to no avail; he was out cold.

Yu Tong casually stood up, estimated the cost for what he had ordered, put a few small coins on the table, threw his pack over his shoulder, then grabbed his weapons and headed for the door.

As he passed by the fiasco going on near the first table, he kicked aside the arm of the unconscious thug to reveal the ornately carved iron bird, a precious weapon he always carried in his sleeve for times such as this.

Carefully he reached down and picked it up then continued on his way out the door. He shook his head in disbelief at what he had been forced to do, then turned, walked outside and began walking into Hefei.

Later in the afternoon, as he was walking through the countryside filled with fields of wheat, apples, corn, and rice, he noticed the sharp contrast between the fields and mountains; flat fertile soil transformed suddenly into a majestic and beautiful formation of sheer vertical rock. Low lying plants bent and twisted in an effort to find the sun. Large splits running upward toward the peak, made the massive rocks appear as though a much larger entity was trapped deep underneath and trying to escape from the millennia of punishment. Sporadically scattered among the fissures were small reliefs barely able to support the swallows and sparrows flying close to the rock in search of twigs and dead grass. He was totally alone, just one small being in the universe.

PUGILIST FROM SHANDONG

Up ahead, he could see a path leading up the hill that was no more than an individual step in the ground for each foot, worn deep into the soil and polished smooth from the years of workers traveling to and from their daily routine of toiling in the fields. But where did it lead to? He stopped to ponder the thought, then after a moment slowly moved on.

Later, as he was making his way around a well-worn hill, he found himself entering a grove of spruce trees that offered relief from the afternoon sun. Their long branches gently reached out from the trunk to grasp a fraction of the essence pouring down from bright golden yellow ball hanging solemnly in the dark blue expanse. As they did, they cast a sporadic pattern of contrasting dark and light shapes across the soft layer of dirt. But even this was enough to help diminish the onslaught of rays beaming down without end.

The heat raining down on the countryside had brought everything including the soft gentle breeze to a complete standstill, so the moment he stepped under the large solitary canopy, he stopped and allowed his body to begin regaining its strength. The sweat continued to pour down every part of his body and his clothing was glued to his skin, so this temporary relief was extremely welcome. After a brief period, he moved on and tried to stay as close to the trees as he could in order to stay under the protection of the long branches.

As suddenly as the sparse grove had appeared, it was gone, and the sun returned with its bombardment of waves of heat.

Moments later he caught a faint smell of old burnt wood. When he walked around the corner of another field of rice, he happened across an abandoned and deteriorating brick manufacturing plant. It was right out in the middle of nowhere. All attempts to keep close to any shade trees were ended years ago when the intense heat from the furnaces eventually killed all the foliage.

Daily, the helpers would have gone out to gather as much wood as possible to satisfy the hunger from the furnaces. While others began the tedious task of mixing water with the red dirt to just the right consistency and then pour the mix into the stacks upon stacks of pre-shaped brick molds. Once each mold was filled, it was laid in the sun to begin drying before being stripped of the bricks, which were then set in the oven to temper. This was a process that had occurred here for centuries, and the surrounding terrain showed its strain from the abuse.

Now all that was left were the charred remains of a series of holes hollowed out of the brick shacks, resembling a beehive with its many uniform openings surrounding a central work area filled with what at one time would have looked like worker bees scurrying about trying to maintain the central command for the entire complex.

No longer were the fires kept red hot inside the ports while stack upon stack of moist mud and straw blocks lay waiting for their turn to cook inside the hot fire. Nor would there be any carts busily scurrying to and fro trying to keep up with removing the bricks from the workers' way and neatly stacking them so they could be sold to nearby masons. Now, as they slowly crumbled from years of neglect, all was silent, except for an occasional whisper from a gentle breeze passing through the area.

Chapter 11

~ A Monkey in Shanghai ~

From the first sight of light the following morning, Yu Tong began another piece of his journey. All day he continued along the small path leading him southward toward his destination. Days turned into weeks and soon he was approaching the great Chang Jiang River near Hukou in Jiangxi Province, which meant he was nearly half way to Hangzhou. Rain on the previous day had been a relief from the previous month of drought and now everything in the fields could continue with its growth. The dry dust that for days lingered in the air had now settled and left behind the clear clean smell of fresh air and sounds of jubilantly singing birds.

While walking up the narrow, quiet lane that gently made its way up the hill to the simple dwelling at the top, he noticed the steady stream of rainwater from the recent downpour that flowed down toward the main street, all the while trying to maintain its existence against the onslaught of the soil to absorb the stream's essence. Upon reaching the street, the

151

small trickle joined forces with other streams and fought back the continual attack from the underlying soil.

The water made its way out into the open road and found access into the drainage ditch along the main road leading out of town. Minutes later as he reached the crest of the hill, he turned, looked back at the serene event happening right beneath his feet, and then began making his way toward the bridge crossing the Chang Jiang River.

As he drew closer, he saw the tall cedar trees that lined the road like temple guardians, each standing erect, still, and strong. With their arms outstretched over the path, they created a canopy, like the guards honoring the emperor as he slowly passed by. At the end of the formidable appearance was the ancient wooden bridge with its platform extending over the almond-colored river and offering everyone who passed by the opportunity to freely cross to the other side and continue on their journey.

He knew this mighty river began flowing eastward from far off in Sichuan Province, then through Hubei and Anhui Provinces and ending its journey by joining forces with the great waters of the China Sea then meandering through numerous cities, towns, and mountain ranges and finally after hundreds and hundreds of miles of twists and turns, finding its destination in the open sea near Shanghai.

After passing under the tall cedars and finally crossing over the aged wooden sentry guarding the vast waterway, Yu Tong passed through Nanchang "prosperity in the South," a city in northern Jiangxi Province dating back over two thousand years, with deep roots of human habitation reaching back into antiquity to 3,000 BC.

Near the center of town he stopped to rest in the shade. His thoughts turned to the question of how many centuries these streets had remained the same; same direction, same layout of businesses and for some the same buildings. After Yu Tong had rested, he decided it was time to press on, so he headed toward the edge of town where soon he would be back out in the open fields again.

Several days later he arrived at the center of Hefei and decided to setup his display of herbs. He looked around to see what businesses were lining the street, and thought if more people arrived, he might be able to make some money by performing with his weapons.

"Hey, mister, what are you selling?" a lady from the nearby clothing store called while sitting next to her front door."

"I have some special herbs and healing liniments," Yu Tong replied and held up a bottle of his special mixture.

"Does it work?" she asked as she stood up.

"Yes, it works very well especially when you apply it with these medicinal patches."

"Will you be there later today when I close my store?"

"Yes," Yu Tong replied as he sat down behind his small display.

"Good!" she said and walked inside.

The sun was just beginning its mid-morning ascent while signaling to everyone that soon it would be directly overhead and all the shadows would be gone. As if on cue people began to walk the street while avoiding the cover of the small overhang in front of the business entrances.

Yu Tong just sat in the sun and patiently waited. An hour later, the sun was finally directly overhead and all the patrons had disappeared. Yu Tong just tilted his round bamboo hat slightly backward and remained still in an effort to stay warm.

Moment by moment the sun continued to inch its way forward and gradually the shadows on the opposite side of the street began to creep out from under the well-worn walkway and crawl across the ground toward Yu Tong.

Ahh… just about the time I finally begin to warm up the sun starts heading towards the horizon, he thought while gazing at the distant trees and observing the change in shadow direction.

If I wait too long most of the customers will be heading home to avoid the dropping temperature.

He stood up and slowly began to loosen up his body from the cold. Several local passersby turned to check out his routine.

"Hey, mister, what are you doing?" a young boy asked as he walked by, clutching his mother's hand.

"I'm loosening my body so I can demonstrate some of my Kung Fu," Yu Tong responded.

"Can I watch?"

"You sure can. Come back in several minutes," Yu Tong said as he slid his feet apart and sat on the ground in a split.

"Wow!" the boy exclaimed just before his mother pulled him into a nearby store.

Yu Tong effortlessly reached forward, grabbed his front foot and pulled his forehead down until it touched the toes. After a few moments he turned and repeated the routine on the other side, then straightened his back, extended his arms straight out to the sides and suddenly jumped up with the arms still straight out.

"Okay, everyone, I will now perform some of my special Kung Fu skills for you," he said the moment his feet came together.

He began a series of kicks and spins from one side of the street to the other. As he turned and prepared to perform back toward his herb display, he noticed the young boy pulling his mother out of the store so he could watch. Yu Tong winked at him and then smiled as he continued his routine.

The crowd began to grow and for the next thirty minutes Yu Tong kept their attention by demonstrating one weapon after another; first a single sword, then his trusty spear, afterwards another series of kicks and punches, and finally his favorite double broadswords.

Soon Yu Tong was completely drenched in sweat and decided to close the performance.

"I would like to thank everyone for stopping by to watch my performance and if anyone has any questions, please come over and ask," he said while extending a formal salute to everyone in the audience just before walking over to his herbal display and sitting down.

"Are you going to be teaching at the Jing Wu Association in Shanghai?" a well-dressed man asked.

"Jing Wu?" Yu Tong asked. He didn't know about this association.

"Yes, it's just starting and they want some experts to help teach everyone about Kung Fu," the man replied.

"Who are the people that are starting this association?"

"It's Huo Yuan Jia and some of his closest allies," the man said.

"Huo Yuan Jia?" Yu Tong exclaimed. "I heard he fought some foreign devil and had no trouble beating him into submission."

"Yes that's true and now they are looking to teach everyone about the superior Chinese Kung Fu." The man clenched his fist tightly and raised it in front of his chest. "If you go there you can apply and if they like what they see you could teach some of the incredible techniques I just watched you perform."

"Shanghai, hmm it sounds very interesting."

"I hope you'll apply, I think your techniques would be a great asset for their association." The man smiled and raised his thumb in approval.

"Thank you for your thought about my Kung Fu. I think I'll begin my journey to Shanghai tomorrow." Yu Tong extended a formal salute to the stranger for his assistance.

"Good, good!" The man said. "I hope I will see you in Shanghai soon."

"Yes you will." Yu Tong answered.

The stranger left and Yu Tong answered questions from the remaining spectators about his training and special herbal patches.

Eventually, everyone returned to their tasks and left Yu Tong sitting alone.

Hmm, Shanghai? "He gazed up at the sky out of the corner of his eye. *If I went there, I know I could impress them with my Tam Tui and Praying Mantis styles.* He began to ponder the possibilities.

I could make some money and not have to perform in the streets or wander so much.

It shouldn't take too long to get there, if I only stop long enough to make some money to eat with. He became more and more excited about the opportunity.

He decided to get something to eat and then get started. He packed his belongings and then turned to find a teahouse where he could eat.

PUGILIST FROM SHANDONG

As soon as he finished with his meal he walked outside and began his journey. For the remainder of the day he kept his pace steady in order to make some distance before the sun set behind the trees.

Early the next morning Yu Tong rose at his usual four a.m. and ventured out into a secluded area where he could perform his daily routine. Even though the air was extremely brisk and without a hint of movement, he adhered to his practice. As the sun was just beginning to cast its first rays of light over the trees, he finished his routine and sat down to give his tired, sweaty body some rest before the start of a long day's walk.

Over the next several weeks he continued his pace in order to make the best time possible. Each day he saw continual reminders that his destination was getting closer and closer, by the changes in terrain, crops, and attire.

I must be getting close, he thought. *I keep seeing more and more of those strings attached to the tops of the long poles.*

He guessed they must carry that electricity stuff he had heard about.

The dirt path gradually began to widen and the ground became smooth and compacted with small tracks worn evenly in the surface from some sort of machine.

Late in the afternoon as he made his way toward the top of a small hill, he heard strange noises and the air filled with an irritating smell. The moment he reached the top, his eyes could not believe the sights that lay before him. Never in his wildest imagination could he have ever dreamed of such a strange and confusing mix.

In his travels he heard about many new inventions that China was importing from the foreign devils, but he never imagined he would ever see them. Now here he was about to come face to face with an entirely new era in the Middle Kingdom's evolution.

Wow! What is all that? He began the long walk down from the hill toward the edge of this large bustling city. He continually saw twinkling of stars coming from the tightly packed houses and buildings.

He thought it was very strange. It was too early and too bright to be seeing stars already and why were they so close to the ground?

He also wondered about the strange smell in the air and that odd beep, beep, beep he kept hearing?

I think I'll sit under this tree and rest while I try and figure out some of this.

He leaned his weapons against the large tree trunk and sat down in the shade.

The moment he rested his head against the tree, a strange machine filled with people passed by on the street below. When it approached a peasant standing in the road, it issued a loud beep.

So that's where the beeping came from. But what's that strange machine?

Ahh... so that's also where that awful smell is coming from, he surmised the moment the fumes reached the area where he was sitting.

He decided to continue into the city to find out about the strings on poles. As he made his way down the hill, he noticed that the buildings kept getting taller and taller. When he got to the bottom of the hill he was amazed to see just how tall each building was and how close together. (Shanghai's population in 1920 was approx. three million.)

PUGILIST FROM SHANDONG

For several minutes he stood and stared at the vast modern city in front of him with so many new technologies; it momentarily took him aback.

"Excuse me, could you tell me where the Jing Wu Association is located?" he asked a stranger the moment his mind returned to reality.

"Go down that road over there and it will take you to Suchuan Road. Once you get there just ask anyone and they can help you find it." The lady he had asked pointed at a road and then continued on her journey.

"Thank you," he headed toward the street leading into the city.

As he walked, the sights, sounds, smells, and overall energy of this bustling metropolis filled his senses to the brim.

Wow this is so different from my hometown or the temple, he thought as he walked deeper and deeper into the city.

The streets were clean and the ground was smooth and hard with what he later learned were cars and trolleys dashing back and forth carrying the masses to their destinations.

Everywhere he looked the architecture seemed so hard and linear; a total contrast to the Feng Shui oriented designs that he was so accustomed to seeing.

"Excuse me, could you tell me where the Jing Wu Association is located?" he asked an old man standing on the street corner next to the sign designating Suchuan Road.

"Yes, if you go about five blocks that way you will see their sign above the front door," the man said as he pointed down the busy street.

"Thank you." Yu Tong replied while extending a formal Kung Fu salute.

159

Several minutes later Yu Tong found the entrance door with the ornately carved sign above it signifying the Jing Wu Association was inside.

He opened the door and as it squeaked from the movement, the young man sitting at the desk inside looked up. "Hello, can I help you? "the young man asked as Yu Tong gently closed the door.

"Yes, my name is Lee Yu Tong and several weeks ago while I was in Hefei a stranger told me that you were looking for qualified Kung Fu practitioners to help teach at your association." Yu Tong carefully placed the weapons on the floor next to the wall.

"Yes we're looking for top quality people to teach, but if we are not familiar with you and what you say you can do, then we will need to verify your skill level. "The young man walked over and began inspecting the well-worn weapons that his visitor just placed on the floor.

"Very well," Yu Tong replied. "When would you like to test my abilities?"

"How about later today?"

"Okay, I'll return in several hours."

"Good, I'll make sure everything is ready." The young man carefully picked up the weapons and handed them to his guest.

Yu Tong bowed and turned to walk out the door but turned before leaving and asked, "Do you know where I can find a teahouse and get some food?"

"Yes, just go down this street another two blocks and you will find a very good place," the young man said.

Yu Tong followed the directions and soon located the teahouse, walked inside and relaxed while drinking his tea and eating some fresh noodles. As soon as he finished, he gathered his belongings and headed back to the Jing Wu Association

"Ahh, you are back," the young man said as Yu Tong entered the front door.

"My master said I should let him know when you returned." The young man bowed to excuse himself and inform his teacher.

After several minutes the young man returned with a guest.

"Hello, I'm Zhao Lianhe, chief instructor."

"Hello, I'm Lee Yu Tong."

"May I ask where you're from?" Zhao asked.

"I'm from Pingdu city in Shandong Province." Yu Tong replied.

"What's your Kung Fu style?" Zhao inquired.

"My family style is the Tam Tui style and I also lived at the Wah Lum Temple and learned the Jut Sow Praying Mantis system," Yu Tong replied.

"Great, great!" Zhao clasped his hands together.

For the next hour the two masters sat and discussed their personal styles, philosophies, and movement theories while drinking freshly brewed tea.

"Okay, now that we have been able to sit and discuss our Kung Fu, I think tomorrow I would like to set up a friendly fighting competition so we can evaluate your fighting skills," Zhao said.

"Very well, what time would you like me to return?" Yu Tong asked.

About ten a.m. all of our students will be gone so it will be quiet and there will not be any interruption."

The two stood, politely bowed and then headed for the front door where Master Zhao helped Yu Tong gather his weapons before bidding him farewell until the following morning.

Yu Tong stepped out the door and into the busy street, looked in each direction, and then decided to return to the hill at the edge of the city.

The following morning Yu Tong woke at his usual time, performed his daily routine and began walking back toward the Jing Wu Association. He knew the hour was still early, so he decided to walk to the teahouse and drink some tea before returning to Jing Wu.

Soon the sun climbed high enough to peek over the tall buildings, so he knew the hour was close to ten. He gathered his weapons and walked outside to return to the Association hall.

"Good morning!" the young man said when Yu Tong entered the front door.

"Good morning." Yu Tong replied.

"My teacher will be with you shortly." He bowed and excused himself to inform his teacher of their guest's arrival.

Several minutes later the young man returned with Master Zhao and another man.

"Good morning." Zhao said. "This is Lou Min; he practices the Monkey style and will be assisting us today. "Zhao gestured for Yu Tong to follow him into the training hall. As they entered the large room, Zhao pointed to the bench next to the wall where Yu Tong could place his belongings.

PUGILIST FROM SHANDONG

"Would you like to loosen up your muscles before we begin?" Zhao asked.

Yu Tong politely shook his head to signify he would not need the time. Lou Min also declined the offer.

"Okay, then we'll begin." Zhao said and motioned for both fighters to step to the middle of the room.

"Again, this is a friendly research match," Zhao said as he bowed to both fighters. They simultaneously bowed to each other.

"Ready? Begin." He stepped back to allow the fighters to begin.

Yu Tong stepped back with his left foot. He could tell Lou Min was not totally focused on the match, so he attacked. First, he launched a series of kicks to drive Lou Min backward. As soon as he saw Lou retreat, he then began a series of punches to drive him back faster.

At the moment when Lou was about to fall, Yu Tong stopped his attack and stood motionless. Lou stood up straight with his eyes wide open and glanced over at Zhao with a startled expression as if to say, *I thought this was a friendly match?*

Seconds drifted by ever so slowly and finally Lou gathered his focus to ready himself for an attack. He began by crouching into a typical Low Monkey stance and then altered his expression to imitate a raging monkey. He charged forward while dodging to the left and right in an attempt to confuse Yu Tong.

Yu Tong stood motionless and waited for his opponent to come within range. The moment Lou was close enough, Yu Tong slipped to the side to attack Lou's unprotected side. Unfortunately, Lou's last dodge maneuver was a clever disguise and it caught Yu Tong by surprise. Lou grabbed his leg and threw him backward; causing him to fall flat on his back.

Without stopping his momentum, Yu Tong rolled over and stood up straight. Without any warning, Lou began jumping up and down in a crouched position; imitating an upset monkey. After several hops he lunged forward to once again attempt to catch Yu Tong off guard.

This time Yu Tong was ready and as soon as Lou was within range, Yu Tong charged straight forward, causing Lou to stumble back and roll over into a seated position.

As Yu Tong pressed forward to continue attacking, Lou spun his feet in a circle over his head to counter any incoming attack and stood back up straight with his feet together, left fist on his hip and his right fist extended toward Yu Tong. Again seconds drifted by ever so slowly as the two fighters stood motionless.

When fighting, change your footwork. Yu Tong heard Ching Yeung whisper in the recesses of his mind. He charged toward his opponent with a series of chaotic steps that gave no indication as to what his next move would be or where it was heading.

LouMin kept a close watch on Yu Tong's feet to detect a pattern. Before he could devise a defense strategy, Yu Tong had closed the gap and was now directly in front of him and still charging forward.

Thud, thud, thud! Yu Tong landed a series of punches to Lou Min's chest just before kicking him in the stomach and sending him rolling backward once again.

For the next thirty minutes the advantage continued to sway back and forth from one fighter to the other; it was obvious these two opponents were very closely matched and neither of them planned to give in.

PUGILIST FROM SHANDONG

Again Lou Min charged forward with his crouching monkey hops trying to confuse Yu Tong. When Lou came within range, he jumped up in the air and tried to kick Yu Tong in the chest.

Yu Tong saw the jump at its onset, so he waited until Lou was in mid-air and then countered with a move called Jade Ring and Chop Step; catching Lou's arm and chopping the opposite side of his neck while simultaneously sweeping his legs out from under him.

Lou's body spun in mid-air and was now horizontal, parallel with the hard floor but still several feet from the ground. For a moment his body seemed to float in space before crashing to the floor.

Yu Tong stepped back and waited for his opponent to recover.

Lou rolled over and struggled to his knees and then began coughing again as he tried to get more air into his exhausted lungs.

After what seemed like an eternity, Lou raised his hand and signaled he wanted to stop.

Quickly Yu Tong rushed over and helped his fallen opponent to his feet and assisted him over to the chair next to Zhao.

"Would you like some water?" Yu Tong asked as he helped Lou sit down.

"Yes please," Lou replied.

"I'll be okay in a few minutes, I just need to rest and breathe, "Lou struggled to say between gasps for air.

"Wow that was quite a fight!" Zhao said as he watched his friend slowly recover.

"Yes, he is definitely an exceptional fighter," Lou replied, rubbing the back of his head.

"Yu Tong, would you care to return tomorrow so that we can discuss your future? "Zhao asked as he put his hand on Yu Tong's shoulder.

"I would be happy to return." Yu Tong smiled at the potential opportunity.

"If you would like, you can sleep upstairs where it'll be more comfortable," Zhao said.

"For today, let's go down to the teahouse so we can talk about what happened here today!" he said and put one hand on the shoulder of each fighter.

The following morning as Yu Tong entered the training hall he noticed several unfamiliar people standing next to Zhao and Lou.

"Ah good morning, Yu Tong!" Zhao said.

"Good morning," Yu Tong replied as he extended a formal salute to everyone in the room.

"I would like to introduce you to some of our other instructors!" Zhao walked over and shook Yu Tong's hand.

"Yes we all heard about what happened yesterday and we wanted to come by and meet you," one of the other instructors said as he walked up to greet Yu Tong.

"They have all agreed that they would like you to teach your Tam Tui at our association." Zhao said excitedly.

"Great, that will be great!" Yu Tong replied.

Over the next month's Yu Tong's life seemed to be settling into normalcy: a place to live, train, teach, and not be concerned about the distant past. But sometimes the past has a way of creeping into the most distant and unlikely places.

PUGILIST FROM SHANDONG

One morning when Yu Tong entered the training hall he saw Zhao sitting on the small wooden bench looking out the window and deep in thought.

"Can we talk a minute?" Zhao asked as Yu Tong placed his weapons on the floor next to the wall.

"Sure, sure," Yu Tong replied.

"I just received a letter from a friend in Qingdao who said he read in the paper that you were teaching here," Zhao began.

"Oh really?" Yu Tong replied with surprise.

"And he said the officials in Pingdu also know about your location," Zhao said.

"So when did the officials find out?" Yu Tong asked.

"I guess several weeks ago." Zhao replied.

Suddenly Yu Tong's interest in training completely vanished from his mind as the thought of what the future might bring filled his senses.

"You realize there's a chance they will send someone to talk to you. Or they'll ask the local authorities to come by and do some initial investigating before determining if they want to come down and continue with their own inquiry."

"Yes I know." Yu Tong quietly replied. "If I stay, then I'm at risk of being arrested until their investigation is completed.

"And if that happens, it will bring shame and misfortune on Jin Wu."

"What do you think you'll do?" Zhao asked as he placed his hand on the shoulder of his friend.

"It seems I don't have many choices," Yu Tong looked at the ceiling, desperately searching for an acceptable answer.

Minutes seemed to stretch into eternity, and the silence he so regularly sought was now becoming deafening.

"I guess if I want to live and train to improve my Kung Fu, I will need to move on. "Yu Tong softly said as he looked around at the place he had called home for the past months.

"Where will you go?"

"Probably south. That way it will be even further from Pingdu and harder for them to find me."

"When will you be leaving?"

"The longer I stay, the more chance there is I'll be found." Yu Tong looked directly at his friend.

"Will everyone else be coming in today?" Yu Tong asked as he slowly stood up.

"Yes they should be here in a couple hours."

"Good, I want to say goodbye to everyone." Yu Tong walked over and picked up his weapons.

"I'll go upstairs and gather all my belongings and come back down when they arrive."

Several hours later Yu Tong returned for the last time while carrying all of his belongings.

One by one each of the instructors arrived and expressed their frustration and sorrow at the prospect of their friend being arrested or taken back to Shandong to serve a jail sentence or executed. Each expressed their gratitude for everything Yu Tong had shared with them and their sorrow for the road they knew he would be traveling.

PUGILIST FROM SHANDONG

Soon everyone was gone except for Zhao and Yu Tong. With a heavy heart Zhao bade his friend good luck on his journey one last time. Yu Tong thanked him for everything he had done for him, bowed ever so slowly to show the depth of his gratitude, turned and stepped out the front door.

Once again he stood all alone. He glanced up at the sky and could tell there were still several hours of daylight remaining. He slowly began walking back towards the hill at the edge of town.

Chapter 12

~Mantis Exits its Cave~

It had been months since he left the Jing Wu Hall in Shanghai. The time spent there remained close to his heart and the friends he made would be remembered forever.

Now once again he was all alone and drifting from place to place in the vast expanse of the Middle Kingdom. Step by step he continued on his journey southward, and each new day always brought a new set of challenges.

Days later upon reaching the Gan River, he decided to follow the river south instead of staying on the main road. He knew this river would lead him through the Luoxiao Mountains and eventually lead to Shaoguan in the northern part of Guangdong Province. From there it wouldn't be long before he reached the ancient seaport of Guangzhou. A city over two thousand years old which had a history filled with excitement, achievement and sorrow. After this great city, he knew the distance to Guangzhou was getting closer.

Hmm…

The terrain is getting continually more mountainous, he stopped at the base of a large hill before beginning the long climb to the top.

The fields are getting smaller and smaller, and the distance from one to another is further apart. He observed while resting in the shade of an old tree.

Wow, it is interesting how they made the fields in a step pattern on the side of that distant hill.

I wonder how long it took to get that step pattern and keep the dirt from sliding down.

I guess when they need to harvest their crops they must carry everything back down that long winding path on their backs, because it doesn't look wide enough to use a cart, he scratched his head.

After an hour of rest he was ready to begin another piece of his journey. As he picked up all his belongings, *I think I will walk until I can see Cenghua City.*

Several hours later upon reaching the top of another hill, he was amazed at how far he could see and how many more hills needed to be climbed. He admired the scenery, shifted the pack on his shoulder, adjusted the position of the weapons, exhaled and began walking down the first of many rolling hills.

As he finished climbing a hill that his legs were telling him would be their last; he saw the twinkling of the lights from Cenghua.

Ahh!…at last, he sat down under a tree to rest.

If I stay here tonight, I will be able to easily make the city before the sun gets directly overhead. He removed all his belongings from his back and laid them on the ground. While watching the distant stars overhead silently twinkle their existence, he decided to sleep under the nearby tree and as soon as his head touched the ground he fell asleep. All was quiet.

As quickly as he drifted off into another night's sleep, he suddenly awoke with the feeling that it had only been a mere second ago that he closed his eyes. But as he looked around he could see that in a short while the sun would be inching its way above the horizon for another day. Sitting up, *Wow! With the fog covering the bottom of the hills, it makes the tops look like the bumps on a turtle's back.*

Standing to begin another day's training, he spotted a tree that would be perfect for his punching routine. After his warm ups and technique practice, he immediately began punching the bark with a variety of close range strikes followed by an equal number of long range attacks. Soon his regimen was fulfilled, so he gathered his belongings and headed down the dew covered hill just as the sun was appearing over the horizon.

For the next several hours he continued his pace and soon found himself looking at the city below the ridge where he was standing.

Good. He glanced down at the meticulously aligned rows of buildings.

Once I get some food I will have time before sunset to see where I want to set up my herb display and performance area.

I wonder what they are growing down there, he made his way down the hill.

I am not familiar with that tall plant.

It's tall like the many fields of corn I saw up North, but I am not seeing any cobs on the stalks.

Approaching the bottom of the hill he was still unable to figure out the species of the plant.

"Excuse me, madam," he said to the elderly woman carrying several tools.

"Could you tell me what plant that is over there growing in that field?" he pointed at the strange plant.

"That tall one or the short one?" she turned and pointed at the field.

"The tall one, I have never seen anything like that before."

"You must be from the North because your accent is very different and everyone around here knows that is sugarcane." She said.

"Sugarcane?"

"What is that used for?" Yu Tong inquired.

"Everyone knows it is made into sugar for cooking!" she shook her head and walked away.

Yu Tong just stood there looking at the strange plant. *Sugarcane? Hmm… that's an interesting plant.* Finally, he turned and headed into town and as with so many places before; he needed to locate a suitable spot to set up his herbs and perform his Kung Fu.

The following morning he walked back into town, set up his herbs and then patiently waited for the remainder of the city to begin their daily routines. As the locals arrived to complete their morning duties, several people stopped to inquire about his herbs and the weapons leaning against the wall.

Days later after making some money from the herbs and performances, he gathered his belongings and began walking towards Guangzhou. The weather improved daily with all signs of the recent winter up North left far behind. No longer did he walk for days with nothing to look at but barren, brown fields and trees stripped of their leaves by the long cold gray winter. Now everything was green and alive with the sun shining bright.

174

PUGILIST FROM SHANDONG

The mountainous terrain ended as quickly as it began so many days before. The small scattered fields were once again wide open and not crowded together. No more terracing on the side of steep hills or long journey's up a continuously switch backing path in order to reach the future harvest. Large wooden carts now replaced the physical struggle of many workers from carrying the equipment or harvest on their backs.

Several weeks later Yu Tong arrived at the outskirts of the ancient seaport of Guangzhou. This city, like Shanghai in the 1920's was already a vast thriving metropolis. As far as he could see there was row after row of tightly packed houses separated only by a narrow dirt street. The calm quiet atmosphere of the open countryside was now crushed by the hustle and bustle of this ancient city.

Wow this sure is a busy place, even on the edges of town. He stopped to allow his mind time to absorb everything.

I should easily find a spot to sell my herbs and perform my techniques.

Maybe I will walk into the city and find a good location rather than staying out here on the edges of town until tomorrow. He began walking down the closest street.

"Excuse me, can you tell me where the center of the city is located?" he asked an elderly man sitting by his front door.

"I sure can," the man slowly stood up and took several steps out into the warm sun.

"Go down this street until it ends and then turn to the right."

"After a while you will see all the construction going on and then you are close." he gestured the directions with his hands and then turned to return to his well-worn stool.

"Thank you for your help," Yu Tong respectfully bowed before turning to continue.

Wow this city is starting to look so modern with all these electricity strings everywhere.

And even the businesses are using it for their lights!

I will walk a little further and see if there are more stores on the street, if there are I will stop here to show my herbs, a sudden breeze began to stir up the fine dust on the ground.

Interesting, the streets are so wide and paved. He looked down the street.

Ahh—good there are a lot more stores.

This should be a good spot to sell some herbs and show my techniques, he carefully placed the weapons against the large building at the corner of the intersection.

Slowly he arranged his herbs, then sat and waited for the remainder of the day while observing the continual stream of people dashing from store to store. Eventually, the sun began to slip behind the rooftops on the opposite side of the street, so Yu Tong gathered his belongings and headed back out to the edge of town towards a secluded spot.

Tomorrow morning that spot will be perfect for training.

The next morning after his training routine, while gathering his belongings he noticed a multitude of clouds slowly marching over the distant horizon.

Ahh —good, if there are more of them behind those, it will be cloudy enough to keep the sun from making it too hot. He bent down to pick up the last of his weapons.

Turning towards the city he glanced in each direction and noticed that he was the only person up and moving about.

I wonder what time the people of this city begin their day.

PUGILIST FROM SHANDONG

After about thirty minutes he finally saw several people entering the Justice Building and reasoned more citizens would be arriving soon to begin their day.

Good.

By the time I get to my spot and get my herbs displayed there should be a lot of people out walking on the streets. He began seeing more and more people.

Instantly he shifted the weapons on his shoulder and increased his pace in order to arrive at his spot as soon as possible.

Great.

There are quite a few people already here. He carefully placed his weapons against the building.

I think today I will just sit and sell my herbs so I can see when the best time will be to perform tomorrow. He squatted down next to the wall.

For the remainder of the morning Yu Tong just sat and watched the routines of the unending crowd. Occasionally, someone would stop to inquire about his herbs or ask him about a specific problem they were experiencing.

As the sun began its slow descent towards the distant horizon, Yu Tong saw a soup vendor slowly pedaling his cart in his direction.

"Hey mister," he yelled as the man neared his corner.

"Can I buy a bowl of soup from you?" the man turned and headed towards his side of the street.

"Sure," the man said.

Jumping off the seat, he quickly gathered a bowl, dipped the long ladle into the freshly prepared mixture and handed it to his customer.

"Thank you," Yu Tong said as he handed his empty bowl back to the man along with the coins for his payment.

"I see you practice Kung Fu," the man pointed at the weapons.

"Yes I've been training all my life."

"And tomorrow I'm going to demonstrate some of my techniques," Yu Tong replied.

"Really?

"I always love watching someone who practices the old art," he tried to demonstrate several hand techniques.

"Have you ever studied Kung Fu?" Yu Tong easily executed a series of punches.

"No, I've always sold soup from this cart since I was young.

"What time tomorrow will you be demonstrating?" the man asked while looking down the street.

"Probably about same time," Yu Tong noticed a young boy across the street excitedly staring at the weapons.

"Good, I'll make sure to stop by and watch," the man began pedaling out towards the middle of the street just before raising his hand over his head and waving goodbye.

It's unfortunate that he never had the chance to train. He does not know what he is missing or where it might have taken him, the shaky cart meandered down the street.

Several hours later the sun once again began to slip behind the distant trees, so Yu Tong gathered his belongings and returned to the secluded spot near the edge of the city. As he leaned back against the large tree a solitary airplane flew high overhead.

Wow, now they have figured out how to fly like the birds, he watched the craft slowly crawl across the sky.

178

PUGILIST FROM SHANDONG

What will they think of next? The plane disappeared behind the horizon.

The following day Yu Tong was setting up his herbs as he thought,

Today I will demonstrate my double swords and maybe some of my Praying Mantis.

I think the man with the soup will enjoy that. He leaned back against the wall of the building.

Hours later as the sun began its downward direction Tong stood up and began loosening up his muscles for the demonstration. Once he finished, he walked out into the middle of the street and yelled, "Okay everyone, I am Lee Yu Tong and I am going to show you some of my family's Kung Fu and weapons."

Instantly, he dropped into a split and then jumped back up while his arms remained outstretched to the sides. He then jumped high in the air, kicked three times and landed in a low single leg stance.

"Wow!" the man with the soup cart exclaimed.

Yu Tong turned and looked at the man, smiled and continued.

"Now I will show you some of my Praying Mantis I learned at the Wah Lum Temple," he looked around at the crowd.

Boom!...Yu Tong stomped as hard as he could on the smooth street and then instantly released a series of strong kicks, punches, grabs, and throws all in a prearranged series designed to an imitate actual combat exchange.

"Wow!" the man said again.

The seasoned fighter continued his demonstration for what seemed like forever, to the man sitting on his soup cart seat. Finally it was over.

"Again, again!" the man cheered.

Yu Tong stood in the center of the street while extending a formal salute to everyone as a sign of appreciation for their audience.

"That was great," the man cheered as he ran across the street to congratulate Yu Tong.

"Thank you, thank you," Yu Tong once again extended a formal salute to his friend.

"When will you demonstrate again?"

"In two days.

"I want to give everyone time to talk about it and tell their friends," Yu Tong replied

"Great, great!" the man said.

"I am going to tell everyone I see that they need to come and watch," he tried to imitate some of the techniques

"Thank you," Yu Tong sat in the shade and wiped the sweat from his forehead.

"Okay, I have to go," the man turned and headed back to his cart.

Months later as Yu Tong was again standing in the street explaining about the show, he noticed three young spectators who seemed less than impressed with the words he was saying.

Throughout the show the audience cheered, except the three young men who were standing with their arms crossed over their chests.

Yu Tong was finishing the show by extending a formal salute to everyone in the crowd and noticed one of the young men walk out into the street and stop a few feet from him.

PUGILIST FROM SHANDONG

"Who do you think you are? "he pointed his finger at the stranger in front of him.

"That wasn't very good Kung Fu and you're in our territory!" he leaned forward and shook his fist.

"I'm sorry, have I offended you?" Yu Tong asked.

"Shut up and don't play with me!

"I'm going to show you what real Kung Fu is like!" he pulled off his shirt and threw it behind him.

"I think you should be careful about what you say."

"Don't tell me what to do old man!

"Ai-yaa!" he instantly jumped forward to kick his opponent in the chest. Yu Tong stepped to the side just enough to avoid the attack and instantly kicked the back leg of his attacker. The young man's body spun in mid-air and his face raced towards the ground while his feet pointed at the sky.

Thud! His face hit the hard surface and immediately the blood from his nose and forehead began to spill around his head as he lay unconscious.

"Hey you two idiots!

"Get over here and get this idiot off the street!" he pointed his finger at the two accomplices.

"Now!" he noticed the two were not moving.

The two scared young men rushed out into the street to gather their still unconscious ally. Without saying a word they clumsily lifted their friend and struggled to carry him off the street. Yu Tong slowly walked back to his belongings on the far side of the street.

"Wow that was incredible!" the man with the soup cart ran towards Yu Tong.

"Do you know who they are?" he stood watching the two struggle with their injured friend.

"Yes, they're from a Kung Fu school not too far from here," the man replied.

"I guess I'll be getting a visit from their teacher," he shook his head.

"Yes, that's definitely true!

"I would be careful; he has a little bit of a temper," the man sat next to his new friend.

"Thank you for the warning," Yu Tong looked down the street.

Weeks later Yu Tong was announcing his performance and as he did, he looked around to see the people in the audience and saw a man standing next to his friend with the soup cart. As the stranger stepped closer to the cart, his friend instantly stepped back.

Immediately the stranger pushed his way through the crowd and into the center of the street.

"Hey you!

"Hey, I'm talking to you!" he yelled.

Yu Tong stopped what he was saying, looked at the crowd in front of him, and then slowly turned towards the stranger.

"What is your problem?

"Why did you beat up my student? "the teacher pointed at Yu Tong.

"I tried to calm him down, but he was insistent on fighting me."

"Liar!

PUGILIST FROM SHANDONG

"My student would never start a fight," the teacher shook his fist at his opponent.

"Well he did the other day while I was trying to perform," Yu Tong shrugged his shoulders.

"Be careful what you say about my students or I will kick you back to where you came from."

"I think you are the one who should be careful."

The teacher clinched his fists tightly together and instantly his body began to shake, while his face turned red.

"Ahhh!" he rushed forward to attack .The moment he was within striking distance he raised his fist over his head to strike his opponent's head. Yu Tong jumped forward and kicked the irate fighter in the stomach; sending him backwards and collapsing on the ground.

"Cough, cough, that didn't hurt," he said between gasps.

Yu Tong stood silently watching his opponent. Gradually the fighter stumbled to his feet and wiped the dirt off his face.

"You will not succeed with that technique again," he said.

Again he rushed forward and attacked; this time with a series of kicks and punches, but each time a kick sped towards his opponent his target vanished by simply stepping back just enough to avoid the impact. Yu Tong continued backing up until he neared the crowd and then suddenly began charging forward while blocking each kick and punching back at the same time. Instantly the teacher began stepping backwards to avoid the onslaught of techniques bombarding his body.

Now as his opponent struggled to keep pace, Yu Tong pressed even harder until the fighter stumbled back and fell next to the soup cart.

"Do not get up and try again!

"Go home and do not return," he pointed down the street.

"I hope you realize there'll be more people coming to challenge you?" his friend walked up while shaking his head.

"Yes that's probably true," Yu Tong sat down.

For months Yu Tong was able to sit, sell his herbs, and occasionally perform his techniques in peace. Unfortunately, this was only a temporary reprieve from the practitioners in the city.

"Hey are you that old man who beat up my friend?" the stranger walked up to Yu Tong sitting by his herbs.

Yu Tong remained silent.

"Hey old man I am talking to you!" the stranger stepped closer and kicked dust in Yu Tong's direction.

"Why are you kicking dirt at me?" Yu Tong stood up and looked at the stranger.

"You beat up my friend and I'm here to teach you a lesson," he threw his shirt behind him and settled into a low stance.

"Is that so?" Yu Tong watched the stranger flex his muscles.

The stranger rushed forward to attack. Kick, kick, punch, punch, punch, but each time a technique neared its target Yu Tong slipped to one side or the other.

"If you keep this up I'm going to be forced to hurt you in order to get you to quit," he stepped back and watched the stranger.

"Bayou think you are that good?

"Well let's find out who gets hurt," the stranger's face broadened from the smile.

He charged forward again, but before he could take three steps Yu Tong stepped forward and cut him off.

PUGILIST FROM SHANDONG

Thud, thud, thud! Yu Tong kicked his opponent in the chest, followed by a low spinning leg circle to sweep his feet out from under him.

Thud, crack! The stranger's head hit the hard ground causing it to split open from the impact.

"Cough, cough, ouch!" he mumbled.

"I told you if you continued, I was going to hurt you.

"So do not try again!" he turned and walked back to his weapons.

The stranger struggled to his knees, then crawled over to his shirt and attempted to stop the bleeding. Eventually, he stood, though very shakily, and staggered back down the street.

Yu Tong just sat and shook his head.

Some people just do not know when to quit, he pulled out his long pipe and began scraping the charred remains from inside.

Months later, "Hey Yu Tong, Yu Tong!" the soup man rushed up to the corner

"Hello, why are you in such a panic today?" Yu Tong asked.

"I just heard some fighters talking over a bowl of soup about how mad they are at you for beating up their friends and they were going to come over here and teach you a lesson!" the man jumped off the seat of his cart and sat down.

"Oh really?"

"Yes and these guys are much better than the earlier fighters!" the man placed his palm on his forehead.

"Hmm, we will just have to wait and see if they are serious and show up."

"You are not worried?"

"No."

"Whew, you might not be, but I sure am!" the man nervously looked up and down the street.

"I have fought much tougher fighters than a few upset kids."

"Really, you are not worried?

"Whew!" he exhaled loudly.

For the remainder of the afternoon the two friends just sat on the street corner; Yu Tong sat patiently while trying to sell his herbs, and his friend continually fidgeted while looking up and down the street.

Again months passed by without any challenges from the local fighters. Then early one cloudy morning just after Yu Tong finished arranging his herbs and straightening his weapons, three men hurriedly walked in his direction.

"Hey you old man get up, we want to talk to you!" the leader of the group said as they stopped within a few feet of Yu Tong.

"What do you want and why do you talk to me with that tone?"

"You beat up some of our friends and we came to teach you a lesson." The leader said as he stepped forward and shook his fist.

"Really? You came here to teach me a lesson about fighting and it takes three of you?"

"No, they are here to make sure I don't kill you!"

"Be careful with your threats," Yu Tong shook his finger.

"I have killed many men while trying to survive, so don't make me add your name to the list!" he turned and looked away.

PUGILIST FROM SHANDONG

"What?

"Ahhh!" the leader stepped forward to punch his opponent in the back of the head.

The moment the punch neared Yu Tong's head, he simply leaned away just enough to avoid the impact and let the fist pass by. Instantly he turned and lightly tapped the fighter's side with two fingers and stepped back. For a few seconds the man just stood motionless, then without saying a word he stumbled backwards against his friend; just before they both fell to the ground.

"Thud," the man hit his head on the ground while his leader landed on top and then tumbled off on to his face.

"What happened, what happened?" the third man watched his two accomplices roll on the ground.

"I told him not to threaten me!" Yu Tong explained.

"But you hardly touched him, so how can he be injured so badly?"

"You three need to be more careful about who you threaten," he sat by his weapons and watched the three strangers.

It had been many months since Yu Tong first arrived in Guangzhou and his abilities as a fierce fighter were causing many in the Kung Fu community to seek him out. Here was a small solitary traveler from the North, who in just months was recognized for his fighting.

Hmm it has been quite a few months and no one has tried to challenge me about beating up one of their friends.

I guess they realized it would be better if they left me alone, he sat and cleaned his pipe.

Eventually, after living throughout Guangzhou, Yu Tong decided it was time to move on.

THOMAS HAASE

I think I will walk towards Vietnam.

I have never been there and would like to see what it is like.

Tomorrow would be a good day to start the journey. He began gathering his belongings.

Early the next morning after he finished his training, Yu Tong securely packed all his belongings, arranged the weapons on his shoulder, looked around at the quiet streets, turned towards the west and began the long slow journey to the edge of the Middle Kingdom.

Chapter 13

~ Time of the Yue ~

Yu Tong's home in the north of Shandong Province seemed so distant. Yet his journey into this foreign land, beyond the southern border of the Middle Kingdom, so real. The roads he traveled, the towns he visited and the people he experienced filled his thoughts.

Which fork in the road should he choose? Should he stay in this village or pass on by? Was this person's technique and style valuable or not? On this journey there were many questions as well as streams and rivers to cross. There were mountains to climb or walk around, forests and fields to pass through.

The rivers could be wild and deep or shallow and calm and the forests so solitary that they kept their secrets to themselves. The fields of carefully tended crops were watched over by their caretakers, who groomed their yield and sometimes allowed a wanderer to sample their harvest. All these things welled up in Yu Tong's thoughts as he made his way onward.

It had been a long road to travel, many days spent quietly sheltered under large magnolia or birch trees waiting for torrents of rain to subside. Other times when there was no cover, the best solution was to walk through the rain and ignore its presence. These were the days when being totally alone reminded him of the singularity of life that he heard about from his family so many years earlier.

Finally, after many miles and many days of solitary travel, he arrived in a distant land. Hopefully, no one here had heard about his problems with the authorities and he could live a simple life in peace.

Living in this mountainous region on the fringes of the Middle Kingdom had a number of advantages as well as disadvantages. Trade from China to Vietnam (Yue land) was very accessible. Even though there were only a few routes traveled back and forth, there were numerous products that Vietnam acquired and over time integrated into their culture.

The language, though spoken in its own distinct dialect, was still written with enough similarities to Chinese that anyone traveling from one to the other could decipher a sufficient number of characters and survive. The food also held many similarities along with its own unique palate of spices and herbs. The people too were so similar yet so distinct in their appearance, manner of dress, and way of thinking.

In this remote village in Vietnam on the western border of China, he noticed the simple houses were all nestled together with the walls of one house being used as a wall for the next. Each family was tightly packed into a small area consisting of a kitchen and several bedrooms. The houses were too small to accommodate amenities like a living room, dining room or foyer. Once the meals were prepared, the family either ate in the kitchen next to the heat from the fire, or went out under the roof overhanging the front door. Chairs, stools or benches were usually in short supply, so squatting was the typical position for eating, talking, or resting.

PUGILIST FROM SHANDONG

While looking at the structures, he could tell that at one time the houses all stood tall and strong but slowly with time and neglect had become worn and faded. These dwellings were now tattered and showing the years of abuse. He noticed the doors, if present at all, were barely hanging by rusted hinges. Numerous strips of scrap wood had been crudely attached to help hold the door together.

The windows were also in much disrepair; barren openings where window shutters once hung bore witness to the need for scraps to repair the doors and walls of these tottering houses, to keep the rodents and larger animals from entering to steal the small amount of food inside.

Sagging roofs struggled to support the tile that had once brightly reflected the wide sky and the passing clouds. Now cracked and faded, the roof tiles no longer protected the inhabitants from the elements; they no longer kept at bay the rain and the wind. Once like a phalanx of strong soldiers the roof tiles now seemed more like a shabby rabble grumbling about higher taxes in the tea houses.

For several years Yu Tong lived a very quiet and normal life; no pressure from authorities, nor anyone looking to boost their reputation by challenging the once-mighty warrior escort. Life was simple.

Sitting in the small, secluded restaurant Yu Tong casually observed the activities in the street. People were busy going about their daily routines, buying food for the household, cleaning the street in front of their stores, repairing a well-worn kettle before the arrival of the evening crowd, and even the children laughing and playing in the street, all seemed to continue at a preordained pace.

As he turned to his meal, he heard the faint outlines of a discussion between two men at the next table.

"So, Mr. Vinh, you think Master Wong is that good at his Black Tiger Kung Fu?" the small round man with no hair said as he cautiously looked around to make sure no one else in the room was listening.

"Yes I do, Mr. Trahn," Mr. Vinh replied. "I saw Master Wong fight with some young braggart from the next village and lasted only a couple of moves before the kid was begging for his life."

"So, what does that prove?" Mr. Trahn asked.

"After he was done I heard him tell everyone around that he was from the south of China and that nobody could beat him, especially not that young kid from Shandong who just moved into town," his friend replied.

"Wow, I heard that young guy was really strong and had techniques like no one had ever seen," Mr. Trahn said.

"Well according to Master Wong, this young guy is only a beginner and should go home and practice more," Mr. Vinh replied.

Instantly Yu Tong's interest in the conversation was piqued and he suddenly found himself forgetting about the food in front of him. Each time they returned to the topic of the Black Tiger master he completely stopped his casual attempt at eating in order to hear all they had to say.

Eventually, the two men finished their meal and made their way toward the door while still arguing about the statements made by Master Wong. As they walked down a small dirt side street, neither of them noticed that Yu Tong had followed them the entire way and was now closing in so that he could hear everything. Soon they stopped at the corner of the street so they could part ways and go back to their individual stores.

Yu Tong quickly walked up and interrupted their conversation and said, "Hey, I heard you say that Master Wong is telling everyone that his techniques are better than everyone else's including mine and that I should return to Shandong and practice more?"

PUGILIST FROM SHANDONG

"Yes, that's what I heard him say just the other day," Mr. Vinh said to Yu Tong.

"Why would he say something like that? I have never done anything to him; in fact I have never even met him."

"I don't know but I do know he is quite nervous about you being here." The man showed obvious signs of nervousness. Meanwhile, Mr. Trahn just stood completely silent.

"Why? I haven't tried to take any of his students," Yu Tong replied.

"I know but he thinks that maybe someday you might try," Mr. Vinh said.

"If he keeps talking bad about me and trying to ruin my reputation, I just might start some trouble to shut him up!" Yu Tong's voice grew louder and more enraged. "You tell him to keep to himself and I will leave him alone; otherwise I will show him just how much this kid from Shandong really knows!"

"Okay, okay I'll tell him," Mr. Vinh said, shaking with fear.

Without saying another word Yu Tong turned and walked back in the direction of the teahouse.

The two men stood completely silent for what seemed like an eternity and then finally looked at each other one last time before parting ways without saying anything.

The following day Mr. Vinh ran into Yu Tong.

"Did you tell Master Wong what I said?" Yu Tong stepped directly in front of Mr. Vinh and stuck his finger in his chest.

Mr. Vinh flinched from the pain of the finger being driven into his soft undeveloped chest muscles.

Yu Tong moved even closer. "Well?" he waited for an answer.

"Y-yes I did." he stuttered, rubbing the spot on his chest where the finger had left a deep dent.

"And what did he say?"

"If I tell you, you might hit me thinking I made it all up!"

"What did he say?"

"He, he said that he wasn't afraid of your Northern techniques because they're childish and weak and you should go home and stay close to your mother for protection," he tried to move away and prepare for a beating.

For a moment neither of them said a word.

Eventually, Yu Tong stepped closer and stared so intensely into Mr. Vinh's eyes that his knees began to shake and said, "You go tell that old man that any time he wants to find out just how strong my Northern techniques really are, all he needs to do is let me know the time and place and we'll see who has better Kung Fu and who should stay home by their mother."

"O.. okay," he turned and scurried back toward his home. The next day while Yu Tong was quietly sitting on a street corner, a man yelled at him, "hey you!"

Yu Tong was deep in thought and did not answer.

"Hey you!" the man yelled again as he stepped off the street and under the overhang of the storefront.

Yu Tong still didn't pay attention to who was yelling at him.

"Hey, Master Wong, where are you going in such a hurry?" one of the storeowners asked as he stepped out his front door.

Yu Tong turned and saw Master Wong heading straight toward him. He quickly stood up and readied himself for the confrontation he knew would happen.

PUGILIST FROM SHANDONG

"Don't you go anywhere!" Wong yelled as he shook his finger at Yu Tong and stepped into the middle of the dry and dusty street. "I came here to show you just who I am, how great my techniques are and let you know your mother is calling you home!"

Yu Tong stood motionless and suddenly felt a strange surge of energy pulse through his entire body and remind him of an earlier time when he had killed a man and had to leave the temple. Without looking away Yu Tong sighed deeply because he knew what was about to happen; he knew what the outcome would be, and he knew what tomorrow would bring.

Slowly he put down his small pouch used to carry the precious herbs, glanced down the street in both directions and saw a small group of people hurriedly trying to get in a good viewing position for the inevitable fight. He sighed once again to release the small pockets of tension welling up in his stomach and shoulders.

As he stepped out into the street and the bright sunlight, his first step caused the fine, dry dirt to puff up and create a cloud of dust that quietly drifted outward and settled gently onto the undisturbed soil surrounding the footprint. Soon Yu Tong was standing face to face with the enraged teacher from this quiet mountain village.

"Mr. Vinh said that you think your techniques are better than mine. Well I'm about to show you what a superior technique looks and feels like!" Master Wong said as he settled into an all too familiar Horse Stance.

Yu Tong knew the style that his opponent had trained in for so many years and he knew that in order to survive this situation he would need to rely on all his training from both his family and the temple styles.

"I have no reason to fight you. But I don't understand why you would tell everyone that my techniques are no good. All I am doing is trying to survive and not bother anyone," Yu Tong said as he held his arms straight out to his sides.

"Don't try and wiggle your way out of this!" Wong said.

Yu Tong dropped his arms and for a few seconds looked up in exasperation at the few small puffs of white floating silently across the midday sky. Then as he returned his vision to the situation at hand, he saw Master Wong ready himself. Yu Tong could tell his opponent was about to attack and try to catch him off guard; he had seen it tried many times throughout his travels in China. So as he waited for the inevitable, he formulated a strategy for his response to the style of techniques he knew this fighter would be using.

Suddenly, just as expected, Master Wong rushed forward, shifting from side to side to try and confuse his opponent.

Yu Tong was not intimidated and stood patiently while his opponent closed the distance. The moment Wong was within striking range Yu Tong saw him shift his left foot and prepare to kick him in the side while trying to draw his attention elsewhere by faking a punch to his head.

Yu Tong waited and then suddenly stepped to his right to avoid the attack and deliver a kick of his own to his unsuspecting opponent's head. *Thud!* Echoed through the silently growing crowd as Yu Tong's foot hit the back of Wong's ear causing him to fall face first into the dry soil and create a puff of loose dirt to rush into the air and fall gently around the face print on the ground.

Instantly Wong jumped to his feet and spat out a mouthful of dirt while rubbing the red welt growing behind his ear.

"You are going to pay for that!" he shook his fist at Yu Tong.

Yu Tong stood motionless and said nothing in return.

PUGILIST FROM SHANDONG

Again Master Wong readied himself with the same fighting position and again Yu Tong recognized his strategy and readied himself for the incoming flurry of techniques.

"Ai-yaa!" Wong yelled as he rushed forward and began throwing an even more furious array of kick and punches.

With each move that sped towards Yu Tong's body, he continued to respond with an appropriate defense followed by his own flurry of attacks.

Wong retreated as Yu Tong continued to press the attack while sensing Wong's nervousness at being pushed backward. So he instinctively attacked even more furiously, backing his opponent up even faster and forcing him to try and defend himself. Without warning, Yu Tong stopped and watched as Wong stumbled backward a couple of steps before catching his balance and walking back to the middle of the area where the crowd had gathered.

Wong again readied himself with the usual stance. Yu Tong smiled inside as he again saw his opponent adhere to his most comfortable fighting position. Wong again attacked

As he charged forward Yu Tong retreated while neutralizing Wong's flailing.

Wong tried to catch his opponent off guard by throwing a series of punches to the head followed by a low kick to the leg.

Yu Tong leaned back out of the way of the first punch but underestimated the distance of the second and was hit next to his temple. As Wong's kick raced in towards Yu Tong's leg, he lifted the foot, swung it backwards over his head, like a scorpion tail and kicked Wong squarely in the face with the bottom of his foot, then continued around and returned to his original position.

The kick took Wong off guard. Its force rippled through his body and caused him to flip over backwards and land on the

197

back of his head. He rolled over onto his face and stood to face his opponent.

All the while Yu Tong stood rubbing the small bruised bone on the side of his head while patiently watching the rage continue to build in his frustrated opponent.

"This time I am not going to hold anything back. I am going to use my most deadly techniques!" Wong screamed as he once again spat out moist soil while rubbing his face and pinching his nose to stop the bleeding.

Without warning, Wong charged toward his opponent. As he raced in and began throwing a deadly flurry of techniques, Yu Tong could see that the intensity of the techniques had increased dramatically and that Wong intended to kill him if he got the chance.

Yu Tong realized what his only recourse would be to Wong's ever increasing intensity of deadly techniques. Again he stepped back and as he had so many years before, he sighed deeply at what he was about to do while accepting the responsibilities and outcome that would surely accompany the actions.

Focus the mind on one target, he remembered his father say.

Master Wong sped forward in another attempt to save face, unknowingly walking into the final moments of his life.

Yu Tong readied himself, and as the first series of punches drifted by his head and found only still dry air, he slipped downward and inside and drove his fingertip deep into the ribcage of his opponent's left side.

Immediately, Master Wong's body went limp and fell to the ground for the last time. First the knees hit the soft soil and the body seemed to stop momentarily, giving the impression that he was still alive. Then the remainder of the energy left his body and as his face lost all expression, he fell forward, his arms limp by his sides, offering no relief from the impending impact.

Slowly Yu Tong stood up and gazed silently at the lifeless body lying at his feet. Once again he began to feel that old familiar feeling that always surfaced following this scenario. Years earlier he didn't experience this sensation until days later. Now for the first time, the feeling began as soon as the fight ended.

He looked around at the many faces of the spectators and noticed their looks of shock. Then quietly one by one, they all turned and headed back to where they were before it all started.

Yu Tong headed back to the street corner and gathered up his belongings. As quietly as the long shadows had disappeared under the doorway, he headed back to his small, simple room where he could be alone and mourn the death of a fellow practitioner in silence.

For hours he sat motionless while thinking about what he could have changed. The bell tower rang once again reminding everyone of the passing third hour. The sound rippled across the rooftops like waves in the ocean

After many hours of quiet thought, Yu Tong's eyes grew heavy and he drifted off to sleep.

The next morning he calmly sat in his meditation position and slowly, moment by moment, the sense of oneness began to fill his entire being like a dense fog slowly sinking to the ground and blanketing all under its path. Soon all sense of time began to slowly fade into the cool crisp morning air and disappear with each breath. All was quiet.

For a while Yu Tong focused on absorbing as much of the sense of being in the moment as possible, then from deep in the far recesses of his mind he began to feel a strong sense of what he must do gradually build and creep its way to the foreground of his mind.

So with a sigh of exasperation he once again chose to travel far enough away so that no one would know anything about the situation. He knew he would have to change his name to avoid any remaining chances for repercussion.

Quietly with a sense of loss welling deep in his stomach, Yu Tong stood up and gathered his few remaining belongings and slowly made his way out of the small room that for so many days had been his oasis from the dark shadows following him continually since his departure from his home years earlier. Now, he would need to move on and find a new location where he might but for a brief period call home and live in peace.

As he reached the street, he glanced back at the worn and weathered dwelling, sighed as memories flooded his mind of the peaceful moments spent inside, then looked down the street to see if anyone was out at this early hour. Fortunately, he was alone so he carefully made his way toward the edge of town and for the last time headed down the narrow road away from this small, secluded village tucked deep within the dense forest.

Soon the sun began to creep up over the distant mountaintops and cast its rays down deep into the valleys below. Walking carefully down the meandering trail Yu Tong noticed the clouds overhead stretched as far as the eye could see. The rolling pattern gave the appearance of a sea of soldiers marching forward to engage their enemy without a single one out of line.

When the wave reached the mountaintops, they seemed to engulf the majestic peaks and hold them deep within their ranks while trying to push back the sun. Finally, after the wave of clouds had passed, the mountains were able to express their joy at being able to endure the clouds' onslaught by once again standing tall and gazing down upon the countryside of tiny villages and patchwork patterns of crops in various stages of maturity.

Throughout the day Yu Tong kept his pace steady and only stopped occasionally by a small stream or lake to drink from the cool clear liquid and refresh himself before continuing on.

Eventually, his efforts brought him to the edge of a small foreign land and back to the fringes of his home. And as the sun began its gradual descent toward the distant horizon, he stopped once again to rest by a calm lake while contemplating which direction he should choose.

He decided to head toward Nanning while drinking a small bowl of water. He remembered it as a peaceful place the last time he was there.

Several days later as he sat quietly leaning against the broad trunk of a large oak tree, his thoughts returned him to the earlier time when he was leaving his home province for the first time. He remembered the many months of slow but continual walking south to escape the past, the countless people he had encountered during his short visits to the countless cities, towns and villages. He wondered how many times he sensed that people were talking about who he might be and other times when no one paid the slightest bit of attention to his presence at all. His life had given him countless memories and experiences, taught him many things and had taken him to amazing places throughout the numerous and diverse provinces.

He sat calmly in the shade with his mind drifting to the past. The calm surface of the water glistening in front of him was suddenly broken by a large brightly colored trout catapulting out of the water to catch a dragonfly hovering close to the surface. The fish could only grasp a single wing before falling back into the calm darkness. The injured dragonfly frantically tried to escape and find safety.

For a moment Yu Tong's attention abruptly returned to the present and as he watched the struggle for life continue along its preordained path, he smiled at the good fortune of one and the bad luck of another. Then with the slight turn of his head his gaze drifted off into the deep blue sky and he returned to his thoughts of days gone by. He remembered the times when he passed through the many long and treacherous mountain ranges.

Walking slowly along the deserted road, he was continuously amazed at the occasional evergreen tree growing high up on the mountainside. These sharp spires were standing solemnly in the cold mountain air, protruding first horizontally and then sharply upwards towards the heavens. Their presence seemed strangely out of place. Nowhere else was there the slightest indication of life. Yet here stood a few sparsely scattered brave souls trying to survive and demonstrate to all that there was hope in the most remote regions.

Soon the outskirts of the city of Nanning appeared in the distance. And late the next day he found himself standing at the edges of the aged city in hopes of peace.

Chapter 14

~ Southern Tranquility ~

F ar out in the remote southwestern regions of the vast and diverse Middle Kingdom lay the small quiet city at the fringes of the long meandering mountain range that started at the water's edge in southern Vietnam and then quietly but continually stretched for thousands of miles north into Tibet and Russia like an old dragon peacefully resting in the warm summer sun.

For those brave enough to venture into this remote area, this city was the last main artery before leaving the Middle Kingdom and heading south into the heavily forested land of Vietnam.

Years earlier when Yu Tong had decided to travel from the hectic world of Guangzhou toward Vietnam, hoping to reach an area where he could live peacefully without worry of recognition, he had stopped in this area and spent many months quietly living among the desert people while trying to learn their unique variation of Chinese and live peacefully. He remembered the residents were unusually friendly and welcoming to even the remotest of strangers and this helped immensely to make him feel at ease.

Now that he had returned and spent the last several months sitting at the same location while trying to sell his medicine to make money, he began to relax slightly about always training in private. Soon he found a small open area with several large trees where he could spend his early mornings and late afternoons practicing and even though it was quite visible for anyone passing by on the small rough and narrow pathway on their way to tend their crops, he continued to spend his time here.

"Hey, Yu Tong, what are you practicing?" one of the locals, Mr. Zhuang, who had befriended the solitary stranger over the months, asked as he was strolling by on his way to visit his cousin in a small village just outside of town.

"I'm practicing my Kung Fu," Yu Tong answered without breaking his rhythm.

"Where did you learn to fight like that?"

"Well, when I was younger and lived in Shandong Province, I was taught my family style of Tam Tui and then my father sent me to a quiet and remote temple to learn a Praying Mantis style.

"Wow! I have never seen anything like that. Could you teach me some of that?" Zhuang asked as he tried to imitate what his friend was effortlessly doing.

"I could but you will have to be willing to do and train the way that I tell you to without any questions," Yu Tong replied as he finally stopped and turned to head back to the small tree offering the only shade in the entire area.

"When could I start?" Zhuang asked with a gleam in his eyes.

PUGILIST FROM SHANDONG

Yu Tong made his way to the tree, then slowly sat down and leaned back against the smooth bark while wiping the sweat from his forehead. He glanced up at his anxious prospect standing directly in front of him and said in a stern voice, "Well if you are really serious about learning, come by tomorrow morning and I'll show you some basics. But you must be willing to train hard!"

"Oh I will … oh I will." Zhuang said.

"Okay then, you go home and take care of your affairs and I will see you early in the morning."

As soon as he was out of sight Yu Tong stood up, walked back out into the open area and returned to his training. Now that he was once again alone he decided to focus his attention for the remainder of the day on applications for all the many movements he had been taught. One by one he executed each movement in the many forms he had learned over the years and then finally after he was satisfied with the depth at which he had delved into each movement, he focused on the specialty training exercises he knew.

After several hours, the sun finally began to set over the snow-covered mountains far off in the distance and Yu Tong gathered his weapons and well-worn backpack and then turned to go to his small solitary abode.

The following morning as Yu Tong was making his way to the open area to train, he saw Zhuang waiting by the large tree where he had left his prospective teacher the day before.

"Good morning, Master." Zhuang said.

"You're early for your first day. Usually new students are late." Yu Tong respectfully bowed in response to the formal greeting Mr. Zhuang demonstrated as he approached his teacher.

"My father was very strict about being on time when you said you would do something," Zhuang answered as he waited for his training to begin.

"Well, it sounds to me like your father was a very old traditionalist and believed in punctuality and the impression it set for others." Yu Tong set his equipment down below the tree, and then leaned against the aged and silent companion to gently stretch and loosen his experienced muscles.

"First you need to open the body up by stretching before you begin any rigorous training. That way you will lessen the chances for injury." Yu Tong said as he turned to begin his new profession as a teacher and gently guide his student through some of the basic ideas involved in his ancient art.

"How often should I stretch my body?" Zhuang asked as he leaned against the tree and imitated his teacher.

"Well, if you want to get the most benefit possible and reduce your chances of injuring yourself while training, you will need to devote time each day to your stretching." Yu Tong stepped back away from the tree to observe his student's technique.

Quietly over the next thirty minutes the two continued to warm up their bodies and prepare for the upcoming rigors of the training.

"Okay, now that we are sufficiently loosened up and our internal energy is beginning to move freely, it is time to start. It will soon be time for the caretakers of the newly planted crops to begin making their way to their fields so we'll want to get as much training in as possible before they arrive so they won't distract us." Yu Tong demonstrated a number of the basic stance positions and their respective punches as Zhuang stared intently at the movements of his teacher.

Over the next several hours Yu Tong slowly and meticulously taught Mr. Zhuang a variety of the basics. Every time he performed one incorrectly Yu Tong would make him go back and practice just that move over and over until it was correct.

206

PUGILIST FROM SHANDONG

"Now see how all that extra practice helped you to execute better punches and kicks?" Yu Tong asked when his student finished another routine.

"My father emphasized the importance of relaxing as long as possible and punching through your target." Yu Tong added while they sat in the shade and quenched their thirst with a bowl of water.

Soon the sun began creeping over the horizon and a few of the workers lazily meandered by on their way to the fields.

"Okay, I think that will be enough for today," Yu Tong said as he watched Zhuang perform the last in a series of movements.

"Are you sure?" Zhuang asked as he tried to keep from showing how tired he had become from the rigorous training. The sweat had been pouring from his body continuously for some time, and his entire body was shaking while the sweat dripped profusely to the ground creating a small pool around him as he stood still.

"Yes, I think you have done enough. When you go home you need to spend some time stretching because your muscles are going to really tighten up." Yu Tong watched Zhuang trying to maintain his upright position.

Zhuang picked up his belongings and turned to bow to his teacher.

"You go home now," Yu Tong said as soon as he bowed in return and then turned to begin his own personal practice.

Gradually over the following months Zhuang began to develop an understanding about the techniques. His body slowly began to reshape and as he punched or kicked he was now showing signs of promise. His movements no longer appeared static and choppy; now they were beginning to link together into a fluid series of attacks and defenses. His eyes and mind were sharper and more focused with less wandering in the middle of a technique.

As Zhuang continued to practice, his family noticed the dramatic changes and one by one they arrived to begin taking lessons. Now what was once an intimate exchange between a student and his teacher had become a group outing and eventually the family asked Yu Tong to teach in their family compound instead of the open area where everyone could observe.

For a while everything moved along quietly and the students progressed rapidly. One day Yu Tong decided it was time to continue his journey and began making preparations to head back towards Guangzhou. Day after day his students tried unsuccessfully to persuade him to stay with them and continue teaching. Once he made up his mind to move on they didn't know or understand that he always stuck to his decision and the decision was final.

Soon the day arrived when he would be leaving and one by one each member of the family stopped by in one final attempt to get him to change his mind and one by one each departed with a deep sense of loss. Finally, Mr. Zhuang arrived to pay his last respects and bid his friend and teacher farewell. And now it was back to the two of them, alone, intimate as it was in the beginning.

Zhuang made no attempt to convince his teacher to stay; he already knew he wouldn't and to continue asking was disrespectful. So he sat and quietly watched as Yu Tong packed his belongings neatly into the backpack his mother had given him so many years earlier. When he finished the two walked to the edge of town and as they reached the small open area where it all began, Yu Tong stopped momentarily to reflect on the memories of an earlier time. Then he turned to his friend and student, bowed deeply while clasping his hands together in a formal salute, looked Zhuang in the eyes and softly said goodbye. No mention of his return or of when they would see each other again, just a simple yet fulfilling bow of respect from his sixty-year-old teacher.

PUGILIST FROM SHANDONG

The following months Yu Tong continued east towards his final destination all the while reflecting on his students and small simple dwelling where he had spent the last few years of his life. Soon he began seeing signs of a change in terrain, design and color of clothing worn by the people and their staple diet through the types of crops being grown.

Walking alone along the small solitary path, he pondered about changing his name in order to avoid any chances of being recognized.

"Hmm, what would be a good auspicious name? I have been to so many places. Which one could I use for my new name?"

As he walked he continued to reflect on the places and ideas for a name that would be appealing.

"I know, I will keep my family name but change my first and middle name"

Oh, I remember, while I stopped in Guangzhou years ago, there was a mountain nearby named Kwan Shan. His mind began to race with enthusiasm over the place and its name.

I could call myself Lee Kwan Shan, after the mountain.

His excitement overwhelmed all other thoughts about the choice.

That's it, I will use Kwan Shan as my name and that will end all the worry about my past. Yu Tong's pace increased with his excitement.

Chapter 15

~ The Fall of Mount Tai ~

Months after leaving Nanning, Kwan Shan finally arrived back in Panyu and was greeted by the familiar sights and scenery he remembered from years earlier when he had passed through the area.

He headed to the center of town and checked out where he could set up his display of herbs and possibly perform.

The next morning after his training he headed down to make sure the spot was still available. Quickly he setup his display and then sat back against the wall and waited for the remainder of the city to awaken and begin another day.

One by one the business owners began to arrive and open their stores. Soon the street began to fill with patrons scurrying from store to store in search of some special item.

Ha, that's game!" He heard old man Liu yell from down the street as he meticulously placed the small white ivory chip into position on the Wieqi (Chinese Go) board thus sealing Master Ng's fate.

The weather was showing signs of a new year with the arrival of spring. The everyday rains now became more occasional and usually ended before noon. People were starting to come out and spend time working in their yard in preparation for the new season. One by one the farmers began to make their daily journey out into the barren fields and prepare for the planting of the year's new crop.

The change in weather seemed to lift the spirits of everyone; Kwan Shan was also affected by the lightened mood. He began to see new chances to make money selling herbs and giving demonstrations. The thoughts of hunger that had gripped him during the winter began to subside. Now he was able to come out in the afternoon hours and set up his small assortment of herbs. He would talk to the farmers and the others who stopped to inquire about his mixtures and remedies.

Occasionally a small crowd would gather as they looked over his medicines, and he would use that opportunity to perform a demonstration for them of his Kung Fu abilities. He hoped that if they didn't buy any herbs they might give him a few coins for his performance.

Shortly after the rain stopped, Kwan Shan gathered his belongings and walked downtown to his usual location and set up his display. He had to get there before the farmers left home for the day to tend their crops. When he finished setting up he glanced down the street. No one was out yet, so he sat down behind his weapons, leaned back against the wall to relax, and waited for the village to wake.

Soon storeowners arrived and surveyed the damage left by last night's storm. After a couple hours the stores were all open, the mud had been pushed back out into the middle of the street and customers began arriving from all directions.

Kwan Shan had arrived in Jian months earlier after having walked for weeks from Jingdezhen. He had heard about the masterpieces of porcelain that were made in this distant city so he traveled southward to see for himself. He wanted to make this city a stop in his travels, but along the way he wanted to travel to Jiujiang to see the famous Mt. Lushan with its many peaks, waterfalls and Three-Tiered Spring.

The immense beauty of the mountain peaks, layered one behind the other and the continual "cloud sea" from the surrounding mist made this a sight like nothing he had encountered. The region contained sheer cliffs of rock climbing toward the sky until they disappeared into the fog.

Waterfalls continually spewed out ice-cold mountain water which fell onto the multi-tiered rock face below. These sights seemed to engulf his being to the point where time simply vanished. He spent days in the area admiring the beauty while walking through the forest. Every day he walked in a different direction to experience as much of the area as possible and each time he never felt as though he came even close to the mountains, due to the continual mist.

Taking this route also gave him the opportunity to travel and stay in areas that were considerably warmer than his home in the distant Shandong. Here he was able to train outside throughout the winter months; back home it would already have snowed several times, greatly reducing his training routine because of space constraints from having to practice indoors. Now he could practice his entire training routine everyday including his favorite arts. This also meant it would be much easier to find food, since the growing season was longer with a wider variety of foods to choose from, and shelter, because now whenever he wanted to sleep he could easily find a small remote area off the main road and sleep for the night outside under the stars.

It had been months since Kwan Shan's arrival in Jian and in that time he had become friends with some of the small business owners. They admired his knowledge of herbal remedies and Kung Fu. Occasionally, a few would walk down to the corner where he set up his display and watch as he performed a variety of Kung Fu skills.

Over the past few months he had been focusing more attention on his double broadsword techniques and had become increasingly proficient at blocking stones that people would throw at him. As he stood in the middle of the street, he would solicit some of the crowd to pick up a stone and try to hit him as he stood and twirled the swords around his body. The owners were always amazed that no one could hit him with a single rock, so every day they returned to see if anyone had succeeded.

Early in the morning shortly after setting up his display, Kwan Shan saw old Liu slowly make his way down the street and stop to talk briefly to Little Zhang, the ironworker and weapons maker, before walking across the street to his favorite Weiqi table. Within a few minutes as Liu sat sipping his morning tea, Master Ng could be seen hurrying down the middle of the street.

The bricks that had been installed years earlier down the center of the road helped to drain the water from the street and give everyone a place to walk after the rainstorms. Now Master Ng could be seen carefully stepping from stone to stone to avoid slipping in the thin layer of mud left on the bricks, while holding his pant legs just high enough so they wouldn't drag on the ground.

Kwan Shan sometimes pondered why a man like Master Ng, who had developed his body and mind to such a high degree through his years of training in Kung Fu, would want to waste so much time and money on a silly game.

He heard about Old Liu from one of his friends and how game after game and challenger after challenger, for years they all stepped up to his inlaid jade game-board and tried their luck in hopes of unseating the old man to gain a reputation as the best player.

Now that Kwan Shan was back, he could tell Old Liu was still regarded as the best Weiqi player in the city of Panyu. He remembered hearing years earlier, that Old Liu had loved the game and played at every chance since childhood. Now after sixty years his expertise at the game had reached a level equal to that of any Kung Fu master's martial technique.

Each morning Kwan Shan would watch Old Liu take his usual route from his small house near the edge of the village. When Old Liu finally made his way to the main street, Kwan Shan watched as he would stop, look up and down the main thoroughfare in both directions, then turned and gaze back down the small alleyway. After a few moments he would turn and head towards his favorite teahouse and Weiqi table.

"Okay Old Liu, just one more game. I can feel a win coming my way," Kwan Shan heard Master Ng plead in desperation as old Liu began to rise from his small stool and stretch his legs.

"Are you sure?" Liu asked in a voice of concern.

"We have been playing for hours and you haven't won yet." He looked back at his friend sitting on the stool and hurriedly trying to rearrange the smooth ivory pieces.

"Yes!" Master Ng shouted as he finished.

"But what about the money you already owe me from today and yesterday?" Liu asked as he stood and watched Ng nervously rearrange the pieces once again.

"Don't worry old man; I'll get your money for you." Master Ng said as he motioned for old Liu to sit back down. Old Liu stood for a moment, looked down at the board and sighed.

"Okay," he sat on the small stool, shaking his head in disbelief.

"You can go first."

Within seconds the two were back totally engrossed in the small ivory pieces covering the rosewood table. Game after game the two played and without fail. Master Ng was always the loser. Soon the shadows began to creep from the corners of the building out into the street. As they did Master Ng grew steadily more anxious about winning at least one game because he knew in a few moments he would need to leave and return to his school to teach.

"It is about time for you to leave isn't it?" Liu asked as he slowly placed his piece into position and won the game.

"Not yet!" Ng answered.

"I want one more chance to beat you before I go." He began rearranging the pieces before old Liu could get up and leave.

"Okay, but this is the last one. I don't want you neglecting your students," Liu said sternly as he turned his focus back to the game.

The shadows continued to crawl out across the street until finally they ran into the walls of the buildings on the other side. There they began the long slow ascent upwards across the shapes of doors and lanterns hanging from the walls. The heat from the noonday sun had relinquished its hold on those trying to survive on the streets below. Now as the sun made its way closer and closer to the horizon, the long shadows began to paint an image across the entire landscape with a mixture of orange and black patches slowly cascading down the walls, across the rooftops, through the trees and out into the open fields. The canvas of this dusty world appeared as though it were slowly melting into nothing. In minutes it would be dark and the lesser light of the moon and the stars would replace the glaring sun.

"That's game," Liu said, but this time without the excitement about winning.

PUGILIST FROM SHANDONG

"It can't be!" Ng exclaimed.

"I was just about to beat you," he grabbed his hair and leaned back on the small stool.

"Shouldn't you be going now?" Liu asked as he reached over to take a sip of tea from the little jade teacup.

At first Ng didn't hear him; he was so overwhelmed with confusion about how he could get so close and then it be gone in an instant.

It was after Liu tapped him on the arm and said it again that he realized what had just happened and with it his last chance to try and even the score for the day.

As old Liu patiently waited, Master Ng slowly began accepting the outcome and knew it was time to go home. Slowly he stood up and paused long enough to glance back at the cold, smooth, black and white squares, gazing somberly at his aged victor just before turning and making his way down the street.

For years this routine continued. Each day Ng would show up early hoping that today was going to be the day. Unfortunately, it never was. Year after year the scenario repeated itself and the villagers grew more and more concerned about Ng's gambling problem. No one dared express these concerns to their friend and teacher because they also knew about his temper. They remembered his Kung Fu prowess from what they had seen years before when he challenged the previous master and killed him after only a few techniques.

As Ng made his way home he heard in the distance the rhythmic sound from the clapper of the town crier calling out the passing of yet another nighttime hour. The sound echoed through the streets followed by silence as the last clap of the bell died out. Just as the bell had gone quiet Ng heard the sharp splat! Splat! Splat! of rain as it began to fall. One by one the drops fell, first in the soft layer of loose soil in the street;

creating small craters where each droplet hit the ground. Soon it ran down the awnings over the stores and finally to the ground. As it intensified it soon covered the entire street with a shiny blanket of turbulent raindrops. The downpour continued throughout the night.

As the sun began to creep up over the mountains, the night slowly turned gray and the outlines of the village rooftops could be seen rising up into the early morning sky. As the wet morning dawned and Ng rose from his slumber, he could see that the streets had turned to an ocean of dark brown mud.

As soon as Master Ng finished his morning meal, he walked out into the open courtyard where the students were beginning their daily practice, to check the weather to see if it was clear enough for him to go into town. Looking up at the gray sky while looking for signs of the day's weather, he noticed the clouds were beginning to break apart and let the morning sunlight burst through on to the ground slowly causing the earth to send up faint whispers of steam. As it did, Ng knew he could rely on old Liu to be downtown waiting for someone to play a game with, so quickly he began to gather his things and prepare for the trip.

This game must have been invented by someone with way too much time on their hands. Kwan Shan thought. *I suppose some people just love to gamble. They will always find a reason and way to gamble, even if they don't do it for money.*

Quickly the two were consumed by their game and oblivious to the passersby who stopped to check out who was winning.

Shortly after the noon hour had been struck as Kwan Shan sat patiently waiting for a customer, he noticed a young well-groomed man who reminded him of some of the scholars he had known back in Shandong Province. His hair was well-kept with the queue expertly braided so that each succeeding braid

218

was identical to the previous one with not a single hair left undone. He wore an outfit that was very clean and shiny without holes, tears or wear marks, nor stains along the bottom of his pant legs from years of walking on the muddy streets. His face and body were strong and healthy, which gave the impression that his lifestyle offered him many pleasures and sufficient food to eat.

Lately, throughout other parts of the country, intense droughts had caused increasing famines. There was a steady stream of starving and homeless peoples making their way toward the larger cities hoping to find work and food. Unfortunately, jobs were scarce and so the people aimlessly wandered the streets looking for whatever they could find.

This young man was definitely not at a loss for food, and as he casually walked from shop to shop, Kwan Shan could tell that he had been formally trained in some form of traditional Kung Fu. He saw from the way the man walked, the way he politely and casually avoided people on the street and the way he carried his steel fan to cool himself from the thick humidity just after the rain, that this scholarly looking man was educated and very practiced.

As he walked with a stride of total confidence; slow, steady and strong, he seemed to be just looking without really wanting to buy anything. Each store he stopped at he would gently pick up some small elegantly carved object, hold it in his palm and use his fingertips to softly feel the faintest depressions in the smooth surface and sense the energy, time and craftsmanship that went into its creation.

After a few moments he slowly returned the object to its original position, looked around for any other items of interest and when he was satisfied he had seen everything, he bade the owner a good day and politely excused himself.

Eventually, he made his way to Little Zhang's shop, quietly stepped inside and began inspecting and handling the various weapons on display near the front door. One by one he tried each weapon with the smooth quiet precision of an experienced fighter searching for the perfect weapon.

"How long does it take to make a weapon like this?" he asked as he held up a long-handled sword.

"Usually it only takes a couple of days," Zhang replied as he stoked the small fire. "Would you like me to make one for you?"

"No, that will not be necessary; I'm leaving tomorrow so I will wait until I return," the young man replied.

Quietly Zhang went back to heating the large flat piece of metal while his visitor continued to inspect the weapons.

"Thank you for your help and patience," the young man said as he walked out the front door.

Without turning around, Zhang raised his hand over his head in acknowledgement and continued with fanning the flame.

Sitting quietly by his small array of herbs and weapons, Kwan Shan had observed the entire route of the scholarly looking young man. When he finally walked into the weapons shop, Kwan Shan could hear his voice and immediately tell he had been raised in the north of China. His accent and pronunciation of certain words indicated he had been schooled somewhere to the west of Beijing.

Now as he stood in the doorway of the weapons shop while looking down the street in both directions, Kwan Shan kept an even closer watch over the stranger, mostly from curiosity to see if he could get any indications regarding his style of Kung Fu.

As he continued to watch he noticed the young man take an interest in the Weiqi game across the street. Over the course of his journey down the street he had seen the game but not paid much attention to it. Now for some reason he suddenly became very interested in the outcome of the current match. Slowly he made his way across the street by carefully stepping in places where others had already walked through the soft mud, leaving footprints behind and giving him a place to step.

As he stood near the table and watched the game, he smiled occasionally as he witnessed Master Ng repeatedly being outplayed. Time after time just about when it looked as if Ng had gained the advantage over old Liu, the wise old man would move one piece and vanquish Ng's efforts in a single moment.

Two more times of the same outcome and now Ng was beginning to become visibly agitated. As he leaned back on the small stool in frustration, he finally looked up and saw the young man standing next to the table and watching the game while fanning his face to ward off the thick humidity that lingered in the hot sun.

It was now about the noon hour and the sun was directly overhead. The clouds had all quietly sped off into the cool shade of the distant mountain range, leaving everyone else to fend for themselves against the rising heat wave. Moment by moment the sun continued to heat up the buildings and surrounding terrain until it drove everyone into the recesses of the few remaining pockets of shade. Unfortunately, with the high humidity from the recent rain and the total lack of breeze even the shaded areas weren't able to offer much relief.

By the time Ng looked back at the game, old Liu had cut him off with a single move, sealing his fate.

"Not again!" Ng exclaimed as he watched Liu execute his final blow to the weak defenses Ng had set up.

"Good move," the young man told old Liu.

"Hey, kid, don't be helping him." Ng glared at the young man.

"I'm sorry, sir, but I was just complimenting him on his playing abilities, and I wasn't trying to help him play." The young man's tone was apologetic and he stepped back to give Ng some more space.

"I've seen you standing there for some time now and every time old Liu makes a good move you have to say something about how good it was." Ng said.

"Excuse me, sir, but I have said nothing during the entire game until just now."

"I heard you, mumbling under your breath," Ng interjected loudly before the scholar could say anymore.

"But, sir, I have done nothing wrong," the young man said.

"Are you saying I'm a liar?" Ng questioned.

"No, sir. I don't even know you, so how could I call you a liar?" the scholar replied.

"Don't try and patronize me, little boy!" Ng snapped.

"I'm not trying to patronize or cause you any trouble, sir; I was just saying I don't know you."

"So are you saying I'm making this up?" Ng stood up and pushed the stool away with his foot.

"Sir, I have said nothing during the entire game," the young man watched the stool slide sideways, hit another stool and then fall on to its side.

"I think you are calling me a liar and I take that as a formal challenge!" Ng's face reddened.

"No, sir, I am not trying to challenge you at all."

Ng stood there as if frozen with nothing to say. Kwan Shan knew he did not want to lose face in front of his friends by backing down from the situation. Ng turned and ran across the street to Little Zhang's store, grabbed a Tiger Fork that was leaning against the wall near the front entrance, and headed back across the street toward the young scholar.

As he neared the center of the muddy street where the few bricks had already begun to dry, the young man slowly closed his fan, tucked it behind his back and took one step back with his left leg to ready himself for what was about to happen.

"Get out here, you arrogant little boy. I'm going to teach you a lesson!" Ng yelled as he pointed at the young man with one finger and swung the Tiger Fork wildly with the other hand while standing in the muddy street.

For a moment everything and everyone on the street stopped, no one moved or said anything as they waited to see what was going to happen.

Finally the young man sighed deeply, stood up from his defensive position and resigned himself to accepting the challenge from Master Ng. Slowly he pulled the front panel of his long jacket off to the side and while holding it with one hand he began to make his way cautiously out into the street.

"There is no need for this," he said as he neared the furious fighter standing in front of him.

Ng just stood completely still with his finger still aimed at the scholar now standing about twenty feet away. Eternity seemed to pass by in the next few moments as the fighters stood motionless while observing each other's stance and position.

Kwan Shan stood up to see the outcome of the challenge and to check out the techniques of the young scholar. But before he could take a step closer to get a better view of the battle, Ng charged the young man. Gaining speed on the muddy street Ng began swinging the Tiger Fork over his head and around his body. He began a series of high and low jabs to try and confuse his young opponent

Unfortunately for Ng, the young man was not impressed and just stood his ground. As Ng drew near the young man quickly stepped backward twice to avoid two of the jabs and as the third strike neared his face, he casually stepped to the side to avoid the attack. As he did, he swung the closed metal fan down hard on top of the wrist of Ng's right hand. A sickening *crack* echoed through the street as the bones in Ng's arm gave way to the sudden impact.

Ng dropped his weapon on the bricks in the street. *Clang! Clang! Clink!*

As Ng reached down to pick up the pieces of his broken weapon, the young scholar flipped his steel fan open and swung it hard across the back of Ng's neck and shoulder. The razor-sharp tips tore through Ng's shirt and opened a large gash in the muscle below as he dropped both ends of the Tiger fork and fell into the soft mud as the blood began to rush from the long deep wound.

Ng frantically tried to reach over his shoulder and stop the bleeding with his left arm. Unfortunately, it was too short to give much assistance, so he tried to shove the shirt he was wearing into the open wound.

The young scholar stood motionless, watching the defeated fighter as he lay in the muddy street trying to slow the bleeding. The disgusted expression on the scholar's face said everything. He had not wanted to fight nor had he wanted to force Master Ng to lose face in his village, but he had to defend himself and his honor.

The scholar knew what the outcome would be; Master Ng would have to leave town because his reputation had just been stained forever. No longer could he live in this village and look people in the eyes after losing so badly to a much younger fighter and all because of his gambling addiction. Afterward, the village would need to go through the process once again of finding a reputable fighter to teach the villagers and defend their homes.

PUGILIST FROM SHANDONG

While the young scholar was deep in a moment of thought about the outcome, "Ai-yaa!" Master Ng yelled as he stumbled to his feet and once again charged forward with another attack.

This time Master Ng changed his attack strategy by rushing directly at his opponent and suddenly at the last minute beginning a series of spins in a low stance. Momentarily, the technique confused the scholar by not giving him any indication regarding Master Ng's next move. While he was waiting for an indication, Master Ng suddenly dropped to the ground on one knee and thrust the points of the fork at the scholar's chest, attempting to surprise his younger and inexperienced opponent. The scholar suddenly recognized the movement from his years of training and began twisting to avoid being struck by the weapon.

He didn't react soon enough and the long point grazed the edge of his rib cage, cutting through the skin without puncturing the lung, and then tearing through the sleeve of his jacket. Without losing any momentum from the spin, the scholar continued his turn and kicked at Master Ng's head while restraining any facial expressions about the intense pain that must be shooting out from his side. As his foot neared its target, Master Ng rolled to his side to avoid the impact and swung his tiger fork over his head in an attempt to chop his attacker's spine while it was exposed.

Again, as the weapon closed in on its target, the scholar jumped toward his attacker while jabbing at his neck with his steel fan.

Master Ng dropped to his side to avoid the sharp points of the fan and thrust his own kick back at the legs of his adversary. The kick struck the scholar's legs, turning his body upside down. The scholar hit the ground with a thud and then twisted to avoid another attack.

Master Ng confidently stood up to face his rival as the blood continued to soak the fabric covering his shoulder.

Cautiously, the pair slowly circled each other, eyes locked. When they stopped, it appeared as though the entire world stopped with them; there was not a sound anywhere in the area because all the spectators had become completely captivated by the battle and stood motionless waiting for the next engagement.

Suddenly the scholar rushed toward Master Ng while opening and closing his steel fan rapidly to distract his opponent and disrupt his concentration.

Master Ng flinched momentarily, and the scholar accelerated his forward momentum. Once he was within range, the scholar thrust the fan toward Master Ng's face.

Master Ng desperately blocked to avoid another deep wound, and the scholar dropped to the ground and spun around to sweep the legs out from under his opponent.

Master Ng's legs became airborne as his head raced downward. *Boom!* He hit the ground on the back of his head and then crumpled into a ball. The tiger fork was no longer a weapon to use against a skilled opponent; now it was an implement attacking its owner as it landed on his face, cutting a deep gouge in his cheek.

The young man looked at the blood dripping from the sharp tips of his fan and bent down to pick up some mud and wipe off the dark fluid slowly thickening on to the metal points. After he finished cleaning the blood from his weapon, he turned, looked at old Liu still sitting at the small table, shaking his head. He glanced toward Kwan Shan, but he had already sat down and returned to his own endeavor. Finally, the young scholar looked around at those standing nearby, sighed heavily and walked away.

Just after he turned the corner and was out of sight, Master Ng's students came running around the corner from another side street to help their fallen teacher. They reached down and grabbed hold of his arms and slowly raised him to his feet. As soon as he could support himself one of the senior students began working on the large wound that extended from just below the right ear across the back and down to the left shoulder blade.

"Ai-yaa!" Master Ng yelled as his student poured tan-colored powder into the wound and then covered it with fresh bandages.

"Okay, Master, we can go now." his student said as he finished securing the last bandage. The other students began carefully carrying Master Ng back towards their school.

Little Zhang stepped down off the sidewalk and walked over to where the fight had just finished. Shaking his head at the incident he had just witnessed, he reached down and picked up the pieces of his weapon, looked at each piece to inspect the damage and then turned and walked back to his shop while mumbling under his breath about how he probably would never get paid for the broken weapon.

Chapter 16

~ A Tiger in Guangzhou ~

Guangzhou: a city of millions perched on the fringes of the southern coast of China and always on the move. For centuries this seaport had been a vital asset to the Middle Kingdom. As far back as 500BC foreign traders would stop here first prior to venturing inland with their goods.

In a city of millions, being proficient at Kung Fu was commonplace and everyone was striving to gain a better position because with it would come more respect and food. Unfortunately, moving upward was extremely difficult and to get high enough in the ranks to be regarded as remotely close to the top ten was even harder. But to actually be one of the ten, now this meant you were quite extraordinary. To be number one, a fighter had to have talents that even the masters aspired to.

Since Kwan Shan had perfected the rare talent of Dim Mak, this meant he was feared above all the rest. Again, this came at a price. Numerous competitors wanted to be number one, and yet they knew the consequences of challenging someone who knew Dim Mak and had a reputation for using it in a fight. Many had heard stories about this man and they in turn passed them on to others.

Challenges between highly skilled masters were common throughout the long history of China. Often, this was due to the ever-present air of position, power, prestige and income connected with the more superior master's skills. Many schools changed hands and styles over and over again as the new kid on the block entered town, challenged the existing master and his school, and if he was extremely lucky and talented, could best the master and take his position in the town.

Kwan Shan was a master of such highly skilled technique and reputation. Yet, with all the advantages that accompanied this position and all the jockeying by so many to get the prize, he still held fast to his training and his simple beliefs. Status and prestige were not of the highest importance to him. He preferred a simpler and quieter life.

In the early morning hours, long before the city awoke, as the sun began to rise and push back the night, Kwan Shan was already out training. He could see the distant hills rise out of the mist from across the Pearl River like an ancient dragon awakening from a long, long sleep. The rolling and deeply forested hills with their emerald green color and the subtle layering of one ridge tucked delicately behind the other resembled the spine and body of this mythical creature. Gradually as the sun crept closer and closer to appearing over the horizon, more and more of the serpent came into view. Longer and longer the body grew and became more defined with the head still far off in the distance.

Slowly the local residents began to move about and begin their daily toil, with the ancient guardian slowly stirring in the background. All the activity beginning on the river with people and boats moving up and down from shore to shore appeared as though the daily tasks of caring for the dragon were being attended to, like worker bees caring for the queen. Cleaning the den, removing unnecessary debris, bringing in the daily food, checking and cleaning every scale on the entire body, and making sure every last detail had been attended to so that the dragon was comfortable.

As with everything in life, all things come at a price. No matter how sweet the nectar or how bitter the wine, nothing is free. Each has its balance, so too with the reputation of being respected throughout Guangzhou as the most famous and feared of the Ten Tigers. Being regarded as the number one of the Ten Tigers of Guangzhou carried with it numerous bags of luggage, each containing a whole set of conditions extremely difficult to fulfill.

As the day gradually began to expose itself to the quiet city, the silence on Do Buo Road was broken by the sporadic sounds of shop doors being opened, shutters tied back, wares being set out for shoppers to see, dogs barking and people coming out to sweep away the dirt from the previous evening. Each person one by one as they stepped out into the morning sun was expecting to be the first to look down the empty streets and then yell at everyone else as to why they were not up yet.

Unfortunately, the moment they glanced down toward the corner, they all saw Kwan Shan already set up and casually sitting on the side of the road. His small bag of herbs and medicine that he had been carrying for years was showing signs of age. The corners were torn and had been re-sewn many times. The fabric was once covered with a bright multi-colored design of lotus flowers in red, green, blue, and white. But now after seventy years it only showed the faded outline of a worn-out pattern.

As he sat quietly watching the mist fade into the shadows, a few of the store owners greeted him before making their way to their favorite teahouse for the morning social gathering.

Kwan Shan just sat motionless, smoking his long thin pipe that he bought ten years earlier, while waiting for a customer to come up and inquire about his medicine.

Later when everyone headed toward their shops to open up for the day, Kwan Shan still sat exactly where he had been when they strolled past earlier. Eventually, Kwan Shan stood up and began slowly practicing a few of his favorite Praying Mantis movements.

A nearby store owner approached him and asked, "Hey, Kwan Shan, what are you doing?"

"Well, I figured I would use some of the time when no one was around to practice some of my techniques," Kwan Shan said without turning around.

"Would you teach me some of your style? "the man asked.

"Sure, I would be glad to teach you a few basic techniques, but I must warn you, I don't teach lazy people."

"Oh, that's okay. I've had to work hard my whole life so I know what hard work is like." The man sat on the ground next to where Kwan Shan's herbs were displayed.

"When would you like to begin?" Kwan Shan asked as he continued to execute the animal-like movements with the precision of a seasoned fighter.

"How about tomorrow morning?"

"Fine, but I begin my practice every morning at four a.m.

"So be here at six," he said without turning around to see the reaction from his visitor.

"That's okay with me. I usually get up early anyway."

PUGILIST FROM SHANDONG

"Oh by the way, can I bring a friend who works for the circus?"

"Sure, as long as he is willing to work and not be late." He finished his routine and walked over by his bag to sit down.

The following morning the two men arrived on time and respectfully greeted their new master with bows.

"Master, this is my friend Kam Wing. He is the one I told you about yesterday." the man said.

Kwan Shan stopped his training long enough to turn, give the stranger a once-over glance, slightly nod his head and then return to his practice.

"Hurry up and loosen up your bodies so we can begin," he slowly made his way through a personal routine while focusing on the precision of each technique.

The two men set their belongings aside and began loosening up their muscles. After a few minutes of light muscle warming exercises, just as they were ready, Kwan Shan turned and said, "Okay, now we will begin."

"First I am your teacher, so you will address me as Master or Master Lee. Only those people who aren't my students are allowed to call me Kwan Shan or Lee Kwan Shan.

"Now I need to show you how to properly stand, punch, and kick. So I will show you my basic stances, punches, and kicks. Then we can move on to learning how to use them.

"When you punch, always punch through your target. Otherwise it is of no use. "Master Lee showed them how to punch.

"Also, you need to learn how to relax as long as possible when punching. Stronger and more powerful punching comes from relaxing as long as possible."

As they went through the various movements Master Lee ensured that they also remembered and associated each name to the specific stance, punch or kick. Occasionally, he would stop their practice long enough to explain the theories behind the use of each position.

"Your stances need to be rooted to the ground in order to be valuable." Master Lee showed them what a poorly executed stance looked like in contrast to a solid strong stance.

"Rooting begins in the mind and is enhanced by the visualizing of your feet buried in the ground and the feeling of your feet sinking into the earth."

Soon what seemed like only moments had turned into hours and Master Lee finally excused the two and told them to return the next morning for their next lesson. Respectfully, the two fixed their dirt and sweat soaked clothing in order to look more presentable, bowed to their new teacher and then slowly made their way back down the street toward the local teahouse.

Over the next several years the two trained daily with Master Lee in the basics to help develop their strength, flexibility and stamina. Following all the basic fundamental techniques that he learned from his father and teacher Abbot Ching Yeung, he then began instructing them in the various forms of prearranged movements. Each one was taught in a slightly different manner.

Master Lee would observe his students' body type, manner of movement, strengths and weaknesses, flexibility and then determine which series of movements would be best for them. Eventually, they would both be learning the same forms, just in a different order, so that he could slowly enhance their individual assets. Daily the routine would always remain the same; first they would begin with a simple standing meditation to help calm their minds. Then they would go through a series of warm-ups and flexibility exercises. Afterwards they would begin training in the traditional forms and weapons. Finally, it was time for the understanding of movement application and fighting theory. Master Lee considered this crucial to developing and understanding the traditional teachings.

Every day after the lesson was finished, Master Lee would return to his corner, set up his small display of herbs and medicine and then spend the remainder of the day selling his products. Day after day this routine never wavered and his dedicated students had progressed very rapidly and were now able to satisfactorily defend themselves. If they chose to, they could also begin teaching other students.

One afternoon as Master Lee sat talking with his new young friend Shek Kin while patiently waiting for a customer, a young woman stopped by.

"Master Lee, my name is Zhang Mei. Could you help me?" the young woman asked.

"What is the problem?"

"Well, I have been searching everywhere for someone who can help my mother's leg and I was told to come see you."

"What is wrong with it?"

"She injured it months ago and nobody has been able to heal her," she said pointing at the spot on her own body where her mother's injury was located.

"I have a special herbal patch that I developed for my training and if you use it faithfully, it should heal her injury," he said showing the woman the medicine.

"Okay, I will buy some," she reached into her pocket for the money.

Master Lee sold her the mixture and gave her specific instructions as to how to apply it.

"Now after you use this for a week, come back and let me know how she is doing."

After a week she came rushing back and could not stop thanking Master for what he had done for her mother.

"Oh thank you, Master Lee, thank you," she said politely bowing.

"My mother said her leg is finally feeling much better and she can even walk several steps."

"That is good to hear. I think if you use this patch for one more week then the pain should all be gone."

"Oh, that will be such good news for her to hear," she placed the new patches in her pocket. "I will let you know how she is doing."

For the next two weeks Master Lee did not hear from the woman, then one afternoon he saw her walking toward him on the street.

"Master Lee, this is my mother Su Wei. I am sorry for not keeping you informed about her.

"After we used the second patch her leg improved dramatically. Then she decided to regain her strength so she could come and thank you personally."

"Thank you so much, Master Lee, I do not know what I would have done without your help," the elderly lady said while humbly bowing.

"I am glad I was able to help," he said while bowing to her in return.

~~~~~

Following that day, Zhang Mei would stop by and greet Master Lee every morning, then thank him once again for his help.

She began to spend more and more time talking to Master Lee and his students and eventually asked to become his student.

PUGILIST FROM SHANDONG

"Master Lee, I have known you for several years and I am impressed with your Kung Fu. Would you consider allowing me to become your student?"

"Well, you have seen how I train my students, so you know I do not allow anyone to be my student unless they are serious about their training," he replied while cleaning the charred remains from his pipe.

"Yes I know."

"If you are serious, then I will accept you," he looked his newest student in the eyes.

"Thank you Master, thank you," she bowed respectfully.

"Tomorrow when you come to class at six a.m., be ready to train and do not arrive late."

"I will be there early. I like to always arrive early for everything."

"Good, I will see you then."

The following day when Master Lee arrived at his training area, he saw Zhang Mei sitting under a tree waiting.

"Good morning, Master Lee," she said after standing up and politely bowing.

"Good morning."

"When my senior students arrive, I will have one of them teach you all of our basics," Master Lee said as he began loosening up his shoulder joints.

"Okay, I will stretch and begin warming up while I wait."

~~~~~

Gradually over the next few years as she continued training, she grew even closer and closer to her teacher until finally one day Master Lee decided he would like to marry the young woman.

"Zhang Mei, I have spent my life alone while traveling from Shandong to Vietnam and here, and now I am ready for a change," Master Lee said after all his students had returned to their homes.

"Over the past couple of years I have slowly become more and more aware of my affections for you," he looked into her eyes.

"I have noticed by your occasional actions, that you have some feelings for me also."

"Yes, Master Lee, my feelings for you have grown considerably," she replied trembling.

He took her hand in his, "Would you consider becoming my wife?"

"Yes! I would be honored to be your wife," her eyes swelled with tears.

"Very well, we should check the calendar to find an auspicious date so it will bring us the most luck," Master Lee held her hand and softly patted her back.

"I agree. A couple should always start their life together on a day blessed with good fortune." She bowed to her future husband.

Several days later after searching the Chinese book for auspicious days, they decided on the day and began to make preparations for the wedding. Since this was a private affair, the only guests were those required by the local government to officiate.

Over the next several years their life together began to slowly ease Master Lee's desire to wander. Now he seemed content to sit on his usual corner during the day and sell his herbs. In the late afternoon he would teach his dedicated students and afterward retreat to his home and wife.

PUGILIST FROM SHANDONG

"Master Lee, will you be home about the usual time tonight?" his wife asked as he opened the door to leave.

"Yes," he replied just before the door closed.

"Hmm, I wonder what that was about," he thought while heading to his corner.

The day turned out to be unusually cool for this time of year. So more customers stopped by to chat and buy his special herbal mixture. Eventually, his routine was finished and he walked back to his house.

"Ah, Master Lee, you are home," she said as he opened the door and stepped inside.

"Yeeess," he cautiously replied while observing the unusual state of cleanliness and decorating.

"Hmm, it looks like you have been busy."

"Oh I just wanted to make everything nice and clean for you," she said while arranging the evening meal.

"And may I ask what the special occasion is that would require this elaborate meal?'

"Please, please eat while it is still hot," she said pushing the bowl closer.

For the next few minutes neither of them said a word, but only focused on the meal.

"Okay, we are now finished with this special meal." He placed the bowl and chopsticks back in the center of the table. "So what was the purpose of all this special attention to cleaning, decorating, and preparing of a meal we only make for the New Year?"

"Wellll…" she began slowly, "I wanted everything to be just right and bring us the good luck."

"Good luck for what? Today isn't any special day on the calendar." He cleaned out the ashes from his pipe.

"I went to my acupuncturist yesterday to find out why I am not feeling well, and we started talking about my mother and how she was feeling and then we talked about the weather and—"

"Okay stop! You are beginning to ramble and not make sense. Breathe, relax and tell me what is going on," he filled his pipe and leaned back in his chair.

"I am pregnant," she softly said and turned to look at him.

Thud! The pipe echoed through the room as it hit the floor and spilled the fresh tobacco.

Seconds seemed like forever. Eventually, when reality shifted back, he turned to her. "Really?"

"Yes," she said in a relieved tone.

"So we will need to make a special area in our bedroom for when the child is born," he said as he looked around the small dwelling.

"Yes we should," she replied and stood up to clear the dishes from the table.

Time passed quickly and suddenly the day arrived for Meiniu, the newest member of their small family, to begin her lifelong journey.

Each day seemed to bring her a continual stream of achievements and growth while her parents struggled to maintain a suitable home. Soon, what seemed like just yesterday had turned into years. Now the little baby was walking, talking, and following her father down to the corner.

I think I should go to Kowloon and see my friends before they pass on, he thought one day as he was packing his belongings prior to heading home. *It has been quite some time since I saw them.*

PUGILIST FROM SHANDONG

"Ah there they are!" his wife exclaimed as he and his daughter opened the door and stepped in.

"Yes, back from another day," he replied as Meiniu ran to see her mother.

"Please sit and I will make you something to eat," she said ,hugging the little girl.

As Master Lee sat at the table, he never said a word about the day. Usually he idly chatted about the customers and a few of the store owners. Throughout the meal he remained quiet as his mind focused on the trip ahead.

"I am planning a trip to Kowloon next week to see some of my old friends," he calmly said as his wife finished cleaning the pots and pans.

"Oh really?" she asked.

"Yes, some of them I have not seen for many years and I want to see them before they die," he explained.

"Do you think it is wise to take a little girl on such a long journey?" she asked while holding her daughter in her lap.

"No, I do not think she should travel that far."

"How long will you be gone?" she asked in a saddened tone, knowing it would be months before he would return.

"I am not quite sure, "Master Lee replied as he cleaned his pipe.

"Do you have everything you will need while you are gone?" she asked as Master Lee packed his belongings.

"Yes, this should be everything," he replied once he had secured the bag with a sturdy rope.

"Come here, little one, your daddy is leaving so give him a hug."

She looked as if she were trying not to cry. "Will we see you again?" she blurted out just before he stepped through the door.

Master Lee stopped, paused slightly then turned around and looked her in the eyes. "Yes," he said while reaching out to pat the top of his daughter's head.

Slowly he turned back toward the door, adjusted the pack on his shoulder, stepped out into the morning sun and then reached back to quietly shut the door.

Chapter 17

~ The Fighting Imposition ~

It had been months since Master Lee left Guangzhou, and the image of his wife and daughter still filled his mind. In every city or village he stopped in to sell his herbs and demonstrate his talents, he saw her young face in the children on the streets.

Now he was nearing Kowloon and the prospect of seeing his friends began to creep into his mind and ease the images of his family.

One day months after arriving in Kowloon, Master Lee was sitting on the roadside selling his herbs as the sun ascended the deep blue sky, and the heat rose to try and keep pace. People visiting the shops tried to avoid the glaring rays by hiding under umbrellas. As they walked from street to street, their grip continued to move further and further down the handle as the sun continued to heat up the curved surface.

Master Lee didn't have such a luxury so he was forced to deal with the heat in his own manner. As he sat on the side of the busy street, he continued to focus more and more on the herbs and medicines he was selling, trying to block out the impact from the sun's attack. When that didn't work he put his attention on the extensive array of techniques and forms he had acquired over the years, the long list of forms from his father and family members, from the abbot at the temple, and all the other acquaintances who had been willing to share their knowledge and style with him: other Praying Mantis masters along with masters from a number of other famous and obscure styles, Wong Fei Hung, Luo Kwong Yu, and Sun Yuan Chang to name but a few. Eventually, even he had to seek refuge from the sun underneath the small overhang of a nearby storefront.

As he was deep in thought over a specific form and the application of its techniques, he overheard a group of men yelling at a man as they followed him down Temple Street and out into an open intersection where the traffic was unusually slow.

The moment the man stepped into the intersection, the group surrounded him. One, a tall skinny man in shorts and a dirty gray shirt stepped forward and began screaming in his face. As soon as he finished yelling, another would step forward and continue where the last had left off. Over and over this continued; all the while Master Lee sat near the curb no more than a few feet away, listening and watching the entire ordeal.

The young man standing directly behind the encircled man lunged forward in an attempt to attack him from behind. As he did the man in the middle abruptly turned and stepped slightly to his side, avoiding the foot nearing his back. The moment his stepping foot made contact with the road his other leg sprang into the air like a rocket, catching his assailant in the groin and sending him rolling backwards writhing in pain.

Another member of the outer circle stepped in to try his moves against this lone defendant, and as his techniques drew near their intended target, the stranger casually neutralized each one and returned his own array of punches and kicks, each one making contact exactly where he had intended and dealing the second assailant the same outcome as the first.

One by one the circle of attackers began to dwindle as each attempted to best this loner until it was down to the last member standing confidently by himself. He attacked; it was obvious why he had waited until the end because he was by far the best of the entire group. Each technique appeared as effortless as brushing a fly from your sleeve, each kick a picture of perfection and faster than the blink of an eye.

Still, with all the expertise this assailant possessed, he was not able to make contact with the other man. As each move drew near its target, the man would slip to one side or the other and return a blow that set the attacker on his backside. Over and over he kept getting back up to try again. Eventually, the lone man attacked showing this inferior opponent talent and technique that he had never seen before, and finished the confrontation.

While he stood there taking in all that had just happened, breathing heavily from the energy expended during the onslaught of attacks, he saw an old man sitting near the curb just a few feet away. Sweat was pouring down his face and into his eyes, spots of blood were scattered on the pavement and his clothes. The skinny old man was laughing at him and his performance. He straightened his clothes as best he could and walked over to the spectator who seemed thoroughly amused by the fight and demanded an answer. "Hey, old man, why are you laughing at me?" he stared down at the small figure squatting near the curb.

"Who me?" Master Lee replied as though he didn't know who the man was referring to. "Why, I was just sitting here trying to figure out how you could beat up ten men with techniques as lousy as yours!" his smile gradually grew wider and wider.

"What do you mean? My name is Leung Kun, and I have trained with the best masters in all of Hong Kong for the past five years and they all say my technique is excellent."

"Well it appears as though you have been learning from the wrong teacher," Master Lee said coldly.

Leung Kun drew his head back in total amazement, not believing what he had just been told. It just didn't seem possible that anyone could be so bold as to say his teachers were not very good. These men were the best in the entire city, everyone knew them and regarded them as the best, and if you trained under their tutelage you would also be held in high regard. Now, here was this skinny little old man sitting on the side of the road spouting off about how poor their teaching had been.

For a moment the two didn't say a word but continued to stare intently at each other.

Master Lee could see the shock on the young man's face. He knew the boy was wondering how a skinny old man could be so bold. If he attacked and the brazen old man was truly that good, he would be in for a world of hurt. If he were nothing more than a babbling derelict, then everyone would criticize him for the unnecessary beating.

Master Lee just looked back at this young and arrogant kid; he had seen many like him before, all full of themselves and their supposed abilities. Each one finding out the hard way that life is long and the line of opponents is never ending. And while you may get the upper hand on a few people, there will always be those few who can put you back in your place, and you can't be fooled by their outward appearance or age.

Then without warning Leung Kun said "Aw forget it!" turned around and walked away. Moments later he turned the corner and disappeared.

PUGILIST FROM SHANDONG

Master Lee reached into his pocket, pulled out his pipe and proceeded to light the small charred substance stuck in the bottom.

For the next eight months the two never saw each other.

~~~~~

Life in China for Leung Kun as a restaurant owner over the years afforded him many benefits. The opportunity to cater to the public allowed the chance to fraternize with the local officials and upper class (as long as he was regarded as acceptable, and his cooking skills were good enough to warrant attention.) With this arrived a position in the social status slightly elevated from the common worker. He was able to approach and even converse with local officials and the upper class as long as he remembered his place and deferred to them at all times, especially in moments of condescendence. The ability to have his opinion heard and be afforded some weight (minimal as it might be) allowed his family certain compensations from the local community: finer clothes, servants, and a family residence with a class sufficient to demonstrate to his peers his social standing.

Social gatherings where political policies and communal laws were debated and enforced through subtle inferences implied during conversations with aides to the local magistrate, were at times available to certain owners with the proper social standing. Still, the ancient custom of deference and condescendence was ever present and must be adhered to at all times, for fear of retribution upon one's person, business and especially his family name.

Owning a restaurant afforded the opportunity to keep current on local gossip and the social standings of his competition, along with recent events throughout the province and country. As travelers scurried about their business oblivious to the local events of the day, they inevitably transported distant events, customs and beliefs from place to place, infusing a subtle yet gradual shift in the social, political and religious consciousness of each and every community. Travelers told of their exploits on their journeys. These exploits were usually enhanced and dramatized to make the traveler was appear to be someone of a higher social status to afford them the opportunity to travel so extensively and have such eventful experiences.

Generally, one of the initial points of interest for any traveler was to frequent the local restaurant and become acclimated to the local events and customs. Here were the proving grounds for countless ideas, customs, religious beliefs, political theories and social prejudices. Wars were waged and won against numerous enemies both foreign and domestic within these sparsely decorated walls, while local criminals were dealt their proper punishment by those of a higher social status contrary to current laws, along with the enemies of those in the restaurant.

Owning a restaurant like all other professions had its balance for all the benefits. Days upon days of long grueling hours of unending work in a hot, steamy, cramped and very noisy kitchen, while patron after patron arrived daily all with specific demands and the expectation that their needs should be the number one priority. And if the restaurant was slow to comply, they immediately took it as a sign of disrespect and lack of concern for their social status and immediate needs.

Daily, people from all walks of life arrived to test the wares and fill their bellies, all the while keeping in mind the thought that if today's dishes weren't as tantalizing as the previous day's, they would take their business elsewhere.

Each morning the doors would open to the world with a sense of newness and hope. Every evening the store was closed with its workers feeling tired, dirty and glad to see the end of the day's commotion. In the morning, it started all over again, with buying supplies, stocking shelves, resetting the tables with clean linen and shiny dishes. Sweeping all the floors to cleanse the room and appease the kitchen gods, all this and more long before the kitchen fires heated the heart of the business to an unbearable level followed by the endless noise of pans being heated, food being prepared and cooks bellowing out demand after demand to the helpers and waiters.

Leung Kun's father had worked in the restaurant business since childhood. His father acquired the family restaurant from his father, who acquired it from his father and so on. Leung Kun was expected to continue the tradition.

With springtime, the weather was beginning to change. The long dry season slowly vanished into the far off mountains, and now the rains began to settle in for the season.

Slowly as the sun sank further into the horizon, the darkness of night closed its grip with the aid of the thick air from the day. Soon even the bravest of animals began retreating to the cool recesses in hopes of escape. Unfortunately, none was to be found.

A typhoon had delivered unusual weather the past ten days. During the days the temperature rose into the nineties before ten a.m., followed by a downpour late in the afternoon. And even though the sun had set, the nighttime did nothing to rescue the villagers from the day's intense attacks. It seemed as though someone had turned off the breeze, even though it did nothing but move the thick stifling daytime air. Now, the night had become the day's flanking ally bringing the next wave of attacks to crush the few remaining survivors from the day.

One morning Leung Kun rose unusually early for a Wednesday and went outside to the well for some cold water to splash on his face and neck. As he was retrieving the small wooden bucket from the dark cavern, he noticed a young deer off in the shadows.

Leung Kun grabbed the bucket and settled it on the small brick wall surrounding the well. As he dipped his hands into the cool clear refreshment, the memory of the humid night air's relentless grip slowly drifted away. Now all he felt was inner peace. All was quiet; the world was at rest.

The moon showed but a glimpse of itself from behind the thick white pillars supporting the heavens. Faint sounds of nocturnal creatures scurrying about their daily duties echoed through the trees. Nearby, a fox was making an unusually early surveillance of his territory more in search of a cool burrow to rest in than an early morning meal.

Moments began to merge and time appeared to stand still as Leung Kun's thoughts drifted slowly into the darkness of night. The deer startled Leung Kun as it began making its way closer to the water. Out of the corner of his eye, Leung Kun noticed that his nervous visitor was within only a few feet. Gradually, over the course of several minutes, the deer inched its way closer and closer. Again time seemed to stop as the deer held its position and waited for any slight indication of danger. Sensing no animosity, the deer relaxed its back and shook its head as if to release any tension from the situation.

Without making any sudden movements, Leung Kun slowly eased the bucket down the wall until it came to rest on the ground next to his feet. The moment it touched the ground the deer's ears swung forward having caught the sound of the heavy bucket slowly pressing the dead leaves closer to the earth.

Moments appeared to stop as the two stood within arm's reach and looked into each other's eyes. Leung Kun gazed into the deep dark peacefulness of the spirit of a harmless creature. The deer was looking at a common foe and waiting for a sense of danger or peace from Leung Kun's eyes.

Cautiously, the deer took another small step forward and paused, all the while prepared to escape at the first sign of trouble. Now they were so close they could feel and smell each other's breath. Once more the deer twitched its ears forward to survey the area for danger, but none came. When the deer realized that Leung Kun was not a threat, it leaned its head forward and accepted a small drink from the bucket. First it drank very slowly in order to keep watch over Leung Kun and the situation. Once it felt safe, the sips turned into large gulps until the cool refreshing liquid was gone.

Upon finishing, the deer slowly raised its head from the container and began walking back into the night. Just before the darkness engulfed the visitor, the deer turned its head as if to say thank you, then quickly bounced off into the night.

If all life were that simple, he thought as the darkness closed back in around him. He reached down to pick up the bucket and place it back on the wall, take one last look in the direction of the deer and then begin to make his way back to the house.

"Leung Kim, come on, we need to get busy and finish all the preparations for your father's birthday!" his mother said the moment she saw him turn the corner near their house. He ran the final distance and in no time was entering the front door.

"Where have you been?" she inquired as soon as he stepped in the door.

"I went out to get a drink from the well because it was so hot and I couldn't sleep." He sat down to tie his shoe.

"Well you sure were gone a long time for just a drink of water."

"Really? I thought it was only a couple of minutes."

"No, you were gone for almost an hour!" she stacked platters on top of each other and handed them to him. "Now, take these platters down to the restaurant and be careful; the bottom ones are very delicate, so don't drop any."

All day long the preparations continued until every table was covered with exquisite dishes stacked nine high. On the bottom was a very large bowl of perfectly carved and auspiciously arranged vegetables. Second, were perfectly arranged shrimp around the edge of a slightly smaller bowl and pointing towards the center at the sweet sauce. Third, roast pork filled a bowl to overflowing and was carefully placed in the center of the shrimp. Next, boneless chicken covered in sweet sauce laid waiting for its praise of elegant appearance. Atop the chicken was a large fat goose cooked to perfection and cut into finger-size portions. The sixth bowl of boneless fish seemed to float effortlessly over the lower bowls. Thinly sliced strips of beef cooked to a chocolate brown and tender enough to melt on your tongue were centered above the fish. The final two dishes were even more elegant and ornate than all the others combined. Roast duck filled the eighth bowl to its rim and the room with a soft smell of herbs. Finally, the entire array was topped with a whole fish subtly inviting all to come and sample its splendor.

Promptly at six o'clock the guests began arriving and within minutes the room was filled to capacity. They strolled through the restaurant, admiring the elaborate display adorning each table. Master Lee entered the room and went directly toward Leung Kun's father's table to extend his congratulations and pay his respects before taking his seat at an adjoining table.

Leung Kim's father was a very wealthy man in the community, so as the evening progressed, many of the local business owners and village residents stopped in to pay their respects and extend congratulations to the guest of honor. Afterward, since Master Lee was also well known as a great Kung Fu master, they each dutifully moved to his table and again paid their respects.

Leung Kun was finally able to find a moment and slip out of the kitchen long enough to make an appearance in the dining area. After greeting the guests closest to the kitchen, he began to make his way towards his father's table.

As soon as he turned the corner and entered the main seating area, he saw an old acquaintance seated at the table directly next to his father. There sat the old man who some months earlier had ridiculed him regarding his Kung Fu training. Obviously, the old man didn't notice Leung Kun's entrance or if he did, he made no attempt to show he knew who it was.

PUGILIST FROM SHANDONG

As he approached his father, and paid his respects, Leung Kun couldn't help but keep an eye on the old man. *How dare he come into our restaurant on such a special occasion*, he thought.

"Hey, Father, who is that man sitting over there at the next table?" Leung Kun whispered in his father's ear.

"Oh, that is my good friend Master Lee Kwan Shan. He is a very famous Kung Fu master all over the province."

"Oh," Leung Kun replied, not knowing what else to say. *He must be a really good friend to my father. I think I'll go ask him if he remembers me.*

Cautiously he made his way around the tables, exchanging greetings with all the guests and making sure he could see the old man the entire time. He didn't seem the least bit concerned. Either he didn't remember or didn't care, because he hadn't shown the slightest sign of concern.

One by one the people at the table got up and mingled with the remaining guests. Soon no one was left at the table but the man who had insulted him. Leung Kun now stood directly across the table from the old man and as he looked him in the eye he shouted, "Hey, old man, do you remember a couple months ago when we were down on Temple Street and I was fighting with that group of people and beat up five of them?"

The old man didn't give the slightest indication that he knew what this young man was talking about.

"Hey, Master Lee, do you remember when you told me that my Kung Fu was lousy and that I learned from the wrong teacher? Now I ask, what was wrong with my techniques that day on Temple Street?"

Again he got no response. After a long pause the old man responded with a puzzled look on his face, "I don't know what you are talking about. I never said anything like that."

Leung Kun didn't believe a single word he said, since he knew this was the man who had insulted him on the street. Again he pressed the old man for an answer.

"Master, do you remember back when you were selling medicine on the side of the street and I was fighting with those other guys. Then after I beat them, you said, 'Hey young guy, where did you learn to fight like that?'"

Still Leung Kun got no response.

As Leung Kun was standing there, he could see Master Lee was thinking about what this young guy was saying and the possibility that there was some truth to it. As he gazed around the room and stroked his long white beard, Leung Kun could see he suddenly remembered as his eyes opened wide and the memory quickly rose out of the shadows of his mind.

"Oh yes, now I remember!" he coyly replied.

Leung Kun could see Master Lee begin to steadily glow more and more as he thought about that memorable day.

Leung Kun said, "Well I came over here to see you and get an answer, so tell me."

As Leung Kun's temper continued to rise, Master Lee sat at the table and stroked his long beard while observing the other guests in the room.

Just about that time, Leung Kun's mother appeared from the adjoining room, as she did Leung Kun watched as Master Lee realized that she was his mother. In a flash the coy expression disappeared from Master Lee's face and was replaced by one of surprise. Master Lee then turned and looked back at Leung Kun and said,

"Oh is this your father?"

"Yes, he is my father!" Leung Kun snapped.

PUGILIST FROM SHANDONG

"Oh, I am very sorry. I did not know. Tell you what; if you would be so kind after the banquet we can go someplace quiet and I will be happy to show you the problem with your techniques, "Master Lee said. "Please, please sit down and have some tea and we can talk while we wait for the other guests to leave."

With his temper still boiling over the previous comments, Leung Kim continued to stare at Master Lee. Soon his emotions calmed down and he then remembered the celebration in progress. Reluctantly, he sat at the table and tried to exchange small talk while waiting for the others to leave.

After about an hour most of the guests had left, and Master Lee said, "Okay, if you would still like to go we can now go and attend to our business."

By now Leung Kun had cooled off and was beginning to anticipate the coming so-called "lesson" so he replied in a polite manner, "Sure, sure I would be most happy to go with you and learn how to improve my Kung Fu."

Master Lee stood and silently made his way toward the door with Leung Kun the respectful junior following behind, partly out of respect and also so that he could check out his movements as they meandered through the crowd.

Once outside he turned to Leung Kun, pointed towards a dark street and said, "Let's go this way, I know of a small area where we won't be disturbed."

Leung Kun didn't say a word, just nodded in agreement and gestured for Master Lee to lead the way. The two walked for about ten minutes, turning down this street, winding through dark alleys until they finally arrived at a small side alley with a single kerosene lamp hanging from a post about halfway to the next turn.

"Okay, this is the place," Master Lee said as he walked over to the nearest door and removed his jacket.

Leung Kun stood in the intersection, looking in all directions for any sign of trouble. Confident it was safe, he walked part way down the alley, turned toward Master Lee and asked, "So what are these great improvements I need to make to my Kung Fu?"

Master Lee removed his shoes from his feet, picked up some white chalk he found near his jacket and rubbed over the entire end of each shoe. Afterward, he took each of his shoes, placed them on each of his hands to form mittens, and tied them with a small string braided from strands of grass. When he finished he stood up and looked at Leung Kun standing under the light with his hands on his hips waiting for an answer.

"Okay now, this is what I want you to do, "he began as he started walking towards his pupil. "You can attack me with whatever technique you want and as you do I will only attack you in return.

"That's right, every time you attack me, I will only attack and not defend at all." Master Lee concluded.

"Okay." Leung Kun shrugged and prepared for the lesson

Once he finished preparing himself, Leung Kun turned toward Master Lee only to find him standing in the exact spot and position as before. He hadn't moved, nor had he put his shoes back on his feet. He just stood there, short, skinny, barefoot and wearing only a pair of pants and his shoes on his hands.

As Leung Kun approached his opponent, he remained cautious of the situation and thought he should take his time and be careful, because if the man was so willing to fight at such an old age, he must be pretty good. Step by step he moved closer while continuing to watch Lee's position for any sudden surprises.

Master Lee never moved from his original spot and continued to act as though he wasn't the least bit concerned.

PUGILIST FROM SHANDONG

Once he was close enough, Leung Kun sprang into action without the slightest indication or warning. His first strategy was to jump directly at Master Lee and try to kick him twice in the stomach and punch him in the temple simultaneously. As he began the first kick towards the lower stomach he, noticed that his opponent never moved but only stood there as if waiting for the foot to make contact.

Then out of nowhere Master Lee twisted sideways and punched Leung Kun's leg just above the ankle barely hard enough to redirect the foot. As the second kick started to draw near his chest, Master Lee turned to the other side and hit the foot directly in the center of the arch.

Leung Kun finished the assault with a hook punch to each temple.

Lee simply stepped to the center and simultaneously tapped Leung Kun on each elbow joint.

With each of the initial attacks, Lee never exerted much force. He had evaded each movement of the attack with just enough power to leave a chalk mark on Leung Kun's body.

Following the first wave of attacks the moment Leung Kun landed, he immediately tried to sweep Lee's feet out from under him.

Again Master Lee waited and then simply lifted his leg just enough to let his opponent's leg pass underneath. The moment it did, Lee stepped behind it and attacked the knee joint from the back.

Leung felt the attack to his knee, changed strategy and spun around to attack Master Lee's groin. Just as he was about to hit Lee, the old man shifted back just enough for Leung to be only able to touch his pants and then stopped any forward progress by hitting Leung in the shoulder joint.

Huh, he's not that good. Each of my techniques just barely missed hitting him. It's a good thing I wasn't trying to hurt the old man, otherwise he would be lying on the ground crying for help, Leung thought as he stood up and gathered himself for the next attempt.

"I've seen better attempts made by little children. Are you going to attack or just throw your hands around like a little girl?" Master Lee asked as he applied more chalk to the shoes.

"Very well, if you want me to hit you I will, but it won't be my fault if you get seriously injured," Leung replied.

Without warning, Leung rushed forward to try and catch Master Lee while he was sitting on the ground. Just as he was about to grab him around the neck from behind, Master Lee reached up, slapped his hand away and punched him under the chin.

"I'm not ready yet." Master Lee said.

Leung stumbled backward more from the surprise of being hit than from the actual attack. *How could he know I was going to do that? I didn't make any noise at all. I guess if he wants to play that game from now on I won't hold anything back, I'll hit him as hard as I can and won't care how he likes it.*

Leung readied himself by sitting in a deep stance and staring intently at his opponent. Slowly he took one step forward but this time it wasn't going to be directly at him. His first step was a half circle outward to the right then the next was a half circle to the left. This continued with each successive step until he made his way around to the side of Master Lee.

At that moment Master Lee turned and looked down at his foot giving Leung the impression that he wasn't paying attention. Suddenly Leung moved in for another attack. This time was going to be different because now his opponent was unaware of his advance. As he moved within range he struck out with his left hand toward Master Lee's temple.

Just as the fist was about to make contact, Master Lee's head seemed to disappear and the sleeve of Leung's shirt grazed his hair. Master Lee's head reappeared on the back side of the punching arm, followed by a single finger strike to Leung's fifth rib.

Leung countered with a right palm strike to Lee's stomach. This was met with a Crane's Beak Strike to Leung's throat. As Leung leaned back from the throat strike he tried to kick dirt in Lee's face, but was stopped by a punch to the inside of his leg.

I can't believe this old man, he thought to himself. Every time I attack it appears as though I'm going to hit him and then he disappears. Nobody has ever been able to stop my punches before.

Over and over Leung attacked Master Lee always with the same result. He would attack and Lee would always stop him. The two moved in and out of the shadows, from one side of the street to the other. At times their movements were like a fluid and rhythmic dance; other times there were long moments of hesitation followed by sudden explosions of techniques.

After about forty-five minutes Leung Kun realized he had totally underestimated this old man. His thoughts of using his superior speed and strength to conquer this frail-looking opponent and validate his teachers' expertise were soon abandoned. Gradually, frustration began to overwhelm his thinking like a thick cloud of smoke billowing from the dense dry underbrush, and filling the entire forest, while chasing out all who had previously inhabited the area.

"I have been polite and never tried to really hurt you and you have avoided all my techniques, but now I will show you my real power!" Leung Kun said as he started back toward Master Lee. This time he tried to bombard him with a series of kicks to different parts of the body, using all the strength he could gather.

First, he focused on the knees, faking to the left and striking the right. This was followed by kicks to the stomach, from the side then from downward and finally upward angles. To most opponents any one of these attacks would have been sufficient, but this was no ordinary challenger. Master Lee was a quiet force to be reckoned with.

As usual, the entire flurry of techniques that Leung combined and threw at Lee were all met and neutralized. Then suddenly, just as abruptly as it began, it was over.

Leung stood crouched next to a post on the side of the street gasping for air. He never looked up to see how his opponent was feeling. All he could do was focus on trying to get more air into his tired lungs. His clothes were soaked with sweat and dust and seemed to weigh on his tired muscles. Slowly after an eternity of gasping, he turned to make sure his opponent was still alive. Since he was stronger and much younger, Leung figured Master Lee would have to be near death from the match. As his eyes caught a glimpse of his opponent, they suddenly flew open in surprise.

"I don't believe it, you're not even tired!" he blurted out in total amazement between gasps.

"As I told you before this all started, you learned from the wrong master and your technique is still lousy!" Master Lee roared in a very condescending tone.

"Now, once you can stand up, carry yourself over to that mirror in the window on the end of the street and observe my 'old man' techniques."

Clumsily Leung grabbed the post and finally stood upright, wiped some of the sweat from his forehead and began stumbling toward a small mirror in a store window reflecting the previous moments of humiliation. The moment he stepped in front of the mirror and saw his reflection his eyes drew open even wider. There before him stood the image of a man beaten and tired with small white spots all over his clothes. Upon closer examination, he realized just how badly this old man had beaten him. Each spot was directly over one of the "Death

PUGILIST FROM SHANDONG

Points" he had heard about. He realized that if Master Lee had hit him with more power, he would be dead right now.

"I don't believe it!" he exclaimed as he stood within inches of the glass checking every inch of his body.

"Now do you believe me when I tell you that you learned from the wrong master?" Master Lee finished putting his shoes back on his feet.

"Master Lee, your technique is so fantastic. You hit me over and over with your Dim Mak but I never felt anything. Now I can see just how great you really are!" Leung made his way back down the street towards his opponent.

As soon as he was close to Master Lee, he dropped to his knees and reverently said, "Master Lee, I have trained for many years and always thought my techniques were unbeatable. Now I see that I am but a mere beginner and if you will accept me I would like to be your disciple."

"Come along, boy, let's go have some tea and discuss your future." Master Lee stood up and then reached down to give his bruised pupil a helping hand to his feet. Slowly they began to walk back toward the restaurant

Leung Kun turned to Master Lee and said, "Master Lee, if you would like, I will run ahead and have some tea and food prepared for you."

"Very well." Master Lee glanced at all the small white spots covering his young adversary's clothes.

Leung Kun ran toward the restaurant in hopes that someone was still working in the kitchen. Luckily the head cook was still cleaning up when he arrived, so he ordered him to begin heating water for tea and rice. As he did Leung Kun started preparing other vegetable dishes to serve with the rice. Within minutes, Master Lee arrived to find a single table set up with several dishes of food and a large pot of tea waiting for him.

THOMAS HAASE

Chapter 18

~ Felling of a Giant ~

Over the years of traveling throughout Guangzhou, Shacheng and Kowloon, Master Lee had made numerous friends, acquaintances and mutually respected colleagues. Those who knew him well knew his high quality morals, ethics and principles regarding life and the martial arts. He always viewed his practice as a necessity for longevity, self-preservation and tradition. All those who knew him respected his Praying Mantis and Tam Tui techniques, especially practitioners such as Luo Kwong Yu; another traditional Praying Mantis master. Both had acquired their styles in the northern province of Shandong and eventually migrated south for their own respective reasons.

Living in Kowloon and knowing a northern style of Kung Fu was a rarity. Trying to live a simple life with the reputations of two feared and widely known masters such as them would prove to be even harder to achieve.

Many times Master Lee and Luo KwongYu would be required to demonstrate their prowess while defending their livelihood and their lives; each time someone was needed to officiate the challenge and verify the rules were followed and without compromise.

One by one the challengers came to test their skills in hopes of enhancing their reputations by defeating the expert masters. One by one they all went home with less than they arrived with; the ego is a heavy load to carry and maintain against someone of Master Lee's and Luo's abilities and because you come from afar it only means an even longer journey home.

~~~~~

The morning began as many others had during the previous months for Master Lee: arrive at work by seven a.m., work until noon before a short break, then after a thirty-minute lunch, head back to work until five or six p.m. The work was grueling for a sixty-five-year-old man with continual lifting and moving of extremely heavy boxes of cargo nonstop until the short break, while the summer sun continued to bear down on the wharf and steadily raise the temperature and humidity.

Inside the warehouse the shade provided by the building did little more than increase the sensation of pressure inside the open space and make everyone feel as though the room was closing in around them. The air was almost thick enough to cut, with no sign of a breeze whatsoever. The smell of sweat mixed with the odor of decaying fish made everything just that much more intolerable.

Just after the noon break as everyone was heading back to work, a young man came running inside. He asked the foreman a question, and the foreman turned and pointed toward the back where Master Lee was working. The young man ran to the back and called, "Master Lee! Master Lee!"

"What do you want?" Master Lee said as the man drew closer.

PUGILIST FROM SHANDONG

"I have been sent by Master Luo KwongYu to fetch you and bring you back to the school."

"Why, can't you see I am trying to make some money here?" Master Lee turned back to his work.

"My master said he needs you to come and be the judge for a challenge from some big Russian fighter." The man said with a tone of desperation in his voice.

After a few moments, Master Lee asked, "When will he need me to be there?"

"Later this afternoon around six."

"Tell my nephew I will be there." Master Lee turned back to his job and tried to make up for lost time.

Hours later, after he had left his job, Master Lee went immediately to his friend's school. When he arrived he walked through the large front door and into a small open courtyard where some of the younger students were busily reviewing their most recent techniques.

"Hey, kids, where is your master?" he asked as they bowed to him upon his arrival.

"He is inside the main school working," The oldest student replied. "He told us to show you to his office as soon as you arrived."

As they walked under the overhang surrounding the courtyard and headed toward the main training area, the sun was beginning to set over the distant rooftops.

Master Lee could hear the senior students inside as they moved through their individual forms and weapon sets. The moment they walked through the door the young student leading the way yelled to everyone inside to come to attention and pay their respects to Master Lee. As they all bowed, Master Lee glanced around the room and saw Luo KwongYu sitting at his desk, totally oblivious to what was happening around him.

"Hey, Luo." Master Lee said after he entered the front door, bowed to the students and made his way over to the small antique desk with ornately carved dragon's claw feet and a large phoenix flying across the front side, sitting in the corner.

"Ah, Uncle Lee." Luo stood up to extend a formal bow to his honored guest.

"What is this I hear about another challenge?" Master Lee said as he reached for a chair nearby and pulled it nearer the desk so the two could talk more privately.

"Yes, I just received this letter this morning and I immediately sent my student to see you and tell you of the news," Luo handed the letter to his friend to read.

"So he will be here in two days and he says he has never been beaten by anyone," Master Lee said as he read the formal letter.

"He says also that his size will help him dominate us small Chinese devils and that we know nothing about how to fight the superior Russian people," Master Lee smiled

"Yes, and he wants to fight out in public so everyone can watch," Luo said.

"So where would you like to set this up, since you have the right to choose?" Master Lee placed the letter back on the desk.

"Well, I guess a good spot would be down by the corner where there is a big open area."

"Do you think that it will be big enough? You know, once everyone finds out they will all be there to watch."

"It will be big enough. Anyone who can't see will just have to wait and hear from their friends what happened." Luo replied.

PUGILIST FROM SHANDONG

"Who else are you going to have judge?" Master Lee asked.

"Just you.

"And I will use my students to make a fence around the area to help keep everyone back."

"Who is going to represent the Russian and make sure he knows all the rules?" Master Lee asked as a young student set down a tray containing a teapot and two porcelain cups. He poured tea into cups and politely served it first to Master Lee and then his teacher.

"According to the envelope that the letter was enclosed in, I guess he found someone locally to represent him," Luo replied.

"Have you contacted them to make sure they know the rules?"

"Yes, they will be coming by my office tomorrow." Luo said as he picked up the small cup steaming from the hot liquid.

The two sat for several hours talking about various subjects and drinking tea. Soon they heard the crier sounding the second bell far off in the distance. So they decided to retire for the evening.

Early in the morning as Master Luo was preparing for his first class, the Russian and his representative came to make a formal challenge. The Russian appeared as the letter had said: big, strong and full of arrogance.

His local representative was a man Luo knew from long ago but had not seen in quite some time, so he knew the man was aware of the local rules for a fight.

The three talked for some time about all the guidelines for the match. When Luo was convinced that the Russian knew what was expected of him, he agreed to the match and then said goodbye to his visitors.

The next day Master Luo rose early to train privately on some of his favorite techniques prior to departing for the fight location. He was just about to finish his training when Master Lee arrived and called him into the front courtyard. As soon as he arrived they both turned and walked back out to the street and headed for the site. Along the way a number of the storeowners came out from their usual morning ritual to wish him well.

As they were nearing the site his students had blocked off for the match, they could see the crowd was already beginning to grow with people who were completely surrounding the circle and many placing bets as to the outcome.

"Hey! Step back so Master Luo can enter the ring," a student yelled while reaching out with his arm to make an opening through the noisy crowd.

Suddenly the chatter of all the spectators ceased as their neighbor made his way into the ring and walked to a spot opposite the foreigner. The air exploded with excitement as the crowd returned to placing their bets.

Clang! Sounded the gong as the center judge tried to gain everyone's attention and begin the fight.

First he spoke in Cantonese to announce the rules to the locals. Then he translated into Russian the same rules and motioned for both fighters' acceptance. With a slight nod the Russian agreed and Master Luo extended his formal salute as an acceptance.

Again the crowd burst into a frenzy of excitement and chaos as the markers called out to those wanting to place a final bet as the two fighters prepared for the match.

Clang! Sounded the gong again to begin the fight.

Slowly the two fighters walked to the center of the circle. Again the Russian only acknowledged his opponent with a slight nod, while Master Luo extended his formal salute with both hands clasped together; one hand closed and the other covering the first.

Instantly, the Russian threw his first punch trying to catch his opponent off guard, but Master Luo reached out and used his two hands in a Mantis Catches Cicada" technique. He followed it with a double palm strike to the chest, sending his opponent stumbling backward. He landed on his back in the fine layer of dirt, raising a cloud of dust and hitting his head on the ground.

As he lay there on the ground stunned, Master Lee smiled, thinking, *this foreigner has got a lot to learn about Chinese Kung Fu.*

Quickly the foreigner jumped up and rubbed his chest, head and shoulder in amazement as he readied himself for the next attack. After a few moments of staring at each other, the big Russian charged once again; this time he tried to use his long reach and leg strength to drive his opponent backward and to the ground.

As he drew close and prepared to make contact with his first kick, Luo casually stepped to the outside of his leg while hooking under it with his hand. He reached under and kicked the side of the big Russian's supporting leg, sending him to the ground once again.

This time Master Lee just looked at the sky and smiled.

The Russian jumped back up and glared at Luo, who stood patiently waiting for the next attack. Moments went by while the Russian appeared to become more and more enraged at the ease at which this puny little Chinese guy could neutralize his techniques. He was so much bigger, so much stronger and he could reach him from so far away, yet this little guy was always able to beat him.

Now the Russian was becoming visibly frustrated. After a moment of preparation, he charged forward throwing a series of kicks and punches simultaneously in an attempt to confuse his opponent and create an opening for his attack.

As the first set of kicks sped towards Luo, he carefully stepped just enough to be out of reach. Before the punches could reach their target, he slipped inside and while chopping the side of the Russian's neck, he swept his feet out in the other direction, one of his favorite moves called Jade Ring and Chop Step.

The Russian's massive legs lifted from the ground and headed toward the sky. Meanwhile the chop to the neck caused his head and upper body to rotate in an opposite direction from the legs. His whole body was floating parallel to the ground for an instant and then landed flat on the ground, again raising a cloud of dust. His body began to spasm as the shock waves from the impact raced throughout his nervous system, and Master Lee could see the tidal wave of pain rushing through him.

His sweaty body lay in the dirt, which stuck to every part that was remotely moist and turned to dark brown mud. He jumped to his feet, wiped the mud from his face, and glared at his little opponent who was patiently waiting.

"I am Russian and way better than you lowly Chinese!" he yelled in Russian while pointing at Luo.

Luo casually looked at him, not knowing what the words meant that his opponent just said, but sensing that the meaning was rude for an experienced fighter to utter.

The Russian settled into a typical Karate stance, trying to show his strength by tensing every muscle. Master Lee knew that Luo was observing the openings available in the Russian's posture that would be potential targets. For several minutes the Russian went through various tension movements meant to build his mental strength and intimidate his opponent. Luo just stood silently, waiting for the theatrics to finish.

Eventually, the Russian stopped his tensing exercises, shook his fist at Luo, then charged forward with another attack.

PUGILIST FROM SHANDONG

His stepping this time had changed to a series of half circle steps while continuously changing his fist and block combinations. With each successive step forward, he yelled "ki-ayy" as loud as possible.

Master Luo calmly stood his ground. The moment he stepped into range, Master Luo jumped backward into a low stance, pulling his opponent with him. As he rolled back on to the ground he kicked the Russian in the chest and sent him flying overhead. The Russian landed head first in the dirt and then collapsed face down.

The large foreigner jumped to his feet in an attempt to show his strength and resistance to any strike by his inferior Chinese opponent.

Once again his futile attempts ended with the same outcome. Obvious cracks were emerging from the Russian's hard exterior; each series of attacks fell short of the expertise of this small Chinese fighter.

The crowd began to murmur about their bets and disperse one by one, each knowing what the outcome was going to be; they had seen a foreigner with too much ego try his best to defeat a true master like Luo and lose badly. Now it was time to head back to work and spend the remaining part of the day telling the story over and over to those at work who couldn't be there.

The defeated and humiliated foreigner crawled to his hands and knees, and then slowly with much effort tried to stand up. His first attempt only saw him lying back on the ground again. After a moment he tried again. This time he was able to stand and eventually his body quit shaking so he could clean himself off.

All the while, Luo stood motionless and patiently waited for his opponent to decide what would happen next. Across the small ring Master Lee watched every move the foreigner made; he had seen others try this same trick. When everyone least suspected, they would jump forward and attack in hopes of trying to catch their opponent off guard. So he stood and watched.

After a few moments the Russian looked up at his small opponent and gestured that he had had enough.

Luo slowly leaned forward and bowed. The Russian returned the courtesy, turned around and walked away.

Master Lee looked at his friend and smiled, then slowly walked back to work.

Without saying a word Luo looked around at what had just taken place, sighed at the thought of it all then turned away and quietly made his way back to his school.

Several weeks later, Master Lee walked over to Master Luo's school to have a chat about the future.

"Hey, Kwong Yu," he said when he saw his friend stepping into the doorway of his school.

"Uncle Lee, how are you?" Master Luo .asked "What brings you here?" the two walked toward his office.

"Well, I came by to let you know I will be leaving soon and heading back towards Shacheng," he replied as they sat down.

"Leaving, but why?"

"You know I have lived here in Kowloon for a number of years," he began.

"Yes," Kwong Yu replied, pouring their tea.

"I have done many jobs from working on the dock and teaching my Kung Fu, to selling medicine on the street, and many other jobs in between." Master Lee stirred the delicate tea leaves in the hot water.

"I am sixty-five years old now and would like to finally settle someplace where I can live out the remainder of my life in peace and pass on my Kung Fu." He began filling his pipe with tobacco.

"I see." Master Luo took a small sip of the steaming tea.

"Will you be coming back this way in the future?"

"Probably not."

"If I can live the remainder of my life in Shacheng, I doubt I will have the opportunity." Master Lee lit the firmly packed pipe.

"Then I guess we should get together every day until you leave so we can discuss our Praying Mantis Styles."

"Agreed," Master Lee replied. "We shall start as soon as we finish our tea."

Over the next several weeks, the two met at Master Luo's school and feverishly practiced, discussed, and researched the similarities and uniqueness of their respective styles.

"Okay, Luo, I will be leaving in the morning." Master Lee said when they finished their practice for the day. "I think we have made some major progress in understanding our Kung Fu."

"I will most heartily agree with your thoughts." Master Luo replied as they sat down for a cup of tea.

"I wish you could stay longer, but if you must leave then I will forever remember you as my good friend." Master Luo extended his hands in a formal salute to his respected friend.

"And I will forever remember you," Master Lee said as he returned the salute.

Early the next morning as the sun began to lighten the sky; Master Lee stepped out of his small dwelling for the last time, turned to look inside, then slowly closed the door and began his long journey toward his home.

THOMAS HAASE

Chapter19

~ When Leopards Strike ~

Months after leaving Kowloon, Master Lee arrived in Shacheng.

Eventually, after settling into his daily routine, he decided to go out to the forest and train in his old location. Quietly with the stealth of a hungry tiger, he rose from his small bed and began preparing for his morning workout. The time was four a.m., and as everyone else slept, he gathered his weapons and without a sound made his way outside into the cool morning air.

Gazing off into the distance, he noticed a light fog unsuccessfully trying to blanket the lower-lying areas, and with the full moon high overhead, the well-worn path up to the mountain was clearly visible. The light breeze blowing through the trees gently whispered the sound of a new day about to awaken, while off in the distance an owl perched high in the tree called out to all that would listen. Along the ground

275

the small rodents scurried about searching for food, ever watchful of the owl overhead.

Walking slowly along the path he'd traveled so many times before, Master Lee gazed up into the night sky and contemplated the vastness of the heavens. The stars that were so numerous and bright appeared to hang effortlessly in the darkness of space and their light continuously shined outward for all eternity, to be seen by countless generations. Amazingly, with all the billions of stars dotting the night sky, none ever infringed upon another. No two ever spent a single moment in competition. The night belonged to them all, small, big, young, and old. His thoughts of the stars' peacefulness in the night sky then drifted to humanity and their years of struggle to act similarly.

Why do so few men continuously try to infringe upon so many? He wondered. *All for material things, which are always temporary.*

They are willing to lie, cheat and steal from each other, ruin the lives of generations of people they have never met, all for the sake of saying – I have.

The stars in the sky so effortlessly co-exist, while man struggles.

Amazing, truly amazing.

I guess nature and the rest of the universe have figured out something that man struggles with and has chosen to ignore, balance." He pondered, as he continued on his journey.

The idea seemed to perplex his very core. As he continued on, the thoughts about the stars drifted through his mind like a slow moving cloud gradually making its way across a clear blue sky, only to be interrupted by the faint smell of jasmine. A scent so distant yet filled with memories of an earlier time. A time when training filled his entire day and life seemed so easy and carefree because the pressures of society were insignificant in comparison to the techniques at hand.

PUGILIST FROM SHANDONG

His thoughts returned to the morning walk by the calls from the owl looking for an easy meal. Sitting high up in the cover of the tall trees, this small winged bird could see extremely well in the complete darkness. But now that the night was beginning to relinquish its hold on the inhabitants of the daylight, the solitary owl had even better vision of its prey.

Suddenly, without warning the bird jumped from the branch high above the view of most ground dwellers. It swiftly and silently swooped down toward the ground and with the ease of picking up a stone from the soft dirt grasped a small rodent with its sharp talons and ascended back into the safety and quiet of the night.

Before long Master Lee found himself crossing the stream where so many years earlier he caught small fish in order to survive the widespread poverty caused during the Japanese invasion of Guangzhou. For so long there was nothing at all for the majority of the city. The viciousness of the invaders was evident everywhere, from the destruction of the ancient buildings and sacred temples, to the widespread stench of death from the numerous corpses lying openly throughout the city.

The low-class Japanese were less than barbarians, for even they had morals and compassion. War was war, but as unfortunate and costly as it was, most battles were fought in accordance with basic rules of engagement.

As he knelt down to drink from the stream, the emotions began to swell inside as he thought about all the atrocities committed by the Japanese. How he hated the Japanese for their actions and how they all deserved to die. All the thousands of people needlessly slaughtered and the others left crippled, homeless, or destitute. Many of his friends from Shandong, Hong Kong, and Guangzhou were either killed, mutilated and crippled, or left with nothing as the foreigners attacked from city to city. As quickly as the thought of the Japanese entered his mind, it suddenly vanished, leaving him with a deep sense of loss.

Gazing forward at the long path ahead, he realized the task at hand, sighed to release the tension from the previous thoughts and pressed on toward his training area. For the next mile Master Lee tried not to think about anything in order to prepare for the upcoming training, so he kept his pace steady and focused on the obstructions along the path.

At numerous locations the walk became more difficult because of the dead trees that had fallen and blocked his way. Struggling to bypass the trees through the underbrush was at times more difficult than climbing over the branches. But it was a small aspect of the trip that he enjoyed immensely, since it gave him a moment to practice various stances and evasion techniques.

At this time in the morning, all was quiet; the air was cool from the soft blanket of light fog. The leaves on the branches barely fluttered in the light breeze, and the sound of each step was muffled by the mist and faintly echoed through the trees, the soft whisper of an approaching predator. Only the keenest ears were able to detect his movements and they became alert to possible danger. None was present, for this was a solitary soul traveling his daily route to a secluded location in search of a better understanding of the many fighting techniques he had learned over the years.

As he walked up the hill, the visibility slowly became worse as the fog grew thicker. Soon, he could only see only a few feet away. With all the many twists and turns, patches of open ground that looked identical to each other, and with well-worn animal trails leading off in different directions, now was when his memory of the trail had to be at its best.

Moments later he arrived at his familiar training site; in a little while when the sun would slowly arise over the far horizon and quietly push the fog into the atmosphere, it would become obvious why he enjoyed this location so much. From the top of this mountain you could see into forever. The horizon was miles away, and cut jagged by the many peaks and valleys of the nearby hills and mountains covered in trees. In the early morning hours just before the sunrise, the view of the landscape as it began to peek above the gray blanket of mist gave the impression of being high up in the Tai Shan Mountains in the remote areas of a secluded monastery.

This was the perfect time for training. Not a single soul was around, the creatures in the forest were still asleep, and the world was at peace. The air was clear and cool and the Qi was perfect for the lungs. Every two hours a different organ in the body would gain the maximum benefit from the Qi in the universe and from four to six a.m. was the cycle for the lungs.

As he reached the open area between the trees that had been a welcome training partner for so long, he set down his weapons and slowly began his morning ritual. First would be the Qi Gong exercises to help stimulate the flow of Qi through the body, loosen the muscles and joints, and sharpen the mind's focus for the upcoming training regimen. This usually lasted an hour or so and afterwards the entire body was alive and ready for action.

Next were the basic stances, kicks, and punches to help send the Qi throughout every cell in every corner of the body and this was then followed by the many prearranged fighting sets with the different weapons or empty-handed.

One of his favorite parts of his training after he had finished everything else was to spend a good amount of time practicing his punches and kicks on one specific tree. This not only helped to develop a deep sense of focus, but also conditioned the body for the impact of actual combat.

Throughout his arsenal were the movements that covered all the angles from which you could be attacked or from which you yourself could attack. So as soon as one strike would hit the large tree and send a bolt of energy deep into the ground and out into every branch, another would be directly behind it from a totally different angle. Over and over this continued through the allotted time he set aside, day after day saw the exact same ritual and series of techniques.

Consequently, after all the hours of being hit and kicked in the same location, thick layer of the trees bark had fallen away exposing the bare wood beneath. All around the base of the tree there were small chards of bark that had given way under the force of the techniques thrown over and over in a continual barrage of attacks, and now even the bare wood was beginning to show signs of wear.

As large as the sturdy tree was, it could not withstand this continual onslaught and the entire tree was beginning to show signs of defeat. Some of the branches no longer produced green new growth for the upcoming spring and at first glance you could tell the energy from the strength of the tree was diminishing; and it was obvious that this solitary soldier was accepting the impending loss of life.

"Hey, Liao, look over there!" a man said while pointing at Master Lee punching the tree.

"Wow. Let's go talk to him and ask him about his Kung Fu."

"Hello, sir, my name is Liao Wei and this is my friend Luo Xin. We are Taoists from Wu Dang and were passing by to visit the Five Immortals Temple and saw you training."

"Hello." Master Lee politely bowed. "I am Lee Kwan Shan."

"What style is your art?" Luo Xin asked.

"My family style is Tam Tui and I also train in Jut Sow (Wrestling Hands) Praying Mantis."

"Hmm, Jut Sow, I have not heard of this style of Praying Mantis before." Liao Wei sat down on the large rock next to the tree. "Where is it from?"

"I trained at the Wah Lum Temple near Pingdu City in Shandong Province." Master Lee sat down and wiped the sweat from his forehead.

"Really? Where is Pingdu?" Luo asked.

"North of Qingdao."

"Oh, okay that explains why we did not know of it. We only traveled south from Wu Dang," Liao replied.

"What is your style?" Lee asked while imitating several animal styles with his hands.

"Oh, I am called Little Leopard because I mainly practice the Leopard Style and Luo is called Agile Monkey." Liao demonstrated some of his specialty.

"That Leopard Style looks like it is quite aggressive."

"Yes it is," Liao said as he finished the movements and returned to sitting on the boulder.

"Tell us about your Praying Mantis," Luo inquired while moving his hands through a series of the Mantis techniques he had learned.

"Well, the style is based on a more solid stance and the use of the hands to act as a mantis as it wrestles its prey into submission." Master Lee stood up to demonstrate some of the techniques.

"We know that a mantis cannot move about very quickly, so the hands must wrestle with the opponent." He executed some of the typical low stances.

"Other Praying Mantis styles use the footwork of the monkey to a higher degree to give them more mobility and their unique style reflects this in their rhythm of movement.

"But we like to imitate how the Praying Mantis actually defends itself and controls the opponent without the fast stepping of the monkey.

"When we utilize the monkey footwork it is to help mobilize the solid low stances" He demonstrated several instances where this idea applied.

"I like how your Leopard Style moves and its usefulness of the cat-like defenses," Master Lee said when he finished his examples. "Would you be willing to teach me some of your style?"

"Sure, and then maybe you could teach us some of your style of Praying Mantis," Liao Wei said excitedly.

"I will be happy to share my style with you."

"I have always wanted to learn some of the Leopard Style" Master Lee stated while trying to demonstrate his understanding of the Leopard movements.

"Oh that is an excellent choice and an extremely effective style," Luo Xin replied.

"The Leopard Style begins like this." Liao Wei performed the opening salute and the first few movements.

"Wow!" Master Lee exclaimed. "It starts like I hoped it would, strong and to the point."

"Yes and from there it gets even better." Liao replied while smiling enthusiastically. "As you execute these moves here, you need to make your steps as fast and agile as a cat.

"Attempting to get in at an oblique angle requires the cat's speed and agility." Liao demonstrated the angular attacks.

"I like how the move makes you twist all your energy up from the back foot into your strike," Master Lee said excitedly.

"As you jump you need to make your body sail through the air like a cat," Liao said. "So make sure to keep the proper angle and use your foot and leg like a tail."

Over the next several hours the three practiced and discussed the theories and applications of this style imitating the mannerisms of a leopard.

PUGILIST FROM SHANDONG

"Okay, now I will show you some of my Praying Mantis Style." Master Lee said as he began to perform several movements.

"That is incredible!" Liao Wei said.

"This style of Praying Mantis will be such an asset to our previous training." Luo Xin said as he tried to imitate what he had just observed.

"Our style begins with a salute like this." Master Lee said as he slowly demonstrated the initial sequence.

"That is such a great beginning."

"Now this is like a Mantis washing its face. Master Lee performed the technique.

"And this is called Bolting the Iron Door Shut."

"Wow! I like the application for that technique." Liao practiced the technique on his companion.

"Now this next move is called Jade Ring Chop Step, and it looks like this." Master Lee effortlessly executed the series.

Again the three masters practiced and explored every aspect of this unique style of Praying Mantis.

Soon the sun began to sink behind the distant hills, signaling the eventual closing to another day.

"Will you be here tomorrow?" Liao Wei asked.

Yes, I am here every morning," Master Lee replied as he began to gather his belongings.

"Then we shall see you just after sunrise."

"Good, we can discuss and refine some more of our Kung Fu," Master Lee said just before heading back toward his home.

The next morning, when the monks arrived, Master Lee told them, "I have some ideas about how to apply some of the movements in the Leopard series. He began the routine he had learned the day before.

"It seems as though you are trying to block and strike at the same time when you are doing this series right here," he imitated the movements.

"Yes you are correct with your thinking, Liao replied and demonstrated on his companion. "As the strike comes at you, you are trying to deflect it downwards and continue forward to strike without retreating or stopping."

"Ah, so you are defending with an attack," Master Lee said as he practiced the movement several more times.

"Yes. And with this movement you are crossing your arms to neutralize the attack and then without retreating you move forward with an attack," Liao said.

"Very good, very good," Master Lee replied as he watched his friend demonstrate the application.

After several more days of training, exploring, and discussing application strategies, the two Taoists had to bid their new friend goodbye and continue on in their travels.

"Okay, Master Lee, today will be our last training session. Tomorrow we will be leaving to continue on to the western provinces," Liao said as he began practicing the movements he had learned.

"Really? Then we better make the most of our remaining time together." Master Lee said as he applied his medicine to his hands.

For the remainder of the day the three continued in their pursuit of refining the movements they had exchanged and then bowed respectfully to each other when they had finished.

Then as suddenly as the Taoists entered Master Lee's life, they were gone.

Chapter 20

~ Stones ~

"**H**urry up with that bag of supplies. We need to go now if we plan on getting a good spot at the market!" Master Lee yelled as he walked past the doorway.

"I'm on my way. I'll catch up with you as soon as I put on my shoes," Sing Yin Tang said as he continued drying himself off after spending the morning on the roof repairing the tiles and re-grouting the seams.

He quickly tied the bag, slipped into his shoes and dashed off toward the main entrance to the compound. As soon as he jumped over the step at the front door he looked down the street to find his master had already covered four blocks and was about to turn the corner and disappear from sight.

Earlier that morning Master Lee had offered Sing Yin the opportunity to accompany him to the market and help sell medicine, provided of course, that he carry the supplies and

287

drum up business. For months he had subtly dropped hints about his interest in helping his master at the market, but each time Master Lee would only look away and say, "Maybe someday."

"Wow, Master, how did you get so far so quickly? I had to run to catch up to you and yet you seem to be barely strolling along!" he asked when he finally caught up to his teacher.

Master Lee just kept on walking as though he never heard anything. Suddenly, he picked up speed, and Sing Yin wondered why. Just as he was finishing the thought, the train whistle blew signaling its departure. Sing Yin shook his head in amazement. Before long they were pressing their way into the train car far enough for the door to close as the engines lurched forward and began slowly pulling away from the station.

As they stood there packed inside the car on their way to the Guangzhou market, Sing Yin thought about all the trips he'd made on this train and how different this trip was going to be. His thoughts were suddenly interrupted when his teacher turned away from looking out the window and said, "When we get there, the best spot is down on the end where everyone comes in. So as soon as we get off the train, I want you to go ahead and get our spot. I'll follow behind in a little while after I stop and visit one of my friends."

"Yes, Master. I'll make sure no one else tries to take it from me," Sing Yin said. "Do you want me to set up the medicine?" He hoped his teacher would allow him to sell something.

"You can, but be careful that no one tries to steal any of the bottles." Master Lee replied as he turned back to the window.

For the rest of the trip neither of them said another word. Master Lee continued to gaze out the window at the scenery of trees, small paths, rolling hills, mountains and row after row of fields. It was now late spring and all the fields were beginning to show signs of the newly sown crops. Each field was artistically carved into endless rows of seedlings reaching to the sun. As the train passed by, the rows seemed to dance like a rhythmic flow of gentle ripples on a calm lake.

Beyond the fields stood the faraway peaks of the Lian Hua Shan mountain range with each peak appearing to effortlessly support the sky and contain the last remnants of the early morning mist. Far below, the small villages bowed in reverence of the majestic guardians high above.

The rhythmic clatter of the cars rolling over the tracks kept a continual pace with the leaning of the cars. One clatter as the car rolled over the next section of track, then twice the car would lean first left and then right.

Soon the rice fields gave way to rolling hills and forests. The fresh smell of pine occasionally separated the thick smoke from the old steam engine struggling to pull the cars.

Suddenly, they could hear the chatter of exotic birds and monkeys calling from far away as the sound echoed through the trees. The soft curves of the hills were covered with small bushes budding with new growth of light green, while just beyond were the thick pine and evergreen trees standing tall and straight like soldiers in formation, with each tree trying to reach a little higher into the sky and grasp more of the sun's rays.

As the small train of timeworn cars neared the trees, the thick damp heat inside eased its grip as the cool shade from under the canopy of green soldiers pushed back the open fields and the sweltering heat.

Darkness engulfed the visitors as the bright sunlight dimmed. Outside the forest, the heat continued to bear down on the fields and its caretakers, while inside all was calm. The sun tried to push through the trees but the umbrella of large sprawling branches kept it at bay. Occasionally, a few lone rays would make their way through to the ground and the small plants would all turn their leaves in that direction and take in what they could before it was gone.

Some of these loners would make their way into the small cars and a rainbow of colors would reflect off the edges of the windows toward the floor, chasing the shadows from underneath the seats. A small child looked up at the rainbow of joy and smiled while reaching upward into the light as if trying to catch some of the warmth and help ease the tension from the crowded car.

The tracks were following the natural shape of the hills, so the cars continued to rock back and forth as the ground rose up, suddenly dropped back down, then to the right or the left. Some branches reached out and stopped within inches of the windows; others had grown completely over the tracks and had left only a small opening for the cars to pass under.

Inside the packed train, the travelers began to ease their grip on trying to keep totally to themselves by withdrawing inside and acting as if no one else was on board, because the solitary rays of sunshine seemed to penetrate to the core of every soul they touched and stir their basic instinct for hope. A number of the inhabitants began talking to complete strangers, occasionally a glimmer of a laugh could be heard and a child played with his mother.

What seemed like hours turned out to be mere minutes, and the journey was coming close to an end. The trees began to show signs of tolerance towards the humans inhabiting their sacred land by allowing a solitary dwelling far off in the distance and just barely visible from the moving locomotive. The dense canopy of shade and the erect ranks of green soldiers abruptly ended and the outskirts of Guangzhou took their place.

Row after row of almost identical houses lined the tracks; the walls and roofs were all worn and covered with dust and smoke from the continual onslaught of the daily passing of trains that carried the multitude of people to and from the city to other major cities and remote villages.

PUGILIST FROM SHANDONG

The doors and windows were covered with simple wooden frames held together with strips of wire and rusted nails. Children played in the dirt next to the tracks without a care in the world, while neighborhood dogs ran to and fro among them. Just outside the front doors leading into the small dwellings, a variety of animals were tied up to help support the family's meager income with milk and meat.

The line of houses seemed to continue forever. There were no roads visible leading toward the tracks, so the pattern lingered on. Eventually, a small path would lead up to the tracks and a small mound of dirt piled up almost to the top of the steel rails, with a dilapidated ramp constructed of old broken boards stacked precariously close to the tracks on each side and in the middle.

This gave the passersby the opportunity to risk crossing dangerously over the tracks without having to go down the street to the main crossover. Two-wheeled horse carts with small platforms on the rear just above the back wheel allowed for the transport of large loads of wood, paper, boxes or an occasional passenger to be carried across town.

The local businesses all opened into the streets facing the passing rail cars. Many owners were out in the sparse patches of open space between the tracks and the buildings working on products, welding metal frames together, hammering nails into a wooden pallet to make a platform to ship a piece of equipment, or repairing an old and torn fishing net. They seemed oblivious to the danger from the massive weight of the speeding cars as they sped by precariously close to the unsuspecting workers. As the train sped by the small businesses, it raised a cloud of dust thick enough to obscure the vision of everyone standing or sitting near the tracks. Everyone on board knew this was a sign of the station.

One by one, the cars all lurched forward as the tiny engine began its slow descent toward the station. People began to gather their belongings and prepare for the hurried exit through the small opening in the side of the car. Gradually the train continued to slow down and soon came to a stop. People began inching closer and closer to the doors, even though they had yet to be opened.

Usually the exiting from the train was extremely chaotic. There was no specific order as to who would get out first, except that whoever pushed the hardest would probably get off first. The doors quickly swung open and the inhabitants swarmed for the door at the same time, pushing and shoving to get out. Yet no one was in such a hurry that they angered anyone else trying to get out or were upset when they didn't step through the door as soon as they would have wanted to. Courtesy was still an underlying quality even in these cramped and often tense situations.

Master Lee and Sing Yin finally stepped onto the platform leading toward the railway station and down to the street. When they got to the main road Master Lee turned to his companion and said, "You go down this street for four blocks and then you will see the market on your left.

"Go all the way to the back and tell the owner you are with me and you want the booth up in front by the street.

"And be careful nobody tries to steal my medicine!" He walked away in the opposite direction.

"I will be back in an hour or so," he said just before the crowd engulfed him and he disappeared.

Sing Yin did exactly as he was told. After finding the owner and securing the proper booth, he proceeded to set up the medicines.

After about two hours Master Lee returned and without saying a word took the spot directly behind the table that Sing Yin had been occupying. He glanced at the contents on the table to make sure everything was still in there. Satisfied, he began to relax and look around at all the other booths selling their wares.

PUGILIST FROM SHANDONG

Next door was a young couple selling intricately carved wood scenes of famous temples in northern China. Each scene was carved from a single piece of wood detailing the grain growing in the open fields, leading up to the layer upon layer of mountains encircling the isolated sea leading to a curved waterfall on the far side of the quiet pool.

Down the small dirt path that wandered past the many other sellers, an elderly man sat sharpening his single-edged razor while waiting for a customer wanting their hair trimmed. His crippled grandson sat wearily on the ground trying to find some way to occupy his time.

Next to them stood a middle-aged man leaning over a large pot of specially seasoned soup and waiting for hungry patrons to stop and demand a sample. Quietly and patiently he continued to stir the secret formulation.

It didn't take long for the sweet aroma to draw hungry customers.

A man stopped, looked down at the large pot with a desperate expression on his face, and inquired about the soup. Without looking up, the vendor reached down, picked up an old wooden bowl from the pile stacked up next to the fire, dipped a large spoon full from the pot and handed it to the impatiently waiting customer. No sooner than the bowl was within reach, the dirty man grabbed it and drank the steaming contents to the last drop. He handed it back to the smiling chef.

"How much for that delicious mix of herbs and spices?" the man asked as he dug through his small pouch of coins.

"Three fen," was the reply from the satisfied man behind the pot as he returned to stirring the steaming mix.

The man dropped the coins into the open palm of the waiting recipient and continued on his way down the dirt path.

Next to the soup man, in an open area completely exposed to the rays from the hot sun, sat an elderly man watching the

293

entire scene while pushing back and forth on the pedal that kept his wood lathe turning. Sweat was pouring from his brow, his torn shirt clung tightly to his frail body, and his faded pants were covered in perspiration, salt stains, and layers upon layers of sawdust.

At his side were the products of many hours spent meticulously turning and shaping rough blocks of hardwood. Each piece was a series of precisely blended patterns of ridges, valleys, v-shaped grooves, and concave troughs followed by uniformly spaced flat areas, then more of the same in an exact pattern, completely unique. Each piece was a work of art.

Some of the finished products were to be used for legs of a table to replace the ones that had broken when a woman's husband arrived home drunk and stumbled into the front room in the dark and fell on the ancient heirloom. Others would be fitted to the leg of a centuries old chair that had broken, while a few after having been turned as simple round dowels would be kept as replacements for a shaky and weather-beaten single-wheeled cart, used for transporting large loads of goods throughout the city.

The continual drone from the tall spire of wood spinning around a single metal point driven deep into the ends of the once rough and sun-drenched scrap of lifeless fibers was overshadowed by loud chatter next door from the fortuneteller describing the details of the future of her unmarried eldest daughter to her nervous, worried, and exasperated mother.

As he unveiled the events he foresaw in the future for the delicate flower on the verge of thirty and now an unwanted girl, the small woman sitting on the wobbly stool showed visible signs of frustration at the thought of her daughter living a life alone at home and without a husband. As her body grew more and more withdrawn over the news of impending gloom, she slowly sank deeper and deeper into the wooden platform until her entire body seemed to melt into the cracks and disappear.

PUGILIST FROM SHANDONG

Then she sat straight up and acted as though nothing had happened, thanked the man for his time, paid the allotted price for the information, stood up and walked away in a most dignified manner to keep anyone from knowing what she had just been informed about.

Master Lee smiled inside to himself as he watched the woman proudly exit the market. After a few minutes of checking out what everyone else was doing in the informal market, he returned his attention to the variety of medicines in perfectly aligned rows in front of him. Some were special mixtures of herbs in a paste form to be used as a poultice for burns and open wounds. Others could heal broken bones and repair pulled muscles or tendons without the need for surgery. There were a few rare mixtures that had been passed down through his family for generations and were only used for special circumstances.

"We need to see if we can drum up some customers to buy my herbs," Master Lee said as he reached in his pocket and pulled out a bottle of dark liquid he kept in his jacket.

"Sing Yin, did you bring the stones I asked you yesterday to find for me?" he poured some golden-colored liquid from the dark bottle into his palm.

"Yes, Master, I did." Sing Yin reached into his small pouch for the rocks he had buried deep under the other bags of herbs.

"Good." Master Lee finished rubbing a generous amount of medicine on his hands and forearms.

"Now, go out there in the middle of the pathway and set up my platform so I can demonstrate for everyone, while I practice my Qigong exercises." He stood up and began loosening up his shoulders and wrists.

Sing Yin grabbed all the specially chosen stones he had found at the village, strolled out into the dusty path and began preparing a small area for the exhibition. He began by cleaning away small rocks and debris and then removed his shoes and leveled the loose soil to make a smooth platform. The ground had over the years become compacted with grooves worn into the soil by all the passersby and now it appeared as if it were a path for carts. The fine film of loose dust blanketing the well-worn grooves seemed to try and hide the years of footsteps continually pounding the soil tighter, but it was in vain. Now a solitary soul appeared and was going to try and wipe away time in but a few brief moments. Soon Sing Yin realized that his task was not going to an easy one, so he began to look around for something he could use to loosen the tight grip the earth had upon this small stretch of ground.

He looked down the road and spotted a man repairing farm tools.

He saw an old hoe sitting in the back corner and decided to ask to borrow it for a few minutes. He walked down the path with a grin on his face.

"Ouch," he heard from a barber's customer who was sitting on a stool with a sheet over his shoulders as the shaky man with the razor-sharp knife slid the blade down the back of his neck.

He approached the craftsman, who was grinding the long curved inner edge of a rusted and well-worn sickle. "Excuse me," he said. "Would you mind if I borrowed that hoe for a few minutes?"

"What do you want it for?" the man replied without looking up.

"My teacher wants to perform an exhibition down the street, and I need to level the ground for him. But when I started to smooth it out I noticed it was really hard. So I figured I could loosen it up with that hoe first and then it would be much easier to level out."

"You are not from this area are you?"

"Why?" Sing Yin asked.

"Because if you were, you would know that the ground here is very hard and it doesn't like to be disturbed. But if you want to try, go right ahead."

Sing Yin walked around behind the pile of broken tools, pulled the lonely hoe away from the wall, and hurried back down to his teacher. As he did he began to formulate a plan for how to best complete his assigned task. First would be to make a few grooves in the soil to help break up the large mass into smaller pieces, then each piece could be broken into even smaller pieces and then pounded into loose soil.

"Where have you been?" Master Lee growled as Sing Yin approached their booth.

"I went down to borrow this hoe so that I could make it easier to level out the ground for you, Master." Sing Yin said as he lifted up the tool in front of his chest. Without saying a word his teacher went back to his exercises as Sing Yin turned and began to try and put his plan into action.

Gripping the hoe tightly at the top of the handle he breathed in deeply and swung the blade over his head and toward the ground. *Thud!* Echoed from the ground as the tool made contact.

Instantly the vibration from the impact traveled up the handle and into Sing Yin's arms. He dropped the hoe and stepped back while a sense of total amazement settled over his entire body.

"What happened?" Master Lee.

"Nothing." Sing Yin replied, trying not to let on how surprised he was with the outcome of his first attempt.

As he reached down to pick up the hoe he turned and looked down towards the old man grinding away on the sharpening stone. Even from a distance he could see the large smile and expression of sheer delight radiate from the man's face as he returned to his grinding.

Sing Yin sighed heavily as he picked up the tool and prepared to try again. *This time I won't be giving in so easily,* he thought as the long wooden handle swung over his head and down toward the hardened earth. *Thud!* It replied once again, but this time he quickly raised the blade and returned it to the ground as if trying to make impact with the unsuspecting earth before it had a chance to prepare a defense. Unfortunately, he was wrong. Thud was the answer he received as the metal edge tried to dig into the ground.

Over and over this continued for about an hour. Soon the tired and sweat-soaked invader came to temporary agreement. The ground would give up some of the very top layers of its precious soil in exchange for Sing Yin's decision to agree that what he had was sufficient for the performance. As he finished breaking up the larger pieces into fine smooth dirt, he looked around and sighed with relief as the once hardened and unforgiving ground was now smooth and soft.

He tried to brush himself off but the sweat had caked all the fine dust to his clothes and bare skin. Now he would just have to wait until he dried off before he could attempt to remove the layers of dust.

"It is ready for you now, Master," he said.

Sing Yin walked down the road and around behind the man still grinding away at the large stone and placed the tool back in the exact same position as it was before he borrowed it.

The man asked, "So how did it go down there with your simple little project?"

"It went just fine." Sing Yin responded, trying not to let on how hard it had turned out to be.

He returned to his teacher before the old man could make any more comments about his plight. When he arrived back at the booth, his teacher had already carried his necessities out into the plot of freshly tilled soil and had begun to arrange his arsenal for the demonstration.

PUGILIST FROM SHANDONG

All the stones were precisely arranged in front of him to show off their beautiful shape, color, and hardness. At his side was a small cloth he always used to wipe away the dirt and sweat from his hands prior to performing. Sitting just beyond the cloth was an array of his special medicine in different sizes and shapes of dark brown bottles. No label was visible on any of the bottles since this was a special mixture that had been handed down for generations through his family, and he didn't want anyone to know what exactly was inside. If they asked he would tell them it was a special blend of herbs designed specifically to heal broken bones and pulled muscles.

"Start trying to gather up some people to watch me demonstrate my power so they can see how effective my herbs are for healing," he told Sing Yin while finishing up with his preparations.

Sing Yin began running up and down the dirt path trying to direct everybody's attention to what was about to happen at the end of the road. One by one as Sing Yin continued, the people began to stroll down to the end to see what was so special about this demonstration.

For years people had been coming to this market to demonstrate their supposed superior abilities at the art of Kung Fu. Little by little the inhabitants of the market had become more and more accustomed to mediocre performances and as far as they were concerned, this time was no different. But still they came, most just to see this old man prove their theory correct.

Within a few minutes the entire area was surrounded with onlookers all curious about this strange assortment of stones sitting completely by themselves. Usually, the other performances would include some sort of demonstration of their weapons prowess, but not this time. Today all they saw was rocks arranged side by side in the middle of a freshly tilled circle of dark brown soil.

"Okay, everybody, watch closely, my teacher, Master Lee Kwan Shan, is going to demonstrate for you his ability to break these rocks with his bare hands, and then you will be able to see just how strong his special herbal medicine really is!" Sing Yin yelled as the crowd drew closer.

"For an hour he has been practicing his Qigong just for this technique.

"Now he will allow you to carefully examine the stones if you like," he continued as he noticed the onlookers becoming more and more curious.

After a few moments, several people stepped forward and reached down to touch the stones. Each turned and exclaimed how hard the rocks were.

"Okay, would everyone please step back and let my master show you the power of his punching technique." Sing Yin began to push the circle of spectators back away from the small area. After a moment, Master Lee looked up at the crowd and casually smiled at a small child standing in the front row. He then stepped up to the first stone, picked it up, placed it on the ground and twisted it a couple times to make sure it was in solid contact with the earth.

A few moments of silence and then his body started to change. The muscles emerged on his forearms, the blood veins in his hand protruded and swelled. His breathing became stronger and more pronounced as he neared the moment of peak concentration.

Without warning he drew his hand away from the rock and with the speed of a lightning bolt his fist came crashing down upon it. The stone shattered into a number of pieces each speeding away from the core at an incredible rate. As it continued to break apart, Master Lee's fist continued downward until it hit the earth and sent dirt flying outward as well. Then as suddenly as it all began, it was over.

PUGILIST FROM SHANDONG

For a moment the entire crowd stood spellbound by what they had just witnessed, and then suddenly everyone started talking at once.

"Wow, that was fantastic," an old woman exclaimed as she held her face in her hands.

"I haven't ever seen a demonstration like that." She turned to check out the expression on her husband's face. He just stood there speechless, with his mouth wide open.

"He did it one time, but can he do it again?" a bystander in the back of the crowd responded.

"He sure can!" Sing Yin yelled back, trying to keep this one negative old grouch from spoiling their performance.

Once again Master Lee picked up a stone and placed it firmly in the dirt, and without warning raised his fist into the air in preparation for the impact. Suddenly the hand came crashing down upon the rock; once again it split into a number of pieces.

Again the crowd was completely astonished by the strength in this old man's fists, but this time even the skeptic in the back was left speechless. As he stood there watching in disbelief, Master Lee reached over and picked up another stone, as he did, the man became even more amazed, knowing that it was about to happen a third time.

Just as before, Master Lee picked up the rock and placed it in the same spot as the other shattered stones. He again raised his fist and gathered all his energy for the final blow. Then, the fist came crashing down onto the stone.

Thud! Echoed the ground as the stone was driven deep into the dirt.

Crack! The bones of Master Lee's forearm gave way to the incredible pressure from the impact.

Immediately the bones pushed the skin on the arm upward and created a sharp ridge in the middle of the forearm.

"Ai-Yaa!" the crowd gasped in disbelief.

"Okay, now you have seen an incredible demonstration of power and strength; now you can come up and check out the herbal mixture that my master uses to heal his broken bones," Sing Yin yelled to everyone before they could begin to leave.

One by one, they came up to check out the herbs, but more so to see the broken limb hanging from Master Lee's side. A number of the spectators bought a bottle and then moved on, some stayed around still curious about the strange protrusion on the arm, while others knelt down to examine the broken remnants and check for any signs of trickery.

After an hour everybody slowly moved on. As they did, Master Lee continued to work on the injured arm by first resetting the bones and then massaging in his special liniment before applying a splint to help support the break.

"What happened, Master?" Sing Yin asked when the last of the curious bystanders had departed.

"Where did you get those stones?" Master Lee asked as he was wrapping the splint.

"I went out by the stream at the edge of the village and found them," Sing Yin replied.

"Was that near that pile of large boulders sitting next to the old dead tree?"

"Yes, Master," Sing Yin said as he bowed his head in shame.

"You idiot.

"Don't you know those are some of the hardest stones in the county? Lee glared at his cowering assistant. "No wonder I broke my arm."

PUGILIST FROM SHANDONG

For the remainder of the day Sing Yin kept to himself and remained completely silent, hoping not to upset his teacher any further.

Finally the sun began to set over the hills covered in statuesque soldiers of green, creating a brilliant pattern of broken and solitary rays of light streaming through the trees and indicating that the day would soon come to a close. Just as the last rays disappeared behind the horizon, Master Lee began to pick up his things and head for the train station.

Sing Yin filled his pouch with the few remaining bottles of medicine and followed his Master, trying not to get to close or make any noise.

All the way to the station, Master Lee never looked back to check on his helper. Making his way through the crowd trying not to bump into anyone, he kept the same pace. As soon as he arrived at the station, he headed straight for the ticket counter, purchased the two tickets and made his way to the open car directly in front of him. Once inside he found one of the remaining seats, sat down, and began to once again work on his injured arm.

Shortly after he sat down, Sing Yin made his way through the door, just as it started to close. Looking around he noticed that his master had taken a seat near the window in the back of the car and that all the other seats were already taken. Cautiously, he made his way toward the back of the car and stood behind his teacher, hoping not to disturb him.

The doors closed slowly and the train lurched forward on its journey back to Shacheng.

As Sing Yin looked around he could see the many people engaged in exhausted chatter about their days' struggle in the city. Some were returning home with large bags full of goods purchased at one of the many markets. Others would be going home with everything they carried with them in the morning, after having no luck selling their wares.

As the cars began to pick up speed, Sing Yin saw the glow from a few lanterns being lit on the streets. Row after row of houses on the streets gradually began to light up from the fires' glow; suddenly, they were gone and were replaced by the thick darkness of the forest.

With the small windows latched open against the side of the car, Sing Yin strained to listen for any sounds echoing through the trees. All was quiet. The birds had made their last call for the evening earlier when the sun was disappearing below the horizon and now were settled in for the evening. The monkeys were all full from their day spent eating fruit and now nestled close to one another. Occasionally, the twinkle of a lone star could be seen dodging between the branches. All else was pure black.

The air turned refreshingly cool as the train made its way under the canopy of trees, a sharp contrast to the sweltering heat that had bombarded the city throughout the day. Within minutes, the cover from the thick blanket of branches abruptly ended and gave way to the open expanse of rolling fields.

Now the passengers could see the deep black sky with its pinholes of light shining through, welcoming the night creatures to begin the evening vigil. A distant star twinkled back and forth from white to blue to white, reminding all that they were not alone in this endless expanse called space.

The moon was just beginning to crawl up over the jagged edge of the distant horizon when the lights from Shacheng village appeared. The cars lurched forward when the engine began to slow as it neared the station; giving everyone a gentle reminder that the trip and their day's toil would soon be over.

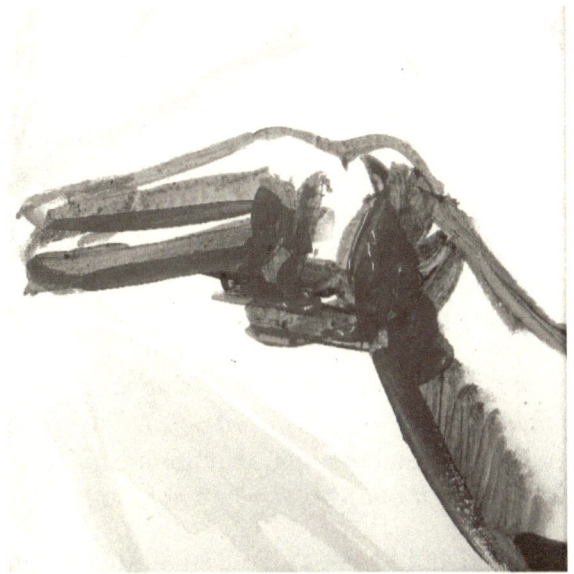

Chapter 21

~ Touch of Death~

A cool breeze softly blew through the streets signaling the close of another summer. The sun gently sank into the horizon. The crops planted in the spring with such anticipation were now harvested and all the villagers were busy preparing for the upcoming autumn season. This had been an exceptional season with sufficient rain to nourish the soil and warm sunlight to stimulate the seedlings' growth. It would soon be time to plant the fall crop of sugarcane and rice and begin the perpetual cycle once again.

Life in the village was now focusing on the upcoming holiday celebration and plans were already beginning for the spring festival in a few short months. This would be the Year of the Snake, so to those who were being favored by the coming year, now was the time to initiate the good luck omens. For many, the idea of receiving good luck from the gods was more of a continual process throughout the year; to others the festival would be another time of rest from the daily grind.

Master Lee strolled down the main street toward his favorite teahouse and he noticed the increased activity among the business owners. Everyone seemed to have a renewed spring in their step while toiling to sell their wares. *Funny it always takes some sort of outside influence to make people happy. When will they learn it comes from inside?* He thought as he turned the corner toward his destination and saw the owner of the teahouse light the kerosene lamp over the front door and then return inside to his customers.

Hmm, I think I'll play a trick on old Chung and put out his lamp and then ask him why it isn't lit yet. As he approached the lamp he stopped and thought, *that lamp isn't very low, I think I'll try to kick it out from here without touching the glass.*

Silently, he stood and focused on the small flickering flame and how he would need to project through the glass tube covering the light. Inwardly he was building his Qi and directing it into his foot. The moment he felt complete accumulation of the necessary energy, he kicked. With a flash the leg sped toward its target like a coiling snake reaching out to seize its prey, and as soon as his foot completed its outward motion and began to return, the flame bent backwards and disappeared.

That wasn't so hard to do, he thought as he entered the store.

"Hey, Chung, how come you didn't light the lamp outside yet?" he asked the owner.

"What? I was out there just a minute ago and started it, and now it's already out?" Mr. Chung exclaimed as he shook his head and made his way back toward the door.

Master Lee did not realize three of the patrons from inside had seen him kick out the flame until he heard them talking.

"Wow, did you see that, I don't believe he is still able to do Kung Fu that well!" one of them exclaimed to his friends as they sat stunned with their eyes and mouths wide open.

PUGILIST FROM SHANDONG

"I, I saw what he did and I still don't believe it! I knew Master Lee was really good at Kung Fu, but I never realized he was that good!" another man at the table said as the tea in his cup spilled on the floor.

Master Lee made his way toward their table, acting as though nothing happened.

"Good evening," he said.

The three men just sat there and stared at him, then after a long pause they all suddenly jumped up and began talking at the same time.

"Master Lee, Master Lee that was incredible. How did you do that, you never even touched the lamp!"

"How did I do what?" he asked, as though he didn't have any idea what they were talking about.

"Come on, Master, we saw the whole thing; you can't pull that 'old innocent me' trick on us."

"Oh that was nothing so let's keep it between us, okay?" Master Lee asked as he moved away toward his own table.

"Sure, sure that's no problem." one replied with a sly grin on his face.

For the next hour the three never moved more than twelve inches from each other, all the while discussing how Master Lee kicked out the light. What kind of training it would take to accomplish such a feat, how each one of them would have done the same thing had they been given the chance and what unbelievable feats each of them had performed when they were young. The more they talked the more unbelievable the stories became and the more trivial Master Lee's ability seemed to be.

Soon it was time for Master Lee to leave, so he rose from his chair, bade his friend farewell and headed toward the door. The moment he approached the three men, he leaned over and whispered, "Now, that incident you claim to have seen is just between us, okay? We wouldn't want anyone to get the wrong impression."

"Sure, sure no one will ever hear about it from us." One of them replied as the other two nodded their heads in agreement.

"Good, I knew I could count on you three fine respectable gentlemen to keep this quiet." Master Lee straightened up and turned to leave. When he stepped outside and turned toward his home, he saw out of the corner of his eye, the three back huddled together deep in discussion. *I wonder if they will wait until I get out of sight before they begin gossiping to everyone else in the place,* he thought as he passed by the window and continued down the street.

The moment Master Lee passed the window and was out of sight, the three men jumped up from their table and went in separate directions to the surrounding tables to tell anyone who would listen what they had witnessed.

"Did you see what he did?" One of them asked a young couple sitting near the window. Without looking up, they shook their heads and continued with their conversation. He ran to the next table, and repeated the question to Master Jiu who also happened to be a Kung Fu master in the village and was regarded as the number one master in Hong Kong.

Unfortunately, he happened to be in the back room so he was totally unaware of the incident. "What are you talking about?" he asked.

"Master Lee, Master Lee," the man said.

"What about Master Lee? I saw him leave just a minute ago, so what?" Master Jiu turned away.

"Did you see what he did earlier? Before he came in the teahouse?" the man asked again.

PUGILIST FROM SHANDONG

"No I didn't, I was in the back room.

"What did he do that was so special that could make you get so excited?" Master Jiu asked without turning around.

"He put out the lamp over the door, he put out the lamp!" the man exclaimed as he sat down across the table.

"So what, he put out the lamp. What's so special about that?" Master Jiu asked as he poured more tea in his cup.

"He never touched it and the lamp still went out."

"What do you mean, he never touched it?" Master Jiu asked.

"We saw him come around the corner and when he got close to the lamp he stopped and looked at it for a long time. Then all of the sudden he kicked at the lamp and the flame went out, but he never touched the glass with his foot, he was too far away," the man replied.

"How could he do that if he was so far away? That's impossible; nobody can do stuff like that," Master Jiu said.

"Yes he did; we all saw him!" The man pointed to his two friends who were talking to people at different tables.

"I am only forty-seven years old and everybody knows I can develop 450 pounds of force when I punch because of my Supreme Ultimate Fist style. So why can't I do something like that?" Master Jiu responded. "I don't believe it. You must be making this up."

"No, it's true. Ask those two what they saw; they were sitting at the same table.

"I guess that means that Master Lee is a lot better than you, if you can't do anything like what we saw him do, just a little while ago." He looked directly at Master Jiu.

"Shut up and get out of my face before I hurt you for what you said." Master Jiu glared into the man's eyes. "I'm really tired of hearing about what Lee can do"

"My technique is as good as his, so I don't know why everybody keeps saying he is so good.

"Maybe something needs to be done about that." He gestured for the man to leave him alone.

Without a word the man bowed his head and backed away from table. He and his friends returned to their original table and furiously chattered amongst themselves with their faces no more than twelve inches apart.

The days passed and the New Year grew closer and closer. All the while the stories of Master Lee's feat grew larger and larger. Soon everyone in the village was talking about it in low whispers among themselves, so as not to upset Master Jiu and feel the wrath of his anger. Only those closest to Master Jiu dared speak openly about what they heard and with each passing day, someone new would approach Master Jiu and ask him if he had heard about the story.

Soon the rage became too much for him and he formulated a plan to get even with the old man. Then the village would quit talking about how great Master Lee was, everything would return to normal and everyone would respect him as the number one master in town.

Quietly in the back corners of the small teahouse, Master Jiu and a few of his most loyal students developed a plan to get even with Master Lee.

"Okay, here's what we are going to do." Master Jiu said as everyone at the table drew in closer. "I am going to invite old man Lee to my new-year celebration."

"I want you to take it over to his school and make sure he gets it. Okay?" he said to one of the younger members at the table.

PUGILIST FROM SHANDONG

"He knows you and won't think anything is wrong when you bring the invitation to him."

"I want you to get one of the best bottles of wine in the restaurant and bring it to my school," he said.

"I am going to make sure that he drinks plenty of wine so that he won't be able to control himself and then I can take advantage of him and beat him up."

"Afterwards, I can take all his students and make him leave the village!" he explained.

Suddenly Master Jiu stopped and cautiously looked around to see if anybody in the restaurant was paying attention to the events in the corner. As soon as he was sure everything was all right he continued with his plans. Now they all drew in even closer as the plans became more detailed and criminal.

"When he comes to the restaurant I will invite him over to my table and offer him some wine.

"I want you to make sure and have this bottle on my table, and don't let anybody touch it!" he said in a very serious tone to his senior student.

"I don't want any of you to start wandering nervously around the restaurant after he gets here. I want everyone to pretend as though there is nothing wrong and we just want to be his friend."

"After he has a couple bowls of the wine, then I'll say something to him to make him mad and want to fight. When he gets up to try something and finds out he has been drinking too much wine, it will be too late, and then I will attack him in front of everybody and they will see how strong I am!

"Ha! It is going to be so great watching him fall on the floor and then have to crawl outside from my beating!"

Finally, with the plans all arranged, and the group quietly strolled out the front door as if nothing had happened and went their separate ways.

Upon arriving back at his school, Master Jiu proceeded to gather all the things necessary to write out the formal invitation that his student would be delivering to Master Lee. Special paper that signified the contents were of a formal matter was folded perfectly and tucked neatly inside an elegantly designed red envelope. The outside was trimmed around the edges with gold and embossed in a traditional Chinese pattern and subtly stamped in the background were small round symbols for good luck.

Each character of the Chinese lettering that was embossed vertically along the sides was surrounded by seven gold stars. This pattern expressed to the recipient sincere wishes for a prosperous new year, while separating a scene of fireworks exploding in the outermost corners. In the center of the invitation's cover was a hand-painted scene of happy children in brightly colored clothes, embroidered with symbols of good luck and playing drums, cymbals, a gong, and lighting firecrackers. Just below a window with an ornately carved lattice screen showed dragons and lions dancing excitedly outside to help celebrate the holiday. Over the top of this invitation was wrapped a single sheet of clean white paper with Master Lee's name perfectly scripted in the traditional style calligraphy and tied with a strip of red string.

Once the invitation was complete, Master Jiu gave it to one of his younger students to deliver to Master Lee. After about an hour, the student returned to say that Master Lee had read the invitation and would be happy to attend the celebration.

The next few days passed quietly without any further meetings by the group. Now it was the eve before the new-year and one by one each of Master Jiu's students and friends stopped by to confirm that everything was in place.

PUGILIST FROM SHANDONG

Early in the morning before the sun crept over the hilltop to announce the new day, a loud clap of thunder suddenly interrupted the silence and then, dense quiet from within the darkness. Moments later, as though the sudden sound rippling through the dark had awakened the clouds silently hanging overhead and stirred them into action, the rain began falling. Unusual for this time of year, the rain brought unexpected nourishment to the fields but also helped cleanse the village for the upcoming new-year celebration. The mild blanket of moisture falling softly without a sound slowly began to fall more heavily and soon turned into a downpour. Within minutes all the streets were covered and the cool morning air turned damp and heavy. Soon the residents of Shacheng awoke to the realization that the new-year had arrived completely cleansed of the past and ready to begin anew.

As the morning lingered and the rain continued, midday arrived while many of the business owners were considering their plans for the new-year celebration later in the day. With the rain still falling, the overall opinion was shifting quickly from the large community celebration toward a series of smaller shows at each business.

The downpour abruptly ended. Gradually, the sun began to break through the clouds and offer a glimmer of hope for the new day, while steadily driving the thunder god back to the mountains, and leaving everyone with the task of cleaning up in the calm after the storm.

Like a soft breeze moving slowly across a still lake, Master Lee made his way into the small restaurant followed by his student. They were met by Master Jiu who politely requested they sit at the table near the back corner of the restaurant. Master Lee acknowledged and quietly they made their way toward the back of the room.

The small table was tucked back in a secluded corner with four simply constructed chairs evenly spaced around the outside. The white cloth draped over the top to disguise the well-worn legs was hand embroidered with a pattern of multicolored plum flowers and a large phoenix surrounded by a five-clawed dragon in the center. Sitting on top of the brightly colored cloth was a small vase decorated in the tradition of the Ming Dynasty.

As Master Lee approached the table, Master Jiu hurried to the guest of honor's chair and offered it to Master Lee.

"No, that's okay," Master Lee headed for the chair on the opposite side.

"No I insist. You are my senior and I insist you take the place of honor." Master Jiu gestured for Master Lee to sit in the special chair.

"Okay, if you insist," Master Lee answered as he started around the table to the chair facing the door. *I wonder why he is trying to be so nice to me all of the sudden. I have been hearing all sorts of things he has said about me behind my back and now he is trying to be nice. I think I will be extra careful while we are here tonight. I don't want him to try and pull anything in front of all these people.* He thought as he sat down and waited for the waitress to bring them some tea.

"Please, Master Lee, I want to try and be your friend. We have had our differences in the past, but I would like to start the New Year as your friend and not your enemy." Master Jiu motioned for his student to come over to the table.

"Very well," Master Lee answered, without even glancing at his host.

Master Jiu said to his student, "Go and get us one of the restaurant's best bottles of wine and three large bowls.

"Master Lee. I have wanted to get together with you for quite some time and I think we should have some wine together on this special occasion." He stood up and respectfully bowed.

"No, that is quite all right," Master Lee responded as he lit his pipe.

314

PUGILIST FROM SHANDONG

One of the things I learned a long time ago from my teacher and father: You never go out in public and drink, because you never know when someone will try to start a fight, he thought as the smoke rose from the end of his pipe. When he finished, he gestured to his host to have a seat across the corner of the table.

"Let's just sit here and have some tea while we talk for a while," he said with a smile and began to pour tea in three small cups. As he did, he could tell that the demeanor of his host suddenly had changed; no longer was he as cordial and jovial.

Master Jiu slid the closest chair to Master Lee away from the table and sat down. The expression on his face changed and his body language spoke of agitation.

Master Jiu's student returned with the bottle of wine and three large bowls. He set them on the table in front of his teacher, arranged the three bowls side by side so that they could be filled with wine and began to fill the first one. As soon as he finished and began filling the second, Master Lee spoke up as he pointed towards the last bowl.

"Hey, don't put any wine in that bowl for me. I don't want any."

"But you must have at least a little, I insist," Master Jiu responded in a mild pleading tone.

"No thank you," Master Lee calmly replied and drank his tea.

Master Jiu abruptly gestured to his student to stop filling the bowls and leave. Once they were alone Master Jiu made small talk with his guests and tried to pretend as though none of this bothered him. His body language told another story.

Over the next few hours, Master Jiu repeatedly tried to get his guest to drink some wine. Each time Master Lee politely declined, took a sip from his teacup and then checked his pipe.

With each decline, Master Jiu's face grew redder and his posture stiffer. Finally, he jumped up from his chair and yelled into Master Lee's face, "Hey, old man, get up out of that chair so that I can kick you!"

"Hey, young man, let's be friends, please sit back down and drink some more tea with me," Master Lee replied.

Without warning Master Jiu suddenly attacked Master Lee over the corner of the table. Standing near the corner, he swung at him with a circular strike.

The moment the fist drew close to Master Lee's body, he calmly twisted to the side and let the technique brush his jacket before harmlessly passing by into empty space.

Master Jiu changed directions and followed the failed attempt with another movement, an attack to the lower spine, while Master Lee was turned to the side. Again he only found empty space as his aged opponent casually leaned sideways just before the moment of impact.

Spinning furiously, he tried to attack the legs of this elusive adversary under the table. With every kick he threw, all he found to kick were the legs of the table. Kick after kick met the same outcome as the punches he had thrown earlier.

Every time Master Jiu tried to hit him, Master Lee would move slightly to the side and evade the technique just as the blow neared its target. Master Jiu continued to throw crushing blows one after another at his guest now turned enemy, but each one missed its mark.

The more he threw punches and missed the more obviously enraged and embarrassed he became.

From the onset, everyone in the restaurant was completely engulfed in the confrontation between the two masters and the flurry of Master Jiu's techniques that continually seemed to find their mark, only to have the old man miraculously vanish from the technique's pathway at the last second.

PUGILIST FROM SHANDONG

As Master Jiu pressed the attack and continued to move closer in an attempt to finally vindicate all the failed attacks, Master Lee casually evaded.

Eventually, Master Lee realized that this young man was not going to quit. So as Master Jiu moved in to make another frustrated attempt, he again casually evaded the momentum by twisting to the side, but this time he turned and with the tips of his first two fingers hit him softly with a Dim Mak technique that paralyzed him on one side of the body.

As Master Jiu lay on the floor trying to move, his facial expression changed from rage to desperation.

His students stepped in and helped him sit back down at the table.

Master Lee realized the severity of the situation and that there would be repercussions, so while everyone inside remained hypnotized by the confrontation and the current situation; he quietly slipped outside into the safety of the dark.

For several days Master Lee remained at his home while allowing the situation to subside. Finally, he ventured out to his favorite teahouse to hear from his friends any news they had heard about the fight.

"Hey, Master Lee, we have not seen you in several days," the owner said as his patron stepped inside the doorway.

"Yes, I have been staying at home to avoid any more problems with Master Jiu and his students," he walked to his favorite seat near the back.

"I hear his arm and leg are still not recovered," the owner said, placing a teapot on the table. "And he is really mad for what you did to him."

"He's mad at me for what I did to him?

"He is the one who started the fight. I tried to avoid fighting, but he kept throwing punches and kicks at me, so I had to do something to get him to stop."

"Well, that is not what he is telling everyone. He says and his students have also been saying you attacked him in his house and hurt him for no reason. We all know that kind of action is very impolite, especially if you were his guest."

"What?" Master Lee jumped up from his chair. Are you serious?"

"Well, he better hope I don't see him on the street, or I might hurt him again," he said as he walked toward the door.

This teahouse happened to be located in a crowded part of the village, so all the alleyways were very narrow. When two people passed each other in the alley, they had to walk with their backs to the wall.

Several days later while Master Lee walked down the narrow alley, moments after leaving the teahouse, he saw Master Jiu approaching from the other direction. As they passed each other Master Lee reached up and grabbed him by the throat. "Do you remember me?" he said, glaring into his eyes.

"Y-y-yes I remember, "Master Jiu replied.

"What is it you are saying about me? "Master Lee pulled his adversary closer to his face.

"I didn't say anything!" Master Jiu exclaimed while his body trembled.

"Liar!" Master Lee leaned in even closer and applied more pressure to the throat. "I have heard otherwise."

"P-please, please, Master Lee, do not hurt me anymore," Master Jiu was now shaking uncontrollably.

"You started all of this, and now people are looking at me like I am at fault.

PUGILIST FROM SHANDONG

"If you want to fight, you can fight with my students," Master Lee said. "I am an old man, so you shouldn't be trying to challenge me.

"I have killed many people before you were even born." He watched Master Jiu's face.

"If you want to fight, fight my students.

But you can't fight with me first, that is not proper martial arts code of respect!

"I should kill you right now for what you have done!" Lee squeezed harder.

"Cough! Cough! P-p-please, please, Master Lee, do not kill me, "Master Jiu pleaded while trying to get the smallest amount of air past the grip on his throat.

As he continued to plead for his life, Master Lee squeezed even harder. Master Jiu legs started to weaken and give out and his voice grew weaker as the lack of oxygen began to take its toll. Then without warning, Master Lee released his grip and watched him fall to his knees and then on to his side while coughing and grasping his throat.

"Oh forget it!" he said, "You are already crippled, so it is not worth killing you." Master Lee turned to continue walking down the alley.

Chapter 22

~ Respect ~

"Hey, you don't belong over here in our neighborhood! You traitor" the store owner yelled as Master Lee's student Chan Wan Ching walked past his store.

"Hey, this is my city too! Maybe you should find a better master!" he yelled back, pointing his finger at the owner.

"My master is just fine, and maybe your master should not be attacking others for no reason, "the store shook his fist.

"Oh really? Why does he only have one good arm then? If he was so good, why did he lose?"

"Hey! You shut up or I will have my friends come and beat you up!"

"Ha! If your friends trained with Jiu Yin, I am not scared at all! I know what kind of Kung Fu they have. So send them over, and I will show them what real Kung Fu looks like."

Several days later as Wan Ching was looking in the window of a pastry shop, he heard, "Hey you! Did you say our Kung Fu does not scare you?" a large man screamed as he ran toward his unsuspecting adversary with his two friends following close behind.

"Why are you yelling at me?" Wan Ching asked.

"You know me, I am a senior student of Master Jiu Yin and I am going to show you some real Kung Fu!"

"So why do you need others to help you out?"

"I don't, they just came along to watch me beat you up!"

"Well, we will see. It may be you they watch getting beat up!"

The large man suddenly lunged at Wan Ching with both fists.

He stepped to the side to avoid the attack and pushed the fists away as they neared his face. "If you try that again I am not going to be so polite," he said while backing away.

"Good, I want to see what your Kung Fu is like when you quit being polite!"

Again the large man attacked, this time he tried a series of kicks.

Thud, thud, thud. Wan Ching blocked the first three.

"I guess one warning is never enough for you," he said while rolling up his sleeves for the ensuing battle.

Wan Ching charged forward with a continual barrage of punches. As his opponent tried to block the first punches, he suddenly changed his style of attack and began throwing numerous rapid techniques.

PUGILIST FROM SHANDONG

Boom, boom, boom! Wan Ching's punches hit the man's head and drove him to the ground.

"Was that supposed to hurt?" he asked.

"No, actually I was just trying to get your attention. If you attack me again, then I will make it hurt."

"We'll see about that," the man charged forward.

The moment his opponent was within range Wan Ching stepped to the side to avoid the kicks and punched the man directly in the chin.

Instantly, his legs began to tremble while his face lost all expression. Then the large man collapsed forward, hitting his face on the ground, and as quickly as the confrontation began, it suddenly ended.

"Hey, what did you do to our friend?" the surprised followers asked.

"I taught him a lesson. Now drag him out of here before I teach you two a lesson also!" Wan Ching shook his fist.

"We will be back when he recovers!" they dragged their heavy friend off the street.

"Good!" Wan Ching yelled as he stepped off the street and into the shade.

Throughout Shacheng over the months following Master Lee's fight, this situation continued to occur between members from both schools, causing the tensions between the schools to continue. Finally, the Shacheng officials scheduled a meeting and invited the two masters and their senior members to gather together to attempt to resolve the disagreement.

"Master Lee! Master Lee!" Chan Lok yelled as he entered the school doors. "I just got a letter from General Chan and it is addressed to you."

"Okay, thank you," Master Lee replied as he took the letter from Chan's hand.

"Hmm, it seems some of the other village elders want to have a meeting. And they are requesting my presence so we can talk about the fighting between the schools."

"Maybe Master Jiu should just leave town and then there would not be a problem," Chan said.

"Now, now, we need to be more tolerant of them," Lee said while writing his formal response to the letter.

The following week Master Lee walked to the other side of the village to where the meeting was being conducted. As he walked inside he noticed several of the senior village members talking at a table and General Chan sitting alone while writing a letter.

"Hey, Chan, what time will we be starting the meeting?" Lee said, sitting across the table from the elder.

"Well now that you are here, we can begin," he said as he put down his pen and pulled out the handwritten notes for the meeting.

"Everyone! Come down here so we can begin," he said while motioning to the others to join them.

"Master Lee," he began the moment everyone gathered around and found a seat. "As you know, there has been some serious conflict between the two Kung Fu schools for the past several months."

"Yes, I am aware of that."

"We called this meeting to see if we could find a solution that is acceptable to everyone."

"I think that would be a wise choice for all involved" Master Lee said as he leaned back in his chair.

PUGILIST FROM SHANDONG

"We would like to hear your wisdom on what a good solution would be."

Suddenly, Master Jiu walked through the front door and casually walked over and sat at the same table.

Master Lee jumped up and yelled, "Hey! What is your problem? I told you before, I am an old man, and if you want to fight, you can fight with my students."

"Please, please, can we all calm down here?" General Chan interjected. "We are all family, so let's try to get along!"

"I have killed many people before you were even born. If you want to fight, fight my students. But you can't fight with me first, that is not proper martial arts code of respect!" Master Lee yelled as he stood and pointed his finger at Master Jiu.

"I am an old man and I do not have many years left, so why are you so jealous of me?"

Jiu Yin looked at the floor.

"You know traditional Chinese customs don't you? You know what you did was wrong and against all the Kung Fu codes of ethics? If you stay in your school, I will stay in mine and teach my students and there will be no more problems."

The entire time Master Lee was yelling, Master Jiu remained silent while looking either at the floor or out the window. He knew based upon the old style Kung Fu customs in China that he was wrong for starting the fight and now had to deal with the repercussions while trying to save his reputation in the village.

"Okay, let's get back to the discussion of how to resolve this problem," General Chan gestured for everyone to quiet down.

"Now, as I said earlier, we need to stop all this fighting and act more like a family." He looked around the room at everyone in attendance.

"There is no reason why both schools cannot survive and be successful here," he continued.

"I agree," Master Lee said as he stared at Jiu Yin.

"What is your opinion, Master Jiu?" General Chan asked.

The room was filled with silence as everyone waited for the answer.

Master Jiu was too embarrassed to reply and just sat looking out the window while everyone waited.

"Okay, let's move on," Chan said. Does anyone here have any problems with this village having two schools?"

Suddenly, as Master Jiu jumped up to leave, his chair hit the floor with a loud crash and without saying a word while looking straight forward, he stormed out of the room.

The entire room was silent.

"I guess we will not be resolving this problem tonight, so tomorrow I will go over and talk to Master Jiu," General Chan said.

"After I talk to him I will schedule another meeting, but for now let's just move on and enjoy a good meal."

For the next several days General Chan tried to locate Master Jiu so they could sit down and talk, but every time he visited Master Jiu's school, he was never around.

After several months of Master Jiu hearing from numerous officials about how he violated the martial arts code of ethics, he realized his reputation had been damaged beyond repair. So he decided to quietly close his school, pack his personal belongings, and move to the Hong Kong New Territories. Little did he know upon arrival, but Master Lee already had many students in that area.

Chapter 23

~Bike Ride Resolution ~

"**M**aster Lee! Master Lee!" his student yelled as he stepped into the compound.

"Yes, Kam Wong, what is it?"

"I just heard from my cousin that there is a Master Ma in Nansha who is talking about your Kung Fu."

"So what is he saying?" Master Lee asked after he put away his writing brush.

"Well, my cousin said he is saying you should take up another career and quit teaching Kung Fu."

"He said what?"

"He said your Kung Fu is not very good and you should give it up." Kam said.

"Who is this guy and how does he know me?"

"He says he knew you when you lived in Guangzhou"

"Oh? And what does he remember about something that happened many years ago?"

"Umm, well, he said he beat you up and chased you down the street afterwards," Kam said softly, while looking at the floor.

"Are you making this up?"

"N-no Master!" Kam took several steps backwards.

"I want to talk to your cousin!"

"O-okay, I will tell him to come by."

"Good!"

Several days later as Master Lee was preparing for his class he heard someone knock on his door.

It was Kam Chin, the cousin of his student Kam Wong.

Master Lee invited him in and motioned for his guest to sit. "So, tell me about this master in Nansha."

"Well, I see him whenever he brings his fish to the market to sell."

"And he told you he knew me?"

"Yes, Master."

"And he told you my Kung Fu was no good and I should give it up?"

"Yes, Master, that is what he said."

"Hmm, do you know where he lives?"

PUGILIST FROM SHANDONG

"Yes, Master, I do."

"Good, I would like you to write it down for me." Master Lee placed the paper and pen in front of him.

"Will he find out who told you about what he said?" Kam asked nervously as he began writing.

"No, this will stay between us," he placed his hand on the shoulder of his guest.

For several days Master Lee thought about what he heard and the more he thought about it, the more it upset him. Finally, he decided to ride down to Nansha and confront his accuser.

The next morning after he finished his morning workout, he borrowed a well-worn bicycle from his friend and began the trip south.

Within minutes he passed through the ornate archway on the edge of town and rode down the small dirt path leading into the open fields. Soon the terrain began to change as he drew closer to the waters of the south China port.

Several hours later he finally arrived at the outskirts of Nansha. As he rode down the small hill leading into town he thought, *Wow, this city is larger than I thought.*

"Hey! Can you tell me where this street is?" he asked as he rode past a peddler sitting next to the rode trying to solicit customers for a haircut.

"Hmm" he said as he looked at the address written on the paper. "Ah yes, now I remember. The man gave him directions, and Master Lee thanked him.

Soon he could see the street sign in the distance, and minutes later he saw the small fishing boat Kam Chin had described. A middle-aged man was working at the back.

"Hey! Are you Master Ma?" he called as he propped the bicycle against the dock post.

329

"Yes I am," he replied as he stood up and turned around. And who is asking?"

"I am Lee Kwan Shan from Guangzhou."

"Really?" Master Ma asked as he stepped backward in surprise.

"Yes, and I would like to know how you know me." Master Lee walked toward the small vessel.

"Well, years ago I lived in Guangzhou.

"One day as I was training behind my father's store, you walked by.

"After watching for a short time you said I should give up my training and find a different career. When I asked why, you just walked away, "he said as he stepped off the boat and on to the dock.

"So, if your technique was not very good, I was probably just trying to save you from wasting your time," Master Lee replied.

"I think if anyone has wasted their time, it is you!"

"I still do not understand why you are talking bad about me after all these years."

"What you said was very insulting and my father was not happy. And after all these years it still makes me very angry! So leave before I show you.

Master Lee's anger boiled over and he jumped forward to close the distance between them to demonstrate he was not afraid of this man's empty threats.

"If you get any closer I will teach you a lesson!" Master Ma yelled as he readied himself.

PUGILIST FROM SHANDONG

Master Lee walked forward and then without warning rushed in with a series of precisely aimed punches.

Master Ma instantly began retreating while struggling to defend himself, as each punch drove him backward. As he frantically avoided the last punch and tried to maintain his balance, Master Lee suddenly stopped and waited.

"So you think you are going to teach me a lesson?" he said while watching his opponent regain his balance.

"Yes!" Master Ma said as he lunged forward without warning. Now I am going to show you what real Kung Fu feels like!" He threw a series of powerful kicks at his opponent.

As each kick sped forward toward its target, Master Lee casually twisted and turned to avoid any contact. Hmm, maybe you should try a little harder. Here, let me show YOU what real Kung Fu feels like!" Master Lee began an even more intense series of kicks and punches.

The first three toe kicks were aimed at his opponent's midline and as Master Ma desperately tried to avoid them, Master Lee suddenly turned in midair after the last kick and kicked successively at each kidney.

Instantly, Master Ma folded over from the impact to his kidneys while wrapping his hands around each side to try and diminish the pain.

"How was that?" Master Lee inquired as he watched his opponent try to regain his focus and ready himself for the next exchange.

"Cough, cough, o-only beginner level!" Slowly Master Ma stood straight up while lifting his hands over his head, he then closed his eyes and began pressing his hands downward while forcefully exhaling. When his hands reached his sides he opened his eyes and glared at Master Lee.

"Now! You are going to feel what my Kung Fu is truly like!" he charged forward.

First he threw several punches in an attempt to lure his opponent into defending his upper body so he could then strike the lower part.

As Master Ma began the first and second punches, Master Lee instantly recognized what his opponent was trying to accomplish, so he jumped to the side and kicked at Ma's rib cage.

The moment the foot reached his side Master Ma twisted to reduce the impact and swung his fist at the back of Master Lee's head trying to catch him unguarded. Master Lee quickly raised his left arm and deflected the punch over his head, which caused Ma to lose his balance and fall on his back.

The moment he hit the ground, Master Lee stepped in and kicked him in the side of his head, forcing Ma to roll over and swallow a mouthful of dirt.

"Phfft. Cough. Cough! You, cough, cough, wait!" he struggled to say as he pressed up to his hands and knees.

"Okay, I'm waiting."

"I have been holding back so far to be polite, but no longer!" MA raged as he stood up and spat out more dirt.

"Good! I am losing my patience sparring with beginners," Master Lee said as he rolled up his sleeves.

Before Master Ma could respond Master Lee rushed forward and released a flurry of kicks and punches designed to stop any seasoned fighter.

As the first punch drew near, Master Ma frantically blocked and tried to avoid the next. The punch arrived before he could move and caught his chin, which instantly caused his knees to buckle, sending him once again toward the dirt. As he was collapsing to the ground, the next kick dislocated his shoulder, causing his body to spin in mid-air before landing.

"Phfft, Cough, Cough!" Master Ma desperately struggled to stand but the bad shoulder gave no assistance, forcing him to use the other weakened arm. Eventually he was able to stand and tugged on the elbow to try and re-set the shoulder.

"Are we finished here?" Master Lee asked as he watched the battered warrior try to regain his composure.

"No!" Ma yelled as he wiped the mud from his face and readied his body with another fighting stance.

"Ai-yaa!" he yelled as he rushed forward to attack while trying to protect the useless arm.

The moment he was within range, he swung his good fist straight at Master Lee's face while attempting to kick at his stomach.

As the punch neared his face, Master Lee blocked it while stepping in to cut off the kick. He then drove a double palm punch into Ma's s stomach and chest, again sending him backwards and to the ground.

"Do not get up!" he said as his opponent lay on the ground. "I have killed many in my lifetime, so do not make me kill you."

Moments passed as Ma lay on the ground trying to draw in another breath of air.

By the time he was able to sit up; Master Lee was pedaling away on his bicycle.

"Here you go." Master Lee said as he handed the bike back to his friend.

"I thought you would be gone longer than that."

"Why?"

"You said you were going to Nansha to see someone."

"I did," Master Lee removed his backpack.

"And you are back already? That was not much of a visit?"

"I was there just long enough to find out what I needed to know," Master Lee replied. "Hey! Will you be celebrating the new Year next week?"

"Yes, definitely!" his friend replied.

"Okay, I will make sure to save you a time in my schedule for a show." Master Lee said as he turned once again and headed for his home.

Chapter 24

~Celebration ~

The sun started to slowly sink into the horizon and changed from bright yellow to a deep orange, signaling the end of another day as well as the ending of another year. While reflecting its brilliance off the few remaining clouds hanging quietly in the sky, it appeared to change their once pure white bodies into floating embers on fire from the intense heat of a burning fireball.

Later in the evening, just before midnight, everyone began the annual cleaning to sweep away the dust that had collected during the previous year and allow the New Year to arrive into a clean and fresh dwelling. Their midnight meal would be prepared with special foods for good luck and auspicious future.

Each year Master Lee and his students would pack all their equipment and walk for an entire month from village to village performing the traditional Lion Dance and Kung Fu exhibition at the numerous businesses to help bring good luck and prosperity for the New Year. Master Lee's Lion Dancing ability was well-known in the area, so all the business owners always looked forward to his return at the new-year celebration.

Early on the first morning of new year, before most of the students arrived, Master Lee looked around the school to see what other supplies and equipment would be needed on their trip around the surrounding villages to help celebrate the upcoming new-year.

"Hey, Chan Lok," he said as his student stepped in the door. "Make sure and pack the drumsticks, cymbals, and gong. Does everyone have all their weapons?"

"Yes, Master." Chan Lok replied as he began packing the musical instruments. "I made everyone gather them together and tie them in a bundle, so it would be easy to carry."

"We will be leaving in two hours and I don't want to get to Huang-gong and not be able to perform."

Soon, all the remaining students arrived with their personal belongings and helped pack the entire array of weapons, music instruments, lion costume, and food into the small two-wheeled cart that would carry the troupe's equipment from town to town.

"Okay, let's get going. I want to be close to Huang-gong by nightfall, so we can arrive early in the morning and begin the celebration before noon," Master Lee said as he began making his way down the dirt street that headed north to their first engagement.

As the troupe made their way toward the outskirts of town, many friends and relatives came out to wish them good luck. For some of the members in the troupe, this was a scene they had experienced repeatedly in their lives. While for others, like Chan Poi, who was only six years old, this was the first time he was permitted to travel with the group and perform during the festival.

After several hours of walking, Master Lee could tell that the youngest member of the team was beginning to tire, so he looked ahead to find a place to rest and when he saw a suitable spot he yelled to the students out in front, "Push the cart over there by those big trees and we will sit and rest for a while.

"We have been walking for three hours and if we stop for a little while now and rest, we can then walk for another couple of hours and stop just outside Huang-gong for the night.

"Chan Poi, go up ahead and start looking for some dry wood we can use for a fire to do our cooking." Master Lee patted the tired boy on the shoulder and sent him off on the errand.

Upon hearing the words referring to food, Chan Poi dashed off into the trees to find small dry twigs and branches to use in the fire.

Meanwhile, the remainder of the group positioned the cart under the trees, removed the belongings they were carrying, and quickly built a stone ring on the ground for the fire. Soon, the fire was blazing, and the pots with rice and vegetables were all suspended above it.

After about an hour, everyone had finished their meal, cleaned the utensils, repacked the cart, and were ready to continue on their journey.

Later that day, as the sun started to descend toward the horizon, Master Lee knew that it would not be long before the dark night sky would be upon them, so once again he began looking for a suitable location to stop for the night.

"Sing Yin. Go up ahead and find a good spot we can set up camp for the night," Master Lee said as the group rounded the base of a small hill.

After about fifteen minutes, the young man returned, ran up to his teacher and said, "Master, there is a nice spot just up ahead."

"Good." Master Lee replied. "We walked quite a distance today and I want everyone to get some rest because you all need to be ready to perform in the morning.

"After we get situated for the night and finish eating. I want to talk about what we are going to do for the celebration performance tomorrow."

Following their meal and the cleaning of the utensils, everyone took a few moments to just sit and reflect upon the events of the day, and gaze off into the dark star-filled sky.

"Okay. Now we need to make sure everyone knows what to do tomorrow during the Lion Dance performance," Master Lee began as he looked at everyone individually, to make sure they were listening.

~~~~~

The Lion Dance was always performed first upon arrival, in order to give the villagers a chance to test Master Lee and his performance troupe. This not only tested their dancing ability, but their Kung Fu technique as well. For each performance, many tests and traps were set up before the troupe arrived, requiring the two performers under the costume to pass through or over, without any foreknowledge about what had been arranged. Therefore, performers had to practice a wide variety of solutions at home, until they attained a high level of proficiency before arriving at the villages.

Master Lee had a very extensive knowledge and understanding of the herbal medicine field. The many years of training and improving his Dim Mak and Kung Fu and preparing herbal solutions for himself and his students had become invaluable and he knew how to effectively neutralize the poisons and defensive nature of the snakes. Many people had attempted this technique only to fail due to a lack of experience and preparation. Now, Master Lee and his team demonstrated the proper technique without a single problem.

Some of the business owners who had their offices on the second floor would tie the envelope to a stick and suspend it straight out from the second story window. The performers then had to build a human platform and stand on top of each other's shoulders until they could reach the string holding the hung bao. Or slip a wooden bowl under the shirt of a younger member's shirt and tie it around their waist, allowing the team to lift up the person and the lion head by balancing the body on top of a stick. When they were high enough, the boy could reach out and cut the string holding the envelope, tuck it into his shirt and then be lowered back to the ground.

Other businesses would set up a couple of sawhorses with a precariously shaky ladder suspended across the top that the lion had to cross. On either side would be an area filled with fresh mud in case the lion fell off. On the opposite end was a large pot with steaming water inside and a bowl floating inside with the lucky money perfectly arranged in the middle.

When the lion approached the test, it would have to perform a special dance to show its understanding of the meaning of the prop. This crude setup was an imitation of a mountain that the lion had to climb up and cross over in order to find the good luck.

Sometimes the owners would arrange a series of delicate porcelain bowls in a row signifying a different type of bridge. The team would have to carefully walk across all the bowls without breaking any and find the good luck on the other side.

"The local residents, to a certain degree, are knowledgeable in the art of Kung Fu, so when we arrive to perform the Lion Dance, they will place the Hong Bao or 'Lucky Money' in difficult places or situations to test our abilities," Master Lee explained.

"Therefore, as the performance begins, we will be required to dance around the entrances of the businesses in a specific manner to bring everyone good luck.

"At the proper moment, the lion has to undo the trap set up by the owners.

"As it approaches the trap, the lion needs to slowly open the lid, and determine what the trap was and how to execute an effective solution. This is the real test: Can a solution be determined and executed during the dance without breaking the rhythm of the drum?

"I have realized that over the years, there are several routines that this village likes to see, and each year they choose a different one to test our abilities." Master Lee drew on the ground with a small stick.

"Here is where we usually start the show." He drew a series of marks in the soft dirt to signify the streets and buildings.

"We will first need to do the opening bow, with the lion and then gradually make our way from one participating business to the next, so we can bring good luck to them for the upcoming year.

"Remember, they will be lighting a lot of fireworks everywhere in the streets and at the front doors of their businesses. So be careful when you are under the lion costume because it will be very noisy, the smoke will be very thick, and it will be difficult to see and breathe." He pointed the stick at the older students who he wanted to be under the costume.

"I want you four to play music, and the rest of you to hold all the weapons during the show.

"Now, when you have finished dancing in front of each business, there will be a special test setup out here in the street.

"You will need to be very careful with whichever test they have chosen.

PUGILIST FROM SHANDONG

"Last year some of you may remember, they had a large basket set out in the street by itself. And you had to get the Hong Bao out from under the poisonous snake inside the basket?" He looked to see who was nodding their head as if they had remembered.

"You almost got bitten because they had it wrapped so tightly with cloth that you couldn't see inside to know there was a snake inside waiting for the cover to be opened.

"Then when you lifted the lid and saw a snake, you got scared and took too long to get the envelope.

"Luckily, I made you put extra gunpowder on your legs and arms, to help sedate and calm the snake and keep it from striking your hands while you were looking for the lucky money, so the snake left you alone.

"If they have the envelope up by the second floor window, you will need to make sure you have that wooden bowl and that twelve-foot pole, close by so you can slip the bowl under Chan Poi's shirt and raise him up with the end of the pole inside the bowl. He is light enough and should be able to balance on the point and still be able to get the envelope while holding the lion head.

"Now, if they have the porcelain bowls arranged with a plank on top and leading to a series of eight-foot-high poles to climb across, you will need to be extra careful, because they like to make sure the poles are not too secure and will wobble a lot while you are walking across the top." He turned to the older students.

"This is when you need to use the breathing techniques I taught you, so you can make yourself light and have better balance.

"If you fall, it will be very bad for my reputation as a teacher, and also bad luck for the business owners. So take your time on the poles and demonstrate the control and patience I have been teaching you when you perform.

"Once you get to the other side of the poles, Chan Biu, you will be under the tail, so you need to grab Chan Poi by the waist and slowly lower him down face first, over the end of the poles, so he can grab the Hong Bao and then lift him back up," Master Lee explained as he animated the technique with his hands.

"Then you have to come off the poles in reverse, so again be careful.

"Remember, you are supposed to imitate a lion going over the mountaintop to get the good luck and then return. So make sure you perform it correctly and can bring good luck to the business owners.

"After the Lion Dance is finished, I want everyone to perform some of their Kung Fu. So make sure you don't forget the movements," he pointed the stick at each student in the group.

"Sing Yin, I want you to do your double rolling swords. Chan Poi, I want you to do your flexibility routine and the Fan Cha (Big Wheel) form. Chan Biu, I want you to do your Tiger Fork.

"When everyone is finished, I will go out and crush a rock with my punches. So Sin Yin, don't bring me anymore bad stones," he scolded as he stared at his student.

"Now, everyone go to sleep and get some rest. Tomorrow will be the beginning of our celebrating the New Year, so let's begin with a really good performance."

The following morning everyone rose early, gathered their belongings, and were ready to begin their walk before the sun rose over the distant hills.

"Is everyone ready?" Master Lee asked as he positioned the small pack on his back.

"Yes, Master," everyone said in unison.

PUGILIST FROM SHANDONG

"Good. Then let's get going before they think we are not going to show up." Master Lee headed down the dirt path.

Several hours later, they arrived in the center of the village.

"Everyone get ready," Master Lee said.

This routine was repeated each time they arrived in all the towns and villages surrounding Shacheng that had invited the group to perform for the New Year.

Chapter 25

~ Big Kwong ~

O ver the years of living in Shacheng, Master Lee had become very close friends with a monk from the small solitary temple on the outskirts of town. Initially, when he arrived in the small Chan family portion of the village he heard from some of the elders about a native of the Northern provinces who lived a quiet and meager life in the local temple. So within weeks upon his arrival he made the trip on foot without really knowing the route except for the few directions he was given by the locals, in order to respectfully introduce himself, and find out which province this stranger came from.

Quietly on one cold spring morning, he gathered his things and mentally made a list of questions he needed to ask. Where was he from, what was his family lineage, what style of Kung Fu did he know? There were other questions he wanted to ask but these were the primary ones he would inquire about first and if time allowed then he would ask the others.

345

THOMAS HAASE

As Master Lee walked along the small dirt path leading from the outskirts of the village towards the nearby mountains, his thoughts drifted back to the time many years ago when he was first heading towards the Wah Lum Temple in Shandong Province. He remembered how his mind was filled with an array of questions and ideas as to how life in the temple was going to be.

Would he be accepted as a student and allowed inside the hallowed, secluded and illusive gates to learn the secrets of the unique style of Praying Mantis, or would they send him home alone, dejected, and totally ashamed about not being allowed to enter even with his father's letter of acceptance? Now, many years later he was having some of the same basic thoughts about the meeting with the monk from the temple.

As he passed the small market at the edge of town he could see the faint outline of the large, silent and majestic emerald-green mountain far off in the distance. It was now late October and the leaves were just beginning to show signs of a slow yet determined release of the intense heat upon the residents of the village. Soon it would begin to cool throughout the day at a steady rate and then taper off just before the onset of the coming New Year celebration. Many of the fields were already harvested and now the owners, along with their workers, were busily preparing the fields for the winter crop.

One by one he continued past the never ending row of plots of land, each a mixture of rich brown soil, interspersed with the remnants of dead leaves and the few remaining shoots of green trying to hold on as long as they possibly could before being tilled under. Each field had an array of workers steadily digging up vegetation, pulling out weeds trying to sprout without being noticed, following wearily behind a lone ox pulling a small and well-worn plow, or spreading manure on the already turned soil before the group of workers arrived to break up the chunks of ground and begin the long task of leveling the soil in preparation for planting.

346

PUGILIST FROM SHANDONG

Soon, as the patchwork of fields faded and gave way to the emerald green leaves on the trees at the edge of the thick forest, the small meandering path began to gradually climb, switch-backing up and around the mountain.

This too brought back memories of when Master Lee was young and walking from city to city and as he headed west from Pingdu toward Jinan just after leaving the temple. On numerous occasions he had to navigate around the tall silent peaks supporting the sky. Before long he found himself on the opposite side after having had to endure many days of intense struggle as he slowly made his way around the aged sentinel, only to find another looming off on the far horizon.

After an hour of steady walking, Master Lee finally began to see the outline of the small, secluded temple. Its outer walls were desperately trying to fight back the onslaught of vegetation climbing over the walls. In some areas tucked away on the far side opposite the main entrance, it was obvious that the vines were winning the battle, since they had already made the long journey over the wall and were beginning their downward march on the inside.

The front gate was a pair of large weathered wooden doors with a number of paint coatings slowly trying to emerge from underneath each other; the doors had originally fit snugly into the opening of stone and brick, but were now beginning to sag from the years of use and continual bombardment from the summer sun.

Inside, the open space behind the entrance was clean and well-manicured with trees lining the main walkway like sentinels waiting for the arrival of the emperor. A small pond gave the appearance of humility. It wasn't boldly placed in the way of visitors as they walked toward the meager shrine; instead it quietly rested near an old oak tree that had grown tall and wide and now its branches stretched far across the open courtyard while offering protection for the small isolated pool filled with an assorted group of brightly colored koi.

The group of buildings beyond the large tree that housed the few solitary monks all needed serious repair. The roofs were all well past the point of being able to resist the onslaught of the spring's rainy season, while the openings for light and fresh air were unable to shut out the bright light from the monthly full moon or the sharp brisk air early in the morning.

Inside the tall, serene, and well-built walls and just beyond the open space was a large incense urn with a trail of smoke rising from the ornately crafted cover. It was situated on a stone platform and raised above the level of the surrounding platforms to signify the importance and reverence designated for its use, since the residents from the surrounding villages all arrived to pay their respects on all the auspicious occasions. Directly behind the urn was the private residence of the abbot, a small, simple, and modest structure giving no indication as to who its occupant might be.

As Master Lee stepped through the open gate he silently bowed to humbly offer his respect to the quiet temple.

"Can I help you?" a monk inquired as he walked towards the visitor.

"Yes, I'm Lee Kwan Shan. I live in Shacheng, but my family is from Pingdu in Shandong Province."

"Pingdu?" the monk seemed to search his memory.

"Yes it's north of Qingdao," Master Lee replied.

"I'm sorry, but I don't know of this city," the monk said.

"That's okay." Master Lee replied. "May I ask your name?"

"I'm called Big Kwong," he said while slowly bowing to his guest.

"I'm honored to meet you." Master Lee bowed to his host. "I heard you were from the north so I wanted to come and introduce myself and ask you a few questions, if you do not mind."

348

PUGILIST FROM SHANDONG

"Sure, sure, but let's go inside and talk over some tea," Kwong said.

After they were seated in Kwong's small dwelling and he had poured tea, Master Lee asked his first question.

"So, Kwong, where are you from up north?"

"Originally, I was from Henan Province but have traveled for so many years, so now I call this temple my home."

"What style of Kung Fu do you practice?" Master Lee asked.

"Well, in my many years of traveling I have learned numerous styles, but I prefer the Shaolin Style," Kwong replied. What is your style of Kung Fu?"

"My family trained in the Tam Tui Style and while I lived at the temple I learned the Jut Sow Praying Mantis system."

"Hmm, Jut Sow Praying Mantis. I haven't heard of that style." Kwong said. "When you come back we will have to research your Praying Mantis."

"Agreed," Master Lee replied.

For the next several hours the two sat and talked about a variety of subjects. Eventually, as the sun began to set behind the tall trees, Master Lee realized it was time to leave.

"Okay, Big Kwong, I think I'll say goodbye for now so I can get home before dark. I will return in a couple months and then we can discuss our Kung Fu in more detail."

"Agreed." Kwong said as walked with his guest toward the front gate.

When they reached the gate Kwong politely bowed to his guest. Master Lee politely returned the sign of respect and then slowly began the long trip home.

~~~~~~

"Hey Chan Lok, I want you to make sure that everyone completes all their exercises and forms practice during this afternoon's class; it has been several months so I am going to go and visit my friend Big Kwong at the temple." Master Lee said as he casually headed toward the edge of town.

Eventually Master Lee turned from the larger path and headed down a smaller, less traveled road leading up the hill to the temple. As he neared the front gate he saw his friend outside the temple working on repairing a section of the small structure.

"Hey, Big Kwong!" Lee shouted as he neared the gate.

"Hello, Master Lee," Monk Kwong answered without standing up or looking to see who was calling his name.

"I came to see you, drink some tea and discuss some fighting strategies."

"So which ones do you want to discuss and try today?" Kwong asked.

"Well, I've been thinking a lot about some specific Praying Mantis techniques and wanted to get your opinion about how to use them," Master Lee replied.

"Okay, let's go inside and after I clean off all the dirt we can practice for a while and see if your ideas are worthwhile." Kwong stood up and brushed the loose soil from his robes.

After about an hour the two masters strolled out of the private quarters of the abbot and into the open area near the front gate. They turned and respectfully bowed to each other to signify their mutual feelings for each other and also to silently announce that they were going to be fighting for research purposes and not for real. They each settled into their favorite fighting positions and quietly stood ready in preparation for the other's first move.

PUGILIST FROM SHANDONG

Moments stretched into eternity as the two stood completely motionless while staring directly at each other. Then Monk Kwong began to carefully step forward in a semi-circle fashion.

Master Lee stood his ground and patiently waited to see what his friend was trying to accomplish.

Suddenly without warning Kwong rushed forward, hoping to catch Lee off guard. As he neared his friend he raised his arm to strike overhead and then followed with a series of kicks to the legs.

Lee had experienced this style of fighting strategy many times before, so he waited until the last possible moment and then quickly stepped to the side to avoid the overhead punch while raising his leg to avoid the multiple kicks.

The moment Monk Kwong's techniques were neutralized, Master Lee began his own series of attacking movements. Unfortunately, Kwong also had many years of experience and as Master Lee moved in to execute his techniques, Kwong would suddenly disappear from range and re-appear somewhere else. Over and over this scenario continued with neither of them gaining the advantage and then during another of Monk Kwong's attacks, Master Lee slipped out of range in a unique manner, catching his friend off guard and kicked him in the stomach with enough force to knock him backwards over ten feet.

"Good kick," he said as he stood back up, realizing the kick had almost killed him, and readied for another attack.

"Are you all right?" Master Lee asked.

"Yes I'm okay." he replied. "Where did you learn that technique?

"That was one I learned from the temple back home." he approached his friend and bowed apologetically.

"After we are finished you will have to show me that technique. In all my years I've never seen such a move." Kwong motioned for Lee to begin again.

For a moment Master Lee stood motionless; not believing his friend wanted to continue, then he nodded his head in acceptance and prepared for another exchange.

This time it was Master Lee who made the first move. First he stepped in as though he was preparing to use some of his Tam Tui style movements to draw his friend into a long range fight. Suddenly without warning he switched to his Praying Mantis style, completely changing his footwork style along with the speed of his attack. Then as he was about to strike, he once again changed back to the Tam Tui style and slipped down under Kwong's defenses while using his ground fighting strategy his father taught him.

In an instant Kwong was once again on the ground; this time on his back from a series of low kicks and sweeps.

Quickly Master Lee rushed to his friend's side, helped him up to his feet and brushed off the dust.

"I think that will be enough for today," Kwong said as he rested his hand on Master Lee's shoulder.

"Okay." Lee humbly replied as he tried to reassure his friend it was not done intentionally.

"Let's go back inside my house and have some tea while we discuss what happened today. You can explain to me about that special technique of yours." Kwong smiled at his friend while rubbing his stomach.

"Master Lee, so tell me about those kicks you used outside." Monk Kwong asked as he poured the hot tea into the small cups.

"Oh they are unique to the style of Praying Mantis."

PUGILIST FROM SHANDONG

"Interesting way of kicking." Monk Kwong leaned back in his chair to drink his tea.

"Oh, before I forget, I brought you something." Master Lee reached into his pocket.

"Here, I would like you to have this." He politely handed the intricately carved iron bird to his friend.

"Wow! Thank you. It's beautiful."

"I had it made many years ago and have always carried it wherever I went, but now I would like to give it to you." Master Lee watched his friend inspect the gift and admire the detailed carving.

"I shall do the same and carry it with me always. Lee. Tell me how your student Chan Poi is recovering from his knee injury."

"It has completely healed. Those special herbs you applied made the recovery so much faster," Master Lee replied.

"Okay, let's go back outside so you can show me more of those kicks you used earlier. I would like to learn how your Praying Mantis style incorporates them when encountering other styles of kicking." Big Kwong stepped outside into the cool air while admiring the iron bird.

For several hours the two fighters exchanged techniques, applications, and fighting strategies until the sun once again began sinking below the trees.

"Okay, Kwong I think it's time I begin my walk back home."

"Yes, I think you should, otherwise it will be quite dark along the path to your house." Kwong bowed to his guest.

"I'll come back in several months and we can continue our research." Master Lee said as he bowed and then turned to begin the long walk home.

Chapter 26

~ Training Area ~

Summertime in Guangdong Province could be unbearably hot and humid with the temperature regularly rising above ninety degrees and making training during the day a constant struggle. A group of the more dedicated students decided to alleviate the problem by constructing a pavilion that would serve as a training area and sleeping quarters.

Hurry up, Sing Yin!" young Chan Poi yelled as he stood at the corner waiting on his cousin to catch up. "Everyone else is already out in the field working on the roof for the new training area.

"We need to hurry because they want to get most of the walls and roof put together before class this afternoon." Chan Poi took off running toward the edge of town while Sing Yin frantically tried to keep up. After running through a series of alleyways, across the small stream that meandered through town, and then through a couple more courtyards, they reached the large open field. They could see from a distance that everyone was busily working to get the main frame assembled so they could put on the roof.

"Where have you two been?" Chan Lok yelled the moment he saw the two appear from between the row of houses.

"I had to wait on my cousin," Chan Poi said as they came running up to the building.

"We need you two to go and find us a bunch of long and intact palm fronds for the roof," Chan Lok said as he began to climb the ladder to work on the main wall frame before they started on the roof.

"How many do you want us to find?" Sing Yin asked as he looked around to see what had been done since the day before.

"Well, we'll need enough to completely cover the roof and the upper part of the walls, so bring as many as you can find."

"Okay, we'll be back in a little while." Sing Yin said as he turned to try and catch up with his younger cousin.

"Hey, Sing Yin! take that rope over there with you so you can tie the leaves together; that way it will be easier to carry and you can bring more of them at a time," Chan Lok yelled.

"Okay," Sing Yin replied as he ran to the opposite side of the building and grabbed the pile of rope lying by the post.

As soon as he had the bundle of rope securely situated on his shoulder, he ran back toward town to catch his younger cousin. In a few moments he arrived at the edge of the houses where Chan Poi was trying to reach the group of large fronds gently bowing downward from the top of the palm tree at the corner of his cousin's house.

The tree was quite old and very tall with many leaves trying to survive on the sustenance from the long thin trunk. Over the years all the previous fronds had been hacked off and used for sweeping utensils, leaving the lower portion of the trunk barren and scared with frayed, splintered and decaying palm shards.

"Hey, Chan Poi, how come you haven't gone up the tree yet?" Sing Yin asked as he neared the tree.

"How?" the young boy asked.

"Well, since you're small and light you can climb up the short stubs sticking out of the tree and cut the good branches from the top," his cousin answered.

Chan Poi dropped the stick and waited while his cousin tied the long knife to his waist. Cautiously he made his way up the jagged tree trunk.

"Now take the rope and tie it around the tree so you can use the knife," his cousin yelled when he neared the top.

Soon the large green leaves floated downward as the boy cut them free from the trunk. After a few minutes he finally removed all the good ones and then began his descent back to the ground.

"Okay, let's go down the street and get those from the tree near your house," Sing Yin said as soon as he removed the rope from the young boy's waist.

The two ran down the dusty path behind the houses and repeated the routine. Soon they had so many leaves they could hardly see over the top and decided to make the long trip back to the field.

"Let's both pull on the rope so it will be easier," Sing Yin said. The two pulled hard at the bundle to get the leaves to slide and then continued along the path without stopping until they reached the open field.

"Let's stop here for a moment." Sing Yin let the rope drop to the ground.

"Whew, those are heavy." Chan Poi sat down in the tall grass to rest, while the sweat poured down his face and dripped onto his already soaked shirt.

"Once we get these out there to where they are working on the roof we'll go over to the other side of town and find another bunch," Sing Yin said.

"Are you ready?" Sing Yin asked after a few more minutes of rest. By the time he stood up his young cousin was already standing, holding his portion of the rope and waiting for his older cousin to tell him when to pull.

"Go!" Sing Yin yelled and the two tugged at the rope to finish dragging the large bundle out to the group of anxiously waiting men who were trying to finish the main roof structure before they had to quit for the day and return to the village for their afternoon training session.

"Hey, Chan Lok, we're going to go over to the other side of town real quick and find some more leaves before class starts," Sing Yin said as the two untied the bundle and prepared to leave.

"Okay, but when you finish collecting the palm fronds, don't come all the way back here, just bring them with you to the school and we'll carry them out here tomorrow," Chan Lok told him.

Later, as everyone was preparing for the afternoon training, Sing Yin and Chan Poi arrived dragging an even larger bundle of long green fronds.

"Hurry up, Master Lee has been looking for you two and he's not happy that you weren't here when class started.

Chan Poi! Sing Yin! You're late!" Master Lee yelled the moment he saw the two warming up in the far corner behind the others.

PUGILIST FROM SHANDONG

"Sorry, Master," they said in unison as they respectfully bowed, then quickly returned to their loosening exercises.

The following day, they all walked to the tall wooden structure standing silently in the cool morning air while waiting for the remaining palm fronds to cover its skeleton and shield it from the intense rays of sunlight. As everyone began to prepare to continue where they left off the previous day, the two frond collectors removed the dew-covered rope from the leaves and glanced around to survey how many more would be needed.

"Now, let's take the bundle of fronds they brought and continue covering the roof," Chan Lok said. "If we hurry, we can finish soon and then we can begin on the second floor."

"What are we going to need for that?" SinYing asked.

"Well, we will need some more posts to tie across from one support post to another.

"And then we will need some boards to cover it to make a floor," Chan Lok explained.

"Now, take Chan Poi with you and go down to that old pile of lumber we saw a couple weeks ago and see if there is anything we can use.

"Bring back all the small stuff first, and let us know if you need help carrying any large beams."

"Okay, we will be back as fast as we can," SinYing said.

"You better hurry, so you will be back in time for class. If Master Lee catches you showing up late again, you know he will hit you with a stick!"

Later, as they were nearing the training area, they saw Master Lee come out the door of his house.

"Good, you're here on time today," he said as he neared the others who had already begun their training.

"Are you finished with your project yet?" he asked as he sat on his chair in the shade.

"Not quite, but it should be soon," Chan Lok replied.

"We just need to finish the second floor," Chan Poi added.

"That will be a great place to train when the sun is hot and when it is raining," Lee added as he motioned for the two to begin their warm-up exercises.

"Yes, and then we can practice longer," Chan Poi added.

"And everyone can also use it to sleep in and avoid the nighttime heat," Master Lee said.

Chapter 27

~ Passing the Torch ~

Now that he was getting into his eighties, Master Lee focused as intently on passing down the art to his students as he had on developing his own training. He now knew what all his teachers had meant when they told him about making sure he remembered everything they taught him so that one day he could pass it down and keep it alive.

It was now 1948 and the world was changing. The era of machines was at hand, with motorized bicycles, machines for people to ride in from city to city, or fly in the sky around the world. Machines to make goods in a fraction of the time it used to take a skilled laborer days to accomplish and machines for killing from long distances.

He knew that the era of skilled fighters like him who followed the ancient traditions, was rapidly coming to a close forever. No longer would there be any skilled practitioners of his caliber who traveled alone throughout the country in a struggle for survival. The need to fight at close quarters during a war or to use a rare and secretive art like Dim Mak were now slowly fading into the pages of history.

The need for a society or a banded brotherhood that would adhere to an ancient code of martial arts ethics and not be held accountable by the local law enforcement was gone. Now, there would be no need to carry your specialty weapon on your back, nor would anyone ever have any need to carry a nickname earned from your peers after witnessing your unique technique developed through a lifetime of training as in the ancient Chinese classic *The Water Margin*, better known as *Outlaws of the Marsh*.

Men and women in China for centuries had devoted their lives to the art of Kung Fu. From an early age they had a unique gift. Their destiny was not that of a businessman, butcher, barber, governor, general or family man. They were destined to be the heroes of the martial arts world, those few inspired legends, stories and operas. They were the Chinese martial arts knights.

Soon all the ancient training regimens required to develop the superior physical and mental abilities would be gone. The world was now moving at a much faster pace and the need for slow and sustained training practices would soon be replaced by quicker and easier practices more acceptable to the new age of impatient practitioners.

During the day as everyone walked to the water's edge to help with the fishing, Master Lee sat quietly in the shade of the trees, smoking his pipe and reflecting on his training and his life.

My life has taught me many things, he reminisced. *I have traveled to so many places and encountered so many people, some good, and some bad.*

PUGILIST FROM SHANDONG

It's unfortunate that I had to kill so many just to stay alive.

He now realized that soon his life would be coming to a close. The light inside that had shone brightly for so many years was beginning to fade. What had been so easy to execute with so little effort when he was young, was now becoming more and more difficult. All the years of training and conditioning that had sustained such a superbly trained martial artist, were now taking their toll.

He was now eighty-two years old and all the practices to develop superior punching and kicking techniques and all the herbal formulations to minimize the deterioration of the body were now catching up with his aged body. His hands and knuckles at times ached from all the training. His fingers once trained to be like steel for use during Dim Mak, now showed signs of age. The mental ability of all the years of training was still sharp, but now the body's resistance was weakening and mild sensations of pain began to appear.

His thoughts suddenly shifted.

I am one of the last remaining masters from the previous century.

Soon all that will remain of our abilities will be the memories of those few souls who will become the caretakers of this ancient art.

They will be left behind with a few of our words of wisdom, techniques, and memories that we told them to pass down and help sustain the art's history.

I have spent my entire life trying to perfect my art

I hope I have done it justice and passed it down well enough so that it will stay alive.

I hope my dear sister has been successful in her life's pursuit.

I wonder what ever happened to my wife and daughter.

Hs heart grew heavy and he smiled while the smoke from his pipe slowly drifted up in to the late afternoon sky.

~~~~~

Early in the morning as the sun rose above the horizon and sent its rays of a new day throughout the land, the air seemed to be carrying the weight of one less inhabitant. All was still. No breeze moved through the trees or stirred the animals to wake. The early morning fog was extremely dense and hung in the air like a large curtain shielding the audience from the players behind. The birds weren't chirping, no dogs were barking, nothing. It is said that animals have a sense of knowing about events not yet fulfilled, and today they appeared as though they knew of an event soon to happen.

As Sing Yin's mother went inside the house to deliver Master Lee his early morning meal, she sensed an eerie presence in the room that chilled her to the core. She noticed that Master Lee hadn't gotten up yet, which was very unusual for him, since he always rose at the same time every morning. As she entered the darkened room a chill again went through her body all the way to the bone. This was followed by a strong sensation in her stomach that felt as much like an intense sickness as it did like a large black hole of darkness drawing everything inside including all emotions.

Slowly and cautiously she crept further into the room, not knowing what she would find. Her thoughts jumped back and forth from the thought of her inner feelings she hoped would go away, to those about what it was that she would find in the room. Step by step she inched her way deeper into the small house.

Eventually she made her way to the table and nervously with her hands shaking, she lit the small lantern. For a moment a feeling of relief rippled through her body, only to be cut short by the thought of having to enter Master Lee's bedroom and see why he wasn't awake. Reaching the door, she noticed that it was still shut tight, which meant that he had not gotten up and gone back to bed. This was a sign that he had not gotten up at all.

Slowly she reached out and softly knocked on the door, not too hard to startle him if he were sleeping but just enough to be heard and gently pull him from his sleep. She waited and listened for any signs of activity inside. After a few moments of silence she knocked once again and then waited. Moments seemed to stretch into forever as she listened for an indication that it was all right to enter. None came.

Now the feeling of sickness and deep dark blackness in the pit of her stomach returned. As she tried to suppress it with thoughts of listening for movement inside the room, the feeling continued to grow and soon overwhelmed any other thought. As she reached for the doorknob, she took a deep breath to try and calm her inner feeling of emptiness. Slowly she opened the door and whispered, "Master," to let him know she was entering the room in case he didn't hear her knock.

Still no response.

Delicately she moved the door open further and slowly brought the lantern into the opening so she could see. She noticed that Master was still lying on the bed. Quietly she walked over and softly touched him on the arm to try and wake him. As soon as her fingertip touched his arm, she sensed that something was wrong. Touching him again this time with her entire hand, she felt that his arm was very cold.

Panic rushed through her body as she pulled her hand away. This time she reached down with both hands and shook his arm very abruptly, but still there was no response.

Reaching for his shoulder, she again shook him in hopes of a response. When there was none she reached up for his neck to see if she could detect a pulse. As her hand neared its destination, she quickly pulled it back and decided to go and get one of the senior students to come and help.

"Chan Biu! Chan Biu! Come quickly" she yelled as soon as she saw him.

"What is it?" he asked.

"Master Lee, Master Lee, I don't know," she said.

"Okay, okay, stay calm, I'll go with you." He stood up and rested his hands on her shoulders.

They made their way into the room and up to the bedside. He too had a sudden feeling of panic rush through his body. Gently he reached over and shook Master Lee by the arm. When he didn't get a response, he reached up and checked the neck for a pulse. The seconds waiting for a response seemed like forever as he waited for the heart to beat. Unfortunately, Master Lee's life had come to an end.

When Chan Biu realized that his Master had died, he bowed his head and sobbed. Sing Yin's mother began to wail uncontrollably.

Others outside heard the sound and came running to investigate. Before long everyone would know what the animals had already been informed about. The sound of dishes crashing to the floor was followed by loud screams of anguish and then wailing, then more doors slamming and more dishes crashing and breaking. All this commotion in addition to the unusually thick fog hanging in the air caused the sound to linger and then slowly travel through the streets and then out into the surrounding hills. As it did, everyone was left with an inner sense of loss and vacancy.

In minutes the entire village had gathered at the doorstep of their beloved teacher only to find that the inner feeling and

PUGILIST FROM SHANDONG

rumor spreading throughout the town were both true – their teacher had died.

One by one as they arrived and were told of the loss, each one began to cry and put their heads on each other's shoulders in an attempt to quell the deep sense of loss. Soon the entire village was standing in the street outside the small house and everyone was crying and hanging their heads in sorrow.

For hours not one person left the house, and the street remained full of mourners well into the night. After the sun had set below the distant hills and the village began to settle in for the night, the sounds of mourners still echoed through the quiet streets. Gradually, with the darkness of night growing closer and closer, the sounds grew more and more faint. Soon all that was left was the quiet sound of the stillness of night.

The next day began like so many before except for the overall sense of loss by everyone in the village. The entire village had experienced the loss of a loved one at different times throughout their lives, but this time it was very different for everyone. None had ever lived or trained with a Kung Fu master of his caliber or reputation. So this loss was even more heartfelt by everyone.

Over the next several weeks his body was kept intact so that students, relatives, friends, and acquaintances from out of town would have the opportunity to arrive and say one last goodbye.

Finally the funeral service was concluded and the town mourned again. For now, it was finally time to put him to rest.

His mannerisms when teaching the movements of his Kung Fu style, along with the experience and understanding of this ancient Chinese art were now a part of history.

His endless stories of China when he was young were now placed neatly next to his mannerisms.

THOMAS HAASE

The many years of training in the ancient, obscure, and deadly art of Dim Mak had finally come to a close.

All his experiences during his travels throughout China floated into the evening sky and merged with the solitary clouds.

He was now gone from his physical body, but as long as his students and family adhere to ancient Chinese tradition, and keep the incense burning; he lives on.

And he still does today, as I too keep the incense burning.

MAP AND DISTANCES

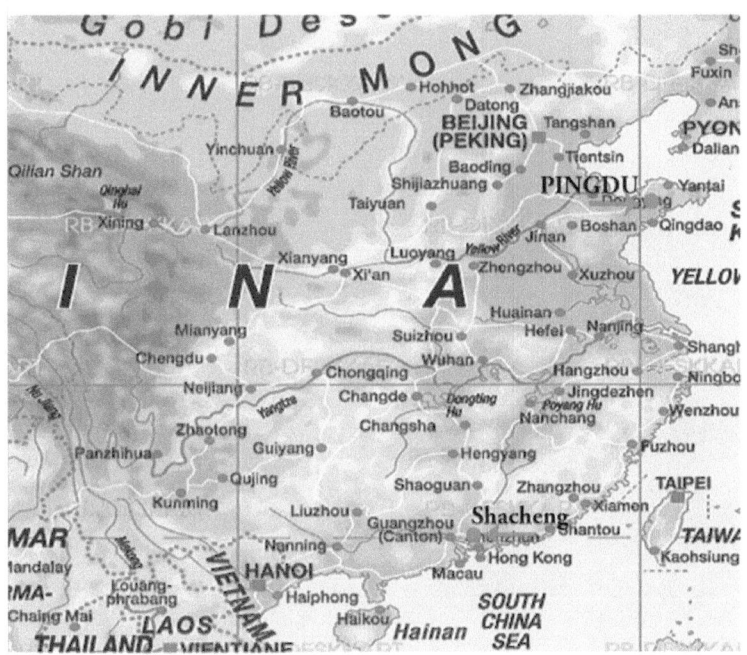

Pingdu – Jinan 164 miles
Pingdu – Guangzhou 1959 miles
Guangzhou – Hanoi Vietnam 495 miles
Hanoi – Nanning 385 miles
Nanning – Guangzhou 357 miles
Guangzhou – Kowloon 130 miles
Kowloon – Shacheng 57 miles

Bibliography

1. China: A New History
   By: Fairbank & Goldman
2. Dictionary of Chinese Proverbs
   By: John Rohsenous
3. Chinese have a word for it
   By: Boye Lafayette DeMonte
4. Chinese – their History and Culture
   By: Kenneth Scott Latourette
5. Chinese Looking Glass
   By: D. Bloodworth
6. Source book in Chinese philosophy
   By: James Wong
7. Chinese civilization and society
   By: Patricia Buckley Ebrey
8. The Forbidden City
   By: Frank Dorn
9. Boxer Rebellion
   By: D. Preston
10. Chinese symbols
    By: Wolfram Eberhard
11. Outlaws of the Marsh
    By: Shi Nai'an, Luo Guanzhong
12. Art of Nature
    By: Guo Ji Liang
13. Gate of Heavenly Peace
    By: J. Spence
14. Strange Tales of Liaozhai
    By: Pu Songling
15. Road to Heaven
    By: B. Porter
16. China Wakes
    By: Kristoff & WuDunn
17. Art of War
    By: T. Cleary
18. Chronicles of Tao
    By: Deng Mingdao
19. Tao Te Ching
    By: R. Hendricks
20. The Chinese
    By: John Fraser

21. Feng Shui
   By: Lillian Too
22. Wah Lum First Fist Form
   By: P. Chan
23. Wah Lum Right Hand Stick/Fatal Flute
   By: P. Chan
24. Wah Lum Double Broadswords
   By: P. Chan
25. Wah Lum Lectures
   By: P. Chan/Thomas Haase
26. Translations from the Chinese
   By: Arthur Waley
27. China Warlords
   By: David Bonavia
28. Boxer Uprising
   By: Victor Purcell
29. The Face of China Photographs
   By: L. Carrington Goodrich
30. Spring Moon
   By: Betty Bao Lord
31. Chinabound
   By: John Fairbank
32. The Dragon Empress
   By: Marina Warner
33. The Heart of the Dragon
   By: Alasdair Clayre
34. Kung Fu Book of Wisdom
   By: Herbie Pilato
35. The Way of Chuang Tzu
   By: Thomas Merton
36. Kung Fu Meditations
   By: Ellen Kei Hua
37. Vitality, Energy, Spirit
   By: Thomas Cleary
38. Chinese Astrology
   By: Paul Carus
39. Secrets of Chinese Astrology
   By: Kwan Lau
40. Hummel, Arthur W.
   Zhili Shandong liang sheng di yu quan tu. [Between 1855 and 1870, 1855] Map.
   https://www.loc.gov/item/gm71005076/.

About the Author:

Thomas J Haase has been practicing the Chinese Martial Arts for over forty-five years, beginning with the Tibetan/ChineseCharging White Crane System: Lightning Fire Mountain White Crane 閃火山西藏攻白功夫派 from the Chengtian Shaolin Temple in Western Sichuan Province, China, near the Tibet border.

In 1982 he began studying Wah Lum Kung Fu under Grandmaster Chan Poi of the Wah Lum Temple in Orlando, Florida.Currently, Mr. Haase and his wife Cynthia operate their own Wah Lum Kung Fu and Tai Chi school in Tampa, Florida.

Over the past thirty years Mr. Haase has written:

Instructional handbooks

Student guides

New Martial Hero magazine articles

Wah Lum Lectures book (transcribed and edited)

Poetry

BOOK ORDER INFORMATION

Additional copies can be ordered through:

Thomas J Haase.com

Wahlumtampa.com/Pugilist-From-Shandong